FOR DUTY AND HONOR

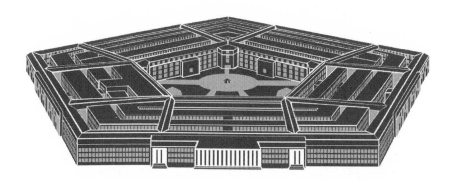

Also by George Galdorisi

Fiction

The Coronado Conspiracy
Tom Clancy's Op-Center: Dark Zone
Tom Clancy's Op-Center: Scorched Earth
Tom Clancy's Op-Center: Into the Fire
Tom Clancy's Op-Center: Out of the Ashes
Tom Clancy Presents: Act of Valor

Non-Fiction

When the Killer Man Comes
Networking the Global Maritime Partnership
The Kissing Sailor
Leave No Man Behind
Beyond the Law of the Sea
The United States and the 1982 Law of the Sea Convention: The Cases Pro and Con

FOR DUTY AND HONOR

GEORGE GALDORISI

BOOKS

Aura Libertatis Spirat

Braveship Books
www.braveshipbooks.com
Aura Libertatis Spirat

Originally published by Avon Books

This is a work of fiction. Names, characters, places or incidents are either the product of the author's imagination or are used fictitiously, and any resemblance to actual persons, living or dead, business establishments, events or locales is entirely coincidental and beyond the intent of either the author or the publisher.

Cover Design by Rossitsa Atanassova

Book layout by Alexandru Diaconescu
www.steadfast-typesetting.eu

ISBN-13: 978-1-64062-055-1
Printed in the United States of America

For Becky

ACKNOWLEDGEMENTS

The Coronado Conspiracy was a relatively easy book to write. *For Duty and Honor* was more difficult and required a great deal of help and support before it reached its final, publishable form. I owe a tremendous debt of gratitude to those who helped make this book a reality.

First and foremost, my family—my wife Becky, our son Brian, and our daughter Laura—provided the support and encouragement necessary for me to continue cobbling together this story through draft after not-good-enough draft. They never wavered in their support.

I received tremendous encouragement from family and friends who read *The Coronado Conspiracy*. Admiral Jim Stavridis, Mr. Fred Rainbow, Captain Dick Couch and Captain P.T. Deutermann provided a tremendous boost as did many classmates from the Naval Academy Class of 1970 who read *The Coronado Conspiracy*.

Special thanks to former squadron-mate, fellow helicopter aviator, friend, and editor extraordinaire, Kevin McDonald. An accomplished writer in his own right, he has an uncanny knack for finding weaknesses in a narrative and making lemonade out of lemons.

Finally, my thanks to the officers, chief petty officers and men and women of the United States Navy. The daily inspiration of watching these professionals at work in peace and in war has inspired my writing. Without their unselfish sacrifice of going down to the sea in ships, there would be no stories like *For Duty and Honor*.

Contents

CHAPTER 1

From a mile-and-a-half away across the hot tarmac, shimmering in the 110-degree heat, the CH-53E Sikorsky Super Stallion looked like a huge praying mantis. Its massive blades hung so low they seemed to touch the ground, and its wide, squat body gave the impression of a big bug—angry and foreboding. All around the bug, the men and women working on her looked like tiny ants trying vainly to overwhelm the insect. Framed by the hangar at the U.S. military's Aviation Support Unit in a corner of Bahrain International Airport, the bug was undergoing its final maintenance checks before its flight.

Inside the hangar, its doors wide open to take advantage of what little breeze there was, two sweating Navy pilots waited as the maintenance chief directed her exhausted crew. Wearing blue coveralls dropped halfway down and tied around their waists, their once-white T-shirts stained with a rainbow of colors—grease, hydraulic fluid, engine and transmission oil—the maintenance crew bent to their task of ensuring their bird was ready for flight.

"Hong, get that hydraulic bowser moved inside."

"Bohem, I told you to clean those damn windshields; how the hell are the lieutenants gonna see where they're flying with that grease you've smeared all over?"

"Peters, get the tow tractor and pull this beast out to the fight line."

"Roger," the last maintenance man replied. Neither he nor his companions moved with enthusiasm. The searing Bahrain heat sucked the life out of them.

Lieutenant Jake Watson and Lieutenant Harold Johnson stood ready, nodding as the chief barked orders. The two pilots were hot, sweaty and dirty too, but at least they'd be flying soon, maybe even bag some night time after their flight taking supplies out to the Navy aircraft carrier in the Arabian Gulf was complete. The chief upset their musings.

"One of you lieutenants mind riding the brakes so we can tow your aircraft out of the hangar?"

"Sure, I'll get it," Johnson replied.

* * *

"I'm ready, Ahmad."

"May you be with him today, Mohammad. Do your duty."

Ahmad and one other companion got out of the van and walked away into the lengthening shadows of the airport building. They never looked back at Mohammad, whose foot had already come off the brake and pressed down on the accelerator, hurtling the van across the tarmac.

The van immediately drew the attention of the Bahraini airport security police, and a police truck started toward them. Mohammad just sped up and turned to head directly for the Super Stallion looming ahead of him less than a half mile away.

As the van accelerated, its carriage started rattling from the weight of the load in back. Mohammad prayed not for his own life—he knew where he would be in the next minute—but that what they had set up would work properly. The Bahraini police truck was a quarter mile back and gaining.

* * *

The maintenance crew walked backwards, keeping their eyes on the blades of the helicopter as they cleared the sides of the hangar. Emerging into the intense heat, the men and women trudged on, just hoping to get another hot, dirty evolution over with.

Johnson saw the van first. He blinked in disbelief. Then, instinctively, he started to climb out of the aircraft and shout to his crew. "LOOK OUT! GET AWAY FROM THE BIRD, GET AWAY FROM THE BIRD!"

The men and women moving the helo just stared at Johnson. What the hell was the lieutenant talking about? Maybe the damned heat had gotten to him. Then one of them turned around and saw what he saw.

"GODDAMMIT, STOP, STOP!" one man shouted at the van.

Only a hundred yards away now, Mohammad had the accelerator on the deck. The van was shaking violently, protesting both the weight of the C-4 explosives it was carrying and the speed the driver was demanding. Mohammad suppressed an urge to yell; he wouldn't give the infidels the pleasure of hearing him scream.

As the van's objective became clear, the maintenance crew started to run away from the bird, looking to their officers and their chief for some rationale for what was happening. There was none.

Yards away now, Mohammad gripped the steering wheel so hard he thought he would bend it. The men and women were scattering, and he could see fear in their faces. Perhaps they prayed to their god. What futility in that, he thought.

The van smashed into the helicopter right on its nose, impacting the chin bubble. The wire connected from the bumper of the van, and threaded back through its interior, was linked to the detonator and set it off, causing the van's cargo to explode. Investigators would eventually be able to pinpoint the exact spot where the van struck the helo and calculate it was carrying approximately 400 pounds of C-4 explosives.

The noise was deafening and the fireball was spectacular. This was followed by another, bigger fireball as 10,000 pounds of fuel in the aircraft ignited. The first explosion killed the half-dozen of the crew close to the Super Stallion instantly, while the second mowed down several others who had managed to scurry a little farther away. What the flames and the heat didn't do, the flying shrapnel did.

Those killed instantly were perhaps the most fortunate, as others who were farther away died more slowly, their bodies ripped apart by metal fragments that seared their torsos and limbs. Emergency vehicles converged on the scene—too late to help most of the helo's crew.

Urgent messages went up and across the U.S. military chain of command. CNN had a crew on-scene in less than four hours. At Fifth Fleet Headquarters in Manama, Bahrain; at the National Military Command Center in the Pentagon; at the National Security Council in the Eisenhower Executive Office Building; in the White House Situation Room; and in other headquarters; they all knew what had happened, but they couldn't answer the question, *who had done this?*

CHAPTER 2

Two weeks later

Fourteen Americans had died in suicide van attack on the Navy CH-53E detachment. The president had been sufficiently moved—or his image-makers had told him it was the right thing to do—to invite the families of the victims to the White House to present posthumous awards for the men and women who had died in the blast.

He had barely noticed her, but as other family members queued up to talk with the president, or be comforted by the First Lady, a small black woman walked up to the national security adviser, Michael Curtis.

"Are you Mr. Curtis, the national security adviser?" she asked.

"Yes, ma'am, I am."

"I'm Margaret Johnson. Harold Johnson was my son."

"Yes, ma'am," Curtis continued. "We are all saddened by his death—and the death of his shipmates—"

She wouldn't let him finish. "Mr. Curtis, tell me my Harold died for a reason. Tell me he didn't die just to keep the price of gasoline down."

Curtis was thrown off guard. Why was she asking him this? "Ma'am, your son was a fine patriot and he—"

Again she cut him off. "Don't patronize me, Mr. Curtis. You didn't know my Harold, so you can't know that. His daddy did three tours in Vietnam—Army infantry—made it home in one piece, but the war took too much out of him. He died when Harold was little. I raised him and his two sisters alone.

Harold got a scholarship to North Carolina State. The Navy recruited him to be a pilot. They don't have many black pilots, you know. He was a Super Stallion helicopter commander. Took me inside of one when I made my first

4

trip to his squadron, then had one of his buddies take this picture of me and him in front of it."

As she finished her sentence, she fished a well-worn picture from her straw purse and handed it to Curtis. It showed Harold Johnson in his flight suit, standing in front of his thirty-ton Super Stallion with his arm around his diminutive mother. It contrasted sharply with the more recent scene at Dover Air Force Base when fourteen flag-draped coffins had arrived on the C-17 Globemaster.

"Tell me this fine boy didn't die for nothing, Mr. Curtis."

Holding that picture and seeing the tears well up in her eyes had a sobering effect on the national security adviser. He knew what he had to do. He couldn't open his mouth unless he made that commitment.

"Ms. Johnson, Harold didn't die in vain. I promise you we'll punish the people who did this."

"Harold loved his country...don't let his country let him down." She was sobbing now, and Curtis was about to lose control. He had to do something.

"Ms. Johnson, please let me introduce you to the president. I know he'd be disappointed if he didn't get to meet you," he said, while gently taking her elbow in one hand. Then he tried to give her the picture back.

She walked the way he steered her, but she looked at him with resolution in her eyes—those eyes he would never forget.

"No, you keep this picture, Mr. Curtis. I remember what Harold looked like—I want you to remember too."

"Yes, ma'am."

"I want you to keep this on your desk until justice is done."

All he could muster was another, "Yes, ma'am."

As Harold Johnson's mother talked with the president, the great man comforting her with soothing words, and the First Lady hugging her, Curtis turned away. Damn the president! He knew what the problem was. He knew how to get to the enemy. They *were* the enemy too, every bit as much as if they had landed on our shores and killed those Americans. Curtis knew he'd have to energize the National Security Council soon.

CHAPTER 3

Six weeks later

The Nimitz-class nuclear aircraft carrier USS *Carl Vinson* sliced through the 85 degree waters of the Arabian Gulf, her two nuclear reactors propelling her in excess of 30 knots. Displacing almost 100,000 tons, *Carl Vinson* parted the waves with her bow, her four 20-foot screws biting into the Gulf waters with incredible torque. Yet for all her power, the massive ship seemed to glide through the water almost effortlessly.

Built in Newport News Shipyard at a cost of well in excess of four billion dollars, *Carl Vinson*, like her sister Nimitz-class carriers, was one of the eight wonders of the modern world. Almost 1,100 feet in length, her flight deck encompassed four-and-one-half acres. Over 240 feet from her keel to the top of her main mast, she dwarfed other warships. On her flight deck and in her hangar bay, over sixty of the most sophisticated warplanes on the planet comprised her striking arm.

Over five thousand officers, chief petty officers and sailors lived and worked in this floating city. The ship was perhaps the greatest engineering achievement the United States had ever constructed—a weapon of war deployed to the seven seas to keep the peace. *Carl Vinson* was in the Arabian Gulf doing exactly that, her crew going about their everyday duties that kept this behemoth functioning. Their routine was just that—routine—until....

"GENERAL QUARTERS, GENERAL QUARTERS, all hands man your battle stations, go up and forward on the starboard side, down and aft on the port side. Zebra must be set in twelve minutes, now General Quarters."

Lieutenant Anne O'Connor shot up in her rack in the small stateroom she shared with Lieutenant Chrissie Moore. O'Connor was in the Alert 15 crew and was supposed to be able to get her F/A-18E Super Hornet off *Carl Vinson's* deck in the next fifteen minutes, ready to refuel the thirsty, fuel-guzzling, F/A-18E/F Super Hornets and F/A-18C Hornets being scrambled to defend the carrier. She had been dozing—it had started off as reading—when the 1MC general announcing system had shocked her awake. Within seconds, she was groping around on the deck trying to put on her flight boots. She knew that if the ship was going to general quarters, she would be launching soon.

"Now launch the Alert 7 fighters," the voice on the 1MC intoned. "GQ time, one minute."

Launch the alert? This could be trouble, or could it be a drill? She didn't know which, but you always had to assume the worst. O'Connor knew the entire defensive package lineup by heart. The MH-60S Seahawk plane guard helo was sitting on spot four on the carrier's angled deck, its pilots watching the temperature gauge creep slowly past 40 degrees Celsius. They would launch first.

Two Super Hornets were in Alert 7, their pilots already in their aircraft so they could get off *Carl Vinson's* deck in seven minutes. They would be the first DLIs—deck-launched interceptors. Then her aircraft, as well as one other refueling Super Hornet in Alert 15, would be the next to go, taking station overhead the ship at 7,000 feet, ready to refuel the thirsty fighters. Two other Super Hornets were also in Alert 15; they'd be next off the catapults—the "cats." After that, the Alert 30 launch: another helo, the E-2D Hawkeye radar control aircraft, the EA-18G Growler jamming aircraft, and two more Super Hornets rounded out the package. If all those aircraft had to launch, she knew the carrier could be in serious trouble.

"Chrissie, what the hell time is it?" O'Connor yelled as she wrapped the long laces of her left boot around her ankle and back again. *Damn, what sadist makes these things this friggin' long?* she thought.

"Only 0830," her roommate, who was still in shorts and a tee-shirt and lounging in her upper bunk, responded. O'Connor was a "nugget" pilot on her first deployment, and Moore was just a few years senior, so they had one of the smallest staterooms on the ship. Theirs was typical of those that junior officers inhabited on *Carl Vinson*—a set of bunk beds, several lockers, two pull-out desks built into the lockers, and a small sink and mirror. The room was austere—almost stark—although they had dressed it up as best they could.

"What? 0830?" O'Connor shouted. "We're not supposed to be flying until 1000. I can't believe this," she said as she slid the second boot onto her right foot and struggled with the too-long laces.

"GQ time, two minutes," the voice said.

"Better get moving roomie, sounds serious," Moore said—with just a hint of sarcasm—as she rolled out of her top bunk and began to put on her flight suit. She needed to show up in the Stingers' Ready Room too, but she wasn't part of the ready alert crew. There was no need for her to panic, plus she was almost sure this was a drill.

O'Connor was perplexed. GQs were usually carefully orchestrated events aboard the Gold Eagle—*Carl Vinson's* nickname—even in the Arabian Gulf. An unannounced GQ was a rarity, and one where the ship actually launched fighters in response to a threat was even rarer. Even lowly JOs knew that something was up.

O'Connor was also worried. Not of what would happen in the air—she was every bit as courageous as her fellow pilots. Nothing that could happen in the air worried her; she had trained hard for her mission. Once airborne she knew she'd succeed.

No, she was worried because of Bingo. Commander Craig "Bingo" Reynolds was the Stingers XO—executive officer—and he was not the kinder, gentler type. The Stingers JOs thought he was a throwback who existed for one reason and one reason only—to make their lives as miserable as possible. As a brand-new lieutenant, O'Connor had absorbed more than a fair share of Bingo's wrath. She didn't know if he was trying to make it hard on her because she was one of only four women officers in the squadron. She was terrified because he would be in the Stingers' Ready Room and would see her come in late.

The Alert 15 crew was supposed to already be in the VFA-113 Ready Room—Ready Room Four—not in the rack. However, since entering the Gulf, the admiral had them in alerts—from Alert 7 to Alert 30—almost continuously. The problem was that being in Alert 15 broke their crew rest cycle and that meant missing out on flying later in the day—or that night—if they were stuck with Alert 15 duty.

They had cut a deal with the squadron operations officer that if they could get back to the ready room in less than five minutes after GQ sounded, he would let them slide back to their staterooms during Alert 15. This wasn't altruism on the ops officer's part. Having his pilots waste their crew day standing Alert 15 meant that he could come perilously close to not being able to fill the flight schedule and this might cause the Stingers to miss sorties. In the intensely competitive world of naval aviation it wouldn't be the squadron exec, but the squadron commander himself, who would have the ops officer's head if they missed sorties.

"GQ time, three minutes," the voice on the 1MC intoned, as O'Connor sprang to her feet and bolted toward the door, determined not to get burned on this one, not as a pilot, and not as a woman. Dammit, dammit, dammit, why hadn't she just left her flight boots on?

Her mind was racing as she flung the door to her stateroom open, leaving her roommate behind. Room 03-95-L—the Navy way of numbering everything on a ship: 03 standing for the third deck above the main deck, 95 standing for the "frame," or numbered divisions that started at the bow and ran aft—each frame marking off approximately four feet on these Nimitz-class carriers—and L standing for living space—was a long way from her ready room. Her stateroom was just starboard of the ship's centerline, as was the back entrance to Ready Four, almost ninety frames aft. But moving on the starboard side passageway meant traveling through the Blue Tile Area, the Flag Spaces that were home to Rear Admiral Michael "Heater" Robinson and his staff.

The ever-present sentry frequently stopped anyone who wasn't on the admiral's staff who was trying to pass through. She changed her route to the port side, a few dozen steps longer. Besides that, that was the direction of the "flow" during GQ—moving up ladders and running forward on the starboard, or right, side of the ship—and opposite that on the port, or left, side. A "ship thing" that most pilots didn't pay much attention to, but now it was working to her advantage.

She turned right out of her stateroom and headed athwartships—Navy slang for anything running perpendicular to the ship's centerline—at a full run, then turned left, picked up the fore and aft passageway, and started at full sprint toward Ready Four. Every three strides, she would lift her feet a bit higher and pull her arms and legs in just a little closer to avoid the "knee knockers" that punctuated the ship's main lengthwise passageways every five frames. Sailors moved aside instinctively as O'Connor barreled aft with a look of semi-desperation in her eyes.

Anne Claire O'Connor came by her bent for naval aviation naturally. The only child of now-retired Captain Jeff "Boxman" O'Connor, who had flown F-4 Phantoms in Vietnam and gone on to command his own carrier air wing, she had grown up in the midst of the lore of naval aviation. An honor student and varsity athlete at Coronado High School in southern California, she had won an appointment to the U.S. Naval Academy and had excelled there as a swimmer. Tall, slim and attractive, at five foot nine and a lithe 130 pounds, Anne O'Connor turned heads. She knew her good looks didn't help her blend as a naval aviator—there were fewer than two dozen women among *Carl Vinson's* over two hundred pilots and naval flight officers. Unlike everything else she did in her life, she failed in her mission to not stand out.

O'Connor gauged her progress aft along the port side passageway by familiar landmarks: back door to the Flag Mess, Flag Intel, TFCC—the Tactical Flag Coordination Center, CATCC—Carrier Air Traffic Control Center, *almost there, athwartships passageway, yes!* She hung a hard left, and began to slow down as she passed the Shrikes Ready Room, then hung a right and was at Ready Four.

"GQ time, four minutes."

O'Connor heaved a sigh of relief. Okay, so far, so good. Now the hard part. *This has got to look casual.* She didn't like playing this kind of ruse, it went against her basic sense of honesty, but they were doing it for the greater good, weren't they? *BS, Anne,* she told herself, *quit rationalizing.* Just get into the ready room, get the brief from the SDO—squadron duty officer—and get in your aircraft.

O'Connor took a deep breath as she pushed the back door to Ready Four open and looked around furtively. No Bingo. Yes, there was a God! What she saw was just the usual assemblage of pilots filing into their chairs. If he or she wasn't flying, a pilot's GQ station was in the Ready Room. She grabbed her survival vest from her chair and walked up to the harried SDO.

"Anne, the other refueling pilot is already in his aircraft—he walked a minute ago."

"GQ time, five minutes."

Her fellow JOs looked at her with a mixture of bemusement and concern—bemusement that they weren't the ones who'd been caught napping, literally—and concern the Stingers would look bad if she didn't launch on time.

O'Connor wheeled to sprint out of the ready room, almost colliding with the squadron ops officer as she did. She heard the sound of the shuttle traveling down the catapult track as the first Super Hornet launched from cat 4. That shuttling sound was followed by the reassuring *pop* as the cat stroke was absorbed and the energy was directed through the ship. The first Alert 7 Super Hornet had launched. This was looking less-and-less like a drill. She had to get into the air and gas those aircraft.

"GQ time, six minutes."

O'Connor turned left out of the ready room, ran forward, and then turned right, heading outboard toward the skin of the ship. She continued outward to the hatch that led out to the starboard side catwalk.

She pulled the handle securing the hatch and opened the huge door, taking her outside, and then turned left and up the seven steps to the catwalk.

"GQ time, seven minutes."

The searing heat hit her. Summer in the Gulf, not a cloud in the sky, and even at this hour, the temperature was over 100. The radiated heat off the flight deck made it feel at least 15 degrees hotter, and the combined thickness of her flight suit, torso harness, and survival vest made her start sweating instantly.

Clack, clack, clack—the sound of the shuttle as the second Alert 7 Super Hornet roared down cat 3. O'Connor bounded up the steps to the flight deck. Then the ship shuddered again with the force of the cat stroke.

"GQ time, eight minutes."

The Alert 7 Super Hornets got airborne a minute late, O'Connor thought. *That won't happen to me.* Now the pressure was on her and her wingman in Alert 15. If this wasn't a drill, she'd need to refuel the strike aircraft ASAP.

Sweating more profusely now, she dashed past the bomb farm—the staging area for the bombs and missiles jammed between *Carl Vinson's* island structure and the edge of the flight deck. Her bird was just aft of the island, in position to taxi to the cat.

"GQ time, nine minutes."

No time to preflight her aircraft again; she'd done that when they'd set the alert last night. She climbed up and her plane captain followed, ready to help her strap in.

"GQ time, ten minutes. Zebra set, main deck and below."

O'Connor grabbed the NATOPS pocket checklist and worked her way through the pre-taxi checklist. Start APU—the auxiliary power unit—start both engines, power up the cockpit avionics. It was the familiar sequence she'd completed a hundred times before.

"GQ time, eleven minutes."

Checklist complete. She saw the yellow-shirted director standing just a few feet in front of her ready to taxi her aircraft. A thumbs-up from O'Connor let him know he could start moving her Super Hornet. She started to taxi to cat 4. Another Super Hornet was already on cat 3 completing its final hookups.

As she taxied into position, the flight deck crew hooked up the holdback bar and the launch bar to the nose gear of her aircraft. The huge JBD—jet blast deflector—moved up into position behind her aircraft to protect planes and people from the blast and heat of the Super Hornet's two powerful engines.

To her right, the other aircraft was just starting to run up its engines, the heat running up the JBD and making the air around it shimmer.

"GQ time, twelve minutes."

The final checkers gave O'Connor's aircraft the last look-over. She completed the final items on the checklist.

* * *

One deck below the flight deck, in the ship's TFCC, Heater Robinson had seen enough. His Alert 7 fighters had gotten off the deck in time and were already talking with strike—the controllers who directed the aircraft toward the engagement area—and his Alert 15 crews would be off the cats early. He was satisfied he could defend *Carl Vinson*. Robinson put his hand on his TAO's—tactical action officer's—shoulder.

"Call it off Steve," he said as he turned and left TFCC, walking the few steps through the War Room back to his cabin.

Lieutenant Commander Steve Rawls picked up the Bogen phone—*Carl Vinson's* internal communications system—which linked him to the ship's commanding officer, Captain Craig Vandegrift.

"Captain, this is the Flag TAO. Stand down from the alert launch."

"Admiral's orders?" the captain asked. Vandegrift had been burned before by junior staff officers who had misinterpreted the strike group commander's orders, and he didn't want that to happen here.

"Admiral's orders," Rawls responded.

"Roger," Vandegrift replied. He picked up the phone connecting him to *Carl Vinson's* air boss in the Primary Flight Control Tower, one deck above.

"Stand 'em down, Boss."

"Aye, Captain."

* * *

O'Connor did the "cockpit wipeout," ensuring that all of her controls were free. The Super Hornet was running its engines at full power as the "Shooter" in the launch bubble prepared to launch the strike fighter.

"Secure from General Quarters. Secure from General Quarters. Stand down the Alert 15 package. I say again. Stand down the Alert 15 package."

DAMMIT, O'Connor thought. *All of this and we don't go flying. What's wrong with this boat?*

There was nothing wrong with *Carl Vinson*, or with what had just happened. Tensions in the Arabian Gulf were rising, and Heater Robinson wanted to make sure his strike group—and especially his pilots—were ready for anything. An unannounced GQ got everyone on their toes and kept them there.

O'Connor looked out on the waters of the Arabian Gulf and into the perpetual haze that hung in the skies. As she got ready to taxi her aircraft back to its original position on deck, she wondered what part she would play in any conflict. One thing she did know—she'd be ready.

CHAPTER 4

The National Security Council meeting wasn't going well. National Security Adviser Michael Curtis had tried his best to form a consensus among the many players—each with a seemingly different agenda: Secretary of Defense Bryce Jacobs; Secretary of State Philip Quinn; Attorney General Victor Creazzo; the DNI—Director of National Intelligence—Peter Hernandez; and the chairman of the joint chiefs of staff, Admiral Jake Monroe, but consensus was not to be had. The president wanted answers, and all Curtis could get from them were questions. In the years he had known the president, he'd learned failure wasn't in his vocabulary. He'd go to the mat one more time.

"Look," Curtis began, looking toward the Secretary of State. "We have to get to the bottom of this. Don't our people in the field have any leads?"

"They do," Quinn replied, "but none convincing enough to take action."

"I agree," Monroe added. The JCS Chairman was an oftentimes vocal critic of the use of U.S. military forces for anything but the most compelling reasons. "We can't be certain of who did this."

"We're pressing hard to try to obtain that information," the DNI said. "We just don't have many in-country sources."

"We don't have the right information, and until we do, I say we shouldn't move," Monroe added.

"Gentlemen, I agree with the chairman," Jacobs said. "We must be certain before taking any overt action."

Curtis pressed again. "Mr. Secretary, I understand the need to move deliberately, but as the evidence mounts that this terrorism might be Iranian sponsored, we should have contingency plans, don't you think?"

"We have those plans," the secretary of defense replied, "but it takes presidential direction to implement them."

"Yes, I know that," Curtis responded, "but we need a comprehensive intelligence estimate."

"We *are* striving to know more. We have operatives trying to get that information," the DNI said.

"We may not have all the time you think you need," Curtis replied. "The president is firm he wants to take action to stop these attacks."

"We need to take the right actions though, Michael, not just lash out," the secretary of state offered.

"WE'RE NOT JUST LASHING OUT!" Curtis shouted, smashing his fist on the desk.

And so it went. The president's key advisors couldn't agree on what action to take, or whether to take any action at all.

"Let's break for lunch and reconvene at one-thirty," Curtis said, hoping that a midday respite would help them break the gridlock.

* * *

After the others filed out of the room, Curtis reflected on the events of the past several months. America had suffered a rash of terrorist attacks. Although there was not yet a smoking gun, strong circumstantial evidence pointed to Iran. The Iranians denied responsibility for any of the attacks.

He was staggered by the attacks' ferocity and confused by their seeming randomness: the suicide van attack on the U.S. Navy CH-53E detachment in Bahrain; the explosion in a marketplace frequented by Americans in Kuwait City; the truck that exploded in the neighborhood populated by American expatriates in Dhahran, Saudi Arabia.

They didn't suspect ISIL—the Islamic State. That cancer was focused on its own brand of terrorism—especially taking hostages and beheading them—not just terror for terror's sake.

The members of the NSC suspected the Iranian regime, but no direct link had been found—yet.

But his president demanded action. Patrick Browne was acutely aware of the opinion polls. Those polls, fed by constant commentary from officials of the administration Browne had supplanted, as well as by a stream of editorials bashing his "do nothing" policy on terrorism, had him sinking rapidly.

Similar polls indicated most Americans believed Iran supported state-sponsored terrorism. The fact that there were active terrorist training camps in Iran made a compelling case to launch attacks against the camps at the very least. The president didn't want to seem to jump to conclusions, so he turned it over to the NSC, not directing, but strongly hinting, what an acceptable finding would be.

Curtis was frustrated by the inability to deliver that finding. There were consistent themes for the attacks. They had targeted Americans and were destabilizing to an area that the United States wanted to keep stable. With over two-thirds of the world's proven oil reserves and close to forty percent of the world's daily oil production, the Arabian Gulf littoral was an area of enormous importance to the United States, as well as to its principal allies in Europe and Asia. Even though the United States was now a major energy producer, any disruption of this flow of oil from the Gulf would be enough to send the western economies into a tailspin. It was a situation that demanded action.

Curtis determined there would be action, smoking gun be damned. President Patrick Browne wanted to be justified before striking back at anyone and wanted the situation painted in black and white, not the muted grays Curtis had to deal with. Curtis knew he needed to focus the energies of the nation against the Islamic Republic of Iran.

Even though it was crafted by one of the president's predecessors and was one of his foreign policy "victories," the nuclear deal with Iran had done nothing to stem the tide of Iranian-instigated terrorism. Sure, it sounded good on paper—keeping Iran from getting a nuclear weapon in the next few years—but what that president and his team didn't get was that Iran was playing the long game and they knew they would get the bomb eventually. With that knowledge in their back pocket, Iran felt more free—not less—to use terrorism to keep the United States off balance and support its long-term goal of being the dominant power in the Arabian Gulf.

Curtis trudged back to his office knowing he'd have to face that picture of Harold Johnson and his still-grieving mama again.

CHAPTER 5

Anne O'Connor and Mike Hart entered the sea combat commander's module within *Carl Vinson's* CDC—Combat Direction Center—to get their briefing from the destroyer squadron commander, Commodore Jim Hughes, prior to launching on their ASR—armed surface reconnaissance—mission. Though many of her fellow pilots just wanted to be in the air flying, O'Connor enjoyed taking the time to see the big picture as the commodore briefed them on the surface plot.

"Okay," Hughes began, "you can see it here on our fusion plot. Up north we've got two of our ships doing maritime interception operations. We want you to go up there and have a look. Check in with USS *Benfold*; she's the on-scene commander."

"WILCO, sir," O'Connor replied. She enjoyed going on these missions—they were more tactical than flying endless circles in the tanker track. Hughes liked to use Airwing aircraft aggressively on ASR missions throughout the Gulf.

"After that, I want you to check out our Maritime Prepositioning ships anchored north of Jebel Ali. They're up here as part of a Marine Corps exercise. We've had reports of small boats approaching them, but no one has been able to identify a country of origin."

"Do you think they might be Iranian Revolutionary Guard Corps boats?" O'Connor asked.

"We don't know; anything you can give us would be great."

"Roger, sir," O'Connor replied.

O'Connor was struck by the fact the commodore always brought the air-crews working with him into his module to give them the big picture. If her damned exec, Bingo, were half as gracious, her life as a JO might be more bearable.

"We'll talk with you when you get airborne."

"WILCO, Commodore, we'll come up on the net ASAP."

The fact that she'd developed this association with Commodore Hughes said a lot about Anne O'Connor as a professional naval officer. She loved to fly, but flying was just part of what she was about.

* * *

"Admiral's in TFCC!" the petty officer shouted as Heater Robinson returned to his Tactical Flag Coordination Center. Announcing the admiral's presence in TFCC was more than protocol—it let the Carrier Strike Group One watchstanders get a jump on thinking through answers to anticipated questions from the admiral.

Robinson was well-liked, but he brooked no inattentiveness among his watchstanders. He expected them to have a complete tactical picture at all times. Pity the Flag TAO who didn't know where every strike group ship and aircraft was, where every potential hostile platform was, and who hadn't thought through what actions the strike group needed to take.

The admiral didn't need to say anything to inspire this sort of activity. His physical presence, as well as the intense training he had put the entire strike group—and especially his staff—through during *Carl Vinson's* workups were sufficient motivation. Robinson was a big man—six foot four inches tall and a hefty 240 pounds—and had a commanding presence. He looked like he could strap on a jet and duel with any one of the fighter pilots in Carrier Air Wing Seventeen, *Carl Vinson's* embarked airwing.

After graduating from the Naval Academy and earning his wings, Robinson had flown F/A-18C Hornets and then F/A-18E/F Super Hornets. He had come up through the system before duty with multi-service staffs was a necessity, and he still boasted more flight hours and traps—carrier arrested landings—than any pilot onboard *Carl Vinson.*

Steve Rawls was still Flag TAO, and rose as the admiral entered TFCC. TAOs recognized the best way to head off questions from the strike group commander was to start briefing him immediately upon his arrival in TFCC. There was much to tell. Dominated by two LSDs— Large Screen Displays—on the port bulkhead of the small space, this nerve center of the strike group's activities was only 15 feet by 30 feet and looked much smaller. On the left-hand LSD was the ACDS—Advanced Combat Direction System—display, a radar depiction of contacts within several hundred miles of *Carl Vinson*. On the right-hand LSD was the NTCS-A—Naval Tactical Command System Afloat—with a depiction of every ship and aircraft worldwide.

Flanking the two LSDs were a series of smaller displays showing a variety of information: the commercial air routes crisscrossing the Arabian Gulf, the PUs—participating units—in the data link connecting the ships in the strike group electronically, the latest weather briefing, the status of aircraft in the air, and a wealth of additional information. To the uninitiated it overwhelmed the senses, but to the experienced watchstander it served to increase his or her SA—situational awareness.

Closer to him than the LSDs, at the T-Table, the TAO had two other officers manning the surface and air displays. Both officers studied their monitors. They knew the admiral's rules—if it appeared on their screen, they'd better know everything about it.

To his left, several OSs—Operations Specialists—manned a variety of consoles, all of which drew information from multiple sources: ship's radars, aircraft radars, IFF—Identification Friend or Foe—interrogations, link inputs, and visual sightings. They put this information into the system, which, in turn, fed the LSDs. To the right were status boards displaying all matter of information: from ship call signs, to warfare commander assignments, to positioning data on key contacts. Interspersed throughout TFCC were a half-dozen radio speakers, all monitored by a TFCC watchstander.

Rawls began to brief the admiral on the tactical situation. Using his laser pointer, he walked around the left-hand LSD.

"Admiral, lots of activity this morning," he began. "We're gonna let the two Super Hornets we launched do a little tracking for the commodore before we bring 'em back aboard." Rawls was a "black shoe," a surface warfare officer, who was still trying to figure out what he was doing on an aircraft carrier briefing an Airedale admiral.

"That accounts for the good guys," the admiral responded. "What do you make of what the other side's doing so far?"

"Activity in Iran today is consistent with their actions over the last few days. Couple of jets out of Bushehr, others out of Shiraz—and of course their P-3 patrol plane making its standard MARPAT," Rawls replied, using the military acronym for maritime patrol.

"Okay, seems pretty normal," the admiral replied. "What's the situation on the other side of the Gulf?"

"Nothing much over there. Kuwait's running some training flights that make it out over the water from time to time, and the Saudis have a patrol aircraft—as well as a few jets—up this morning. All of it is pretty routine."

"Got it. Anything else?"

"No, Admiral, not really...."

Robinson could tell something about the air activity bothered his TAO. "Go ahead Steve; what's on your mind?"

"Well, Admiral...you know...I'm not an Airedale or anything, but I've been standing TAO for a while, and this is just a theory I guess, but Iran is flying at a higher rate than they were a week or so ago."

"Yes, I know. But do you make anything of it?"

"Sort of. It seems that their flights are...well...more organized."

"More organized?"

"Yes, sir. I know this sounds weird, but weeks ago they were flying from different fields at dissimilar times and going in random directions. Sometimes they'd come out over the water. Remember the time two weeks ago when we were in the northern Gulf and their two aircraft were flying out over the water? We went to GQ and got all spun up. Turned out they were just doing practice runs against their patrol boats."

"I remember that. Things were tense for a while, weren't they?"

"They were, Admiral. But now they don't do that anymore. Other than the MARPAT P-3, we haven't seen an Iranian aircraft get its feet wet in three or four days. And there's something else. They don't just launch at random times and go in different directions. A large number of their strike aircraft launch around the same time and go off in the same general direction over the desert—it even looks like they refuel en route. Then they all form up and come back to the southwest at the same time. It sure looks a little funny."

"Perhaps so. Certainly worthy of us putting some analysis into, don't you think?"

"Yes, sir, I sure do," Rawls replied.

"Good, then talk with Rocky and his intel folks and let's take a hard look at what they're doing. I'm going back to my cabin."

Robinson walked through the War Room and back into his cabin. He sat down and considered his conversation with his TAO. Every professional instinct he had gave him pause. What Rawls had described to him sounded ominously like the Iranians were practicing mirror-image strikes against his ships. If the aircraft formations Rawls described flew in the opposite direction, they would be on top of him.

He had a feeling that the theocratic regime in Iran was poised and ready to inflict devastation on his ships. It was a thought that filled him with dread. How had he missed what Rawls had just told him? He needed to act; protecting his ships was his most important job.

He reached for the KY-68 secure phone on his desk. A push of the intercom button and his administrative people connected him with Fifth Fleet Headquarters and his immediate operational boss, Vice Admiral Harry Flowers. His flag lieutenant, Lieutenant Mike Lumme, did as the admiral asked and stayed in the Flag Cabin and listened to Robinson's end of the conversation. It was shorter than either of them expected.

"Good afternoon, Admiral Flowers," Robinson began.

"Yes, sir, we're training hard out here—" he continued, but Flowers interrupted him.

"Yes, Admiral. I had something I thought I needed to bring to your attention—"

"Yes, sir. It is a rather large concern—"

"Admiral, if I may—"

"No, sir. We *have* been observing Iranian air activity—"

"No, sir, I'm sure that your intelligence people have been observing it too—"

"Admiral, the level of activity has picked up, and the patterns of activity—"

"No, Admiral, if I may continue. I have concerns we may need to take more of a defensive posture—"

"Yes, sir. I said defensive posture. It's only prudent—"

"No, I don't think I'm raising any alarm bells unnecessarily—"

"No, sir, you are certainly in charge of naval matters in the Gulf, but I'm—"

Lumme watched as the admiral suddenly pulled the receiver away from his ear. He looked visibly pained.

"Did you lose the connection, Admiral? Shall we call again?"

"No, Mike, we're done. I just need a little time alone."

"Yes, sir," Lumme replied as he beat a hasty retreat.

* * *

One hundred and fifty miles away, at Fifth Fleet Headquarters in Manama, Bahrain, the man who had been at the other end of the clipped dialogue with

Robinson stood at his desk and completed that conversation. "WE'LL SEE WHO THE HELL IS IN CHARGE!" Flowers shouted as he slammed the phone handset down.

Small, pale and gaunt, Flowers was the complete physical—and in many ways, psychological—opposite of Robinson. Flowers had only recently taken command of Fifth Fleet as the Navy commander in the Arabian Gulf and intended to set the tone early for his expected two-year tour. Word would spread to follow-on carrier strike group commanders that he wasn't someone to be dealt with lightly. Strike group commanders indeed. He wielded the real power. He'd decide how U.S. Navy forces would be used.

Flowers's career in the Navy differed as much from that of Robinson as their respective physical appearances did. A nuclear trained officer who grew up on surface ships, Flowers had a disdain for Airedales. He'd succeeded in a series of junior officer jobs on now-obsolescent nuclear-powered cruisers by his scrupulous adherence to the regulations and procedures of the Navy's nuclear-power program.

Flowers had never commanded a Navy carrier strike group and had little empathy for the predicament Robinson found himself in. After command of a frigate and subsequent command of a cruiser, Flowers had gained notice for his performance in a series of Washington assignments, many with the Navy's Naval Reactors organization.

Most recently, he served as the Navy Inspector General, where his job was to inspect other Navy commands and find fault or uncover wrongdoing. It was an assignment that suited his temperament, and he earned enough recognition uncovering scandals that—partly to assuage a Congress that criticized the Navy for not policing itself—he was given his current command.

The only tour Flowers had had on an aircraft carrier was his two-year stint as RO—Reactor Officer—aboard the aircraft carrier USS *Dwight D. Eisenhower.* While this was typically a tour where nuclear surface officers learn to live with, and appreciate, their aviation counterparts, Flowers's disdain for aviators only grew as he constantly bickered with *Eisenhower's* commanding officer. During this tour, Flowers usually took his meals in his stateroom to avoid eating with his fellow department heads—a luxury *Eisenhower's* executive officer allowed him only because Flowers outranked him by several years.

Flowers called his chief of staff, Captain Roger "Bolter" Dennis, an aviator, into his office. He wanted to get to the bottom of what Robinson was telling him.

"Chief of Staff, does our intel have anything changing recently regarding threats in the Gulf?"

"No, sir," Dennis responded.

"Any change in THREATCONs?"

"No, sir."

"Any thoughts on why the strike group commander might be worried?"

"No, Admiral."

"Any reason why the strike group shouldn't carry out the exercise the way we told them to?"

"No, sir, no reason at all...." Dennis was beginning to see why the admiral was quizzing him. As the chief of staff—as well as the senior aviator on the staff—he was accustomed to receiving the admiral's wrath against aviators.

"Is it clear, then, who is in charge of naval forces in the Gulf?"

"Crystal, sir."

"Good, Chief of Staff, I'm glad we agree on that."

As Dennis departed, Flowers had a few moments to reflect on why the Navy had sent him here: They wanted him to die professionally. Few Fifth Fleet commanders had ever risen to four-star rank. It seemed counterintuitive, given the importance of the Gulf region. One would think the naval forces commander here would be an important player. But CENTCOM—the United States Central Command—was almost always commanded by an Army or Marine Corps officer, and the focus was on land and air warfare and on checkmating the premier land power in the region, Iran.

This meant that when it came time to take military action, Navy forces were relegated to a supporting role. Flowers recalled operation Desert Strike against Saddam Hussein. Precluded by political considerations from striking Iraq from bases in the Middle East, the Air Force blocked attempts to use Navy carrier-based aircraft already in theater. Instead, Navy jets had been used to escort B-52s that were flown from Barksdale Air Force Base in Louisiana to launch cruise missiles against Iraq. The bottom line remained—there was a strong prejudice against using naval forces in this theater.

Flowers wasn't going to spend two years commanding Fifth Fleet merely to have it be a sideshow for the Army and Air Force. That would guarantee that he'd labor in obscurity for two years, only to be shuffled off to some nondescript job and then into retirement before he was ready. If Robinson was too timid to use his precious strike group aggressively, he'd direct the efforts of the group himself.

During his career, Flowers had developed a network of officers who were in some way beholden to him: officers whose careers he had pushed, others whom he had spared when he could have ended their careers abruptly, others hoping to garner favors when he gained his fourth star. Flowers kept meticulous files and had already called in some markers. More would be called in soon.

He summoned one of his yeomen. The admiral didn't bother to use the man's name. He'd be of little long-term use to him.

"Yeoman, I want you to place a call to the NSC—that's the National Security Council—" he said gratuitously. "I want you to reach a Captain Perry. Tell him I want to talk with him immediately."

"Yes, sir," the yeoman replied. He'd learned never to question the admiral's orders, even if he knew that the time zone difference meant it was early morning in Washington, D.C.

"And another thing, yeoman," Flowers shouted after him. "Get the operations officer in here right now."

Captain Carl Mullen appeared within two minutes after extracting himself from a meeting. It wasn't fast enough for the admiral.

"About time, Ops O," Flowers snarled, not even looking up.

"Yes, sir," was all that Mullen could offer.

"Are we monitoring *Carl Vinson's* flight schedule?"

"Yes, sir," Mullen offered.

"I want to be briefed more thoroughly on their operations every day. How many sorties did they have yesterday?"

"Admiral, I'll have to consult my message traffic, but I believe that it was just over one hundred—"

Flowers cut him off. "Just over a hundred. We've got the biggest damn exercise going that we've had here in years, and that's all they can muster? How many of those were strike sorties?"

"I think about forty-five," Mullen replied.

"Forty-five?" Flowers said as he shot out of his chair. He'd barely calmed down from railing at Robinson, and now he was boiling again. Didn't these people understand? The damn Air Force was getting too big a piece of the action and this timid admiral on *Carl Vinson* was only generating the minimal number of sorties. Flowers would be damned before he'd let Robinson torpedo his ambitions.

Flowers pointed his index finger at Mullen. "You talk to those people now— I mean right now. I want all the sorties they can generate. I want simulated strikes. Why do they think we send a carrier to the Gulf, just to defend itself? I want that message sent loud and clear!"

"Yes, Admiral. I'll get right on it," Mullen replied.

As Mullen left, Flowers collapsed back down into his chair. Why was this so damn hard? Once he talked to Captain Perry, things would change in the Gulf—and his star would rise one way or the other.

CHAPTER 6

President Hasan Ibrahim Habibi sat in his office in the heart of Tehran. He'd been president of the Islamic Republic of Iran for just a year following the assassination of his predecessor. He recalled the tumultuous days following that event, as well as his struggle to hold together the country's diverse radical, pragmatic and conservative factions. He didn't think the nation would survive another such upheaval.

Habibi had just finished chairing a factious meeting of the Supreme National Security Council. He had been unsuccessful in forging a consensus among the clerics, diplomats, and top-ranking military officers as to how to deal with the Islamic Republic's deteriorating economic condition and spiraling internal unrest. The coalition of conservatives and pragmatists he'd cobbled together was under intense attack by the radical faction, which seemed singularly focused on the Ayatollah Khomeini's doctrine of permanent revolution—something that had remained in Iran's DNA long after Khomeini's death. The exchanges still rang in his ears.

"We must continue to expand our oil exports," the Interior Minister began. "We can dramatically boost oil revenues by increasing our exports to Europe, and especially to Asia—"

"But not to the United States," interrupted the Supreme Council's secretary, and a representative of spiritual leader Ayatollah Rebaz Nateq-Nuri. "The Americans still refuse to buy our oil and they've poisoned the Paris Club of Bankers. We had to negotiate a dozen different debt agreements to refinance our loans—at exorbitant rates."

"You're correct, we cannot trade with the United States," the Interior Minister responded. "But we can't let that deter us from generating the revenues we can."

"I agree," Habibi added. "We must boost oil exports. The opportunity for increased revenues has never been better."

"You think we can buy off our people with more money?" another man asked. "Do you think that's the way to solve our problems?"

"I do!" Habibi shouted. "You forget that our unemployment rate is almost twenty percent—among our young men it's almost twice that. You recall the riots just a few miles from this building last year, as well as the riots in Mashhad, Araq, Ghazvin, and Shiraz. General Najafi, how many were killed and wounded in the rioting in Araq?" he asked the chief of the armed forces.

"Over forty killed, several hundred wounded, Mr. President. But it was all handled quickly."

"Indeed it was," Habibi continued, knowing the next answer, but wanting the general to say it himself. "But did you handle it with your forces alone?"

"My forces?"

"Yes. Was it your forces alone that you used, or did you have to rely on the Basij Militia?"

"Yes, the militia was of some help."

"And the anti-riot force sent all the way from Tehran? Were they of 'some help' too?"

"Yes," Najafi answered.

The debate continued, Habibi driving for a moderate, pragmatic approach. Above all else, he wanted to ensure European and Asian nations continued their policy of engagement with the Islamic Republic rather than follow the position of the United States, which seemed to never have recovered from the shah's overthrow.

But not all those present at the meeting participated in the debate. Listening, but non-communicative, had been the minister of foreign affairs, Ali Akbar Velayati. Habibi knew Velayati was influenced by a former Foreign Ministry official, Hossein Jahani. Jahani was strongly anti-American and was now the chief financier of the terrorist training camps within the Islamic Republic, as well as the architect of the recent terrorist attacks in the region.

Although most of those advocating Khomeini's doctrine of permanent revolution, like Jahani, had been purged from formal government positions, many had built a strong power base in the Revolutionary Guard, as well as in the Basij Militia. Abiding the terrorist training camps while denying their existence was a compromise Habibi felt he had to make to avoid having his revolutionary credentials questioned.

These were the internal conflicts that Habibi pondered as he sat in his office. Sometimes he felt he was single-handedly holding together the divergent groups within his nation. He had placated the radicals by allowing them to pursue their so-called permanent revolution. He was surprised—and relieved beyond words—that the United States hadn't yet found a smoking gun. How long he could maintain this precarious balance was a question he was afraid to ask.

Chapter 7

"Launch complete, launch complete," *Carl Vinson's* air boss, Commander Jack "Boomer" Davison, said over the ship's 5MC announcing system as the last Super Hornet climbed out ahead of the carrier. Davison would have much rather been in one of those Super Hornets than in *Carl Vinson's* Primary Flight Control on the ship's O-10 level high above the flight deck, but he'd had his share of flying tours, including command of the VFA-195 Dambusters.

Carrier Air Wing Seventeen's package was inbound to take station over western Iraq to monitor air activity in Syria. While much of the Islamic State's infrastructure in both Syria and Iraq had been destroyed, ISIL still had pockets of fighters in both countries. But there was a new threat.

What Carrier Air Wing Seventeen was doing was, in many respects, a replay of what their predecessors in other air wings had done almost a quarter century ago during Operation Southern Watch. In those days the mission was to monitor the Iraqi regime, which was oppressing its Kurdish minority subsequent to Operation Desert Strike. Those operations continued for years and had become routine.

Now Iraq was rebuilding with United States help and was also taking back much of the territory ISIL had overrun over the past several years. But there was a new concern in the greater Levant—it was Syria. Racked by years of civil war, the Alawite regime had finally beaten back the Islamic State and was free of that threat, at least for the moment.

But the Syrian regime had hardened its stance and was hell bent on squashing those segments of their Sunni majority that had been most restive during—and subsequent to—the so-called Arab Spring. The United Nations had finally brokered peace—of a sort—and had imposed restrictions on Syria's formidable air force regarding where it could, and couldn't, fly. Syria was complying—up to a point. But as had been the case a generation ago during Southern Watch, it was left to the United States—and specifically the U.S. Navy and U.S. Air Force—to maintain airborne patrols to enforce the U.N. mandates.

Lieutenant Brian McDonald was part of "Package Charlie," the third group of aircraft the Navy had sent up today to maintain airborne patrols to monitor Syrian military air activity. As the group of four Super Hornets, two Hornets and one EA-18G Growler all finished taking their drinks from the Air Force KC-135 tanker over south-eastern Iraq and got ready to "push"—move toward their patrol station—it occurred to him this wasn't a bad way to spend the day.

Sitting in Fighting Redcock 104, McDonald twisted his neck to the right and looked over at his wingman, Tiny Baker, in Fighting Redcock 106, who gave him a nod. Back to his left, a section of Super Hornets from the Shrikes of VFA-94 flew along with them. All the Super Hornets were armed with two AIM-7 Sparrows, a single AIM-120 AMRAAM missile and a full gun load. To his right, two Hornets flew in tight formation armed with two Sidewinders and a single AMRAAM. The Growler, with its sophisticated jamming pods, rounded out the package.

McDonald loved what the Super Hornet could do as a flying machine, but he was even more impressed by what it could do as a weapons platform. In the air-to-air mode, the aircraft used the APG-65 radar to track multiple targets simultaneously and then engage targets using the full range of air-to-air missiles in the Navy inventory. In the air-to-ground mode, McDonald's Super Hornet could use all Navy precision guided munitions: laser-guided bombs, SLAM, Maverick and Harpoon. For McDonald, the Super Hornet was a joy to fly and operate.

* * *

Well to the northwest of Carrier Air Wing Seventeen's package, at Tha'lah Military Airbase in Syria's As-Suwayda governance region, Raid Abd Bakr climbed into his MIG-25 Foxbat and went through his pre-flight checks prior to taxiing. He had a single AS-6 training missile slung under his aircraft. He was scheduled for a training hop, a GCI—ground control intercept—flight that would take him close to Iraq's western border and near—but not into—the no-fly zone the United States and its allies enforced. He considered his good fortune. His assignment with the 766 squadron at Tha'lah would ensure he experienced more flying than his compatriots at other airfields.

The GCI flight was excellent training. The ground controller would fly him over the vast Syrian Desert—a continuum of wide stony plains interspersed with occasional sandy stretches and long, wandering wadis. Bakr's job was to follow the instructions of the controller precisely. It had been over two weeks since he'd last flown, and he knew he was rusty, but this was a good way to regain his proficiency.

Bakr taxied his MIG out to the end of the airfield's single runway. Once there, he checked in with his GCI controller. All the controller was to him was a disembodied voice that would keep him safe. He jammed the throttles forward, powered his aircraft along the runway, and lifted his MIG up into the early afternoon sky.

* * *

Shortly after *Carl Vinson's* package Charlie took off, Air Force Captain Brad Weiss was airborne in his U-2S "Dragon Lady" aircraft. Launching from Prince Sultan Air Base in the Saudi Arabian desert, Weiss figured this would be another routine mission. He considered his good fortune being part of the Beale Air Force Base U-2S squadron detachment assigned to forward-stage at Prince Sultan. Now Weiss was where the action was, not cooling his heels at an obscure Air Force base outside Sacramento, California.

The U-2Ss patrolled the sky along the southern edge of the no-fly zone. Weiss would use his aircraft's cameras to take pictures of Syrian positions on the other side of the no-fly zone, seeking bits and pieces of intelligence regarding Syrian troop movements, flights, or missile positions.

Weiss didn't lack for courage, but he felt incredibly vulnerable as he flew this mission. "Alone and unafraid" he and his squadron-mates called it with their pilot's gallows humor. There were no routine missions as far as he was concerned. Even a half-witted Syrian pilot could shoot him down. He took some comfort in the fact that the Air Force and the Navy put fighter packages into the air whenever the U-2S flew in order to protect his defenseless aircraft.

* * *

As package Charlie approached CAP station Colorado, they anchored over a convenient geographic checkpoint. The Super Hornets and Hornets set up their racetrack patterns, while the Growler took a jamming station south of them. Flying their north-south racetrack enabled the jets to have at least one section of fighters pointing toward Syrian airspace at all times, ready to engage any Syrian jet that threatened the U-2S. Further to the south, the ever-present Air Force AWACS radar plane kept a wary eye on everything in the air, ready to provide an instant alert should a Syrian jet make a threatening move.

Brian McDonald was flying one of the sections, teamed with Shrike 300, piloted by the Shrike's executive officer, Commander Tim "Benny" Tallent. The Shrike exec was years senior, so McDonald was content with flying his wing. Once package Charlie was on station, Tallent radioed the AWACS and told the controller that the U-2S was cleared to begin its mission.

* * *

Raid Bakr began the first leg of his GCI hop with a mixture of exhilaration and frustration—exhilaration to be in the air once again, but frustration that his jet wasn't operating to his liking. His gyrocompass was acting balky and his standby compass was out of the aircraft, no doubt removed to place in another aircraft with more severe material problems. Worse still, his radios produced a great deal of static.

He frequently had to ask the GCI controller to repeat his instructions. The condition of his aircraft was annoying, and bordering on unsatisfactory, but he wasn't about to return to base and wait—who knew how long—to fly again. He'd just make the best of it. Flying south across the Syrian Desert, he was thankful there was a GCI controller at all. There were no navigational landmarks in this vast wasteland.

* * *

"Roger, Joker," Brad Weiss said as the AWACS controller cleared him to begin his flight along the northern edge of the no-fly zone. He activated his cameras, banked right, and headed for his first way-point. He had a specific flight path he needed to follow. The AWACS had cleared him along his route and that meant his defensive CAP station was set—didn't it? Was it Navy pilots flying protection today? What if they had an emergency on the aircraft carrier and they had to be recalled? He felt the hair on the back of his neck stand up.

* * *

Raid Bakr found himself speaking more and more loudly just to make himself understood to his GCI controller. He knew the enlisted man at the other end was most likely a conscript and just trying to do his job. Senior officers were monitoring his flight and if he didn't perform well it wouldn't be the controller who'd be censured, but him.

"Turn now—"

"Say again, control, you are very garbled!" Bakr shouted.

"Four-zero-nine, I say...turn...one...five...."

"You're broken, say again."

"I say...turn...."

He thought he understood the command and the turn didn't seem exactly right—south-south-east—but the radios were getting worse and picking up every second or third word was the best he could do. He stared at his fuel gauge and tried to concentrate on managing his fuel supply. *Let's see, at a speed of 450 knots, consuming*...he thought as he did his mental calculations regarding how long he could stay airborne.

* * *

The Package Charlie section continued to fly lazy race track patterns over their anchor point as they surveyed the landscape below. Brian McDonald was alone with his thoughts in his Super Hornet. He was broken out of his musing by an unexpected call from the AWACS.

"Shrike 300 and flight, Joker, over."

"Go ahead, Joker," Tallent replied.

"Three-zero-zero, I've got a bogey headed south-southeast, type unknown, about ninety miles from your posit."

"Roger, Joker, say intentions?" Tallent asked. He'd been doing this long enough he realized the AWACS was good—but not perfect. They had radar "ghosts"—false images—just like any other radar. Tallent wanted more info.

"Shrike 300, on its current course, contact will pass within fifteen miles of the U-2 in ten minutes. We have a problem."

"Joker, Shrike 300. Rules of engagement are pretty clear on this one. It's your call if we engage."

"Roger, 300, checking...wait."

"Joker, 300, say range to bogey."

"Shrike 300, Joker. Bogey still closing our man, now inside of thirty miles, request you commit. Vector three-two-zero, seventy-five miles."

"Roger, Joker. We're committing on the bogey, bearing three-two-zero for seventy-five."

Tallent banked his bird hard, and McDonald followed. They had practiced this dozens of times. Was this the real thing?

* * *

Raid Bakr continued on his path. His fuel calculations complete, he looked out at the formless desert below trying to pick up some landmark—anything that would tell him where he was. The GCI controller wasn't helping, though Bakr did note the pitch of his voice in his almost inaudible communications pick up.

* * *

Weiss continued on course, but listening to the conversations coming from the AWACS made a tight knot form in the pit of his stomach. He was as brave as the next man, but the AWACS needed to tell him to reverse course and steer out of danger away from the Syrian intruder. When were they going to call him?

* * *

Aboard the AWACS, the mission commander had less than a minute to make two decisions. The first was relatively easy. He called Weiss on the secure net.

"Dragon, this is Joker. You're steering into danger. Turn right now, reverse course, and come to a heading of 250. Acknowledge."

"Joker, Dragon, WILCO," Weiss replied as he banked his U-2S as hard as he dared and retreated toward safety.

Satisfied that his charge was turning away from danger, the AWACS mission commander made his second decision.

"Shrike flight, this is Joker. Dragon is clearing the area. Target at your one o'clock, forty-five miles. Stand by to engage. I say again, stand by to engage. Out."

Tallent and McDonald quickly rehearsed their procedures as they simultaneously shed their disbelief this was happening. They determined that the best tactic was for Tallent to engage the MIG-25 at long range with his AIM-120 AMRAAM missile. McDonald would be ready with his shorter-range missiles if his flight lead missed.

* * *

Raid Bakr was shouting now, trying to make the GCI controller hear him. Damn these radios. His instincts told him he was on this leg for too long a time, but the Syrian military booked no freelancing by its pilots. His shouting seemed to have some impact. Now the controller was talking loudly and excitedly. What was he saying? The high pitch of his voice started to make Bakr anxious.

* * *

"Shrike flight, bandit declared hostile. You're cleared to engage. I say again, cleared to engage," the AWACS mission commander said.

Satisfied that he was lined up for a good shot and cleared to fire, Tallent turned on his fire control radar. Immediately, he had contact.

"Shrike flight engaged with the bandit bearing zero-four-zero."

* * *

The display was unmistakable to Raid Bakr. His ES—electronic surveillance—gear picked up the Super Hornet's fire control radar as soon as it came on. But how could it be? He was targeted? Bakr called his GCI controller and then his survival instincts took over.

* * *

"Fox three," Tallent shouted, stating the obvious but following procedures nonetheless. The AMRAAM missile coming off a fast-moving aircraft travels at over 1,500 miles an hour. It headed straight for the MIG-25. It would take less than two minutes to get there.

* * *

Raid Bakr didn't know what was coming, and he didn't know what was to soon hit him. He mustered all the flying skills he had learned in all his years of flying and yanked and banked his plane wildly to try to defeat the unseen foe.

* * *

Aboard the AWACS, the mission commander and his crew tracked the AM-RAAM missile as it sped toward the MIG.

McDonald spotted it first. "Shrike 300, flash, twelve o'clock. No chute."

"Roger 104, we're breaking off," Tallent replied. "Break. Joker, Shrike flight, splash one bandit, returning to station."

"Roger, Shrike 300," the AWACS mission commander replied. He prepared a short, pre-formatted message to his command element over his secure net. Simultaneously, the U.S. Navy E-2D loitering off the coast had picked up the transmissions and was preparing a similar message to send to *Carl Vinson's* CDC.

As the operators in the field followed their well-rehearsed procedures for pushing this information up the chain of command, it was only a matter of minutes before the word of this shoot-down reached the National Military Command Center in the Pentagon. A short time later, this same information arrived at military headquarters in Damascus.

CHAPTER 8

U.S. Army General Daniel Xavier Lawrence sat at his desk at CENTCOM Headquarters at MacDill Air Force Base in Tampa, Florida. Sensitive to Arabian Gulf nations' concerns that the U.S. "footprint" in the Gulf was too large, the United States had set up the command responsible for military activities in that region at this Florida base.

The CENTCOM Commander directed activities in the Gulf from this distant headquarters and that situation led to the challenges he was now dealing with. Tensions were heating up in the Gulf and he wasn't there. The only senior officers in the Gulf Area of Responsibility—AOR—were Air Force Major General Anthony Gaylord, running air-watch operations monitoring Syrian air activity, and Vice Admiral Harry Flowers, the U.S. Navy's Fifth Fleet commander. Lawrence could barely tolerate the Air Force and couldn't abide the Navy at all. He was getting his information secondhand, and from officers in whom he had no confidence.

CENTCOM was the most unique of the nine Unified Combatant Commands assigned operational control of United States combat forces. Other Unified Combatant commanders—like the U.S. Pacific Command headquartered in Honolulu, Hawaii and the U.S. European Command headquartered in Stuttgart-Vaihingen, Germany—had vast forces continually under their command and were also located in the area of their operations. Conversely, the CENTCOM commander had fewer than two thousand full-time military personnel permanently assigned to his headquarters located seven thousand miles from where the action would be in a conflict.

The theory had it that in time of crisis CENTCOM would deploy to the Gulf and would draw forces from its component commanders: the Army Forces Central Command (ARCENT) at Fort McPherson, Georgia; Central Command Air Forces (CENTAF) at Shaw Air Force Base, South Carolina; Naval Forces

Central Command (NAVCENT) in Manama, Bahrain; Marine Corps Forces Central Command (MARCENT) at Camp Lejeune, North Carolina; and Special Operations Command Central (SOCCENT), also at MacDill. That was the theory, but Lawrence had seen that theory come apart during Operation Desert Strike in 1996 when the CENTCOM staff hadn't moved forward. He wasn't in control of the situation and it bothered him deeply.

Control was what had propelled Lawrence to four stars in the Army and what had made him one of the most powerful men in the U.S. military. His looks accentuated that power. Lawrence had been a boxer at the U.S. Military Academy at West Point and still practiced in the ring. At just over six feet tall and a lean 180 pounds, he looked like a professional athlete and appeared to most to be a decade younger than his fifty-four years.

He was just finishing his first cup of coffee and going through his message queue when his executive assistant—his EA—Colonel Carter Samuels knocked and walked into his office.

"Yes, Carter?" The general looked up and immediately sensed alarm in his assistant's eyes.

"Sir, General Gaylord's on the line. He says there's been a shoot-down."

"Shoot-down!" Lawrence exclaimed. "One of our planes?"

"No, sir, a Syrian Foxbat."

Samuels left and put Gaylord's call through.

"Lawrence here," the CENTCOM Commander said, picking up the phone on the first ring.

"General, good morning. Our AWACS just reported that one of our jets just shot down a Syrian MIG-25 over their territory. It was heading right for our U-2 when it was shot down."

"Heading for our U-2? Why? When?"

"Just ten minutes ago; I called you as soon as I could. We've made our voice report to the National Military Command Center—and to your command center, of course. But I wanted to call you personally."

"Who the hell shot at him?"

"It was one of the Navy Super Hornets off *Carl Vinson*."

"Navy? I told you we had to keep the Navy out of the box. God-dammit! Who gave the shoot order?"

"Our AWACS gave the final order, General—in accordance with the rules of engagement," Gaylord replied.

"Fuck the ROE!" Lawrence shouted. "I'm the God-damned unified commander. Did you ever think of consulting me?"

"General," Gaylord protested, "there just wasn't time—"

"Wasn't time? You let that Navy cowboy Flowers screw the pooch on this one. When the hell is he going to call me? I want that Navy pilot debriefed and a full transcript sent to me."

"Yes, sir," was all Gaylord could offer. Lawrence wasn't thinking clearly—he was barely thinking at all. There was never time to check such things through. U.S. aircraft had been playing this cat and mouse game—first with Saddam Hussein's Air Force, and now Syria's—for a long time. Now something had happened.

"Send me a full report, General. I want to see anything else about this shoot down before it goes out to any other commands."

"Yes, sir," Gaylord responded.

Lawrence's EA was the next to receive a blast.

"Carter, get in here!" Lawrence shouted. Samuels was there before the general's finger was off the intercom button. "Get Admiral Flowers on the line." Samuels was gone as quickly as he had appeared.

Lawrence was too agitated to sit down, so he paced back and forth across his office. Finally, his deputy director for intelligence brought in the charts that he'd asked for.

Lawrence spread the large map of the CENTCOM AOR on his desk—he had little use for the electronic maps others used. He had a fascination with geography and spreading this chart out and staring at it helped focus his mind. Looking at the sprawling AOR, which stretched over 3,000 miles from east to west and almost 3,500 miles north to south, he reminded himself of the complexity of the twenty countries that comprised the area. In addition to the Gulf littoral states of Bahrain, Iran, Iraq, Kuwait, Oman, Qatar, Saudi Arabia and the United Arab Emirates, his AOR stretched to the borders of Kenya and Tanzania in the south; to the borders of Egypt and Libya in the west; to the borders of Iran and Azerbaijan in the north; to the borders that Pakistan shared with China and India in the east.

While looking at the map helped focus his mind, it increased his frustration. How the hell did they expect him to manage the complex interactions in this area from his headquarters in Florida? How was he supposed to safeguard—from seven thousand miles away—a region that was the juncture of major maritime trade routes linking the Middle East, Europe, South and East Asia and the Western Hemisphere? He'd find a way to get himself and his staff into the AOR or bust.

The intercom rang again. "General, I have Admiral Flowers on the line," his secretary said.

"Put him on," Lawrence replied, pushing the maps aside, "and tell Samuels to get on the line, I may want to replay this one."

Having their executive assistants listen in on their calls was a time-honored tradition of senior military officers. They felt their time was too valuable to take notes on their conversations, so the EA was assigned to listen in and keep a transcription of what was discussed. Little wonder rumors and leaks abounded throughout the military.

Lawrence let the phone ring several times as he settled back into his chair. Finally, he picked it up. "Lawrence, here."

"General, this is Admiral Flowers. How are you this morning?" the admiral began, knowing what Lawrence was calling about but not certain of what his reaction would be. He found out immediately.

"Not worth a damn, Admiral. How in the hell did you let one of your planes shoot down a God-damned Syrian aircraft?"

"The MIG was making a beeline for our U2, General. I'd say that we probably saved our pilot's life." Flowers was taking a hard line. He would show Lawrence who had the real clout in the CENTCOM AOR.

"You say we probably saved the pilot's life. What do you base that on, your extensive experience in the AOR, or your actual combat experience?" Lawrence asked with a heavy dose of sarcasm. He had no respect for Flowers. But now this...this...*dilettante* was defying him.

Flowers was undaunted and brushed off the personal and professional slight. "General, I think if you—"

Lawrence cut him off. "No, Admiral, now you just go into the listen mode. You didn't think, that's the God-damned problem—you and whoever is in charge of your strike group launching these guys over Syria without having control over them. You just started blasting away. Are you responsible for those Navy jets?"

"Yes, I am responsible—"

"You are, huh? So you've spent time on *Carl Vinson*—in your capacity as fleet commander?"

"Yes, General, I've been out to *Carl Vinson*."

"Yes. I'm sure you have. And you've visited the ready rooms and talked with the pilots, correct?"

"Well, General—"

Lawrence knew the answer and poured it on. "And since enforcing these U.N. sanctions is so important, you've impressed on them *personally* the delicacy of the situation over Syria. You've explained to them how they should use force only as a last resort. You've done that, haven't you, Admiral?"

"No, General, not exactly."

"Not exactly?"

"No, General…well…I mean I haven't personally done that. I didn't feel that that was my role. The strike group commander—"

"Let me understand this," Lawrence interrupted once again. "You're there in the AOR full time. You have one carrier strike group working for you. You have assets that can take you out to the carrier anytime you want—hell, you can embark in the carrier full time for all I care. But you haven't made the time to take an interest in something so important and have left it up to some cowboy out there on the carrier. You must be awfully busy doing other things. It's just not clear to me what those things are."

Flowers hadn't expected his conversation with Lawrence to be pleasant, but he hadn't anticipated the attacks to be so personal. "General, I will fix the problem. You have my assurance on that."

"You're the God-damned problem! You and that idiot in charge of your strike group—Robinson—isn't that his name? He's supposed to be some hotshot flyboy. You haven't heard the end of this!" Lawrence shouted as he slammed the phone down. Samuels winced as he pulled the phone away from his ear.

"Mandy," the general yelled, loud enough for his secretary to hear, "you got that call placed to the chairman yet?"

"We'll get a call back as soon as he comes out of the NMCC, General."

Lawrence was frustrated beyond words. He needed to be where the action was. He couldn't do his job from this desk in a building half a world away. He was going to be in charge, and he was going to be in control.

CHAPTER 9

Carl Vinson had been at general quarters for over three hours. Immediately after the E-2D Hawkeye had reported the Foxbat shoot-down, Captain Vandegrift had sent his ship to GQ to prepare for the worst. The ready alert fighters and a tanker package had been launched and some of the aircraft in the just-returned Package Charlie had been refueled and immediately sent up again.

The handler—the officer responsible for positioning the carrier's aircraft in the hangar bay and on *Carl Vinson's* flight deck—wasn't as well-prepared for this contingency as he might have been. As aircraft were re-spotted—moved to different positions on the flight deck—a heavier burden fell to the airborne tankers to keep gas in the air.

Anne O'Connor was piloting one of those tankers. Immediately after the Foxbat shoot-down she had been pulled off her ASR mission, brought back to the carrier, hot-refueled, and sent aloft as one of the primary tankers.

She was running tanking circles at 7,000 feet and 250 knots high above *Carl Vinson*, and she'd just refueled her third fighter. There were more coming. Navy fighters are notorious gas hogs and use a lot of fuel during their launch and initial climb out—so much so that it was necessary to top them off with fuel before sending them on their mission. O'Connor had been airborne for a while, and coming on the heels of their long ASR mission, she was getting a little ragged.

As she motored around the tanker track making endless left-hand turns, she spotted the next fighter on her list of planes to refuel—Fighting Redcock 104—Brian McDonald's jet. It reminded her of how being a naval aviator—or even being a naval officer—was such a near thing for her.

Like all of the 1,200 or so new plebes, Anne O'Connor entered the U.S. Naval Academy on a sultry day in June. She was determined to become a naval officer and then earn her naval aviator wings.

O'Connor had an intense plebe summer and was ready to begin her academic year. She hit the ground running, becoming a peer leader among her classmates, making the varsity swimming team, and keeping up with her studies—though that part was harder than she'd anticipated. She made no secret of the fact she was focused on naval aviation and collected naval aviation squadron stickers to post in her room.

A month after Christmas, during a period known at the Naval Academy as the Dark Ages: when the Annapolis sky is perpetually gray, when the joys of Christmas are a distant memory, and when spring seems too far away to even think about, O'Connor hit a tough spot. Her grades were slipping badly. She was starting on the swimming team, and she didn't want to back off on that joyful activity. Swimming was more than just something she did—it helped define who she was.

She'd been dating a former midshipman on the Academy men's swimming team who had quit the Academy a month earlier and transferred to USC, where he accepted a full swimming scholarship. O'Connor had been offered a swimming scholarship at USC out of Coronado High. She turned it down to attend the Academy but received an e-mail from the Southern Cal swimming coach reminding her that if she ever changed her mind, a scholarship was waiting for her.

Her company officer, the adviser for the hundred-plus midshipmen assigned to a company, was a non-athletic surface warfare officer who wasn't enamored with athletes, prospective aviators, or women for that matter. He had chewed her out about her grades and told her how stupid she was to be playing a varsity sport. The low ebb hit when she flunked her second math exam in a row and then came down with the flu, missing several swim meets. Her friend at USC was texting her every night to try to persuade her to drop out and come join him there.

Brian McDonald was a first class midshipman in her company and had already been selected for naval aviation. Although O'Connor wasn't in his squad there were informal networks within the company. When he learned a fellow midshipman interested in naval aviation was thinking of quitting the Academy, he summoned her to his room in Bancroft Hall, the Academy's cavernous dormitory.

"Midshipman O'Connor, reporting as ordered," she said as she knocked on Midshipman First Class McDonald's door at 2100 on a Tuesday night. He had picked the time because he knew his roommate would be in the library cramming for an exam.

"Come in, O'Connor. Stand at ease."

"Yes, sir," she replied. She didn't know why she'd been ordered to show up here, but if a plebe was called to a first class midshipman's room, it was never a good thing. *He's probably going to rag on me about my math grades.* This might be the final nail in the coffin that was going to make her decision to quit the Academy that much easier.

"I guess you're wondering why I called you down here," McDonald began.

"Yes, sir, I was." *The less you say, the better,* she told herself.

"This may take a while, why don't you grab my roomie's chair and sit down."

"Yes, sir," she replied. Upperclassmen never invited plebes to sit down in their rooms. She sat at attention in the chair.

"I understand that you've been having some trouble with math?"

"Yes, sir, but I'm studying hard, and I'm going to math help sessions twice a week."

"Well, calc is pretty tough stuff. I figure you must be studying because you're not around the company area much; you must be at the library."

"Yes, sir, I'm there a lot."

"One thing I noticed when we do room inspections is you've turned your room into an aviation shrine. You have an awful lot of stuff, memorabilia and all that."

"Yes, sir, I think what I have posted is all within regs."

"O'Connor, relax, will you? You look like Artoo-Detoo without his can," McDonald said.

That finally drew a smile.

"Look, a company is a tight place," he continued. "I think I know you're interested in naval aviation. Am I safe in saying that?"

"Yes, sir, more than interested, I've wanted to fly since I was five years old."

"Okay, so we have something in common. You know if you graduate from this place, and can pass your flight physical, you're virtually a shoe-in to go to naval aviation training."

"That was my goal when I came here."

"It's also no secret that you're thinking of dropping out and transferring to USC."

"Yes, sir, that's right. If I can't get good enough grades to stay here, I want to go somewhere where I can finish my education—"

"And what happens to flying?" he asked, interrupting her.

"After I graduate from USC, I can look into that—"

McDonald interrupted her again. "O'Connor, look, you haven't been to all the briefings I have. The Navy is downsizing. They don't need that many pilots. If you go to USC on a swimming scholarship, they aren't going to let you join NROTC. And if you don't graduate from here or an NROTC school, the chances of getting into naval aviation are almost zero."

She hadn't considered what he was telling her.

"Here, I want to show you something," McDonald said as he produced a thick photo album. It was filled with pictures of his naval aviation summer training. There were pictures of him on USS *John C. Stennis* working and flying with their Super Hornet squadron; pictures of him in Pensacola, Florida, home of the Navy's Blue Angels; and pictures of him in various kinds of flight gear. As he went through the book, she was caught up in his contagious enthusiasm for flying—the same kind of enthusiasm she had months ago when she'd entered the Academy.

Finally, he closed the book. "Well, what do you think?"

"It seems like you're really looking forward to flying. I think you'll make a great pilot."

"So will you, O'Connor."

"I don't think I'll be one—or a graduate of this place."

"Look, O'Connor, I called you in because I didn't want you to give up your dream. I was in a tough spot two years ago—in my sophomore slump—when someone did for me what I'm trying to do for you."

She finally looked up and made the first real eye contact with him.

"Don't you see? I can tell that you love naval aviation. Who do you think I want in my squadron flying wing on me—you, or someone who just picks naval aviation out of a hat on service selection night?"

"Yes, sir, but I can't hack the math," she replied. Everything he was saying was so true—she desperately wanted to fly—but she wouldn't if she flunked out or transferred to USC.

"Bullshit, O'Connor," he replied loudly, startling her. "Everyone says that at first. The math sucks and it's as boring as flying is fun."

He pushed a sheet of paper across the desk. "Here, recognize any of these names?"

"Yes, sir, these are all midshipmen in our company."

"More than that, they're all going into naval aviation. Each of them has volunteered to tutor you. My personal recommendation is Frank Noonan, he's a real math whiz. Or there's Mary Williams, she took the same course last year that you're taking now. But you can pick who you want."

O'Connor looked at the piece of paper. More than just a list of names, he had detailed what math courses each of them had already taken, as well as what math courses they were currently taking. This wasn't some off-the-cuff thing; he had put a lot of time and effort into the list.

"Sir, I'll think about this. I'll think about this a lot; I really will."

"O'Connor, I'm counting on you to do more than that. We're gonna get you over this math speed bump, and over this flu, and back in the pool and winning swim meets for us. Then we're gonna get you out of here and into the fleet and flying, you got it?"

With that McDonald rose, and she did as well. He extended his hand.

"I'm looking forward to you flying on my wing, O'Connor, so don't screw it up," he said as they shook hands.

"I won't, sir."

That encounter with Brian McDonald had been just the tonic. She received an extraordinary amount of help, and while her math grades weren't pretty, she got through. She was soon back in the pool winning her events and ultimately lost interest in USC.

She had never found a way to formally thank him for doing what he did, and there never seemed to be an end to his helping her. After he graduated he kept in touch, writing her e-mails occasionally when he was going through flight training and also sending her a little something to keep her psyched up for naval aviation—a squadron patch, a picture of a fighter aircraft, or some other sort of aviation memorabilia.

O'Connor had gone to Pensacola after graduation. The constant moving from base to base as she began flight training, coupled with McDonald's embarking on his first carrier deployment, caused them to lose touch. Now, years later, they found themselves in the same Airwing.

She tried to thank him, but he downplayed his role, insisting she had done it all herself and pointing out that one of her classmates from their company, Jake Roach, who was flying with HSM-73, had availed himself of the same type of help. O'Connor and Roach were friends, and as they compared notes, they realized just how influential McDonald had been in getting them to where they were now.

O'Connor put those thoughts out of her mind as Fighting Redcock 104 moved in to refuel. It took only a few minutes to give the Super Hornet the 2,000 pounds of gas it needed. As 104 broke away she allowed herself a look at McDonald's jet and saw his head turn toward her. No eye contact was possible behind those darkened visors, but she was sure that she saw a head nod. *Still checking on me,* she thought. *Brian McDonald, making sure I'm doing all right.* Those thoughts were broken as Fighting Redcock 104 drifted back behind her aircraft to wait until his wingman, Fighting Redcock 107, refueled.

Fighting Redcock 107 was halfway through refueling when the E-2D called. O'Connor could tell instantly that there was a problem.

"Ninety-nine," the Hawkeye pilot began, using the collective call sign for all the aircraft in the air, "this is Sun King 601. We've got a Super Hornet with an AMAD PR caution light. We need to bring him aboard immediately. Break. Shrike 305, we're doing a pull-forward now to clear the flight deck for you. Hold ten miles aft, signal delta. Expect a straight-in approach."

* * *

"CAG LSO to the platform."

The announcement over *Carl Vinson's* 1MC told everyone that an emergency was in progress. An aircraft carrier's launch and recovery cycles are stable, fixed events, and the LSOs, or Landing Signal Officers—the pilots who guide the planes to touchdown over the flight deck—are always on station before a scheduled recovery begins. When an LSO has to be called to the platform unexpectedly it invariably means that an aircraft had to land early, often with an emergency.

The emergency was an AMAD PR caution light on Shrike 305, one of the Super Hornets returning from the box. The AMAD—Aircraft Mounted Accessory Drive—powers the Hornet's generators, as well as its oil and hydraulic pumps. An overheated AMAD could lead to the loss of the aircraft. The Super Hornet needed to land immediately.

On an aircraft carrier carrying over 5,000 people it's usually impossible to be singularly focused on any one event for long. Hundreds of important things go on every hour of every day. When an Airwing aircraft has an emergency, however, the ship's focus is riveted on that bird.

Sitting at their scopes in CATCC, *Carl Vinson's* operations specialists picked up Shrike 305 as soon as it was handed off by the E-2D. Clearing all other aircraft out of the way, they set him up for an extended straight-in approach, rather than a carrier "break," where the aircraft flies over the carrier and then breaks left abruptly to enter a downwind leg for landing. A straight-in would minimize the strain on the aircraft's hydraulic control systems as the affected engine was shut down. On the bridge, the captain called for more speed so *Carl Vinson* could have additional wind over the deck. On the flight deck, on the LSO platform, and in Primary, the first team was at the ready to get Shrike 305 back on deck safely.

The air boss got things moving, booming over the 5MC. "On the flight deck. Let's get in the proper flight deck uniform. We've got a Super Hornet with an emergency coming in for a final approach. Get cranials on and buckled, sleeves rolled down, excess personnel clear the flight deck. Make a ready deck."

Shrike 305 rolled onto a ten-mile final approach following the course of the ship. The pilot, Lieutenant Paul "Weasel" Weisbrook, nursed the jet along, making the minimum control inputs required to keep it heading toward *Carl Vinson.*

CCA—Carrier Control Approach—handed the jet off to the LSO, and the next voice Weisbrook heard was that of the CAG LSO, Lieutenant Commander Mike "Dobie" Gillis.

"Shrike 305, paddles contact, call the ball."

"Paddles" was the name for the landing signal officer and was a throwback to the days before the "meatball" glide slope indicator that gave the pilots a more precise way of guiding their jet safely to the deck. In the days before the meatball, the LSO, armed with two signaling paddles, directed the jet to the deck and used his paddles to wave the jet off if its approach was out of parameters. Now, the LSO worked in sync with the meatball and gave the pilot advisory—and sometimes imperative—commands. He needed to make this approach a good one. No one knew how long the Super Hornet could go without having its hydraulics fail, causing the loss of the pilot and his aircraft.

"Three-zero-five, Rhino ball, four-point-eight, single-engine," Weisbrook said, telling the LSO he had sight of the meatball; how much fuel he had, 4,800 pounds; the nature of his emergency; and using the nickname for the Super Hornet—"Rhino."

That was the last transmission Weisbrook was expected to provide; all he was supposed to do now was fly the ball and follow the LSO's directions.

Gillis worked him in. "Roger ball, Rhino, single engine, working twenty-five knots. You're on glideslope...ooonnn glideslope."

Weisbrook's jet ballooned above glideslope, and Gillis was on it immediately. "You're going a lit-tle high."

Gillis was the best LSO in the air wing—that's why he was out there. Gillis's modus operandi was to talk in almost a whisper while working his pilot down. As Shrike 305 got closer, Gillis's voice got even softer.

"On glideslope...ooonnn glideslope."

Weisbrook drifted left of centerline, and Gillis jumped in again.

"You're lined up left."

Gillis was coaxing, cajoling, and putting body language into his voice. He wanted to make Weisbrook feel like he was in the cockpit with him, that he too felt the mushy controls.

"You're going low...power."

Weisbrook added a shot of power to get back up on glideslope.

"You're drifting left."

Shrike 305 was closing rapidly, inside one-quarter mile, only seconds away from the deck. Gillis could see the aircraft wallowing. He could feel Weisbrook's tightness as he tried to fight through the degraded hydraulics. Talking much more rapidly now, he coaxed the Super Hornet in.

"A lit-tle power...right for line-up."

The jet began to settle.

"Power, POWER!" Gillis shouted.

SLAM! The ship shook as 38,000 pounds of Super Hornet smashed onto Carl Vinson's deck at 135 knots—just over 150 miles per hour. Weisbrook had been low, and Shrike 305's tail hook caught the number one wire, the first wire on the deck. As soon as he hit, Weisbrook pushed his throttles full forward—standard procedure as a precaution in the event that the tail hook didn't engage the wire—so his aircraft would have enough power to leap back off the deck. Anything less than full power and the aircraft would settle and crash into the water.

The opposing forces of the number one arresting wire catching the Super Hornet, and the full force of his throttles trying to thrust the plane forward, whipped Weisbrook back in his seat as he absorbed the punishing Gs that accompany every carrier landing.

The air boss boomed over the 5MC. "On the flight deck, let's get a tractor and tow bar on 305, chop, chop!"

One deck below, Heater Robinson walked out of TFCC and back toward his cabin. The pressure on his people was increasing and he could do little about it. If only the leadership would decide how they wanted to use his strike group, then the dangers his pilots were dealing with would be worth something.

CHAPTER 10

Much of the business of the U.S. military carrying out the nation's mandates is routine. Hundreds of thousands of military people are deployed each day across the globe, but their actions usually receive little notice. Even those working directly for the commander in chief pay scant attention to the activities of forward-deployed Navy strike groups, Marine Corps air-ground task units, Air Force wings, and Army brigades.

However, when a crisis occurs, the president is surrounded by a large number of civilian and military advisors. The shoot-down of the Syrian Foxbat was no different and the White House Situation Room was rapidly filling as more-and-more people filed down to the West Wing basement.

The president entered the Sit Room conference room. Most of his key advisors—Michael Curtis; Defense Secretary Bryce Jacobs; chairman of the joint chiefs of staff, Admiral Jake Monroe; and the DNI, Peter Hernandez, were already gathered. The secretary of state was still en route.

Curtis stepped forward to brief the president. *How ironic*, he thought. Just a day ago he and many of the principals present had met to try to evolve a plan to deal with Iran. Now another state, Syria, had apparently tried to shoot down a U.S. military spy plane.

"Michael, let me have it; what do we know?"

"We don't have a complete picture yet, Mr. President," Curtis began. "We're just getting fragmentary reports thus far."

"Well, what *do* we know?"

"We do know several things," Curtis continued. "We know that at 0722 Eastern Standard Time, a strike-fighter off USS *Carl Vinson* shot down a Syrian MIG-25 Foxbat. We know we had a U-2S flying along the northern edge of the southern no-fly zone at that time. The AWACS reported that the MIG was heading directly for the U-2. We know we haven't heard anything from the Syrian government."

"That's fine, but we don't know why. Do your boys know anything, Peter?" he said, turning to his Director of National Intelligence.

"Not as much as we'd like to, Mr. President. We don't think this is part of an overall offensive plan. There've been no troop movements and no increase in air activity. There were no precursors to today's event."

"Other theories?" the president asked.

"Another theory is that this may have been a defector," Hernandez continued, "That's a pretty low probability, because the pilots flying out of Tha'lah Military Airbase are thoroughly screened."

"Go on," the president probed.

"Another theory," the DNI continued, "is that this guy might have been a rogue pilot who just wanted to start a conflict on his own. But we discount that one the same way we do the defector theory."

The president let his stare tell the DNI he should come to the point.

"Based on what little we do know, the most convincing theory that we can come up with is that this pilot just got lost."

"Got lost?" the president asked.

"Yes, sir; got lost."

The president held up his hands as if waiting to catch something that was going to be thrown. Monroe came to his colleague's rescue.

"Mr. President, it's a plausible scenario. Their pilots aren't nearly as well trained as ours; they're almost totally dependent on their ground controllers. It's beyond belief that a controller would tell a pilot to threaten one of our aircraft and just as unbelievable that one of their pilots would attack one of our planes."

"So you're saying that this poor bastard may have just strayed across the border by mistake?"

"Yes, Mr. President," Monroe replied.

"And we shot his ass out of the sky?"

"Yes, sir."

"God-damnit, Jake!" the president shouted. "Are your guys out there *trying* to start World War III?"

"No, sir; they're not," Jacobs replied. "The reaction times are so brief that the pilots must act quickly. You can imagine the disaster if one of our U-2s were shot down. It's unfortunate that this happened, Mr. President, but I think everyone acted properly."

"Disaster if our U-2 was shot down...'unfortunate' that this happened? Don't you all see what you've just done?"

"Mr. President," Jacobs continued, "we had no intention of starting anything. From what we know thus far, our forces exercised prudent precautions. We're conducting a full investigation, and if culpability is found, we'll be swift in handing out punishment."

"Jake, who the hell is in charge out there?" he said, turning toward the chairman of the joint chiefs.

"Sir, General Lawrence is the commander of the Central Command, and Admiral Flowers—"

"I know the God-damned chain of command!" the president interrupted, "but who's in charge of the carrier sending these trigger-happy pilots up where they can start a war?"

"Admiral Mike Robinson is the strike group commander. I've served with Mike—"

"Yeah, yeah," the president interrupted again, "and you're gonna tell me what a fine fellow he is and how he's doing a great job."

"Yes, sir," the chairman said. "He *is* doing a fine job. I'll contact him and ensure that he remains mindful of the rules of engagement and keeps things from escalating out of control."

"You do that, Jake, and don't wait too damned long."

"I'll do it immediately, Mr. President."

"All right," the president continued. Turning to Curtis he said, "Someone get Secretary Quinn on the line. I want to know what the situation in Syria is." Then, turning to the secretary of defense, he said, "And I want to know what our options are—our full range of options."

Curtis welcomed the order to contact Philip Quinn. It got him out of the blast radius of the president's wrath. But more importantly, it got him away from the immediate conversation about Syria. He was certain this was just some tragic accident—a mistake by a second-rate pilot flying for a third-rate air force. But it had distracted the president from the long-term menace in the Gulf. How long would it take to get their focus back in the right direction?

The national security adviser didn't come by his opinion on Iran because of any ingrained prejudice, and certainly not just because of recent events. He saw in Iran a power that had the potential to threaten the United States and its interests much more directly than Iraq had in 1990 when it invaded Kuwait. There were a wide array of facts that supported his reasoning.

Iran possessed a more than a dozen Chinese made Hegu fast attack craft and had fitted them with C-802 surface-to-surface missiles. These craft gave Iran a mobile, anti-ship missile capability that could be used against merchant or naval shipping.

More ominously, Iran was equipping its aircraft with air-to-surface missiles. The C-801 had been fielded on Iranian aircraft operating out of the Bushehr airfield. F-4s taking off from Bushehr could be launching deadly missiles at *Carl Vinson* only minutes after takeoff.

The national security adviser also knew Iran possessed hundreds of Chinese-made Silkworm and Seersucker anti-ship missiles and had positioned them along its coast flanking Gulf shipping lanes.

One of the more troubling aspects of the Iranian arms buildup was its growing submarine force. Iran had obtained three Kilo-class diesel-electric submarines from Russia. In addition to torpedoes, they each carried twenty-four mines. The potential for these submarines to choke the Strait of Hormuz was real.

What made Iran's military capabilities so worrisome was the long and deep animosity that the ruling Iranian mullahs had against the United States. The Iranian clerics had convinced themselves the United States wouldn't rest until their theocratic regime no longer ran the Islamic Republic. They viewed America as a long-term, implacable foe.

Of course, one of their planes hadn't just been shot down by one of ours. Curtis had no doubt Iran would try to somehow leverage its position as innocent bystander.

CHAPTER 11

President Habibi heard the intercom and felt the hair on the back of his neck rise. He thought he knew what this visit was going to be about, and he didn't want to be engaged in this way. But he had no choice.

"Minister Velayati to see you, Mr. President," his secretary said.

"Send him in," Habibi replied, trying not to sound annoyed, or even resigned.

"Good afternoon, Mr. President," Velayati said as he entered. The minister of foreign affairs was a tall, spare man who was a decade younger than Habibi.

"Good afternoon, Mr. Foreign Minister. My staff wasn't able to discern an agenda for this meeting. How may I help you?"

"I think you know why I'm here. You've heard, I'm sure, about the downing of the Syrian plane by the Americans."

"I have, but what concern is that of ours?" Habibi measured his words. Velayati never asked for a meeting unless he wanted something.

"I think it concerns us very much."

"And how is that?"

"The Americans can only focus on one thing at a time. They'll conjure up all kinds of reasons to justify punishing the Syrians. They'll ignore us completely while this is going on."

"What does this mean to us?"

"It means we have an opportunity to rid the Gulf of the Americans."

"I don't share your compelling need to drive them out. They want to keep oil flowing through Hormuz just as do we. You seem to forget what supports our economy."

"I know very well, but all commerce is on their terms."

"Be that as it may," Habibi continued, "we gain no advantage by going against the Americans, none whatsoever."

"And you see no advantage if the Americans focus their wrath on Syria and if such a conflict weakens them?"

"You can't think this incident will spark that. Surely this shoot-down was an accident. There will be saber rattling, angry words, and then it will all be papered over," Habibi replied.

"Perhaps so, but I'm not talking about this incident. I'm talking about all that we're doing, and must continue to do, to keep the pressure on America to make their presence in the Gulf ultimately too costly."

"So what is it you are asking me to do?" Habibi probed.

"Nothing, Mr. President."

"Nothing?"

"No, nothing. Nothing at all."

"Then why have you come here?"

"Because you know actions are underway that will deter the Americans from honoring their commitments here. They're being undertaken by our martyrs, many of whom have gone to paradise already."

"If I know of these actions as you say I do, why are you telling me this now?"

"Because these actions must be stepped up. We've been doing this at a low level of intensity for a long time. We're getting results, but those results are minor—a pipe bomb here, an explosion in a marketplace there—they haven't had the desired impact. We need your assurance you'll look the other way as we intensify these preparations."

"Why would I want to provide these assurances?"

"It's not for me to make judgments about the way you're discharging your duties as president of the Islamic Republic."

"Tell me why I should follow your lead on this."

"I'll tell you, only because you insist. I shouldn't have to remind that the Imam, Ayatollah Khomeini, preached a doctrine of permanent revolution. As the leaders of the Islamic world, it's our job to carry this out."

"So you question my revolutionary credentials?"

"You've said it, Mr. President."

"You propose to carry on these actions against the Americans with my acquiescence? If I give you that, you'll validate my credentials as a revolutionary in the cause of Islam?"

This was exactly where Velayati wanted the conversation to go, because it enabled him to play his trump card.

"I will, as will Ayatollah Rebaz Nateq-Nuri," Velayati replied with a flourish.

The mention of Ayatollah Nateq-Nuri, the country's religious leader and, by law, its commander in chief, set Habibi back. Velayati was too cautious to play this card cavalierly. He must have already consulted with Nateq-Nuri.

Habibi was all too aware of the power of the Islamic Republic's religious leader so he proceeded carefully. "Mr. Minister, if you've already consulted with Ayatollah Nateq-Nuri, why are we having this conversation?"

"As you know, there's strong precedent among our clerics to disassociate their temporal and spiritual activities. He must remain aloof on many of the more mundane issues affecting the day-to-day things we do to run our government—"

Habibi wanted to say, *So, Mr. Minister. You want to insulate Ayatollah Nateq-Nuri and let me take the fall for having knowledge of such activities should they backfire*, but he held his tongue. Instead he said, "Mr. Minister, I see your point."

"You do?"

"Yes. If there's consensus this must be done, I'll not stand in the way, but I insist that you keep me informed."

"Of course, Mr. President."

"That is appreciated. Now, are you prepared today to tell me of the activities you have planned?"

"Well, not completely. I don't keep all of the details in my head, but I can tell you what I know."

"That will be sufficient."

"Very well. First, you know that we currently have just a dozen camps where those who support permanent revolution train."

"Are all of these camps active?"

"No, not all. The Imam Ali camp east of Tehran is our largest camp. It's there we're training members of the Saudi dissident groups, especially the Hezbollah of Hejaz and the Organization of Islamic Revolution."

"Yes, and the other camps?"

"The Nahaveand camp in Hamaden southwest of Tehran is a training ground for Hezbollah. The Husseini camp is just south of our capital outside of Qom and is active training Turkish militants. The Alyeck camp is to the northwest near Qazin. These camps are operating at maximum capacity already, and we need to bring others online."

"You've told me enough about the camps; now tell me what else you're doing that I must know about."

Velayati laid out the outlines of his plan and Habibi listened.

CHAPTER 12

The admiral's chief of staff, Captain George Sampson, knocked on the door to the strike group commander's cabin.

"You wanted to see me, Admiral?"

"Yes, COS, come in please." Admiral Robinson rose, walked over to the large sofa in his office, and invited his chief of staff to sit down.

Sampson could see that Robinson was in one of his reflective moods.

"COS, you know our role is becoming more and more complex. Remember when our mission was defined only as naval presence?"

"I remember, Admiral."

"Desert Storm changed that, didn't it? Now we've inherited all these new responsibilities. This expanded no-fly zone over Syria demands constant patrolling."

It was a rhetorical question, and Sampson didn't bother to answer. He just let the admiral continue.

"There's not much margin for error. I know that I'm not telling you anything that you don't know."

"No, sir," Sampson continued. "I wouldn't be so bad if enforcing this no-fly zone over Syria was our only mission."

"You're right," Robinson continued. "Do they have any clue how many assets it takes to enforce United Nations sanctions? And that doesn't even consider ISIL in Iraq and Syria. We've beaten them down for now, but who knows how long that will last?"

"It's all tough work, Admiral."

"That's what Exercise "Swift Sword"—planning contingency operations against any state that threatens our interests in the Gulf littoral—is all about. I've just got to be damned sure we're ready."

"I think that we'll be more than ready," Sampson offered.

"Good. Thanks for listening, George," he said as he rose. "I think we're on the same page on this. Let's get the other players together."

As he opened the door to the admiral's cabin, and motioned for his key advisers to enter, Sampson recognized that while this was a familiar scenario, there were aspects of it that seemed different from previous trips to the Gulf. Something had changed. The admiral was gathering his closest advisors in his cabin to try to determine just what.

Robinson sat down at the head of the table and motioned for the others to sit as well. Gathered there were his chief of staff; *Carl Vinson's* commanding officer, Captain Craig Vandegrift; CAG, Captain Ryan "Wizard" Foster; Captain Jim Hughes, his destroyer squadron commander; and his operations officer, Captain Bill Durham. Foster broke the ice.

"Admiral," he began, "we've been working with CVIC and the intel folks at Fifth Fleet to come up with target sets for Exercise Swift Sword and I've got some problems with them."

"What kind of problems?"

"They give us target sets, and they are focused on hitting the Iranian Navy hard in port. It seems like we're doing overkill on the navy boats—ah, ships—and ignoring everything else."

"Like what?"

"The size of the strikes we're sending into Bandar Abbas and Bushehr are huge, I mean, big, big, packages."

"How big?"

"Well, sir, 'bout twenty to twenty-four plane raids."

"At each one?" Robinson asked.

"Yes, sir."

"And what's the timing on these raids?"

"They say that the fleet commander wants 'em pulled off simultaneously. Don't get me wrong, Admiral, we want to train the way we're gonna fight—if that's the way we're gonna fight."

Turning to Vandegrift, Robinson asked, "Skipper, can you get that big a package off the deck given the sea room you have?"

"As long as the wind keeps coming from the northwest; I've got plenty of sea room. No problem getting them off. Recovery gets a little tougher with the way visibility drops so rapidly at night."

"Some of these exercise strikes are at night, aren't they?" Robinson asked, looking back toward Foster.

"Yes, Admiral, they're day and night." CAG spread out a flow sheet which showed the multiple strikes on each of Iran's two major naval bases.

"The way their staff is directing it, we're doing three major attacks on each base. Of course, this is only training, but the way they're coming at this, being so directive, makes me just a little curious."

"Me too," Robinson replied.

"Then there's the weaponeering," Vandegrift added.

"What about it?" the admiral asked.

"Well, sir, as I'm sure you remember all too well from your tour in command of a carrier, building up the bombs is often the long pole in the tent. When CAG and I initially looked at this, we felt that cluster bombs would be the best weapon for what we were trying to accomplish. The blast and frag pattern that we'd get would put the Iranian boats out of commission for a long time. Then we could move on to strikes against terrorist training camps, which was the purpose of this 'exercise.'"

"That makes a lot of sense to me," Robinson replied.

"Us too, Admiral," Foster said. "But the Fifth Fleet staff guys told us to use laser-guided bombs. They said we wanted a probability of kill to…well…they said to send the Iranian Navy to the bottom."

"Why do they want to do that?"

"We can't get 'em to say," CAG continued. "You know what it's gonna take to do that. More bombs, a lot more accuracy, riskier packages and all that. We're certainly willing to do that, but we kind of feel like mushrooms as we try to plan for all this—"

"Kept in the dark all the time and fed shit?" the admiral offered.

This direction from Fifth Fleet bothered him. His staff, ship, and air wing had proposed constructing this exercise so it involved simulating blasting the Iranian Navy with cluster bombs that could be dropped from high altitude. These would explode at a predetermined height above the Iranian boats, raining down small bomblets and rendering them out of commission for a long time.

The use of laser-guided bombs, which allowed aircrews to guide a 500, 1,000, or 2,000-pound bomb directly onto the target, would increase the probability of sinking the vessel it hit. But this tactic required the attacking aircraft to hold a laser designator on the target for the entire time of the bomb's flight, a much riskier flight profile. The admiral was dead set against his pilots taking unnecessary risks.

"It's strange," Robinson continued, "damn strange."

"Exactly, sir, and it gets even stranger. The commodore can fill you in."

"Admiral," Hughes began. I've been getting a lot of guidance from the Fifth Fleet ops folks regarding ship positioning for Swift Sword. They're telling me to forget about maritime interception ops and bring my ships into position to simulate threatening Iran. They want me to bring my Tomahawk shooters into launch baskets. That isn't a problem; the plan has always been to use Tomahawks to neutralize their integrated air defense system—"

"Isn't that what we've been doing?" Robinson asked.

"It is, but we're doing more. In addition to the Tomahawks we have programmed against IADS," he began, referring to their integrated air defense system. "They're telling us that we need to pour Tomahawks into their naval bases at Bandar Abbas and Bushehr—"

"In addition to the TACAIR strikes?"

"Yes, sir. They want a high probability of kills at both those bases. Additionally, they want Tomahawk shots against the airfields at Shiraz, Bushehr, and Omideyeh. They've given us a long list of targets."

"What kind of Tomahawk inventory are we talking about using?"

"That's just it. The way they have us shooting them on the first two days of this 'exercise' we all but run out of TLAMs at the end of day two. I mean, no reserves, and no backup missiles for the later salvos."

"Anything else?"

"Yes, sir. They told us to move our cruisers in close to Bushehr and simulate pounding it with naval surface fire support."

"Who do they envision providing air defense for the carrier?"

"They said that we can cover that with our deck-launched interceptors."

"CAG, you got that covered?" the admiral asked.

"No, sir, not even close. With strike packages this big, and with the short turnaround time between strikes, I'm pressed to just make the flight schedule for the strikes—and that's if our availability is great."

Robinson looked around the table. His senior commanders were staring at him almost blankly. What they were being told to do by Fifth Fleet just didn't track. "Exercises" like Swift Sword often mirrored reality, and if they practiced that intently for something, then at least at some level it was being considered as a real scenario. If that was the case, then it tracked even less well. He was aware of the concern with the Iranian terrorist training camps. But this new level of escalation—sending their navy to the bottom, destroying their air force, using guns to pound their naval bases—this all signaled something more ominous.

"All right, here's what I want you to focus on for now," Robinson began. "Plan for the exercise, cooperate with the Fifth Fleet staff as best you can, but don't degrade the defense of this task group. Is that understood?"

The nodding of heads around the table signaled they understood.

"Plan simulated strikes for Swift Sword, but give 'em a reality check. Until someone explains to my satisfaction why we're doing what we're doing, it's business as usual. We're *not* going to try to run strikes we can't put together and support. We're *not* going to run our supply of Tomahawks to zero. We're *not* going for overkill when we have a discrete mission that we can execute with far less cost. Are we clear?"

"Yes, Admiral," was their collective response.

As the last officer left his cabin, Robinson was momentarily alone with his thoughts. Thus far, he hadn't been able to convince his seniors of the potential dangers to his strike group. He looked at his secure phone and determined to try to explain the situation to Admiral Flowers again. As he lifted the receiver, there was a knock on his cabin door.

"Come in," he said.

"Hello, Admiral," his communications officer began. "We just received a SPECAT message, and I wanted to get it to you right away."

The commo had his full attention. SPECAT messages were Special Category messages, those of such importance, and needing such a degree of privacy, that only one staff radioman was allowed to handle them. Were they finally going to take action against these terrorists?

* * *

Just forty frames aft of where the admiral and his senior commanders were planning their strategy, junior officers were also planning. They were devising ways to deal with the potential that some of the aircraft in any actual strike against Iran might be shot down.

In Ready Room Five, home of the Battlecats of HSM-73, several officers bent over a chart and planned their CSAR—Combat Search and Rescue—training mission.

"Okay Jake," the squadron's air intelligence officer began, "We've mapped the route of flight for your birds. For these missions you'll ingress the coast right here—"

"For all our missions?" Lieutenant Jake Roach, one of the Battlecats' aircraft commanders, asked. Roach didn't like interrupting the AI, but these were life-or-death missions.

"Yes. I've got the other routes on different charts, but they're the less-likely scenarios."

"Okay, I see it. Do these circles represent all of the Iranian surface-to-air missile batteries?" Roach's copilot asked.

"All of the fixed ones, the mobile guys are just too hard to pin down," the AI continued. "Now, these small black circles represent all of the AAA sites we've charted."

Roach and his co-pilot were new to this game. HSM squadrons flew the MH-60R helo that was optimized for missions like anti-submarine warfare, reconnaissance, electronic warfare and other "high-end" warfighting tasks. What that meant was that their version of the Seahawk airframe was packed with tons of gear and had little space in its cabin. For that reason, flying these CSAR missions was not in their usual playbook.

But early in their deployment, their sister squadron, HSC-6, which flew the MH-60S which didn't have all that mission gear the MH-60R did and was optimized for CSAR, had suffered a major crunch. Two of its helos had collided on the flight deck, severely damaging both birds. Another HSC-6 helo had made a hard landing and ruptured its fuel tanks. The squadron was down three birds.

CAG had directed HSM-73 to take all the mission gear—dipping sonar, sonobuoy launcher, and more—out of two of their aircraft and make them "slick" birds capable of going on CSAR missions. Roach and his squadron mates were happy to be doing a mission that felt more "real" than their other missions like anti-submarine warfare—ASW—which pilots often referred to as, "awfully slow warfare."

"I think we've got it," Roach replied. He turned to the representative of Team Three. "Your guys are riding with us for these missions, you got any questions?"

"No," he replied. "You boys just get us to the SAR dot where your guy needs to be rescued; we'll do the rest once we get on the ground."

"We'll get you there. You snake-eaters just live for this stuff, don't you?"

"That we do."

The SEAL had to think a bit about what he'd just said. He didn't like telling Roach, or any of the other HSM-73 bubbas, half-truths. The SEAL platoon missions, including Combat Search and Rescue, would be flown with the HSC-6 Indians, as well as with the HSM-73 Battlecats. The helo squadron pilots had established a close relationship with the SEAL and his team.

That's why it pained him to deceive these men and women. Sure he was with SEAL Team Three, but while all of his men were SEALs through and through, he wasn't. Oh, his service record said he had moved up through the ranks, had made chief petty officer, and then had been commissioned as a result of especially heroic action, but he wasn't entirely what he seemed.

Rick Holden was CIA. That was his parent organization, and that was where he began his career after graduating from the University of Virginia. He'd been part of many operations with the agency's clandestine services. After Holden was involved in an operation that went bad, the agency needed to make a decision regarding his future: keep him working in clandestine services, assign him a headquarters position, or cut him loose from the agency altogether. The first choice was just too dangerous, Holden balked at the second, and all agreed he was too valuable an asset to lose completely.

Therefore, a cover was set up. The service record of Chief Petty Officer Rick Holden, ostensibly just brought on active duty from the Navy Reserves, appeared in the Navy Personnel Bureau. Holden was provided with comprehensive information regarding the SEALs so he could appear to be what they wanted him portrayed as—a Navy SEAL chief who had been in the reserves for approximately ten years. He was then assigned to a SEAL team and deployed as an assistant platoon leader. He was just supposed to keep his head down, blend in as a SEAL, and be on-call to the agency.

However, while assigned to USS *Coronado,* Holden became caught up in a scheme by senior military officers who caused a major military operation to fail in an attempt to have the president impeached. Holden and a Navy intelligence officer discovered this plot and thwarted the conspirators. This heroic action earned him a commission as a naval officer. The agency let his cover continue to play out by having him make this enlisted-to-officer transition in the SEAL community.

Holden enjoyed his role as a SEAL, and now that he'd been commissioned, he was enjoying life as a naval officer. He wanted this to continue for as long as possible, but he didn't know how long that would be. And he didn't know what role he might have in the hornet's nest that was the Arabian Gulf.

CHAPTER 13

The Syrian Air Defense Force is an independent command within the Syrian Armed Forces and administers a vast air control and air defense network. The Force controls twenty-five air defense brigades, each with six SAM—surface-to-air-missile—batteries. It is equipped with 650 static SA-2, SA-3 and SA-5 launchers, 200 mobile SA-6 and SA-11 launchers, and over 4,000 anti-aircraft guns.

The Syrian air control and air defense network has a pyramidal structure. Observers at scores of posts feed tracking data into the system. This information is, in turn, fed into intercept operations centers—IOCs. Like spokes in a wheel, the IOCs send their information to regional sector operations centers—SOCs. These SOCs control the entire land mass of Syria.

The Hama SOC is responsible for the area around Damascus, including the area along the northern edge of the no-fly zone. Hama, along with the three other SOCs, feeds its information to Air Defense Headquarters in Damascus, thereby providing the Syrian high command with a nationwide air picture.

It was this system that alerted Syrian political and military leaders that Raid Bakr had been shot down. A replay of tapes showed the path of his aircraft, the path of the American U-2S spy plane, and the attack profiles of the American fighters. It looked like what it was—an unfortunate accident. Still, those in the Syrian command structure needed to report what happened to the Syrian president.

Once he had sorted out the details of the incident, Chief of Staff of the Syrian Air Force, Lieutenant General Sa'b Hassan Muzakim, prepared to call the chief of the Armed Forces. The general picked up his command center phone and was linked to Syrian military headquarters.

"General Ayad, you have heard, no doubt, about the unfortunate shoot-down of our MIG-25."

"Yes, I have."

"All of our forces are on alert. Radars at multiple sites have detected no movement of American planes outside of their normal patrol patterns."

"So you don't think this is a prelude to an attack."

"No, I don't. I think that it was just a tragic blunder."

"We're reserving judgment. You'd better come up with answers quickly. Our president isn't a man of infinite patience."

"Yes, General." He could feel the full wrath of Syria's president falling on him, and he didn't think that any of his higher ranking military colleagues would step up to protect him. He called Hama.

* * *

Raid Faud Muhammad was the chief of air controllers at the Hama air control facility where the GCI controller directing Raid Bakr's aircraft worked. He and other officers had reconstructed events and had determined that the controller, Sergeant Majid Khadduri, had simply blundered. There were reasons for this: he was inexperienced on the piece of gear he was operating, he was in a brutal watch rotation, and the communications with Raid Bakr's aircraft had been extremely poor. All of these were excuses, and excuses weren't what his seniors wanted to hear. He would question Khadduri himself. He knew what he wanted to hear, and what the sergeant must say.

A small group was gathered in the Spartan office in the basement of the Hama control site. Supervisors and more experienced controllers stood around the periphery of the room. In the center of the room was a small table with two chairs. Muhammad sat in one chair, and Khadduri sat in the other. The raid offered Khadduri a cigarette, which he gratefully accepted.

The sergeant had been well coached. Muhammad drew deeply on his cigarette and smiled at Khadduri.

"Sergeant, do you know why I'm here?"

"I think so, sir."

"It's about the tragic loss of Raid Bakr. You understand no one is here to blame you for anything."

"Thank you, sir. I've been a loyal soldier, and I've performed my job diligently. No one has worked harder learning all of their systems—"

Muhammad stopped him. "Sergeant, no one is questioning that at all. We want you to tell us about the American trickery."

Armed with that code word, Khadduri began to relate the tale that he'd been coached to tell. He was controlling Raid Bakr's aircraft precisely as he'd been instructed. He knew exactly where he was sending him and had calculated sufficient margin of error to keep the aircraft safe. But then, in the later stages of the flight, as the MIG-25 came to its closest point of approach to the edge of the no-fly zone, an American Growler aircraft began jamming his station. He switched frequencies and did everything else he'd been instructed to do to break through the jamming, but to no avail.

At this point in his story, Muhammad interrupted him. "Sergeant, you know the capabilities of all American aircraft. If the Growler was close enough to jam you, it could have shot a HARM missile at you—destroying you and your entire station."

"Yes, sir, I considered that, and I alerted my supervisors. But I knew I needed to continue to try to communicate with my aircraft."

"What happened then, Sergeant?"

"It became very confusing. Many of my circuits were jammed, but I was trying so hard to do my job—"

"Yes we all know you were. Just tell us what you recall."

"I heard a voice I didn't recognize giving orders to Raid Bakr, Khadduri continued. "The communications were scratchy, but it sounded like he used the same kind of instructions I use. I heard Raid Bakr question him about his orders, but the controller said that he was to do what he was told."

"This from a controller to a pilot in our air force?" Muhammad asked.

"Not only the controller, sir, but another voice. The conversations were broken, but when Raid Bakr questioned the instructions he was receiving, another voice came on the same circuit and shouted at him to follow instructions. Seconds later, I thought I heard him yelling about American aircraft. Then I heard nothing."

Muhammad looked at the sergeant, who was now starting to shake. His hand was barely able to hold his cigarette. Finally, he began to sob.

"There was nothing I could do. They were jamming my station. I tried to break through to my aircraft. I knew the risk, but I kept trying to transmit. They were too powerful for me. It's not my fault, it's not."

Sergeant Khadduri continued to sob. But he had told his story well, and Muhammad reached over and patted his shoulder.

* * *

Lieutenant General Sa'b Hassan Muzakim answered the intercom that jangled his already frayed nerves. "Yes, what is it?"

"Raid Faud Muhammad wishes to speak with you," his secretary said.

"Send his call in—and close that door."

As he picked up his telephone and settled back into his chair, the general listened to what the major told him. It had gone exactly as planned. The chief of staff of the Syrian Air Force would report this to his superiors. He knew he was safe for now.

CHAPTER 14

"Gentlemen, the admiral," Mike Lumme announced as a stone-faced Heather Robinson walked into Carrier Strike Group One's War Room. Adjacent to the admiral's cabin and close to both TFCC and SUPPLOT —Supplementary Plot—where much of the most sensitive intelligence *Carl Vinson* collected was analyzed, the War Room was the location for meetings where Robinson gathered his key warfare commanders and principal staff members.

Dominated by a massive table in the center and twelve high-backed chairs surrounding it, the War Room emphasized function over aesthetics. An over-sized chart table dominated the port bulkhead, and small desks filled the forward and after bulkheads. A large projector loomed over the table and pointed at a screen on the starboard end of the room.

"Seats, gentlemen," Robinson said as he sat down at the head of the table. Sitting at the table were Captain Sampson, Captain Vandegrift, CAG Foster, Captain Hughes, Captain Bill Durham, and Captain Rocky Jacobson. The admiral had called this meeting to review preparations for Exercise Swift Sword.

The meteorology officer began the briefing. After he projected an array of charts, the admiral asked just one question.

"What's the weather prognosis over Iran for the next week?"

"Pretty much the same trend we're seeing now, Admiral. Westerlies will be strong. The shamal will kick up dust storms and increase the haze over most of the country. If you have no other questions, I'll be followed by the assistant intel officer."

"Morning, admiral," the staff assistant intelligence officer, began. "I've been asked to focus on the Iranian Navy. We assess their navy as posing a significant threat to our strike group."

"Let's focus on where they are now, in their ports," Robinson replied.

The officer called up another slide on her power point briefing. "Admiral, this map shows the three Iranian naval districts; the first district at Bandar Abbas in the south; the second district at Bushehr in the north; and the third district at Bandar Khomeini—"

"What you're telling me is fine, but let's get to the point; I want to know the positions of the Iranian ships in each port."

"Yes, Admiral," she replied as she clicked ahead a few slides.

As she did, all eyes in the room were on Robinson. They knew he'd had secure phone conversations with the Fifth Fleet commander. Swift Sword was an exercise—a major exercise—but an exercise nonetheless. These exercises were disguised with enough papering over that the target nations weren't supposed to feel threatened, but their purpose had hardened in the past year.

Exercise Swift Sword would be more aggressive than any exercise in recent memory. The movement of additional forces into the area, simulated strikes deep into Iran, simulated blockade of Iranian ports and other actions all seemed quite real. This led to the strong suspicion that offensive action might actually take place. The staff knew only what they carried in their classified folders, but the admiral was privy to additional information. Some tried to read that information in his eyes.

The assistant intel officer finally found the slide she wanted. "Admiral, imagery has confirmed the disposition of Iranian naval forces you see on this slide. The major concentrations are, of course, at Bandar Abbas and Bushehr. At Bandar Abbas they have their three Kilo-class submarines, as well as a couple of Sumner Class DDGs, some SAAM Class FFGs, a number of patrol craft, and some Hengham Class LSTs, as well as about a dozen Revolutionary Guard Boghammars."

"Good. Continue," Robinson said.

"Yes, sir. At Bushehr they have no submarines, of course, but that's where they have their large concentration of missile boats, mainly the French-made Kaman, but also some smaller boats. The Revolutionary Guard keeps almost twenty Boghammars here."

The previously blank TV screen mounted on a bulkhead over her left shoulder came on and presented a photo of the Bandar Abbas naval base. As Robinson listened, she went through a number of these photos, showing the position of every Iranian naval vessel. The same scenario continued with photos of Bushehr naval base.

"Subject to any additional questions, that concludes my brief."

"Thanks. Now the question is; what do we do with this information?" Robinson said as he got up and strode to the front of the War Room.

"All right, folks, now I'll tell you where what we're going to do. We'll press ahead with Exercise Swift Sword. First of all, we're not going to be distracted by this incident over the box. CAG, your boys did a fine job up there. If anyone wants to second-guess, they're going to have to second-guess me. While we're doing Exercise Swift Sword, the Air Force will pick up all of the air patrol missions over Syria. Wizard, you feel like your folks have given them a good enough pass down."

"Yes, Admiral," Foster responded.

"Good. Now our focus is on Swift Sword. I don't need to tell most of you, especially many of you who've served in the Gulf before, that sometimes these 'exercises' turn into full-fledged operations. Now nobody's saying that we're getting ready to thump up on Iran, but you know what they've been up to, and you know what could happen. That's why we want to do this 'exercise' with as much realism as we can. I want bombs on airplanes, your first teams in the aircraft, and ships really at GQ—not some halfway compromise—and people practicing like the real McCoy could happen tomorrow."

Robinson paused a moment to let what he was saying sink in.

"But remember, there's life after any exercise and there's life after any strikes we might do. We'll complete whatever mission we're given—but we'll defend this strike group at all costs. I want you to plan this exercise, but don't stretch it so thin that we can't take care of ourselves."

The heads around the table nodded.

"Okay, I think that I've taken up enough of everyone's time. I appreciate all of the hard work that's gone into your planning."

Robinson walked back to his cabin. He sat down heavily in his chair. He hoped that he hadn't let his anger spill over onto his people. He opened his message folder and re-read the SPECAT message that he'd read with disbelief right before the meeting.

OPIMMEDAITE
FROM: JOINT CHIEFS OF STAFF
TO: CARSTRKGRU 1
BT

SECRET SPECAT FOR ADMIRAL ROBINSON FROM MONROE//Nooooo//
MSGID/GENADMIN/JOINT STAFF//
SUBJ/(S) CRISIS OF CONFIDENCE //
RMKS/1. (S) HEATER. WE GO BACK A LONG WAY AND I TELL YOU
THIS IN STRICTEST CONFIDENCE. DESTROY THIS MESSAGE AFTER
YOU READ IT.
2. (S) I'VE JUST HAD MY ASS ROUNDLY CHEWED BY THE PRESIDENT
OVER THIS FOXBAT SHOOTDOWN. I'M SKIPPING ECHELON AND
NOT TELLING THE THEATER COMMANDER OR YOUR IMMEDIATE
BOSS, HARRY FLOWERS. I'M TELLING ONLY YOU. THE PRESIDENT
WAS A HEARTBEAT AWAY FROM FIRING YOU OVER THIS INCIDENT. I
HAD TO PROSTRATE MYSELF TO KEEP HIM FROM DOING SO. YOU'VE
GOT TO GET IT TOGETHER AND KEEP YOUR GUYS FROM STARTING
A WAR. I'VE SHOT MY SILVER BULLET, HEATER, ANOTHER SCREW-UP
AND I CAN'T BAIL YOU OUT AGAIN. WARM REGARDS, JAKE.
DECL/X4//
BT

Reading it again didn't help Robinson understand it any better. Had his longtime friend forgotten what it was like out here? He'd helped him once, but now it was clear that he was stepping away. What could he do? He stared at the STU-III secure phone for a few moments and then picked it up.

CHAPTER 15

The president sat at his desk in the Oval Office and fiddled with some paperwork. He put the papers down and rubbed the bridge of his nose. Patrick Browne wasn't a particularly big man, but he was a man of presence. At just under six feet tall and a well-built 200 pounds, he still looked younger than his fifty-eight years. He had that perpetual hail-fellow-well-met look about him that was so helpful to anyone in public office.

As he swung around in his Kevlar-backed chair and stared out the pale blue bulletproof windows, he was too preoccupied to enjoy the trappings of his office. He brought his gaze inside the room and looked for a moment at the American flag to his left and the presidential flag to his right, hoping to find some inspiration.

He was waiting for his national security adviser to update him on the Iraqi Foxbat shoot-down. He'd directed his press secretary, Pete Lockhart, to fend off the press with the standard sop that he served up in such situations: "The president was conferring with other leaders." Anything to buy some time.

His secretary ushered in Michael Curtis, along with vice-chairman of the Joint Chiefs of Staff, Air Force General Alfred Cutler. Curtis also brought along his military assistant, Navy Captain Tom Perry.

"Come in gentlemen and sit down," the president said, motioning for them to sit as he walked to the sofas in the center of the Oval Office. "What are the facts as we know them?"

There was momentary silence, but then Curtis nodded, indicating that General Cutler should begin speaking.

"Mr. President, the chairman sends his regrets, but he thought it best to remain in the NMCC. It appears the shoot-down of the Syrian MIG was just an unfortunate accident. The consensus is the plane was the victim of sloppy GCI procedures and crossed into the no-fly zone."

"How far did it cross before he was shot down?"

"Less than five miles," Cutler continued. "However, Mr. President, it was heading directly for our U-2S aircraft. The on-scene commander had to make a decision, and in this case I think he made the right one."

"It appears that he may have done just that, General," the president replied, and then continued, "I think, under the circumstances, our Navy pilots did the right thing." Then, looking at Captain Perry, he added, "Don't you think so, Captain?"

"Yes, sir, I do," Perry replied, and then drawn in by the president's encouraging eyes, he continued. "But Mr. President, all this shoot-down does is distract us from our primary focus in the Gulf. It—"

Curtis cut him off. He didn't mind showcasing his bright Navy captain with the president—hell, Perry worked eighty-hour weeks, and was as loyal an assistant as had ever served him—but he wasn't going to let him dominate the conversation. "Mr. President, if it's all right, may we close out this matter before moving on to the next one?"

"Certainly, Michael. I understand the Syrian pilot was killed."

"Our pilot reported the Syrian plane exploded, and he didn't see a parachute, so it's extremely unlikely he survived."

"I see. What's the Syrian reaction been?"

"It's been a bit mixed. On the one hand there's been no indication of stepped-up military activity on their part, suggesting they're not using it as an excuse to take aggressive action. So on the military front, things are calm."

"And on other fronts?"

"It's confusing thus far, but we have indications the Syrians are claiming that we lured their aircraft across the border with electronic deception so we could have an excuse to shoot it down."

"Did we?" the president asked.

Cutler subtly signaled Curtis that he wanted to answer, and Curtis nodded his assent.

"Mr. President, I can tell you absolutely we did not. But we think it's a plausible ruse by the Syrian military. At some level—probably at several levels—heads would roll for a blunder of that type. Therefore, it's likely someone in their military would blame us for doing this so they could save their own skin."

"So what are you all recommending?"

"I think we should just wait it out, Mr. President," Curtis replied. "We should tell the truth, and I think that we'll have the high ground in the court of world opinion."

"I agree," the president replied. "Now, this wasn't all you wanted to talk about, was it?"

"No, sir," the national security adviser continued. "As Captain Perry alluded to earlier, this incident shouldn't cause us to lose focus on the other side of the Gulf. The situation in Iran continues to worsen. As you know, Iran has supported terrorist training camps throughout their country for a long time. For the past few years, the activity there has been fairly steady, but lately it's picked up dramatically."

"What do you make of it?"

"There are a number of different scenarios, but perhaps the worst is that the Islamic Republic is just biding its time and continuing to train more terrorists. Then, at some time, they'll strike simultaneously throughout the Gulf, primarily at our military forces, our embassies and consulates, as well as at concentrations of American citizens."

"When would they do this—and why?"

"The 'when' is an open question, Mr. President," Curtis continued. "The 'why' lingers from the days of our support for the Shah. It's almost the chicken and the egg scenario—the same convoluted logic we used to go through with the Soviets—do we threaten them because they threaten us, or do they threaten us because we threaten them? But be that as it may, there's the feeling in some intelligence circles the mullahs believe the United States won't be satisfied until their clerical regime is overthrown. We know the Arab Spring worried them deeply. The intelligence community's consensus is that Iran's leaders think acts of terrorism will cause us to back off from our commitments in the Gulf."

"Do they feel that threatened?" the president asked.

"I'm afraid they often do, Mr. President, and our rhetoric in the past hasn't helped any."

"Our rhetoric in the past?"

"Yes sir," Curtis continued. "We've tended to blame Iran for terrorist acts over the years, many of which couldn't reasonably have been attributed to them."

"Where do you assess we stand now?"

"If this scenario plays itself out in a negative way, we'll likely have little notice terrorist attacks are about to happen. We need to be prepared to strike back the instant an attack we attribute to Iran occurs. Only by coming at them with disproportionate force can we dissuade them from follow-on attacks."

"And you're sure we can sort out the source of an attack, I mean, can we tell with certainty whether it was carried out by Iran, or by ISIL, or by someone else?"

"Mr. President, we've been dealing with ISIL long enough to understand their patterns pretty well. They don't like the fact the United States has a presence in the Gulf, but they're clever enough to leverage our being there to draw more recruits to their cause. When they conduct a terrorist attack, they always claim credit for it and get what they've done out on social media. I think our intelligence community has a great track record of sorting out the source of terrorist attacks," Curtis replied.

"All right, I see your point. If we know its Iran, then what?"

"As you suggested, we need to be certain it *is* Iran. If it is, we need to move quickly with a disproportionate response."

"We seem to have a lot of forces in the area. I'd think that that's something we could do—attack them right away, I mean."

"Yes, Mr. President. But those forces can't respond with a strike on short notice. They have to apportion missions to various platforms and then train to hit those targets in order to ensure a high probability of destroying them."

The president was frustrated. "Look, I know that I'm not a military man, but is it really that complex to hit a bunch of terrorist training camps out in the middle of the Iranian desert?"

Curtis deflected the question to the vice chairman. "General?" he said, looking at Cutler.

"Mr. President. Our goal would be to strike the camps, but we need to ensure we're putting our forces at as little risk as possible."

"Well certainly, General. That sounds prudent."

"In order to do that we must neutralize their IADS—their integrated air defense—their air force, and their navy."

"Yes, well, all right. How do we do that?"

"Mr. President, we practice such scenarios."

"I assume we're conducting these drills now."

"Yes, we are," Cutler continued, "and we're directing particular attention at their navy."

"Their navy?"

Perry shifted forward on the sofa and looked at the national security adviser. He wanted to speak. Curtis nodded his consent.

"If I may, Mr. President," Perry began. "The Iranian Navy poses the greatest long-term threat to our interests in the region. While more than fifty percent of their military equipment was destroyed in their war with Iraq in the eighties, their Navy was relatively unscathed. What's more, they've added substantially to that navy and it now poses a threat to our carrier strike groups. Additionally, they could, given their mine-laying capability, close off the Strait of Hormuz."

"Would they do that?" the president asked.

"We assess they would if provoked."

"What damage could they do to our Navy?"

"None, if we strike them first. That's why we think that an attack on their navy is crucial to the success of any operation, as well as to the safety of our forces."

"That sounds reasonable."

General Cutler jumped in. "Yes it does, Mr. President. It is just a question of degree, not kind. There are several ways to go at their navy. One scenario would have us put their navy out of action long enough to guarantee the success of our strikes and ensure the safety of our carrier strike group. Taking another approach, we could make a more robust attack on their navy and sink it, eliminating it as a threat for years. That's the approach Captain Perry here advocates, but it will take a lot more horsepower to achieve that level of destruction."

"Yes, I can see it would," the president responded.

"We don't need to make a decision today, Mr. President. But should we ultimately wind up in some sort of strike scenario, we'll have to make a decision on which route to go," Curtis replied.

The president looked at Perry. "You're concerned about the safety of your Navy, aren't you, Captain?"

"Yes, Mr. President, I am."

"I am too. General Cutler, I know it'll take some level of effort, but if Iran lashes out at us and we need to retaliate, I'm not comfortable with leaving them with much of their naval force intact. Hell, I thought we realized that from all those years of dealing with Saddam Hussein. Anything we didn't obliterate, he just rebuilt and put back into service. Captain Perry, you've provided a compelling case."

"Thank you, Mr. President," Perry replied. He was flattered he was being complimented by his commander in chief, but he was more satisfied that he'd pushed forward the agenda of his mentor, who was on-scene seven thousand miles away.

CHAPTER 16

Package Foxtrot had completed its mission patrolling the no-fly zone and was returning to the carrier. Brian McDonald was happy with the how things had gone. The
eleven-aircraft package had been almost double the size of normal patrols, and his
pilots had performed well. Now all that remained was getting back aboard the boat.

To someone standing on a modern Nimitz-class aircraft carrier, the ship
looks huge, monstrous and awe-inspiring. It dwarfs any other ship in the U.S.
Navy, and makes the few aircraft carriers possessed by other navies seem puny.
That's a perspective shared by all but about two hundred and fifty of the five-
thousand-plus people aboard *Carl Vinson.*

To the pilot in the aircraft making an approach to a carrier, the "boat"—as
the pilots irreverently call the vessel that's officially classified as a ship—looks
as big as a postage stamp. Throw in a bit of a sea state, and that postage stamp
begins to pitch and roll and do any number of gyrations. Add darkness, and the
degree of difficulty goes up geometrically. Add marginal weather—the kind of
weather McDonald and his fellow aviators were experiencing now—and the
difficulties involved in getting a fifteen-ton aircraft flying up to 150 miles per
hour to hit the spot on the deck between the one and four wires—a distance
of only 120 feet—tested the mettle of even the most experienced pilots. When
aviators referred to flying as "hours of boredom punctuated by moments of
terror," this was the terror they were talking about.

McDonald knew this would be a tough night back at the boat. As the aircraft
left the box and went feet wet, they would first check in with Red Crown, the
Aegis Cruiser, USS *Shiloh,* who would ensure that the aircraft were all friendlies
and that a hostile aircraft had not joined the large gaggle of U.S. planes. Then
the aircraft would all head for the marshal stack—the airspace between fifteen
and thirty miles behind the carrier—and await their turn to land.

Aboard *Carl Vinson* the air boss encouraged his troops to hang in there for the night's last recovery. It was 2330 and this recovery wouldn't be complete until past midnight. *Carl Vinson* had been flying fixed wing aircraft since 1100, and helos before that, and the flight deck crew had been on duty continuously—save for a brief respite in the short time between launch and recovery cycles. It was a brutal pace that was taking its toll. The Air Department team went through their normal routine of handling the last recovery.

Petty Officer Donald Parker was one of the sailors involved in the recovery. It was his job to push the rake, a device that shoved the arresting gear off any obstacles as it was pulled back into position after it had been stretched by a landing aircraft.

Parker had been up since before sunrise. "Parks" as his buddies called him, was on his first deployment and was looking forward to seeing his wife and two-year-old son when *Carl Vinson* returned to her home port of San Diego, California.

The Super Hornets were the first aircraft out of the marshal stack. McDonald was number three and listened as he heard the lineup for the aircraft in his package.

McDonald heard the call as the first aircraft made its approach, "Stinger 405, on and on, three quarter-mile, call the ball."

"Four-zero-five, Rhino ball, four-point-two."

"Roger ball, Rhino. Deck's moving, working twenty-eight knots. You're on glideslope," the LSO replied.

"Roger."

So the conversations went, with the LSOs bringing in the first two Super Hornets. Each had good passes, Stinger 405 caught the three wire, Stinger 402 caught the four wire. McDonald was next in the groove.

The LSOs knew each pilot's habits, how they handled their aircraft and how they would react to correction calls. They knew how much each pilot would advance the throttle at the call for power. There were subtle differences, but in the high-stakes game of putting an aircraft on a moving flight deck, those were the finesse factors that spelled the difference between disaster and a successful landing.

As one of the more senior pilots in the squadron, McDonald was a good "ball flyer," and his LSO tended to give him less direction than he did to more junior pilots.

"One-zero-four, on and on, three-quarter mile, call the ball," the LSO said.

"One-zero-four, Rhino ball, four-point-four."

"Roger, ball, Rhino, working twenty-eight knots."

As he approached the ship, which was pitching at a steady rate, the LSO saw him begin to settle below glideslope. "A little power."

McDonald corrected, working hard to keep the ball in the middle of the green datum lights. As he approached the ramp, the ship slid right.

"Come right," the LSO directed.

As McDonald made his lineup correction he settled again, and the LSO was on top of it. "Power."

THUD! McDonald put his Super Hornet in the right spot, the three wire. This one would bump his landing grades a small decimal point higher.

Another Super Hornet was next for landing. Eight more aircraft to go.

On the flight deck, Parker pushed the three wire McDonald had caught back toward the center line to ensure it didn't snag. He had long since sweated through his clothes. He was debating whether to try to grab some mid-rats—the meal that was served on the mess decks around midnight—or to just grab a shower and hit his rack.

Parker had been trained to go back behind the "stubby" tow tractor or the N-16 crash cart after he pushed the wire. That would protect him if anything untoward happened on the flight deck—an aircraft crash, something flying off the aircraft, a wire snapping. But it would take several dozen extra steps to do that and Parker was exhausted. He just leaned on the tail pylon of Battlecat 703, one of the helos parked next to the island. There, in the shadow of the helo, he escaped everyone's notice as he waited for the next recovery.

"Shrike 306, call the ball."

"Three-zero-six, Rhino ball, four-point-seven."

"Roger, ball, Rhino, working twenty-nine knots."

Shrike 306 drifted left of course.

"You're lined up left."

The fighter corrected but settled, and the ramp took a big dip which the pilot chased.

The LSO transmitted again. "Power."

Shrike 306 gave them a shot of power, too much, and drove himself high as he got in-close.

"Easy with it. *EASY!"*

It wasn't the best approach he'd ever seen, but the LSO knew the pilot and knew he was a good ball flyer. He also knew the weather wasn't getting any better, and he needed to get everyone back aboard.

SLAM. The Super Hornet landed a little long and caught the four wire, which started its run-out. Then disaster struck. The cross deck pendant, the center part of the arresting wire, snapped. With a sickening sound much like a gunshot, the wire whipped through the air, moving with incredible speed. Men and women everywhere instinctively hit the deck. In the tower, even the air boss and his crew ducked. Shrike 306 was already well off the deck and climbing out.

But it happened too fast for Parker. Holding on to the side of the helicopter, he watched the Super Hornet hit as he had done thousands of times before, and he watched the cable start its run-out. He heard a noise, but he was too startled to comprehend what it was. The cable moved so fast that he never knew what hit him—at least that's what they would tell his widow and young son. The cable hit him just above the waist and cut his body in half.

The cable might have kept going and thrown him over the side, except for Battlecat 703. It slammed his broken body into the helo and then lopped off 703's tail pylon, leaving it a mangle of metal, cables, control tubes and wires as it slowed down its inertia and came to rest in the "junkyard" area aft of the island.

The mini-boss saw it first and reflexively buzzed the captain. "Captain, mini-here. Yes, sir, I saw it. Cable snapped. We've got a man-down. Need a 1MC call."

The air boss was already booming over the 5MC, "On the flight deck, there's a man down, man down near the after-portion of the island."

The mini-boss grabbed the UHF radio transmitter and called to the aircraft still in the air, "Ninety-nine, we have a snapped cable and an injury on the flight deck. Delta easy, I say again, delta easy." Delta easy is the signal for all aircraft to loiter around the carrier at their best fuel conservation altitude and airspeed.

Next, the Bos'n mate on the bridge made his 1MC call. "Man down, man down. Man down on the flight deck, vicinity of the island. Away the medical alert team, away. MAN DOWN!"

Five decks below the flight deck, Petty Officer First Class Adam Pierre grabbed his gear and joined two other medics as they raced out of medical and headed toward the flight deck. They burst out of the interior of the island and headed for Parker. Pierre was the first to reach him. He instantly recognized it was too late.

The air boss and the mini-boss knew too. Someone had to tell the captain. The air boss knew he had to be the one.

"Captain, the man down on the flight deck is Petty Officer Parker. He...he didn't make it."

Vandegrift listened impassively, and then said, "Okay, Boss, let's get the flight deck cleared and get those aircraft on deck."

* * *

Six decks below the bridge, Heater Robinson hung up the Bogen phone after listening to Vandegrift tell him of Parker's death. The chairman of the Joint Chiefs of Staff had chastised him for shooting down a Syrian pilot. He wondered if Jake Monroe—or anyone else sitting in their air conditioned offices in the Pentagon, in the Eisenhower Executive Office Building, or in the White House—cared one whit about men like Parker who were dying so that the United States could do nothing in the Gulf.

CHAPTER 17

Syria's president called in his key leaders in the wake of the Foxbat shoot-down. He wanted to determine what had happened and decide what he should do next. He'd already made up his mind, but he wanted validation from his top military commanders. It was surprising he still thought he was getting sound advice. These men weren't fools. They knew what he wanted to hear and understood the penalty for not telling him exactly that.

Lieutenant General Muzakim, Air Force Chief of Staff, spoke first. "We've investigated the loss of our Foxbat and have determined it was the work of American warplanes that lured it across the border and then shot it down to provoke an incident with us."

"Why would they do such a thing?"

"Their motives aren't entirely clear," Deputy Prime Minister Aziz interjected. "The United States doesn't like our government and they accuse us of persecuting our Sunni majority and the rebels who have tried to overthrow our government."

"Perhaps. But how is it that one of our aircraft, flown by one of our best pilots, could be lured across the border by such a simple ruse?"

"Excellency, the Americans spend a great deal of money on jamming and deception aircraft such as their Growlers. This is the aircraft that jammed our control center. Unfortunately, the best technology we're able to purchase from Europe is not as advanced as that in their aircraft."

"When this jamming occurs, don't our pilots and controllers take precautions?"

"They do. However, it appears the Americans evolved an elaborate plot. Looking back now, we've been jammed and deceived before but it never had this disastrous result."

He turned toward his minister of defense. "General, is there no way that we can defeat this?"

"We continue to explore ways of getting better equipment. I have a delegation in China looking at some of their most modern gear."

"I understand, but will the Chinese sell the equipment to us?"

"They've shown that they'll sell their arms to whoever will pay them. You know how much they sell to the Iranians. The Chinese want to increase their sales throughout our region."

The dialogue continued, with the assembled underlings telling the Syrian president exactly what he wanted to hear: The Americans had lured Raid Bakr across the border. Syria didn't have the sophisticated equipment to defeat this tactic—but they were going to get it. Syria's president seemed satisfied by the explanation, much to the relief of all.

Finally, the minister of defense spoke. "We aren't merely waiting for new equipment to keep the American warplanes at bay. We've moved many of our aircraft from our northern airfields to our southern ones. Additionally, we're moving our mobile surface-to-air missile sites every day. We'll impossibly complicate the American's efforts."

"So, you guarantee that we'll not have an incident again?"

"Yes, we've moved decisively to achieve this."

CHAPTER 18

"Come in," Heater Robinson said in response to the knock on his cabin door. His senior aviators filed in: Craig Vandegrift; Boomer Davison; Wizard Foster; Captain Walt "Stretch" Purcell, the Deputy CAG; and Bill Durham. They were all in a somber mood.

Robinson looked around at the sea of morose faces. "Gents, we all mourn the loss of Petty Officer Parker. I know all of you are troubled by what happened, especially by an accident that was so avoidable. Don't misunderstand the reason for this meeting. I'm not here to tell you that you must do better or try harder."

"Admiral, we all feel the loss of Petty Officer Parker," Vandegrift began. "It was a tragic accident that could have been prevented."

"What have we learned so far regarding what happened?"

"We're just beginning the investigation," Davison responded. "But one thing we know is that Petty Officer Parker had been up since 0430."

"Since 0430?"

"Yes, sir. We had flight quarters at 0530 to launch the COD to the beach to pick up pax. Then we took the CH-53E hits with cargo and mail. After that, we launched two MH-60Ss to push parts to the small boys. By that time, we were setting up for our first full launch and it didn't let up after that."

"I read you, Boss," Robinson responded.

"Admiral, Parker was completely exhausted. He just let down his guard. He should have been standing behind the tow tractor. No one saw him, otherwise one of my flight deck supervisors would have made him move," the air boss continued.

"Has the pace picked up all of a sudden?" the admiral asked.

"Air Boss painted an accurate picture of yesterday," CAG interjected, "and no, yesterday wasn't an atypical day. The pace has been building gradually ever since we entered the Gulf."

85

"It certainly is higher than when I had a carrier command over here," Robinson added. "But what's changed specifically?"

"Admiral, there are the daily P-8 flights. Commodore needs 'em to do surveillance, we know that, but the Fifth Fleet staff now wants us to put up CAP to protect them," he said, referring to combat air patrol—fighters sent up to protect other aircraft. "Those guys patrol just about all day long, and that's a lot of CAP sorties."

"I see. Anything else?"

"Nothing major, Admiral. Seems like Fifth Fleet used to let us use CTF-53's Super Stallion helos all the time to bring parts, pax and mail out to us. They're holding them back more now; they say it's for 'higher priority missions.' That makes us launch a few extra COD flights every day."

"So we're getting nibbled to death on the margins, is that it?" Robinson asked. It was a rhetorical question, and no one answered.

"Ops O, what does your counterpart say when you speak with him about this?"

"Admiral, I'm on the phone with their ops officer several times a day," Durham began. "I challenge him on each one of these new requirements, and he's hard pressed to explain why they're laying them on. He hints pretty strongly Admiral Flowers is coming up with these ideas on his own."

"We're saying we've pushed it to the limits, but it's a problem of our own making. That tells me it's nothing that can't be fixed."

Vandegrift chimed in. "Admiral, we've got to find a way to make sure what happened to Petty Officer Parker doesn't happen to another sailor."

"There's only one of us here who can take point on this, fellas. I've got the ball; let me run with it a while."

CHAPTER 19

At Fifth Fleet Headquarters, Admiral Flowers sat at his desk reading the day's intelligence summary. The news wasn't encouraging. The Syrians were still posturing in the wake of the Foxbat shoot-down, and the Iranians were stepping up their terrorist training and starting to filter some of those terrorists to locations throughout the Gulf. He'd marshaled sufficient U.S. forces in the Gulf to do something about it—now he just needed to be able to move forward.

He hadn't been satisfied with the *Carl Vinson* strike group commander's preparations for Exercise Swift Sword. He wanted to see the strike briefs in person, not just some vanilla, watered down "executive summary." Robinson had protested—God, he had some nerve: didn't want to fly that many people in, tied up a lot of helo assets, all manner of excuses. He'd told him that he could either fly them in from the carrier's position over a hundred miles away, or he could anchor his carrier at Bahrain Bell and enjoy a shorter flight.

Flowers thoughts were interrupted by the buzz of the intercom.

"Yes?"

"Admiral, Captain Perry is calling," the yeoman said.

"Put him through."

Seconds later, Perry was on the line. "Good day, Admiral."

"Hello, Tom. What's the word from Washington?"

"Admiral, the news is good. We had a positive session with the president. I laid out all of the advantages of striking the Iranian navy hard and I think I was convincing."

"That's great news. Exactly what did he say?"

"He said"—Perry paused for effect—"we should sink their navy."

"Not just take it out of action?"

"No, sir. He said sink it."

"That's great work. You keep in the loop, you hear. I don't want anyone getting cold feet and changing their mind."

"I won't let that happen, Admiral."

"I know I can count on you, Tom."

Flowers was interrupted by another buzz of the intercom.

"Yes!" he said sharply.

"Admiral," the yeoman began, "Admiral Robinson and his staff people are here."

"I'm on an important call to Washington; have the chief of staff take them down to the conference room. I'll get down there when I can."

As the yeoman relayed the message to Admiral Robinson, Captain Dennis, who could hear the yeoman's conversations from his office, appeared and greeted Robinson. "Admiral, welcome. The boss is momentarily tied up. Won't you join me in our conference room?"

Robinson wasn't quick to anger, but he was doing a slow burn. Flowers had summoned him to the Fifth Fleet Headquarters and insisted he bring his senior staff members and strike leaders. It had taken two of the carrier's MH-60S helicopters to haul the group. Robinson had complied, not because it made any sense, but because Flowers was his superior commander. And now he was too busy to personally greet the only other Navy flag officer in the entire theater of operations?

"All right, Chief of Staff," Robinson began, "lead the way. My folks are already down there and we might as well get started."

Dennis led them down the corridor toward the conference room. The Fifth Fleet staffers—as well as his own people—stood as Robinson entered the room. Robinson sat at the center of the large table.

The Fifth Fleet operations officer, Captain Carl Mullen, began. "Admiral, gentlemen, thank you all for coming. Admiral Flowers wanted to review the preparations for Exercise Swift Sword."

"We've got our plan pretty well laid out," offered Robinson's ops officer, Bill Durham. "We've transmitted those to you via message, and I think we've met your requirements."

"You've done an outstanding job," Mullen continued. "We just wanted to look at your plans in a little more depth."

"I know, Carl," Durham replied, "but you know as well as I do this level of detail, having our strike leaders brief the conduct of their simulated strikes for this exercise, is a little bit unusual."

"I know, but you've got to understand the importance of this exercise. I'm sure when Admiral Flowers comes in he will share some of his insights with us," Mullen replied.

"That's right," Dennis offered. "We just wanted to get all the major players assembled in one—"

"Stop!" Robinson shouted as he shot up out of his chair. "Maybe we need to wait for your boss. I've brought a dozen of the most senior people from *Carl Vinson* here today because your boss summoned us. We're working sixteen hours a day to put this damned exercise together to your specifications. But when you interrupt us in the middle of our preps to come here and present the plan so you can nit-pick it to death. We don't have time for that—"

Robinson was looking at Dennis and Mullen and noticed their eyes were slowly moving to the right, toward the door at his left. He turned and saw the small, spare frame of Admiral Flowers standing in the doorway. He'd evidently heard at least some of Robinson's monologue.

"Admiral Robinson, you've had your say. Now please be seated."

Robinson mustered all the control he possessed and sat down.

Flowers went to his chair without stopping to shake Robinson's hand. "We welcome all of you from *Carl Vinson*. I know you might be a bit busy, but we wanted to bring you here to explain our plans, which evidently get lost somewhat in translation in the miles from my headquarters to your flagship," he began.

"Those of you afloat just don't have the big picture. I'm going to tell you what the big picture is."

All eyes were riveted on the Fifth Fleet commander.

"The big picture is that I'm not going to let you people on *Carl Vinson* waste everyone's time husbanding your precious strike group. You didn't come all the way here to worry about just defending yourselves.

"You're here to do the national will. That includes threatening Iran so they stop their terrorist activities. Exercise Swift Sword could turn into an operation at any moment. Therefore, we're going to train the way we're going to fight. I don't want any halfhearted, watered-down strike packages; I want everything you can throw into this."

Durham replied. "Admiral, we're just trying to balance—"

Flowers cut him off. "Balance? I don't want to hear about balance, Captain. I want you to build strike packages that put the fear of God into those damn people. Don't think for a moment they aren't watching what you're doing during your practice strikes. And should we take this further..." He paused for effect. "We're going after their Navy. We're not going to put it out of action. We're going to sink it. Iran won't have a navy when we're through with them."

The contingent from *Carl Vinson* had never heard anything like this and his own staff members had never seen Flowers this animated.

"Now that we understand each other a little better, Admiral Robinson, why don't you have your people brief us."

"Certainly, Admiral," Robinson replied. "My Ops O will lead off with the overall campaign plan, followed by CAG, and then the various strike leads for strikes during the first phase of the *exercise*."

Each briefer presented his portion of the plan and each time, predictably, it wasn't enough. As the Fifth Fleet commander expressed his dissatisfaction at each step along the way, Robinson assured Flowers that things would be changed to meet his requirements.

Finally, the briefings were complete. Flowers absently thanked everyone. He left the conference room as abruptly as he had entered.

Back in his office, Flowers settled into his chair, buoyed from making his points, but drained by the effort. He wouldn't be another forgotten Fifth Fleet commander. He would be remembered as the man who sent the Iranian Navy to the bottom of the Gulf.

CHAPTER 20

Anne O'Connor bent over her right leg, which was propped up on an NC-8 electric power cart on *Carl Vinson's* flight deck. During the limited time the ship wasn't conducting air operations, Boomer Davison opened up the flight deck for jogging. O'Connor and many others planned their schedules around this time, as the flight deck was the only place to run on this ship.

As she stretched, she looked around the flight deck for familiar faces, looking for someone to jog with. She saw Jake Roach and Rick Holden running toward her. Roach and O'Connor had been classmates in the same company at the Naval Academy and had been friends since then. She waved at Roach as he came toward her.

"Hey, Anne," Roach said, raspy and a bit out of breath.

"Hey Jake, hey Rick." She had seen Holden around the ship, especially with Roach and the other HSM-73 bubbas.

Roach was running with Holden—it seemed like the natural thing to do, given how closely HSM-73 worked with Holden's SEAL platoon.

"Anne, you just getting ready to go?" Roach asked.

"Yeah, I'm gonna give it a good couple of miles anyway. You hot, sweaty boys want to join me?"

"Not me," Roach replied. "This SEAL has run me into the ground."

O'Connor really did want to have someone run with, so she pressed. "Come on you guys, just a lap or two."

Roach was silent, his hands on his knees, trying to catch his breath.

"Sure, I'll give it a few more turns around the deck," Holden chimed in. "Ol Jake needs to get a little nap. He isn't as young as he once was."

"Great," O'Connor replied. She really didn't know Holden and was surprised he'd agreed to run with her. What would they talk about?

As Roach walked toward the catwalk, O'Connor and Holden headed for the "stream," the group of runners going in clockwise circles around the deck. They were silent for a bit. Finally, O'Connor spoke up.

"Rick, you're the OIC of the SEAL platoon, right?"

"Sure am. Jake says you're a Super Hornet pilot. How's that bird to fly?"

Roach had been telling Holden about her?

"It's a great aircraft; flies like a dream," she replied. "I see you and the HSM-73 pilots together. You do a lot of flying with them?"

"Yeah, that's the only reason I knew what you flew. Jake and the other ring-knockers spend about half their time talking about their days at the Academy. I think that's where your name came up."

O'Connor saw him flash a broad smile.

"Oh, sure, and I'll bet they told you some wild stories. I take it you didn't go to the Academy. Where'd you go to school?"

"Oh, I went to UVA. But that was a long time ago."

"So you're one of those really smart guys," she kidded. "Did you go ROTC, or just decide to come in after you graduated?"

"No, I bummed around after college at a few different jobs before coming into the Navy," he replied. "I see flight ops have been pretty intense lately. Guess that's good for all you pilots, right?"

"Well, I didn't come on this pleasure cruise to catch up on my reading. You've probably noticed we're spending a lot of time in alerts. No flying there…just getting baked in the cockpits of our aircraft."

Well, yeah, guess that's not too much fun."

"So how is it for you SEALs? Not much to do but work out every day, right?"

"Yep, putting that high-priced UVA education to work."

"I could sure go for that."

"Who knows, the way the Navy is changing, maybe they'll be women SEALs one day and you can join up."

"Maybe it'll snow in August in the Gulf," O'Connor replied.

O'Connor was enjoying the light banter with Holden, and she would much rather talk with a man who wasn't in the Airwing. Holden was "safe," and she was mildly curious about the SEAL mission.

Talking with Holden was safer than talking with any of her fellow pilots. As a naval aviator, where everyone is supposed to have the "right stuff," she felt she couldn't confide in her fellow aviators. She didn't have that problem with Holden.

"You up here running every day?" he asked as they completed their second lap around the flight deck.

"Not every day. Sometimes I'm so drained after flying all day that I just bag it. I don't imagine you SEALs have that problem. We pay you guys to work out every day, don't we?"

"Yep, and I'm trying to give the Navy their money's worth."

Holden found O'Connor easy to talk with, but was guarded about his professional past. Beyond that, he wasn't sure how involved he should become with any woman. During his last assignment, before he was Lieutenant Rick Holden, he'd been close to someone—someone with whom he had shared life or death experiences. He knew she cared for him, and he cared for her—but they wanted to give a relationship that had burned in the crucible of shared danger time to mature.

They were both Navy and were assigned to commands a world away from each other. They e-mailed and texted frequently, and although there were no definite plans, they felt they could have a future together. With this history with Laura Peters in his mind, Holden wasn't looking for a relationship with anyone else right now.

* * *

One deck below where O'Connor and Holden were now making their fourth circuit of the flight deck, Heater Robinson sat in his cabin alone. First the angry SPECAT message from his friend, Jake Monroe, then the needless death of Petty Officer Parker, and now this humiliating experience at the hands of Admiral Flowers.

Robinson was not so much staggered by the personal attacks, or even by whatever impact this would have on his professional reputation. What angered him was his country's vacillation and its unwillingness to act. It was holding back and running only exercises that sapped both equipment and morale when it should be striking the enemies of the United States. He had faith the system would eventually do the right thing, but that faith was being sorely tested.

CHAPTER 21

Patrick Browne was pacing. He'd planned to make his economic stimulus package the crown jewel of his first term as president. The fact this major package of tax cuts was going to be announced right before his reelection campaign kicked off was just a serendipitous bonus he told himself. He'd told himself this so many times that he actually believed it. But one foreign crisis after another diverted his attention.

The president was still pacing when the door to the Oval Office opened. Michael Curtis led a large group into the office. It included Bryce Jacobs; Philip Quinn; Jake Monroe; Peter Hernandez; Lieutenant General Robert Allen, the JCS operations director; and Andrea Wilson, the deputy secretary of defense for international security affairs.

Once the president gestured for them to sit, Curtis began. "Mr. President, we wanted to update you on the situation in the Gulf. First of all, we believe the situation in Syria is stable for the moment. They will saber-rattle for a while, but we don't expect any additional threats to our forces. Admiral Monroe has confirmed this with CENTCOM."

"Admiral?" the president asked.

"Mr. President, I've been in constant contact with General Lawrence. The Syrians have been grinding away at this story we lured their aircraft across the border. We feel the real story will come out, they'll realize their guy just screwed up, and they'll drop the issue."

"No chance they'll try to use it as a pretext to step up operations in the region counter to our interests?" Wilson asked.

"We really don't think so," Monroe continued. "They're too weak now because of U.N. sanctions."

"That's good," the president replied.

"Yes, sir," Curtis said. "On the other hand, the extent of Iranian activity is sobering. It appears they may be planning something major soon. Mr. Hernandez has some additional details. Peter."

"Mr. President, the Iranians have put a number of terrorist training camps back on-line and have intensified the activity at others. We've seen the highest-ever level of activity at these camps based on imagery and HUMINT."

The statement startled the president, since HUMINT—human intelligence—indicated the United States had agents in Iran reporting on the activities in the terrorist training camps.

"Go ahead, Peter."

"We're beginning to see a flow of people out of the camps. We suspect these men are being sent to perform various missions. It's not just the fact this is happening, but that it's happening in such numbers. We simply don't have the capability to track every person who leaves one of these camps."

The president simply nodded.

"Mr. President, we've zeroed in on Gulf nations known terrorists are entering. We've raised the threat condition in these states and warned American citizens about the threat. Our next step could be to have U.S. citizens leave these countries—voluntarily, of course."

"No, no," the president said. "I don't want to start a wholesale panic. Raising the threat levels is an overt enough act. I don't want us overreacting."

"Mr. President," Quinn chimed in, "no one is overreacting. Our intelligence community has presented a clear threat. We may want to take other, more definitive, action."

"What kind of action are you talking about?"

"One option that would have an impact would be a demarche to Iran, warning them that any terrorist activities would be met by disproportionate force."

"Isn't that a little strong?" the president asked. "Do we have to issue a demarche to every nation that might threaten us? I'll have to think about that one."

"Of course," Quinn replied.

Curtis hadn't been in favor of the secretary of state's demarche idea. He was glad the president had vetoed it.

What Curtis had put into effect was much more comprehensive than any diplomatic demarche. Working with the Chairman of the Joint Chiefs of Staff, as well as with General Lawrence at CENTCOM, they'd put together Exercise

Swift Sword. They hadn't kept the exercise a secret from the secretary of defense or from the president, but they'd billed it as just another routine exercise.

What the president didn't know was that the exercise was designed to simulate massive strikes into Iran with the objective of setting back their military capability at least a decade, perhaps two. A terrorist act could be the trigger to put that plan into action and turn the "exercise" into actual strikes. They didn't want any diplomatic posturing to derail what they were doing.

"Mr. President," Curtis said, "I believe the secretary of state has presented a viable option, however, a demarche to Iran might tip our hand. There's evidence that the Iranian clerics wouldn't be deterred by a demarche, and that it even might have the opposite effect and cause them to act sooner and unleash more terrorists throughout the Gulf."

Quinn knew he was being outmaneuvered and backed off as gracefully as he could.

"Of course, Mr. President, a demarche is only one option you have at your disposal."

"I see," the president responded. Then he began issuing instructions. "Peter, I'd like you to take a hard look at just what's going on with respect to Iranian-sponsored terrorist activity in the Gulf. Bryce, I want you and Admiral Monroe to continue this exercise you're conducting and be ready to respond massively to an attack."

Patrick Browne surveyed the room. His principals were taking notes on their tablets to record his instructions. The press would report he had "taken charge," and soon he could put this untidy business aside and return to his domestic agenda.

Curtis smiled to himself. He had his victory. The president's instructions would take so long to carry out that a major terrorist act was bound to happen. Exercise Swift Sword would soon be turned into an attack on the Islamic Republic of Iran.

Curtis left the Oval Office quickly; he had work to do. His first phone call would be to Captain Perry. The Fifth Fleet commander would be called moments after that. He wanted to be sure Flowers was ready. This was the opportunity they'd waited for.

CHAPTER 22

One of the things the U.S. government does least well is keep secrets. Although they had no well-placed spies in the sense most people understand the word, Iran recognized it was in their best interest to stay tapped into the decision-making apparatus of the nation that threatened them. A secretary here, a summer intern there, a media person with the appropriate contacts, and they had the capability to discern moves the American government intended to take. There was a well-established funnel to channel this information back to the Iranian capital.

Ali Akbar Velayati and General Abdollah Najafi had asked for meeting with the President of the Islamic Republic. Hasan Ibrahim Habibi thought it odd these two men should ask for an audience together. He ushered them into his office. Minister Velayati spoke first.

"Mr. President, thank you for seeing us on such short notice."

"No affairs I deal with are so important I cannot make time to see you and General Najafi. How may I help you?"

"Mr. President," Velayati continued, "when we last met, I told you about actions we were taking to make the infidels think twice about their presence in the Gulf—"

"And I told you that I don't share your urgent need to expel the Americans from the Gulf, Mr. Minister," Habibi interrupted.

"You did, Mr. President. But in spite of your concerns, we felt we must step up our actions. I have men in place ready to strike, and what General Najafi will tell you will convince you this is the right course."

Habibi was puzzled. "General?" he asked.

"I'll come right to the point, Mr. President. We've received disturbing information from our contacts in the United States. The Americans may be planning an attack."

"What makes you think such a thing is possible?"

"There are several indicators an attack is imminent."

"What are they?"

"First, the foreign minister has learned the U. S. Department of State is crafting a demarche accusing us of fostering terrorism and threatens to attack our nation if there is a significant terrorist attack anywhere in the Gulf."

"Anywhere in the Gulf?"

"Yes," Velayati replied.

"That's outrageous. Have the Americans gone mad?"

"Our diplomats assure us this demarche hasn't been issued yet, but it's being considered. The fact that it's on the table is troubling."

"I should say it is, General Najafi. You said there are indications of an impending American attack."

"The actions of their navy cause us a great deal of worry."

"I think we've seen an increase in activity after the shoot-down of the Syrian Foxbat but none of that seemed directed at us," Habibi replied

"The Americans work hard to conceal what they do. But they're menacing us in a direct and specific way."

"How so?" Habibi asked.

"The Americans are conducting an exercise called 'Swift Sword.' It's supposedly an exercise to test their naval and air forces in the Gulf. But the object of this exercise is clear; it's our Islamic Republic. Our Orion aircraft have been monitoring this exercise," Najafi began, using the nickname for their P-3 MARPAT aircraft. "They tell us the thinly disguised practice strikes the Americans are conducting are aimed at us. We're certain they intend to hit our naval bases at Bandar Abbas and Bushehr. There's also evidence they'll attack into the heartland of the Republic."

"Are you certain?"

"More certain than I've ever been. But these attacks won't only be conducted by the carrier *Carl Vinson,* but also by the dozens of aircraft of the so-called AEF that the traitors to the Islamic cause in Qatar have allowed to move into their nation," Najafi continued, referring to the American Air Expeditionary Force at Qatar's Al Udeid Air Force Base. "The American admiral on *Carl Vinson* has made trips to Qatar to confer with his Air Force colleague."

"Are we so poorly defended?" Habibi asked.

"Yes, Mr. President. It shames me to tell you this, but our forces are just too weak to withstand the American onslaught."

Minister Velayati chimed in. "Mr. President, this is why I'm moving forward to use the men we have trained in our camps. The Americans plan to hit us anyway; we won't make our situation worse by striking first. In just a few days the American aircraft carrier will make a port call in Muscat. We'll strike them there—"

"Strike the carrier?" Habibi interrupted.

"No, that's too hardened a target. We'll strike at their people."

"Then what do you think the Americans will do? Aren't you making it certain that they'll strike us?"

"They intend to strike us anyway," Najafi offered.

"Yes, I understand, General. But Mr. Minister, won't this just enrage them and lead to devastating attacks against us?"

"The Americans have a long history of running away from crises when they lose large numbers of their people. Look what they did in Lebanon when the Marine barracks there was bombed. And you recall that they got out of Somalia when they saw video of their dead soldiers being dragged through the streets. They have no stomach for these kinds of personal losses."

"What if they don't react as you predict?" Habibi asked.

"We—General Najafi and I—have considered this possibility and have set a plan in motion to raise the stakes so quickly the Americans will surely leave the Gulf for good."

"Raise the stakes—higher than killing a large number of their sailors?"

"Yes, Mr. President," Velayati continued. "The Americans won't rest until our regime is destroyed, or until they recognize it's too painful for them to hurt us. We're increasing that threshold of pain."

"How?" Habibi asked.

"By the time the attack in Muscat is complete, our agents in America will be ready to take these attacks to the American homeland."

Habibi looked toward Najafi for affirmation, but he just nodded agreement with what Velayati was saying.

"Mr. President, that's all I'm prepared to say at this time, but I assure you that if we're struck, we'll strike back harder."

"But if they don't choose to run as you assume they will, the American carrier will strike us again and again. General Najafi, you just told me that our defenses are too weak and will be overwhelmed."

"Mr. President, the *Carl Vinson* poses the biggest threat. Eliminate that carrier and we can survive whatever blow the Americans can deliver. I'm not a political person, but I think the court of world opinion would be with us if we lashed back after the Americans strike us."

"So, how do you propose to strike the Americans?"

"We don't many weapons that can successfully attack a carrier. Our missiles are good, but the Americans are adept at thwarting them with their Aegis cruisers. We have little chance of penetrating the ring of steel around the American carrier," Najafi replied.

"But if our surface combatants can't reach them, then surely our aircraft can."

"Our pilots fly obsolete aircraft like the F-4—a plane the Americans used during the Vietnam War—the F-6, and the F-7. Even the F-14 Tomcat, one of our best planes, is one the Americans phased out decades ago, and we're constantly in need of spare parts that we can only get at exorbitant prices on the black market."

"I've never been briefed on any of this," countered Habibi.

"This is normally not something that we'd raise to your level, Mr. President. The bottom line, however, is an attempt to attack the American carrier with our tactical aircraft would be a suicide mission for our pilots, and one that would have no chance of even wounding the carrier."

"What do you propose then?"

"Our scientists have worked diligently to revive our nuclear program. The nuclear agreement we made with the Americans years ago has given us the flexibility to cheat in ways they never anticipated. Progress on this new weapon has been slow, as we're impeded by western embargoes. But we've come up with enough enriched uranium to build a low-grade nuclear device. This device is undergoing testing. We—that is, with your concurrence—propose to put this device on an aircraft and destroy the American carrier."

"But you've just told me the Americans can shoot down our jets with impunity. How do you propose to deliver this weapon?"

"That will take some finesse. What we'll do is put it on one of our transport aircraft. That aircraft can then take off from Shiraz International and fly toward Kuwait City," Najafi replied.

"Will this fool the Americans?"

"Yes, and here's why. Our government, in cooperation with the International Civilian Aviation Organization, has recently established a commercial airline route between Shiraz and Kuwait City. This is now a normal path for commercial airline traffic, and because of the relatively short distance between the two cities, these airliners rarely climb above ten thousand feet. This path goes right by the area where the American carrier operates. Our plane will join the airliner route, spacing itself in sequence with the normal flow of traffic. Then, when it's close to the carrier, it will head toward it and drop its weapon."

"What will happen to the crew? Surely the Americans will shoot them down."

"The Americans won't be able to react in time," Velayati chimed in. "And even if they shoot the plane down after the weapon is detonated, the crew has been selected well. They're prepared to die for our cause."

"I understand your plan, gentlemen. We must discuss this within the Supreme National Security Council. Such an action is something that must be decided only after much prayer and debate."

"Yes, Mr. President. But we must not pray too hard or debate too long. The Americans must be taught a lesson and taught one soon," Velayati said.

As the two men left his office, Habibi slumped down in his chair. Events were spinning out of control. He no longer felt that he could effectively lead his country.

CHAPTER 23

Commander Carrier Air Wing Seventeen, Captain Wizard Foster, was displayed on a polished brass plate on the door. Below it was the air wing's logo—the rainbow and eagle's head. Above the door was a small brass enunciator light with green illuminated, indicating Foster was in his cabin and didn't have a visitor.

Commander Alex Fitzgerald could have knocked and walked right in, but he paced nervously outside of CAG's door. Fitzgerald was the Airwing Seventeen flight surgeon and was wrestling with an issue of doctor-patient privilege. CAG was his boss, and he had made it clear he wanted to know everything about the health of every aviator aboard *Carl Vinson.* Fitzgerald was torn, but ultimately his loyalty to his boss won out.

"Enter!" Foster said in response to the loud knock on his door.

"Hello, CAG," Fitzgerald began. "I apologize for barging in. If this isn't a good time—"

"Naw, anytime's a good time for you, Doc," Foster replied. "What's on your mind?"

"CAG, I have an issue I could have tabled under the rubric of doctor-patient privilege. However, you've made it clear you wanted to know about the health of all of our aviators."

"Yes, I did, Doc." Foster replied. He knew what kinds of corners aviators sometimes cut to keep flying when they shouldn't. Hell, he'd pulled some of those tricks when he was a lieutenant—taking Motrin to kill the pain of athletic injuries, flying with a cold, taking meds and then piloting a jet when he shouldn't have been flying at all.

Sometimes he thought Fitzgerald was a bit too anal about this. Pilots knew their limits. What minor faux pas had the doc discovered?

"I appreciate your dilemma. So tell me what you know."

"CAG, well, this isn't exactly about an Airwing aviator—though it is about someone who flies with the Airwing—occasionally, that is."

"Okay, Doc, who would that be?"

"This is hard for me to discuss; it involves a very senior officer—"

"Doc, for Chrissake! Who the hell are you talking about?"

"CAG, it's Admiral Robinson."

"Admiral Robinson? Doc, are you serious?"

"Yes, sir, dead serious, and I think his condition may be grave."

"Doc, what the heck is going on?"

"It started a few days ago. The admiral asked me to come up to his cabin. He said wanted me to give him something to calm his nerves—"

"Calm his nerves?" CAG interrupted. "Did he look nervous or upset to you?"

"You let me come to many of the flag briefs, and I've noticed the admiral doesn't look the same as he did when we began the deployment—"

Foster interrupted again. "Hell, Doc, none of us do. We're in the Gulf. This is hard, stressful work. We just lost a man on the flight deck. Sure, he's probably stressed. What did you give him?"

"Sir, on his direct orders, I prescribed a mild sleeping sedative. But that's not the point."

"Well, what *is* the damn point? So far nothing you've told me sounds like any of our business."

"CAG, I persuaded the admiral to let me take his blood pressure and listen to his heart—just so I could prescribe the right meds. His blood pressure is sky high—170 over 110. His heart is racing and his pulse is too. And he just...just...looks bad."

"What did you do then?"

"I suggested we do a more robust battery of tests like blood tests, an EKG, those sorts of things, but he told me he didn't need any damn tests."

"When did this happen?"

"It happened two days ago. I know now I should have told you right away. But, sir, he's a flag officer and a patient."

"Doc, you did the right thing; thank you for coming to me with this. For the moment, though, why don't we just let this sit? The admiral hasn't flown much since we've been in the Gulf. I'm not worried from the standpoint of an aircrew being on medication."

"Yes, sir, but from the standpoint of his overall health?"

"Right, Doc. I'll find a way to bring it up with him."

"Thanks CAG. I'm glad...well...I'm glad that I came to see you."

"I am too, Doc."

As the door shut behind his flight surgeon, Foster now understood just how much stress Robinson was under. He wanted to help him, but he wasn't sure how to do it.

* * *

Fifty frames forward of where Foster was wresting with what his flight surgeon had told him, Anne O'Connor was pulling on her flight suit for another hop. She was one of the high-time pilots in her squadron for this month, and she was rubbing it with her roommate.

"So Chrissie, are you in *double-digits* for flight time this month yet? If you're not, I *may* bag out of one of my hops and let you take it."

Moore sat at her desk reading an e-mail from "the beau," as O'Connor referred to her fiancée. She knew she was pouring through that missive, and that she could run her recklessly, knowing she wouldn't be focused enough to think of a good comeback.

"No, I'm getting plenty, roomie, but you may be getting too much. By the way, *Brian* stopped me in the p-way the other day asking how you were doing."

"McDonald?" O'Connor asked, feigning surprise.

"Oh, cut it out, Anne. You know who, it's always *Brian*."

That hit a nerve. "Chrissie, you know there's nothing going on with me and McDonald, don't you?"

"Sure I do. I know he's just this big mentor guy from the Academy. Aren't there a bunch of you he's looking out for?"

"Yep, he's great as a sounding board about stuff like career patterns, good flying jobs, that sort of thing."

"Hey, I think it's great. Maybe I run you because I'm a little jealous. Even though we had a big NROTC unit at Notre Dame, we don't have this worldwide network like you ring-knockers do."

"I think McDonald keeps checking up on me because I need the most help. Maybe that's why I'm hogging this much flight time.

"I guess," Moore replied. "But, what's up with that guy you've been jogging with? Anything there?"

"Chrissie, now that you're engaged I know what you're up to. You can't stand for me to be single," O'Connor chided back. "No, there's nothing there. You know how it is, I confide in you, but that's it. I don't dare talk to any guys in the Airwing, there's just too much scuttlebutt. Rick is, well, safe. He's older, and he's just easy to talk to."

"I think that's great, go for it. You're not gonna stop talking to me now, are you?"

O'Connor knew Moore was running her now. It wasn't just that she was her roommate, or that they were squadron-mates, or that they did a lot of things together—it went beyond that. She was her confidante. She told her everything: every victory, every defeat, every worry, every crisis. The thought she would ever stop talking with her was so bizarre she pushed it out of her brain.

CHAPTER 24

The national security adviser sat at his desk going over his notes, waiting for the other participants to assemble in the Cabinet Room. Michael Curtis was edgy, but comfortable with his role as national security advisor. Power was what had attracted him to public service and what had driven him for the last thirty years. Nowhere but in government service at this level could a person rise to a position where they could exercise this much power. Sure, elected officials had to be allowed to believe their positions let them wield the power, but ultimately it came to men like Curtis. They were the *real* decision makers.

It hadn't been an easy or a direct path. His family connections and educational credentials gave him a favorable starting position, but that position was crowded with thousands of young hopefuls like him. Curtis had simply outworked, outfought, and outmaneuvered the competition to become the principal adviser to the president.

Curtis was determined to best his historical competition, too. As he thought about some of the national security advisers to past presidents—Henry Kissinger, Zbigniew Brzezinski, Colin Powell, Brent Scowcroft, Tony Lake, Sandy Berger, Condoleezza Rice, and others—it occurred to him only a few had wielded the full range of power he could employ. Others had either been unwilling or unable to use the office as a tool to craft a foreign policy agenda that met the nation's vital interests.

Curtis thought of himself as a lone marksman delivering the single shot to the threat to bring it down permanently. Iran was that threat and was a nation that posed a compelling danger to the United States. He wasn't unhappy the Iranians were unleashing terrorists throughout the Gulf region—and maybe further than that.

He knew the United States was prepared to respond to a terrorist attack with disproportionate force. He had the ability to steer that response in a way that wouldn't just persuade the Islamic Republic to cease its terrorist acts for the moment, but would render it incapable of posing a threat in the ensuing decades. He wanted that to be his legacy.

His principal military advisor, Captain Tom Perry, had helped him evolve an effective plan for doing this. They had presented this plan to the president, emphasizing the need to destroy the Iranian Navy. The only way the plan could go awry was if the Iranians didn't give the United States a reason to attack. He would ensure that didn't happen.

Curtis strode into the Cabinet Room where the small group had gathered: Admiral Monroe, Peter Hernandez, Andrea Wilson, Lieutenant General Allen and Captain Perry. He got right to the point.

"The president has given specific direction regarding our actions in the Gulf. Our role is to ensure that the unified commander is prepared to carry out the president's desires should a terrorist act occur. Admiral Monroe, I'll leave that to you and to General Allen to ensure CENTCOM is prepared to do this."

"We'll see to it, Mr. Curtis."

"Splendid. Peter, I want you to continue to share intelligence with the Pentagon. If Iran is responsible for a terrorist act, and if we start shooting, Admiral Monroe will need detailed information regarding the position of Iranian forces, especially Iranian naval forces."

"Yes, sir, we can do that."

"In the event any of our forces are struck, we must be prepared to respond with overwhelming force. Nothing short of that will dissuade them from striking us again."

"Mr. Curtis," Monroe begin, "you're speaking as if the Iranians have already attacked our interests. We may want to wait a bit to be sure we aren't being preemptive."

"Admiral, we have to be ready for any contingency. General Lawrence and Admiral Flowers feel sufficiently alarmed to have put their forces in a higher state of alert. I'm just asking us to make commonsense preparations."

They all knew there was more to it, but they dared not confront the national security adviser. They'd go along with the plan—at least for now. How long they would have to do this, they could only speculate.

For his part, Curtis needed a spark to ignite his plan. He was determined he'd get that spark and get it soon.

CHAPTER 25

Tuesday was a no-fly day aboard *Carl Vision* as the ship steamed en route to its port call in Muscat, Oman. It was a long way to travel from their operating area in the northeastern Gulf—over 500 nautical miles—but to everyone aboard *Carl Vinson* it was an important trip. The pace of operations for their past several weeks had been unrelenting. Everyone—from Admiral Robinson to the newest seaman or airman—needed to recharge their batteries. Muscat, with its close-in anchorage, as well as logistics needed to support an aircraft carrier like *Carl Vinson,* was one of the few good port calls in the region.

Heater Robinson sat on the Flag Bridge watching the scores of sailors on the flight deck work on their aircraft. His chief of staff and his Airwing commander stood by him.

"Admiral, looks like we've got everything on track for our port call," George Sampson said.

"I think so, Chief of Staff. Boy, these kids are ready for some liberty."

"They are," Wizard Foster replied. Then he continued. "Admiral, so, how is everything else going? I know that we're keeping you super busy. Are you getting enough time to sleep and work out?"

"Never enough, but I'm doing okay. How about you?"

"Just fine. You know you've got senior commanders who can take on more if you need us to."

Robinson looked him quizzically.

"Flag Bridge, Chief of Staff," Sampson said as he picked up the ringing Bogen phone. "Roger, we're on our way down."

"Admiral, that was the Staff TAO. He says that Admiral Flowers wants to speak with you. He says it's urgent."

"It usually is, COS,"

What does Flowers want now? Robinson asked himself as he moved down the five decks with the CAG and chief of staff in tow.

As he entered the War Room, Mike Lumme met him outside of TFCC. "Admiral, Fifth Fleet is on the phone. We can't seem to transfer it to your cabin, some IT glitch. Would you mind taking the call in TFCC?"

"No problem, I'll get it there."

"Admiral Robinson here," he said as he picked up the phone.

The Fifth Fleet flag lieutenant put his boss on.

"Hello, Admiral Flowers."

"Robinson, what's your location now?" Flowers asked.

"Admiral, we're entering the Western Traffic Separation Scheme. We should pass through the Strait of Hormuz on time."

"Of course. Never want to be late for a port call," Flowers snarled.

So that was it, Robinson thought. Flowers had been dead set against this port call. Now he was going to grind him about it.

"No, sir, we don't want to be late now that we've laid on our logistic requirements for Muscat."

"No, of course you don't. But will you be ready for the next phase of Exercise Swift Sword when you come out of that visit?"

"Yes, sir, we will. We got our Airwing up to speed with night landing currency, and we've already identified the pilots we have to qualify the first night out of port. We'll be ready."

There was a pregnant pause before Flowers continued. "You sure as hell better be ready in all respects when you sortie. And another thing, I saw your message regarding force protection plans. They looked a little sketchy to me. Don't you believe there's a threat out there?"

"We do," Robinson replied. He had scanned the force protection plans—he couldn't say that he'd read them thoroughly—but they'd looked adequate. "I'll review them again and if there are extra measures we need to take, I'll add them and beef up our security."

"See that you do. You're the one who pushed for this port call—over my objections, I might add—and we finally let you have your way to throw a bone to the political wonks who want my ships to visit every damn port in this theater. You just make sure you protect your people. Is that clear?"

"Crystal, Admiral."

CHAPTER 26

Peter Hernandez had left the National Security Council meeting determined to ensure that his organization did all it could to solve the Iranian conundrum.

As he strode into the National Counterterrorism Center—the NCTC—at Liberty Crossing in McLean, Virginia, he was met by his EA who led him to his executive conference room.

"Ladies and gents, you all know why we are here," the DNI began. "Events in the Gulf are heating up fast. We want to be able to give the NSC our best estimate regarding threats to Americans. Let's go around the table and see what we have."

Marty Adams spoke first. "Sir, we don't have a complete picture of the extent of terrorist infiltration into the countries around the Gulf littoral. We feel confident that due to the extent of the training that went on in the Iranian camps, there's a high probability that any terrorist activity in the next several days or weeks would be logically attributable to Iran."

"Logically attributable to Iran might not be quite enough to rain destruction down on their country if some group somewhere gets pissed off and blows something up, Marty."

"Got it, sir."

"Okay, what else?"

Sam Lipman spoke up next. "We've come across information which may help us point the finger at Iran. Airport security at Bahrain International found two bags with explosives in the luggage unloaded from a flight from Tehran. Dogs lit on the stuff. Security there speculates the passengers who transported those bags fled. The Bahrainis are working hard to try to ID who the luggage belonged to."

"What else?" Hernandez asked.

"There's one more thing, sir," Adams added. "We've learned that four Hezbollah agents entered Muscat on a flight from Tehran almost a week ago. Muscat is a convenient jumping-off point to travel to other locations such as Qatar, Bahrain and Saudi Arabia, but no one can confirm they've left Oman, and their arrival came soon after the port call for *Carl Vinson* was announced. We assess they may pose a threat to the carrier or its crew."

"We announce our carrier visits?" Hernandez asked.

"Not exactly announce, sir," Rear Admiral George Baldwin, the NCTC deputy director, replied. "There are long-lead time items incident to a carrier's visit: arrangements with husbandry agents to procure supplies, permission to fly in that country's airspace, rerouting of the logistics train that brings supplies from the States, those sorts of things. By the time the carrier arrives it's no secret."

"That certainly doesn't make our job any easier, does it?"

"No, sir, it doesn't. Normally it's not a problem, but we might want to modify our procedures when the terrorism threat is high."

"Good, thank you." Turning back to Adams, Hernandez said, "Marty, what else do we know about this situation in Oman?"

"Ambassador Young and the USDAO will brief *Carl Vinson* on the potential threat. The carrier will be anchored out, so they should have no trouble with security for the ship itself. We're confident they can make the crew aware of how to protect themselves while ashore."

"It's hard to make, what, three thousand sailors, inconspicuous."

"Five thousand," Baldwin offered.

"Admiral, didn't you have command of a carrier strike group deployed to the Gulf a while ago?" Hernandez asked.

"Yes, sir, I did. *Abraham Lincoln* Strike Group some years ago."

"If you were the strike group commander, and you knew what we know now, what would your concerns be?"

"Well, whoever is supporting these terrorists—Iran, we have to assume—is probably not pleased with the government of Oman for letting the carrier go there in the first place. So they probably want to lash out, not only at us, but at Oman as well. I don't see an attack on government buildings, they're well protected and that wouldn't make the connection with the United States. What my greatest fear would be is their attacking a large group of my sailors."

"How would they accomplish such a thing?" the DNI asked.

"My guess is that if there really are terrorists in-country bent on hitting us, they'll probably look to target a hotel where we have a large group of sailors staying. The Omanis don't have the type of security we have seen the Bahrainis put up in places like the Manai Plaza."

"How do we protect against that? What recommendations can we push up to the NSC?"

Hernandez was stuck. Of all the bureaucracies in government, the intelligence community was perhaps the most conservative, and depended on never being wrong. To predict something with certainty, and then have it not happen, was professional suicide. The DNI had succeeded the intelligence community because he'd avoided getting burned by a wrong guess. Now he was on the spot in a time-sensitive situation where he had to make a call.

"Well sir," Baldwin continued, "Mr. Adams has given us what sounds like pretty reliable information that these Hezbollah agents are in Muscat. They just left the camps where they trained. Iran's rhetoric has been getting more strident. We don't know for certain they intend to strike at our people, but it might be wise to deny them the opportunity to do so."

"What are you recommending?" the DNI asked.

"We can suggest canceling the Muscat port visit for *Carl Vinson*," Baldwin responded.

"How would the Navy feel about that?"

"If their people were in harm's way, I think they'd be glad they weren't going there."

The discussions continued for a protracted time. The more they talked, the tougher the conundrum became. Finally, their meeting broke up. As everyone departed, Baldwin stayed behind.

"Mr. Director, I don't want to press, but if we want to do something we need to move quickly. *Carl Vinson* passed through the Strait of Hormuz hours ago."

Hernandez finally decided he had to take action. He would call Michael Curtis.

"Thank you, Admiral, I'll take it from here."

CHAPTER 27

"Anchored, shift colors!" The call over *Carl Vinson's* 1MC was followed by the long blast of the ship's whistle. Simultaneously, the National Ensign flying from the mainmast was hauled down, while the Union Jack was raised on the bow, and another National Ensign was raised on the stern. It was a military maneuver that had occurred on *Carl Vinson* hundreds of times before.

As *Carl Vinson* turned and pointed up into the wind at her anchor, deep inside the berthing compartments throughout the ship the mood was festive as the crew prepared for the first liberty they'd seen in over a month. Civilian clothing came out of lockers and there was a race to get to the hangar bay to join the lines of sailors waiting to go ashore.

* * *

At the Muscat InterContinental Hotel, officers from various squadrons and departments aboard *Carl Vinson* who had flown in on the COD a day prior to make arrangements for admin rooms were settling in. The InterContinental, which fronted a beautiful beach, was the hotel of choice for *Carl Vinson*. Her young, aggressive manager, Andrew Cox, was determined to make his hotel *the* place to be.

The InterContinental's spacious lawns were being roped off and a bandstand was being built to accommodate a battle of the bands that would, Cox hoped, draw even more of *Carl Vinson's* crew to the hotel. Throughout the Omani capital, everyone—from cab drivers to merchants—knew the InterContinental was where sailors would want to go.

At the InterContinental's imposing entrance, two men were washing the large glass inner and outer hotel doors. The doors were washed by a contracted maintenance crew. The men completed the outer doors, moved through the entry area, and began working on the inner doors. The InterContinental's clientele was too busy to notice that one of the men was taking measurements of the height and width of the doors. Their washing complete, the two men melted away as quietly as they had come.

* * *

In *Carl Vinson's* War Room, Admiral Robinson gathered his commanders for the final meeting they'd have for the next few days. He wanted to ensure they were ready for Phase II of Exercise Swift Sword.

"CAG, I know we've got concerns about aircraft availability. How is it looking for resupply of spare parts while we're here?"

"Not too bad, Admiral. There are a lot of spare parts waiting for us in Muscat. The supply channel's working pretty well."

"Good," Robinson replied. "Commodore, how are we covering things in the Gulf while we're in port?"

"We've got things pretty well set," Jim Hughes replied. "I've turned over Maritime Interception duties to DESRON 50 and they're embarking in *Laboon* in the Northern Gulf. We're not real deep, but we can cover it for the four days we're here."

"Great. Ops O, how's the schedule of events looking for Phase II?"

"Admiral, we've been over this with Fifth Fleet staff," Bill Durham replied. "We've tried to narrow the scope of this exercise, but they keep insisting we add more and more events."

"I've got that, thanks. Before we put sailors ashore we need to ensure our force protection measures are tight. Captain, have we done everything we can?"

"I think we have, Admiral," *Carl Vinson's* CO replied. "We've taken all the measures that Fifth Fleet requires us to take."

"And we think that we'll be all right with what we've set up?"

"We've taken all the reasonable precautions that we can. We've set a curfew for our people and have briefed them thoroughly on being cautious while they're here. I think we're okay, sir."

"Good. These people deserve all the liberty we can let them have, but we've got to keep 'em safe."

* * *

Just a few yards from the War Room, George Sampson, dealt with the plethora of details incident to a carrier's making a port call. He didn't have time to go through the morning ritual of reading his message traffic. Had he done so, he would have noticed that the threat assessment for Oman had just been increased to the highest assignable level.

* * *

In a tiny garage a few miles from the InterContinental, several men were packing a van quickly, but with care. It wasn't a complex task—the van was large, and their explosives were powerful. Bringing the bomb material into the sultanate had been laughably easy; they could have readily brought in much more. The size of the van had been selected specifically to do the job and just fit into the orifice it needed to.

* * *

Aboard *Carl Vinson*, in the Blue Tile Area, Mike Lumme helped Admiral Robinson with his uniforms as the admiral and other senior officers prepared for the obligatory round of calls on Omani dignitaries.

The admiral wasn't in a good mood—he still had a junior officer's love of liberty and viewed these calls as a waste of his time. Worse, he couldn't start the calls until he welcomed the Naval Attaché aboard—and he wouldn't be there for another hour. He'd just as soon wave off all of the diplomatic niceties, but then that would give Admiral Flowers just one more thing to be on his case about.

CHAPTER 28

Admiral Flowers sat at his desk reading the morning's message traffic. His duty officer had reported *Carl Vinson* was anchored off Muscat, and it just served to remind him how angry he was that he'd been overruled regarding the carrier's port visit. Flowers didn't like being overruled. Hell, in his last job as inspector general no one dared overrule him. He knew this fight was over; he'd move on to the next one. He would turn up the gain on Exercise Swift Sword and run it at a level of intensity never before seen in the Gulf.

His chief of staff knocked and then entered from the private hallway. "Admiral, Intel and Ops wanted to get on your calendar this morning as soon as possible," Dennis said.

"What's the issue; can't it wait for the staff meeting at 1000?"

"They don't think so, Admiral. It has to do with intel reports about the threat condition in Oman. I don't have all the details, but they're ready to present them as soon as you're available."

"Okay, five minutes, my conference room."

* * *

"Seats, gents," Flowers said as he entered his executive meeting room. He surveyed the faces around the table. In addition to Dennis, the group included his operations officer, Captain Carl Mullen, his intelligence officer, Captain Don Fraser, and his legal officer, Commander Mike Oakes.

"Okay, let's have it," Flowers began. "You all asked for this meeting."

"Admiral, we've just come across some disturbing intelligence," Fraser began. "The report indicates there are at least four Hezbollah agents in Muscat, and we assess that there is a probability they'll try to attack our sailors. I got this report via

116

flash precedence message at 0200 this morning. I elected not to awaken you, Admiral. However, I sent a message to Admiral Robinson's staff on *Carl Vinson* to alert them."

"Good, have we gotten an acknowledgement they've received it?"

"No, sir; we haven't been able to establish comms on any of our normal nets," Mullen interjected. "What we wanted to do was see if we need to revisit this port call with *Carl Vinson* and perhaps see if we should consider waving this entire thing off."

"I want those nets established ASAP; I don't care how many of our comms people we have to inconvenience."

"Yes, sir," Mullen continued, pressing Flowers as far as he dared. "But do you think we need to call off this port call?"

"Call off this port call? You gents seem to have an awfully short memory. I've been against this port call from day one. It interferes with the biggest exercise that's been conducted in this AOR in years. I pushed this up the chain once and got told to sit down and shut up. This report of terrorist activity came down the chain of command, so if they know something more than these 'suspicions,' then they can wave this off."

The discussion among his advisors continued as Flowers emphasized that the CSG One staff and *Carl Vinson* needed to be notified immediately of the danger that they might encounter in Muscat. Hardheaded as he might be, Flowers drew the line where the safety of Navy Bluejackets was concerned.

Their discussions were interrupted as the yeoman pulled the door to the conference room open. "Admiral," he began, "there's a Captain Perry on the line for you. I told him that you were in a meeting, but he insisted I tell you it was important he speak with you."

"Tell him I'll be right there," Flowers replied. Then, turning to his staff, he said, "I'm dissatisfied with the lack of progress in contacting the strike group staff. Ops O, go over to the Watch Center and make something happen. I want Admiral Robinson and his people to know about the dangers they may face." With that, Flowers got up and headed for his office.

"Hello Tom," Flowers began once he was at his desk. "My staff said you had something urgent we needed to discuss."

"Good morning, Admiral," Perry began. "I'm sorry to pull you out of a meeting but things are moving quickly here."

"I'm sure that they are, Tom." Flowers rarely displayed this degree of familiarity with officers who were junior to him, but Perry was an exception.

Not only was he his protégé, but Perry was his link with the National Security Council, and he was the only one who could provide him with details of the NSC's deliberations.

"Admiral," Perry continued, "as you know, intelligence is pouring in strongly suggesting there may be some kind of terrorist attack against American forces in Muscat. We haven't gotten a formal intelligence community report yet, but all the circumstantial stuff points to it."

"I know that, Tom, and we're working on warning the *Carl Vinson* Strike Group. We'll have them take all possible precautions."

"Admiral, these are strong signals. No one here is ready to say an attack is going to happen, but it looks extremely likely. Can't we at least call off the port call?"

"Look Tom, it's too late for that. We have a huge liberty party ashore already. We're trying every means possible to alert the strike group's leadership to take all reasonable precautions."

"I know, Admiral, I just—"

Flowers cut him off. "You just keep me posted...hear?"

CHAPTER 29

Anne O'Connor and Chrissie Moore, as well as two other VFA-113 Stingers' officers, alighted from the taxi in front of the Muscat InterContinental Hotel. As they did, a doorman dressed in traditional garb, with a heavily jeweled dagger hanging from his belt, made a deep bow. As they fished their bags out of the trunk, they were in a festive mood anticipating four days of liberty.

For O'Connor, this would be a welcome break. The flying had been great, and she was at the top of her game professionally, but she felt a bit isolated on *Carl Vinson*. There was no one she could confide in except her roommate. Sure, she was a member of the Stingers' Ready Room, but she was one of only four *women* pilots. And she couldn't just hang around with them, that would make it look like they were a scared, clucking mess. Besides, Laura Meechan was recently married and all she could talk about was her husband, and Kate von Dressel was so stuck up that *no one* wanted to talk with her. Even Moore wasn't much fun anymore, now that she was engaged to a P-8 pilot and spent hours a day e-mailing and texting him.

O'Connor was almost paranoid about having anything that even vaguely resembled a relationship with any of the male aviators in the Airwing. There were too many horror stories about women officers who had gotten tangled up in Airwing romances.

That's why she'd agreed to play tennis with Rick Holden. He had played on the tennis team at the University of Virginia, and she'd played tennis before she'd dedicated herself to varsity swimming at the Naval Academy. Since graduation, she'd found herself getting back into tennis. What they were doing was just tuning up their games—nothing else—and it wouldn't give anyone on the ship anything to talk about.

As the OIC of the SEAL detachment, Holden was an outsider too, not part of the inner Airwing group, though the HSM-73 bubbas were doing their best to adopt him. O'Connor felt she could talk to him and not have every word make it back to the Airwing. It was going to be fun—she just hoped that her game hadn't fallen apart too badly.

* * *

In a small garage in the heart of Muscat's downtown area, the men were finished packing the DHL van with 600 pounds of high explosives. The van had just been reported missing that morning, and Omani authorities had assured the company they'd find it quickly.

* * *

As Anne O'Connor, Chrissie Moore, and their friends entered the lobby of the Muscat InterContinental, they paused to take it all in. The interior of the hotel was built around a huge atrium with lush plants, a cascading waterfall and multi-level walks. In the middle of this scene stood a tall shaft with three elevators which whisked passengers to their rooms.

O'Connor and Moore were part of the Stingers' admin, but the summer rates at the InterContinental were reasonable, and Moore had talked O'Connor and Meechan into springing for a room of their own. They'd hang with the guys in the squadron admin, but wouldn't have to stay there at night amidst the piles of beer cans and snoring males—to say nothing of having to fight a dozen guys for one of two bathrooms. Blend as they might, the women felt they had to draw the line somewhere.

O'Connor and Moore finished checking in and walked to the elevator for the quick ride up to the ninth floor. They found their room and pushed the door open. Immediately below their room was the InterContinental's enormous swimming pool, half-covered to accommodate those who needed the shade, and open at the near end. Beyond that was a large, lush, grassy area. To the right was the tennis complex. This was perfect.

* * *

A small, nondescript car moved out of the garage and proceeded down the narrow alley. The van followed a respectable distance behind. It didn't need to follow too closely—that might arouse suspicion. They had driven the route before many times; there would be no surprises.

* * *

Rick Holden, Jake Roach, and some of the other HSM-73 bubbas got to the InterContinental and checked into their admin. Holden was enjoying his professional and personal association with HSM-73. Anne O'Connor had been a fun surprise, too. There was no one else on the ship who was much of a tennis player, but she was. He knew she had to be careful about the semblance of any kind of shipboard romance, but playing tennis seemed innocent enough.

That's why Holden felt a sense of dread every time he checked his e-mail from "his friends." He didn't want this to end. It occurred to him that this new life was blissfully less-complex than his old life with the CIA. There was a lot to like about going to sea as a Navy SEAL and flying as part of a Combat Search and Rescue team.

* * *

The car led the van through the streets. There were three men in the car, and one man in the van.

Chapter 30

Carl Mullen, burst into Fifth Fleet's TFCC. He hovered over the watch-standers working phones and radios. He shouted at the command duty officer, demanding to know why he couldn't get through to CSG One aboard *Carl Vinson*. Admiral Flowers had ordered him to have the word of a probable attack against Navy personnel in Muscat passed to Admiral Robinson's staff, but he was unable to make that happen.

"Commander, it is beyond belief that you can't raise *Carl Vinson* on any net."

"Captain, I'm trying," the command duty officer replied. "I can't raise them on Task Group Command. I call, but no one answers."

"Are you trying UHF satellite or HF?"

"I'm using HF. We don't have good UHF coverage here."

"What else are you trying?" Mullen asked.

"The STEL line isn't synching up, I think they have bad crypto. I'm trying to use the KY-68, and it sounds like I'm going out, but they're not answering it at their end."

"What do you mean not answering? I've been aboard *Carl Vinson*. Their KY-68 is in TFCC and its manned twenty-four hours a day in port and at sea. I can't believe this."

The command duty officer was a ninety-day reservist sent to Fifth Fleet Headquarters in Bahrain to serve his active duty time. These reservists weren't there long enough to be given real jobs, so they were made permanent watch-standers. It was a source of consternation for the Fifth Fleet staff members, and they constantly bitched about the lack of professionalism of the people manning their TFCC.

"Captain," the command duty officer offered, "without actually being on *Carl Vinson*, I can't tell you what their problem is."

There was nothing else Mullen could do here. He directed the watch team to call the staff information operations officer—the N6—and tell her to untangle this mess.

With the departure of the operations officer, the command duty officer was able to focus on trying to contact *Carl Vinson.* Ninety-day reservist or not, he was determined to do his best to warn his fellow Navy men and women. He assigned one petty officer to keep working the KY-68, while he had another draft a flash precedence message to CSG One spelling out the danger. Even with all the voice nets available he knew a flash message, which was pushed through the system faster than others, would reach the staff immediately. That done, he walked through the door and entered the Staff Intelligence Center. He encountered another ninety-day reservist standing the intel watch.

"I've got to get word to *Carl Vinson,* and I can't raise them on any of our nets. I'm drafting a flash message now, but do you have any way I can get to them faster?"

"Yeah, I think so," the man replied. "We've got classified e-mail via JWICS," he continued, referring to the network that carried top secret messages. "Sit down at our terminal and bang something out."

"Great, lead on." This would be shorter version of the flash message he had just dictated. He sat down at the terminal and typed:

FLASH
FROM: COMFIVEFLT
TO: CSG1
BT
SUBJ: TERRORIST THREAT
PASSED FROM FIFTH FLEET COMMANDER TO ADMIRAL ROBINSON. DELIVER IMMEDIATELY.
THERE IS AN EXTREMELY HIGH PROBABILITY THAT TERRORISTS IN-COUNTRY OMAN WILL ATTEMPT AN ATTACK ON U.S. NAVY PER-SONNEL AT A PUBLIC PLACE IN MUSCAT. HOTELS HOUSING LARGE NUMBERS OF CARL VINSON SAILORS ARE CONSIDERED ESPECIALLY VULNERABLE. RECOMMEND LARGE GATHERINGS OF CARL VINSON PERSONNEL BE AVOIDED AND EXTRA SECURITY PRECAUTIONS BE TAKEN.
DECL/X4//

Satisfied he had done his best, he returned to TFCC to see if any progress had been made on getting through on any radio nets.

* * *

Aboard *Carl Vinson*, the CSG One spaces were full of staff officers and enlisted sailors moving about, most departing on liberty, but a few preparing to stand their watches. The transition between the underway watch team and the in-port watch team, which had just one watchstander in TFCC, was not as seamless as it should have been.

Operations Specialist Second Class Doug Lewis was assigned the TFCC radio watch, but he was also the security petty officer charged with ensuring all safes were locked during in-port periods. He'd been chewed out by the ops officer during last in-port period for not checking an obscure safe in the back of the ops office and once was enough. He figured he could leave TFCC for a few minutes.

* * *

In Fifth Fleet's TFCC, the command duty officer hovered over the harried petty officer as she tried the KY-68 yet another time. "I'm sure I'm getting through, Commander, but it just rings and rings."

"Okay, just keep at it," he responded.

* * *

An identical ringing punctuated the silence in TFCC aboard *Carl Vinson*. Petty Officer Lewis was checking safes in the operations office across the passageway from the War Room. The only person in the vicinity was Lieutenant Hank Caine, one of *Carl Vinson's* intel officers, who was standing the intel watch in SUPPLOT behind the heavy steel door adjacent to both TFCC and the War Room. Caine didn't hear the insistent ringing of the KY-68 in TFCC next door.

There was a mild *beep,* and Caine looked up to see an e-mail had popped up on his JWICS circuit. *Probably some obscure intel factoid about something an ocean away,* he thought. He almost decided to ignore it, but he glanced up for just a second.

Holy shit! Caine heard himself shout.

Caine stared at the e-mail. He couldn't believe what he was reading. This couldn't be a drill, could it? An exercise?

He pressed the bitch box that connected SUPPLOT with TFCC. "TFCC, SUPPLOT!"

No answer.

"TFCC, SUPPLOT, over."

Still no answer.

Caine picked up his red phone and dialed TFCC.

It just rang.

He dialed the War Room.

No answer.

Caine couldn't stand it anymore. He had to find someone, anyone, to tell.

Caine flung open the SUPPLOT door, and walked the few steps into TFCC. There was no one there. The phone was ringing, but he dared not pick it up—probably some meaningless call—all it would do was slow him down if he had to write down a message.

He turned around and walked into the War Room. It was empty. He looked to his left at the slate-gray metallic door with one large star that led into Admiral Robinson's cabin. Should he call first? Should he knock?

Caine mustered up all the courage he could and turned the door handle. Locked. He turned it again, jiggling it. Nothing.

Suddenly, the door opened. Heater Robinson stood there in his white uniform, his large frame filling the doorway.

"Yes, Lieutenant?"

"Admiral...I...well...we...." Caine stammered. Somehow he hadn't expected to see the admiral himself. An aide, perhaps, but not the admiral. Caine tried to form the words, but his mouth just moved.

"Well, what is it, Lieutenant?"

Caine watched the admiral's eyes grow wide and as he poured out the details of the message.

CHAPTER 31

Andrew Cox had succeeded beyond his wildest expectations. A combination of having one of the finest facilities in Muscat, and his willingness to work with the Navy to provide them with special deals, had ensured a sellout for the entire in-port period. Officers, chief petty officers and sailors had filled his hotel.

*　*　*

The DHL van moved at just under the speed limit. The driver was determined to do nothing to attract attention. With dozens of delivery vans in Muscat, it was easy to blend in. They only had a few miles to travel from their garage to the InterContinental. Their advance car continued to lead the van to ensure they didn't encounter any surprises.

*　*　*

Anne O'Connor and Rick Holden were halfway through their second set of tennis. The heat caused them take more time on the court changeovers every two games. This gave them the opportunity to talk about life on an aircraft carrier, and O'Connor took advantage of the age-old right of a sailor to complain by letting Holden know how she felt like she was under a microscope as one of only four female aviators in her squadron.

*　*　*

Their advance car circled through the InterContinental's driveway. Only two cabs stood by for fares, and they were well off to the right of the main entry. It was late enough in the afternoon that few people were being dropped off. The van would have a clear path.

* * *

Scores of *Carl Vinson* crewmembers were lounging at the pool or at various places around the hotel's expansive lawn. Others were using the fitness club, unwilling to be away from a gym for even a day. Many others were simply enjoying the plush chairs and sofas in the lobby, where the wait staff was having difficulty keeping up with the demand for drinks. Here, in air conditioned comfort, they could do what it was impossible to do aboard *Carl Vinson*—completely relax.

* * *

The driver of the DHL van now had the InterContinental in sight. He continued to glance in his rearview mirror. The van was shorter—by inches—than the entry doors of the hotel. He couldn't aim at them directly—the island displaced from the front entrance prevented that. He would have to come up the circular driveway, and then as he pulled up to the front entrance, he'd have to turn sharply right, crash through the first set of doors, pass through the approximately twenty-foot entry, crash through the second set of doors, then hit the brakes and detonate his explosives.

His comrades had determined that major structural members for the front facade of the hotel flanked the entry doors, and he hoped that the explosion would both collapse at least that portion of the building and also kill everyone in and around the lobby area. He pictured his mutilated body propelled by deadly explosives flying by infidels as they breathed their last breath on earth. The thought pleased him.

* * *

O'Connor and Holden never did finish their second set. Their casual banter had extended so long the next group of players had claimed the court. They headed to the tennis clubhouse and grabbed some Gatorade, and were taking their first sips when the shock wave knocked them both to the ground. They got up and headed for the pile of rubble.

CHAPTER 32

Word of the explosion at the Muscat InterContinental flashed worldwide instantly. Nowhere did this word travel faster than through U.S. military channels. Whatever faults the U.S. military might have, getting the word passed expeditiously regarding major events was not one of them.

Bill Durham had been lounging at the InterContinental pool when he heard and felt the blast and saw portions of the hotel crumbling. He resisted the urge to charge into the morass in response to the shrieks and screams of the injured. He called the CSG One duty officer. Initially, the duty officer didn't believe what he was hearing, but Durham persisted, finally telling the junior officer to go into the "listen mode."

Armed with Durham's report, the duty officer broke out his notebook and turned to the OPREP III—NAVY PINNACLE/FRONT BURNER section, which described the report that needed to be sent in the event of an attack on United States' forces. His first phone call was to Fifth Fleet Headquarters in Bahrain. The second was to CENTCOM. The next was to the National Military Command Center in the Pentagon.

At commands like Fifth Fleet and CENTCOM, each headquarters went through their procedures. At Fifth Fleet, Admiral Flowers's staff concentrated on assessing exactly what had happened and on alerting other Navy forces in the area, as well as notifying U.S. embassies and consulates in the region.

The National Military Command Center received the word of the disaster and passed this information to the National Security Council, as well as to the White House Situation Room. Michael Curtis was informed immediately and requested an urgent meeting with the president.

* * *

Rick Holden and Anne O'Connor had been among the first to reach the pile of rubble that was once the InterContinental. The worked with their shipmates to pull broken bodies from the pile and begin administering first aid. For some, all they could do was hold their hands and comfort them as they took their last breaths.

* * *

As Curtis entered the Oval Office the president asked, "Michael, you said a hotel in Muscat has been attacked—the InterContinental?"

"Yes, Mr. President. We had a large number of *Carl Vinson* personnel staying there. No numbers yet on dead or wounded but the initial reports suggest that the losses will be high."

"Do we know who did this?"

"We may, Mr. President. The intelligence agencies were picking up information that terrorists who had recently departed camps in Iran were somewhere in Muscat. They had to be the people who attacked us."

"We don't want to jump to conclusions, but surely we'd have to think of Iran as the primary suspect."

"Yes, we do, and pending nailing this down with certainty, I recommend we prepare to take action."

"Michael, we don't want to jump the gun. We need to consult with our allies. We need to get more intelligence."

Curtis almost interrupted the president, but he waited for him to finish. This was a time for action, not diplomatic considerations. More intelligence? The intelligence agencies had botched this by not providing timely information about the possibility of an attack. The hostile act Curtis had secretly hoped for had happened. It seemed almost certain they'd be able to link it to Iran. He had to keep the president focused.

"Mr. President, regardless of who did this, we can't just sit on our hands. We have to get forces moving, increase readiness postures, and then follow through with OPLANS. We can't just wait."

Curtis stopped his impassioned monologue long enough to momentarily look up from his tablet. The president sat with his head buried in his hands.

CHAPTER 33

Only the most extraordinary degree of military discipline kept *Carl Vinson* from being plunged into chaos. The ship's crew suspected several hundred of their shipmates were dead or wounded in the carnage at the InterContinental. They knew they had to try to save those they could, as well as begin the notification process for the families whose loved ones had perished in the blast. They also knew this was a terrorist act aimed at the United States, and that they would have to carry out attacks against whoever had perpetrated this crime—Iran, most assumed.

The tragedy galvanized the crew in a way only such events can. As word of the bombing spread through Muscat, *Carl Vinson's* sailors returned to the fleet landing to go back to their ship. As crewmembers streamed into the landing, *Carl Vinson's* administrative officer, Lieutenant Commander Pete Otterey, gave instructions using a bullhorn.

"Listen up folks. I know that you all had buddies in that hotel. Right now, I can't tell you anything for certain regarding who's hurt and who's not. What I need now are medical people, and I need all of them I can get. I want corpsmen, and I want dental techs."

"I'm the Medical Department chief," Senior Chief Petty Officer Don Long said, raising his hand. "I'll take charge of these people. What about medical supplies?"

"I've got Dr. Berg on his way now with equipment and supplies. There will be more to follow."

"Commander, we need to get HSC-6 and HSM-73 primed to start flying the wounded back out to the carrier," Long said.

"Already got that turned on, Senior Chief. Dr. Berg wants us to triage everyone on site and then bring those we can to *Carl Vinson*. The more seriously wounded we're taking to Muscat hospitals."

"Aye, sir. We've got about a half-dozen corpsmen and dental techs gathered up. If it's okay, we'll wait for Dr. Berg's boat to land and then head to the hotel."

"Do it," Otterey replied.

* * *

Back aboard *Carl Vinson*, Admiral Robinson and a portion of his staff were assessing the situation. All of his senior staff and senior commanders had survived the blast. It was a quirk of fate they'd been spared, because most of them had rooms at the InterContinental and could have just as easily been there during the blast.

Wizard Foster had been at Omani Aviation Administration, clarifying the rules they'd have to follow while flying in the Omani Flight Information Region. Craig Vandegrift and Jim Hughes had gone directly to the souk, determined to do their shopping before the hordes of *Carl Vinson's* sailors came ashore. His chief of staff and his operations officer were paying a call on Omani naval headquarters. It was small compensation in the sea of death and destruction, but Robinson knew he needed them to help him turn *Carl Vinson* into a fighting machine again.

* * *

At the InterContinental, the devastation was complete. The blast had collapsed the entire front facade of the hotel, leaving a pile of rubble over two stories high—broken concrete, shattered glass, twisted steel, shreds of furniture, bodies, and even more gruesome, parts of bodies, amid the rubble. Beyond the front facade, the two adjacent sides of the hotel had suffered less damage, but much of the hotel looked as though it could also collapse at any moment. In the lobby, the human carnage was worse. All of those sitting there had been in the direct path of the blast and had probably died instantly.

The first order of business for rescuers on scene was to try to find survivors in the pile of rubble. It was inefficient business, as there was no one in charge. The Omani authorities made a stab at taking control, and the Navy people who had survived the blast were hell bent on rescuing their comrades. They all worked to reduce the size of the pile of rubble and look for bodies—hopefully alive—under it.

The rescuers could do nothing for the dead, save identify them. The wounded pulled from the rubble were brought to the lawn between the hotel and the Gulf where a triage station had been set up. *Carl Vinson's* senior medical officer had been lounging at the pool and was unhurt. He had taken charge of the medical treatment. Holden and O'Connor worked alongside him to save as many of their shipmates as they could.

* * *

The principals were gathered in Admiral Robinson's cabin—his chief of staff, *Carl Vinson's* CO, CAG, the DESRON commander, intelligence officer, and a few others. They had all headed for the boat landing as soon as they heard about the attack on the InterContinental and caught the first available boat back to *Carl Vinson*.

The admiral wasted no time with pleasantries. "Folks, we took devastating losses in the explosion at the InterContinental. It'll probably be hours before we're able to fully understand the number of our shipmates who were killed or wounded. Intel, what do we know so far?"

"Admiral," Rocky Jacobson began, "as we piece together the reports after the fact, it looks like the chain of command tried to let us know the InterContinental was being targeted, but we couldn't get the word to the hotel fast enough."

"I know that," Robinson replied. "As soon as Lieutenant Caine showed me that report, I knew we were in trouble. What I want to know now is who did this. What do we know?"

"From what we've been able to piece together, it appears someone drove a van packed with explosives right through the front entrance of the hotel. The entire front facade collapsed. You've seen the photos, Admiral; it looks worse than Khobar Towers."

Robinson just stared straight ahead. Finally, his chief of staff said, "Admiral, ops o is going to stay on scene directing the rescue effort. Our medical folks are treating the wounded, and we've got people sifting through the rubble looking for survivors. That's the primary focus right now."

"What are the Muscat authorities doing?" Robinson asked.

"They're on scene and trying to help, Admiral, mainly with transporting the seriously wounded to local hospitals."

"I just placed a call to the ambassador. She should be arriving on-scene soon. She'll help coordinate with the local authorities. Now tell me what else we know about who may have done this."

"We don't know a great deal. Eyewitnesses said that the van that crashed into the hotel was a DHL courier van. As you might imagine, the van is nothing but little pieces. We've checked with the local authorities who told us that a DHL van was reported stolen."

"This is a helluva way to find it," Robinson replied.

"Yes, sir," Jacobson continued. "While we're not jumping to conclusions, this attack is likely connected to the Hezbollah agents who were reported to have entered Muscat a short while ago. It seems to track based on what little we know."

"Chief of Staff," Robinson said, turning toward Sampson, "are we about ready to get underway?"

"We are. As soon as the ship has a few more boatloads of sailors aboard, we should be ready."

"Good. Are we leaving enough people on the beach to help our wounded and tend to those we don't bring back aboard?"

"Yes, sir, and Fifth Fleet has a contingent of their staff moving toward Muscat to help the people we're leaving on scene. CENTCOM is sending docs and medics. The Omanis have opened up all their hospitals."

His staff could see Robinson was torn between mustering the full resources of his strike group to help his wounded sailors and getting *Carl Vinson* to sea for what were likely to be retaliatory strikes against Iran. His staff convinced him they were doing all they could for those left behind. It was time to get underway.

"All right," Robinson began. "Captain, get as many of your folks back aboard as you can, but I want us underway in the next four hours. CAG, let's get aircraft pre-flighted and pilots briefed. We need to be ready to put airplanes in the air ASAP."

Robinson rose as the others got up and began to file out of his cabin. He felt he had the weight of the world on his shoulders.

CHAPTER 34

As *Carl Vinson* passed through the narrowest section of the Strait of Hormuz, the perpetual haze made it impossible to see the shore on either side of the ship. The carrier plowed on at a steady eighteen knots, accompanied by her Aegis cruiser, USS *Shiloh,* which had sprinted south through the Strait to meet the carrier.

Craig Vandegrift sat in his bridge chair on the port side of *Carl Vinson's* bridge and surveyed the flight deck below him. Brown-shirted linemen and green-shirted mechanics swarmed over their aircraft installing spare parts that they'd picked up in Muscat. They worked feverishly to put each aircraft in prime operating condition.

As commanding officer, Vandegrift felt the loss of all of *Carl Vinson's* officers, chiefs, and sailors—whether they were ship's company, Airwing, or staff—more deeply than anyone else. He mourned for each of them. Beyond mourning was concern that his ship might not be able complete its mission. The losses among the officer corps were particularly high, and his executive officer, Commander Pete Chanick, had just arrived on the bridge to go over the toll.

"XO, tell me how bad our losses were."

"Captain, you may know some or all of this already. We had at least one hundred twenty-five people killed in that blast. The number still isn't firm, because not everyone's accounted for yet. Many more are badly hurt. Some of those will remain in the hospitals in Muscat, while others are being MEDEVACED to U.S. military hospitals in Europe. We sailed without three hundred eighty people. Counting another forty or so in sick bay and a few score others who aren't in sick bay, but who are pretty banged up, we've got over five hundred people out of action."

"That's ten percent of the crew. Can you give me your sense of the impact on our upcoming operations?"

"Biggest problem is pilots and WSOs in Airwing Seventeen. I've put it all down here," he said, powering up his tablet and showing Vandegrift a columnized sheet with a squadron-by-squadron breakdown of pilots and naval flight officers who were either killed, injured, or missing. The numbers were overwhelming.

"This is really bad. Do you have a list of ship's company people who are out of action?"

"Yes, sir," Chanick said as he showed him the ship's company losses. Vandegrift read down the list, and Chanick could see he was having trouble controlling his emotions. One hundred and twenty-three names. Sixty-seven of those were dead and many others were badly wounded, with twelve in critical condition. The ship's navigator and mini-boss, as well as six other officers, were dead. Vandegrift continued to stare at the list.

"Captain, these are tragic losses, but the assistants to the principals we lost have stepped up," Chanick said.

Vandegrift just nodded as he continued to stare at the tablet.

* * *

Six decks below, Wizard Foster had gathered each of his squadron commanding officers in his cabin—save two. The Checkerboards' skipper had been in his squadron's admin at the time of the blast and was in critical condition and not expected to live, and Cougars' skipper had been killed instantly as he sat in the InterContinental's lobby. Both of their XOs were at the meeting, stepping in—one permanently and the other, they hoped, only temporarily.

"You all know why I've called you together," CAG began. "The loss to our Airwing and to the Navy is staggering. We have dead to bury, families to console, wounded to care for, and teams to build back up."

Foster paused as heads nodded around the table.

"Right now, though, the immediate need is for us to be ready for combat. I know our leaders in Washington are wrestling with exactly what we're going to do, but there's no doubt in my mind we'll be dropping ordnance soon. Regardless of what we're called on to do, the work we've done thus far in Exercise Swift Sword has gotten us up on the step. Use this time to review our target folders and get updated intel on the location of Iranian forces. I want your most senior aviators flying strike lead."

He paused as he surveyed the sea of faces around him. They were all warriors, all about fortyish, with almost two decades of flying experience each. They were somber, but ready to lead their strike teams.

"Someone tell me about how our losses will impact each of the strike teams like the ones you led in the latter stages of Exercise Swift Sword—the portions where we conducted our biggest strikes."

Hound Dog McLain, CO of the VFA-94 Shrikes, spoke first. "We lost some experienced aviators, but everybody is ready to fly extra missions and rain steel down on the bastards who did this."

"I'm sure we all are," CAG replied. "What I want to know is if we have the experience to do what we're gonna be asked to do."

"We do," Hound Dog answered. "Exercise Swift Sword has been going on long enough that we've had the chance to roll a lot of folks through as strike leaders. The biggest challenge is gonna be just total number of pilots and NFOs we can muster."

"I suspected that. Just how bad is it?"

"It all depends on how we strike and how long we sustain it. When we did our SURGEX during workups to see how many sorties we could generate over ninety-six hours, the forcing function was aircrews. By the end of the exercise we were all pretty ragged. Now, if we're going into this with these aircrew losses, it's gonna be awfully tight. We can do it for a few days, maybe, but not for a long campaign."

"I've got it fellas. We've trained the way we're gonna fight and that training is about to pay off," Foster replied.

* * *

Across the Blue Tile passageway, Heater Robinson was waiting for Admiral Flowers to come on the line. This wasn't uncommon. The Fifth Fleet commander had a habit of having his aide get junior commanders on the phone and then have them wait.

"Admiral Flowers is on the line. I'll connect you now sir," the Fifth Fleet aide said.

"Robinson, you got your carrier back in the Gulf yet?" Flowers asked.

"Yes, Admiral, we're passing through Hormuz now."

"Good. There will be missions for you shortly. Just when do you plan on flying again?"

Robinson was having trouble maintaining his composure. This was the first time he'd spoken with Flowers since the attack on the InterContinental. He could have at least expressed some sympathy for the losses the strike group had sustained.

"We're going to continue to do maintenance today, Admiral, but we expect to fly again starting late tomorrow afternoon."

"Late tomorrow afternoon? I thought our ops officers had talked."

"I think they have, Admiral, and we've talked about it out here."

Flowers now felt his orders were being ignored. "You don't need to second-guess me. If it comes from my ops officer, it comes from me. I fail to see why you feel you have to wait so long before you fly again."

"Admiral, we've had some staggering losses. We're still assessing where we stand. We have dead to bury and decedent affairs to take care of. Every pilot in my Airwing lost a close buddy and the ship has lost key people. I have to be sure we're ready to fly before I just start shooting people back into the air. I don't think you understand just how bad things are."

Flowers wasn't going to be challenged like this. He had kept it just below the surface, and now he blurted it out.

"Well, Admiral Robinson, you wouldn't have this problem if you'd done what the hell I told you to do. I told you not to have any of your people—*any of your people*—step ashore until your force protection plan was airtight. Far as I can tell, you failed in that mission."

"We had a good force protection plan that we implemented to the letter of the law after chopping it through your staff. My people did their job to the best of their ability."

"Well, if your people did their jobs, we've found the source of the problem. You let your people down and their blood is on your hands."

Robinson stood up and pulled the phone away from his ear. He looked at the hand piece, looked at the phone cradle on his desk, and then slammed the phone down.

CHAPTER 35

It was at times like this Michael Curtis felt the enormous power of his position. The group of the president's closest advisors had just left, assured they would be notified as soon as the president made his decision. But they all knew the Patrick Browne wouldn't make this choice alone; Curtis would have a major input into the final decision.

"Michael, we've heard the arguments. I take it you're pretty firm on the fact we need to take action against Iran?"

"Mr. President, I recognize the enormity of the decision that you must make," Curtis began. "The decision to launch Desert Storm in 1991 didn't involve such momentous consequences. I think most of your advisors favor swift action to punish the Iranian regime—"

The president interrupted, asking almost rhetorically, "But we don't really have a convincing smoking gun."

"No, we don't, but the circumstantial evidence is all but overwhelming. Philip Quinn told us how strongly the court of world opinion is behind us already—and the full death count hasn't yet been made public. There really isn't any doubt this attack was conceived, planned and supported by the Islamic Republic."

"I suspect you're right," the president responded. "I know you're advocating action beyond hitting the terrorist training camps. Do you really believe that such a step is absolutely necessary?"

"Mr. President, we *must* take decisive action well beyond hitting the camps. The safety of our forces demands it. We must put their air force, and especially their navy, out of action before they can attack the *Carl Vinson* strike group or any of our other forces."

"But do we have the capability to do that?"

"We have the forces in place, and have others moving toward the Gulf. *Carl Vinson* has been rehearsing strikes over the past several weeks in Exercise Swift Sword. We need to issue an execute order, and we need to do it soon."

"When you all were discussing the types of weapons you were going to use, I got the impression you were interested in doing more than temporary damage to their forces and installations."

"That's our goal. Iran is still far and away the most powerful nation in the Gulf. Temporary damage to her military machine would leave her free to threaten us again."

"But there's been change in that country. I've read the reports; the young people there don't blindly follow everything their leaders say."

"Mr. President, the clerical regime in Iran isn't going to change. There's no organized internal unrest strong enough to threaten it. President Habibi is no more than the puppet of the head mullah. He knows the radical elements within the government control the political agenda, and that agenda is to rid the Gulf of the United States. We can fix it now, or we can deal with it year-after-year."

"You're talking about having our people take a great deal of extra risk, aren't you?"

"Not if we do it right. Admiral Monroe is convinced that while it will take longer to hit Iran in this fashion, it involves no greater threat to our forces. We'll need to use the full spectrum of our weapons—Navy and Air Force tactical aviation, as well as cruise missiles—to inflict the damage we need to cause."

"After these attacks are complete, how much will their ability to threaten us erode?"

"Terrorism is easy to run on the cheap, Mr. President. But the important thing is they lose the ability to defend themselves. Once they lose that, and once they've seen us respond to terrorist acts, we're certain they'll think twice about supporting terrorism. They'd be naked to our attacks."

"If we degrade them that much, what would it do to the balance of power in the region?

"Not as much as you might think. We're not going after their army. It doesn't threaten us. Her navy and air force can reach out and touch us. We need to destroy them."

"Our military commanders are confident they can execute this?"

"Yes they are, Mr. President."

Patrick Browne said nothing, but just stared straight ahead.

"Mr. President?"

"Yes?"

"Sir, we need your concurrence to proceed with this plan."

The president paused for a long moment.

"Michael, the case you've laid out is persuasive. It's compelling from a military standpoint and no doubt achievable. But from a political standpoint, it just won't wash. The rule of law has got to prevail if we're to have international credibility. Terrorists struck our sailors, and Iran seems to be behind it. We can take out the terrorist training camps, but I won't authorize taking down an entire nation as we lash out."

Curtis was dumbfounded. The president had seemed so convinced. He had to turn this around.

"Mr. President, if I may—"

The president wouldn't let him continue. "Michael, I have no doubt how strongly you believe in the position you've advocated. But as commander in chief, the final decision is mine and mine alone. I must live with the consequences of our actions. This isn't nation against nation. It's the United States against international terrorism. That's what has struck us, and we must strike there and there alone."

Curtis sat gaping, as if he had been hit in the solar plexus.

The president continued. "Michael, I've benefited from your brilliance for a long time. Now I need to be served by your loyalty. I want to be briefed on strikes against the terrorist training camps as soon as possible while the court of world opinion is still on our side."

"Yes, Mr. President," was all Curtis could say as he left the president's office. He had calls to make.

* * *

Seven thousand miles away, in another presidential office, President Habibi sat at his desk as his foreign minister and his military chief were ushered into his office. Habibi didn't rise, but let his secretary seat the two men.

"Minister Velayati, Habibi began. "The explosion at the InterContinental has completely dominated the international news media since it happened over thirty-six hours ago."

Velayati stared back at Habibi, sullen.

"Mr. Minister, I've yet to see anything on these news broadcasts about our cause or about American attempts to dominate the Gulf. No, what I see instead are pictures of broken bodies and of tearful parents and spouses back in America. I see news reports of American leaders making statements about prosecuting the people who did this, and they're making thinly-veiled references to us as the culprits. The Americans aren't idiots. They know we did this."

Najafi fidgeted in his chair.

"Our radar stations report that far from running away, the American aircraft carrier is coming back into the Gulf. Have we just signed the death warrant for our Republic?"

Both men knew Habibi was enraged. Though he had bought into this plan, they recognized now that the aftermath of this attack was playing out, Habibi might not be willing to take the next steps he must take.

Najafi spoke first. "Mr. President, we've been listening to the American statements—just as you have. Though they saber-rattle, they've not traced this attack to us."

"What about the carrier moving back into the Gulf?" Habibi asked.

"The movement of the American carrier is routine. They're barely through one-half of their standard three-month assignment in the Gulf. They were supposed to come back into the Gulf as a matter of course."

"Except that now they'll rain down destruction on us!"

"They may want to do that, but they must get the carrier into position to attack. We'll have ample warning, and as I told you in our last meeting, we have a plan to neutralize the carrier, and with it, the ability of the Americans to threaten us," Najafi replied.

"You've told me of your plan to have this transport plane embark on this mission. Are you certain this will succeed?"

"Mr. President, nothing in war is certain, but the fact we're using a transport plane on a commercial route makes it virtually fail-safe. Ever since USS Vincennes shot down our Airbus decades ago, the Americans have been paranoid over shooting down another airliner. They take extraordinary pains to double check before shooting at anything."

Habibi just nodded.

"If the Americans take action against us, I'm certain the plan the general has laid out will succeed," Velayati added. "But as further insurance, I've told Jahani to set the plans in motion to have our operatives prepare to take these attacks to the American homeland."

"You spoke of these 'operatives' when we last met, but you were unwilling to tell me anything at all about them," Habibi replied. "Under the circumstances, do you think you might reveal more of this now?"

"I assure you I'm not holding anything back. The reason that I don't know many details is to protect our regime. The less all of us know of the specifics of the matter, the better our regime is protected—"

"Enough!" Habibi interrupted, springing out of his chair. "Everything. I want to know everything you know right now!"

Velayati stammered, but then replied. "Mr. President, Jahani is running this on our behalf. I do know he has several operatives in major cities in the United States. New York and Washington, I'm almost certain, perhaps Chicago, and maybe a city in California. They each have been supplied a cache of a nerve agent which has been smuggled into the United States from Vancouver, Canada. These men await his instructions to release it in these cities."

"What will these attacks accomplish, Mr. Minister?"

"Mr. President, these attacks would only be done to stay America's hand. Terror attacks paralyze them. If their carrier strikes us, we'll strike them in their cities. There's enough pressure throughout America to limit their worldwide commitments. The average American sees no reason to protect corrupt regimes like the Saudis. Attack them in their homeland and kill their women and children in their cities, and they'll demand all of their forces pull out of the Gulf—forever."

CHAPTER 36

"Attention on deck," the VFA-94 SDO said as Admiral Robinson, CAG Foster, and a small number of other staff and Airwing officers entered the Shrikes' ready room.

"Seats," Robinson said. The assembled officers noticed the normally buoyant admiral seemed drained by the events of the last few days.

Robinson looked at the four ready room chairs with a border of black felt framing each of the name tags identifying the aviator who'd formerly sat in that chair. It gave him pause as he shifted his attention to Hound Dog McLain, the Shrikes' skipper, who would lead the first strike against Iran.

The strike group hadn't yet received an execute order to conduct strikes—they'd just received a general warning order—but they expected they'd be told to conduct strikes against the Islamic Republic of Iran's navy, air force, and integrated air defense system, followed by strikes against the terrorist training camps. Admiral Flowers had told Robinson to go into detailed planning and to anticipate getting authorization to execute the plan soon.

McLain was standing in front of the ready room, ready to present his strike briefing. VFA-94's XO, Benny Tallent, would lead the second strike, and his brief would follow Hound Dog's.

"Good morning, admiral, CAG, chief of staff," McLain began. "I'm going to present the brief for Strike Alpha. This will be a coordinated TACAIR and TLAM strike. Then I'll be followed by Commander Tallent, who will brief Strike Bravo—"

Robinson interrupted. "Hound Dog, before we begin, I need to know how long we can sustain these strikes with the officer losses the Airwing's suffered. I know you all can suck it up and press for a while, but we can't do this forever. Tell me how all that has happened impacts your strikes."

"Admiral, this is an eighteen-plane strike—plus twelve Tomahawks—against the Bandar Abbas naval base. Intel shows they've got their ships pretty bunched up, so we can get some pretty good Pks," he began, referring to kill probabilities, "with a reasonable number of missiles, planes, and bomb loads. Even with our losses, I can meet an ambitious flight schedule for the next few days. After that it starts getting harder."

"Go on" Robinson replied.

Foster jumped in. "Admiral, I think Hound Dog hit the nail on the head. Even with our losses, we can strike and restrike Iran for a number of days, perhaps for as long as a week—that's all the bombs we probably have anyway— as long as we're just striking. We've built these plans around having the Air Force fighters in the Qatar AEF fly the majority of our defensive-counter-air and surveillance missions. We all recognize the political sensibilities that would prevent them from doing strikes, but as long as they cover the other stuff, we should be okay."

"And if they don't?" Robinson asked.

"Admiral, if they don't, we could be stretched pretty thin. We've talked with COMNAVAIRFORCES back in San Diego, and as you know, they're making contingency plans to send us aviators from Airwing Eleven."

"I think we'd better put those plans in motion," Robinson replied.

"I'll make that happen," Foster responded.

* * *

While the strike brief was underway, other missions were being flown. Commander Nasty McCabe sat in his F/A-18F Super Hornet, Fighting Redcock 100, ready to launch on his mission. A naval flight officer and the squadron commander of VFA-22, McCabe was flying with one of his junior pilots, Lieutenant Andy Bacon. *Small world,* McCabe thought. When he was a brand-new "nugget" NFO, then-Commander Heater Robinson had been his pilot. He'd learned a lot from Heater. Today, he and Bacon were on a TARPS—tactical airborne reconnaissance pod system—mission to take pictures of Iranian military emplacements. His wingman, Fighting Redcock 102, was running up on another cat.

McCabe loved the Super Hornet. With its APG-79 Active Electronically Scanned Array and AN/ASQ-228 Advanced Targeting Forward Looking In- fraRed Systems, the Super Hornet could track and engage multiple targets simultaneously. Armed with the AIM-120 AMRAAM, the AIM-7 Sparrow and AIM-9 Sidewinder missiles, as well as a lethal 20mm M61A2 Vulcan nose-mounted Gatling-style cannon, McCabe knew they could best any other fighter in the air.

McCabe and Bacon sat on cat 2, waiting for the catapult officer—the shooter—to signal that they were next. The shooter gave them the appropriate signals, and Bacon pushed the throttles forward. The two F414-GE-400 turbofan engines roared with over 25,000 pounds of thrust. After exchanging salutes with Bacon, a petty officer knelt and pointed forward, and the shooter in the bubble punched the firing button. The shuttle ran forward along the track, moving the Super Hornet from zero to 125 knots in less than three seconds. Bacon and McCabe were thrust back into their seats by the force of the cat shot, and within seconds, their aircraft was climbing away from the ship, heading for the mission tanker at 7,000 feet. Fighting Redcock 102 climbed up right behind them.

* * *

McLain and Tallent had given their strike briefings, and now there was a long silence in the ready room as Admiral Robinson let what he heard sink in. The first two strikes would be on the naval bases of Bushehr and Bandar Abbas, and subsequent strikes would be made on these two naval facilities, all of Iran's major air bases, and the Islamic Republic's IADS. Once this four-day-long campaign was complete, the terrorist training camps could be struck and re-struck with virtual impunity.

"Those are good plans, fellas," Robinson said. "Let's send them to the Fifth Fleet ops officer with a little outline of what we have planned for the other strikes. I think we should give Admiral Flowers and his staff as much time as possible to look these over."

"Can do, Admiral," Rocky Jacobson replied.

Turning to his aide, the admiral continued, "Let's get Fifth Fleet on the line. I want to let Admiral Flowers know the strike group is ready."

* * *

McCabe vectored Bacon to his position off the coast of Iran. They were on a mission to get updated photos of the Bushehr naval base to see which Iranian ships were in their berths. Bushehr would be a primary target and knowing where the Iranian Navy was berthed was crucial to the targeting process. As Fighting Redcock 100 leveled off at 12,000 feet heading south-south-east, Fighting Redcock 102 joined on McCabe's wing. Sun King 602, the E-2D Hawkeye from VAW-116, was ten miles to the west and watched them as they cruised just outside the twelve-mile limit of Iranian territorial waters.

McCabe was startled as the AN/ALR-67(V)3 radar warning receiver went off with a sickening, high-pitched tone. He yelled at Bacon at the top of his lungs.

"BREAK LEFT, BREAK LEFT, ACTIVATING COUNTER-MEASURES!"

His pilot needed no further urging as he snapped the stick to the left, chopped the throttles, and dove for the deck in a desperate maneuver to avoid the incoming missile.

CHAPTER 37

As he sat at his desk and looked out on the garden beyond the far end of his office, Harry Flowers grew angrier and angrier. A week ago he would have been furious at Admiral Robinson for being too conservative with his strike group, but now Robinson was seeing things more his way. The strike briefings had been almost exactly what he was looking for: aggressive, comprehensive strikes that would set the Islamic Republic back at least a decade as an effective military force. Maybe the fact his people had been killed and maimed in Muscat had brought the junior admiral around. Flowers had gotten the chain of command under him fixed; now he needed to work on those above him.

He was angry because he'd exploded at General Lawrence and now regretted it, not because he had any angst about arguing with a senior officer, but because he recognized this would just make it tougher to conduct business in the future. Echoes of the conversation still rang in his ears.

"Admiral, you're to have the Carl Vinson strike group hit a total of nine terrorist training camps in Iran. The target list is still being scrubbed, but I've been authorized to provide you with a tentative list so you can begin your strike planning. We want this to be a proportionate response to the terrorist attack against the Muscat InterContinental," the CENTCOM commander said.

"But, General," Flowers replied. "The entire campaign plan we've practiced during Exercise Swift Sword revolves around first taking out the forces that can threaten our strike group and then going after the terrorist training camps once that's accomplished. I can't guarantee that our forces will be safe if they go after the camps first."

"Nothing about combat is 'safe,' Admiral," Lawrence replied. He wanted to say *except in the comfort of a nuclear submarine, where warfare is little more than a glorified video game*, but he didn't. "We have our orders. Now we're supposed to carry them out."

"With all due respect, General, I don't think we've had this plan get a full hearing. If it would be helpful to you, I can be on a plane today and brief the Joint Chiefs on what we intend to do."

Lawrence was dumbfounded. Not only was Flowers accusing him of not understanding the big picture and worse—of not effectively representing his subordinate commander to higher authority—but he was also hinting he was prepared to go over his head and present this plan directly to the Joint Chiefs of Staff. This maverick needed to be put in his place.

"Admiral, I'm going to say this one time, and one time only, so start listening...."

As Flowers reflected on that disastrous conversation, he tried to think of a way to get his superiors to see things his way. He knew he had to get Tom Perry to bend the national security adviser's ear.

"Yeoman!" the admiral shouted, "get me Captain Perry at the NSC."

"Aye, aye, Admiral," the yeoman responded.

Flowers knew that once he put Perry to work, whatever cautions Lawrence had would be inconsequential. He had to admit to himself the fact he could go over Lawrence's head pleased him.

"Hello, Tom," Flowers began once Perry was on the line, "There seems to be a bit of confusion up my chain as to what's going to happen with these strikes in the wake of the hotel bombing. I've got my strike group commander preparing to lay waste to the Islamic Republic's military. I assume you all have those plans we sent you—"

"Admiral," Perry interrupted. He knew the more Flowers told him, the more disappointed the Fifth Fleet commander was going to be. *Damn*, Perry thought, *why do I have to be the one to break the bad news?* Even though he was the admiral's protégé, Flowers might still shoot the messenger. "I need to tell you about the strikes, sir."

"And I'm eager to hear what you have to tell me."

"Admiral, the national security adviser met with the president less than six hours ago. He pressed his case hard for the types of strikes we know we must do. However, the president wasn't willing to proceed on this course. He's only willing to hit the terrorist training camps, and we're not authorized to hit them until we get a detailed execute order—"

"WHAT?" Flowers exclaimed. "What are they thinking? Are you certain of this, Tom?"

"I'm absolutely certain," Perry replied. "The national security adviser went to the wall on this one, but he was rebuffed."

There was silence as Flowers let this all sink in. This tracked with what Lawrence had told him. Now that he knew he could no longer influence the outcome of events and he needed to be "on board" and carry out the wishes of his masters.

"Admiral?" Perry asked.

"I got it loud and clear, Tom. Please convey to the national security adviser I'm here to carry out the president's orders to the letter. We'll plan to take out those camps—and those camps alone."

"Thank you, Admiral," Perry replied.

"Don't thank me, Tom. I'm just doing my job."

The next stage of doing his job was telling Robinson to reorient his plans.

CHAPTER 38

Heater Robinson sat in his chair in *Carl Vinson's* TFCC, next to his Flag TAO. The GCCS—Global Command and Control—readout on the large-screen display showed how his forces were distributed throughout the Gulf. *Carl Vinson* was in the central Gulf, in position to deliver air strikes against the Bushehr and Bandar Abbas naval bases. *Shiloh* and other ships were in their launch baskets in the Northern Gulf, ready to launch Tomahawk cruise missiles against the Bushehr naval base. Other Tomahawk-equipped units were in the Southern Gulf, ready to hit the Bandar Abbas naval base in southern Iran.

Airwing Seventeen was in a state of constant rehearsal, launching simulated strike packages that were mirror image strikes into Bushehr and Bandar Abbas. Other aircraft were conducting ACM—air combat maneuvering training—getting ready to defend against any Iranian aircraft that might try to challenge the strike group, AIC—air intercept training—practicing vectoring fighters to attack various enemy targets, as well as other missions such as the reconnaissance mission Nasty McCabe was flying near Iran.

Suddenly, an excited voice broke into the Strike Group Command circuit.

"This is Sun King 602 on guard! Report from Fighting Redcock 102. Fighting Redcock 100 has been hit. Fighting Redcock 100 has been hit! Mayday, Mayday, Mayday!"

The admiral stared at his TAO as the E-2D pilot continued his report on guard. "This is Sun King 602. Fighting Redcock 100 has gone down. He reported a missile lock on, then no transmissions. Fighting Redcock 102 saw the missile hit. One-zero-two reports no chutes, repeat, no chutes from 100."

The watch team in TFCC stood in silence as Robinson stared at his TAO. "Who's in 100?" the admiral asked.

"Pilot is Lieutenant Bacon and his wizzo is Commander McCabe, Admiral," the TAO replied, using the Navy slang for Weapons Systems Officer—WSO.

"Tell the captain to send the ship to General Quarters. This could be the prelude to something bigger."

"Yes, Admiral."

The E-2D continued transmitting on guard. "This is 602. Appears to be a missile fired out of Bushehr. It went straight for Fighting Redcock 100. Sun King 602 is scramming to the west."

The ship's 1MC blared, "General Quarters, General Quarters, all hands man your battle stations. Now launch the Alert 7 package."

TFCC soon filled with senior CSG One staff members. Sailors broke out sound-powered phone sets, and watchstanders donned their flash hoods and gloves. The chief of staff, the ops officer and others crowded in. Orders were shouted by anyone who had something to say.

"Get back to Sun King. Ask him again about chutes."

"Let's get the war council formed. Meet in the War Room in ten minutes."

"We need to get a SAR helo up toward Sun King's position."

"TAO, have you called Fifth Fleet yet?"

Robinson knew his staff was doing everything possible to make sense of the situation, but he also knew what "no chutes" meant.

"GQ time, one minute," the voice on the 1MC continued.

"I'm going to my cabin to call Admiral Flowers," Robinson said.

Robinson walked the few steps back to his cabin as he had walked them hundreds of times before, but this time he had trouble putting one foot in front of the other. How tragic to lose two good men—and especially to lose Nasty McCabe. It seemed like yesterday he had taken him up on his first hop in a fleet squadron. They'd flown together in Operation Iraqi Freedom. Why did he have to die like this?

He sat down and dialed the Fifth Fleet commander himself. After a brief word with Flower's yeoman, Robinson was put through to his boss.

"Robinson, sorry to hear about the loss of your aircraft," Flowers began. "We heard the transmission from the E-2D on guard. We'll get to the bottom of it in time, but it appears your Super Hornet strayed into Iranian airspace."

"Admiral—" Robinson began, but Flowers interrupted him.

"Look, I know you're going to defend your crew, but I don't have time to get into a pissing contest with you over whether they did or didn't violate Iranian airspace. There are more important things we need to talk about. Had you not called me, I was about to call you."

Robinson was about to snap at him, but the senior admiral continued.

"I'm going to tell you something you won't like; you won't like it a bit. Off the record, I'm as angry as you're going to be."

Robinson had no idea what the Fifth Fleet commander was talking about. With his deepening shock over the loss of his aircrew, and his increasing rage at Flowers for writing it off as a crew screw-up, all Robinson could do was listen.

"I've just been told all the preparations that you're making to strike the wide spectrum of targets in Iran must immediately cease. You'll be provided an execute order soon to conduct strikes against terrorist training camps, and only against these camps. There will be no other targets and no collateral damage. Do you have that loud and clear?"

"Admiral, you know the danger our pilots—"

"Robinson, I put my professional ass on the line to lobby for more robust strikes against Iran. Hell, I had to convince you this was what we should do when you first got here. I pushed hard for comprehensive strikes, and got it shoved back in my face by CENTCOM—"

"I know, Admiral, but—" Robinson replied.

"Don't 'but' me, Robinson, just listen!" Flowers shouted. "I believed strongly enough this was the right thing to do I went over Lawrence's head. Now if you ever tell anyone this, I'll deny it a thousand times. I went straight to the National Security Council, straight to the top. Don't you ever repeat this, but these orders came from the president himself over the protests of his national security adviser. So there's not a damn thing that you or I are going to change down here in the trenches."

"GQ time, two minutes. Now set Zebra, main deck and below."

Robinson was silent.

"It's unfortunate your crew was lost," Flowers continued, "but it doesn't impact the final equation. We aren't going to change the nature of the kind of attacks we conduct. I think your boys screwed up and got shot down because they were where they shouldn't have been."

Robinson was too shocked to even speak. All he could manage was a weak "Yes, Admiral," in response.

"All right, I know you have things to do. If we're only going to strike these camps, then we'd better be prepared to do it right. You and your people get your strike planning done and then get back to me."

"Yes, Admiral," Robinson replied as he hung up the phone.

"Admiral."

George Sampson repeated his name respectfully, but insistently. "Admiral?"

Robinson turned in his chair to face his chief of staff. He'd been staring at the bulkhead for an interminable time after finishing his call with Flowers. His staff knew that calls with the Fifth Fleet commander usually weren't pleasant ones for their boss, but after this call the admiral hadn't emerged from his cabin for over ten minutes.

"Yes, COS?"

"Admiral, we've had two of our SAR helos scour the area where 100 went down. They heard nothing from survival radios, and they see nothing in the water. We vectored USS *Benfold* over there to search with her two helos, but they found nothing. *Benfold* has launched its MANTAS autonomous unmanned surface vessel with a FLIR pod to continue searching the area. That search will go on throughout the night."

Robinson just nodded.

"Admiral, was there any news from Admiral Flowers?"

"Yes, he had news for us. He definitely had news."

Sampson was baffled by Robinson's cryptic replies.

"Admiral, is there anything that you'd like me to do?"

"No, COS, you can go."

Sampson knew enough not to pry.

As soon as his chief of staff left, Robinson buried his face in his hands and wept. When he could finally move again, he pulled open his bottom desk drawer. He dug around in the back of the drawer until he found his old aviator's log books, where every flight he had flown was recorded. He picked up volume three of his four-volume set and found the time when he'd had his command tour.

There they were, flight-after-flight, memories of his CO tour and dozens of flights with Nasty McCabe. He found his first flight with him, a training hop at NAS Lemoore. He closed his eyes and pictured their jet crossing the California coastline and climbing out over the Pacific.

Thumbing ahead several dozen pages, he found their last flight flying off USS *Nimitz* at the completion of their deployment. He recalled thinking then that Nasty would make a great CO one day and it had happened. Robinson had been the guest speaker when McCabe had taken over the Fighting Redcocks just eight months ago. Now he was gone—and they were going to do nothing about it. He buried his head in his hands again.

He'd been completely loyal to his Navy and his nation for over two-and-a-half decades, but this was too egregious, too unbelievable. It couldn't stand. Robinson was too much of a man, too much of a warrior, to turn his back on this. The people who did this would pay, and they'd pay dearly.

CHAPTER 39

Michael Curtis had been up since 0430 and it was approaching midnight when Admiral Monroe entered his office to update him on the Joint Staff's work in selecting a viable COA—course of action—to hit the Iranian terrorist training camps.

"Come in, Admiral," he began. "I know your staff has been working to refine the COAs General Lawrence provided us. Do we finally have one that will pass muster with the president?"

"I think we do, sir," Monroe replied.

"Let's run through it, and your folks can work it up through the rest of the night. We can present it to the president tomorrow."

Monroe motioned to his aide and two other assistants who then set up a laptop computer and a large-scale chart of the Arabian Gulf. He clicked to the first slide and began to walk through his briefing.

"Mr. Curtis, as you can see, the preferred option is a combined TACAIR and TLAM strike against the Iranian terrorist training camps. Since our primary targets are concentrations of people, we'll want to strike at night while the terrorists are in their barracks, and we'll want to hit the camps simultaneously or nearly so."

"That all makes sense."

"As you know, *Carl Vinson* strike group represents our only available striking force in the region. They only have fifty fighter/attack aircraft and a discrete number of Tomahawk missiles. Spreading them around this many camps leaves us pretty thin across the board."

"We've taken a hard look at the situation with respect to our Air Force assets?" Curtis asked.

"We have. You know we have the Air Force AEF in Qatar. State has started a dialogue with the Qataris, but there's little likelihood they'll let us fly out of there if it involves attacking Iran. The Islamic Republic has too much clout in the Gulf for the Qataris to want to risk antagonizing them."

"So *Carl Vinson's* got this lock, stock, and barrel? Can they execute the mission without putting themselves at undue risk?"

"Mr. Curtis," Monroe began, "there's always risk in any military operation. The COAs we've been given represent the best options given the constraints we're working with. We've discussed the option of waiting until we move more forces into the area—you've already been briefed that the *Eisenhower* Strike Group is in the Mediterranean, and could be sent through the Suez Canal and on to the Gulf—but you've expressed the president's desire to move quickly—"

Curtis was losing patience with Monroe. "Admiral, you know waiting isn't an option, so let's not waste time bringing it up again. Are you comfortable enough with the COA we've picked so that we can brief it to the president?"

The JCS chairman was torn. There was only one answer the national security adviser wanted to hear, and only one answer he—chairman of the joint chiefs for just over two years, but a Navy man for three-and-a-half decades—could give. To give any other answer would be to suggest carrier strike groups—the sine qua non of U.S. Navy striking power—were somehow not up to the task.

"Mr. Curtis, I'm comfortable we can do this mission."

"Good. So am I, Admiral. Let's get to it."

Monroe had his assistants gather their materials, and they all departed. He was deep in thought as he headed back to the Pentagon. He was gambling with the *Carl Vinson* strike group. He hoped he was right.

Curtis didn't share the admiral's angst. He was focused on his long-term goal. The JCS chairman was barely out of his office when he buzzed his secretary.

"Ask Captain Perry to step in."

"Yes, sir."

Within moments, Perry materialized. Even at this hour, the national security adviser expected his assistants to be available.

"Tom, sit down," he began as Perry entered his office. "I've just had a session with Admiral Monroe. He's prepared to support the COA we discussed early this evening. You know what this means, don't you?"

"Yes, sir. I know we got set back when the president decided not to proceed in the manner we recommended—destroying Iran's naval and air forces before striking the camps. But if we hit the camps as hard as this COA calls for, it's a virtual certainty the Islamic Republic will lash back against the *Carl Vinson* strike group. *Carl Vinson* can attrite them, and then we can press the attack to units that haven't sortied. We'll accomplish essentially the same thing this way."

"We may. But attacking ships at sea, or shooting down aircraft in the air, is a lot tougher problem than attacking them before they steam out of port or take off from their airfields."

"Yes, sir, you're right. But we've got to believe *Carl Vinson* strike group is up to the task."

"Are they?"

"With some degree of risk, yes, sir. But if that risk is too great, and the strike group gets overwhelmed by the Iranian backlash, then I'm not sure that we're prepared to deal with the consequences."

"The consequences?"

"Yes, sir, the consequences of a U.S. aircraft carrier being attacked and damaged, or even sunk."

"That'd be catastrophic, but think of what the nation's reaction would be, and think how the president's attitude would change regarding how much damage he's willing to inflict on the Islamic Republic."

"I hadn't thought of it in just those terms, sir."

"No, but I have. That's my job. No matter what happens in the next several days, *Carl Vinson* strike group will be the vehicle that brings an end to the Islamic Republic as a regional power."

Perry was dismissed as quickly as he'd been summoned. He left with mixed emotions. His loyalty to his nation, to his Navy, and to his boss was absolute. Was the national security adviser gambling with the lives of the eight thousand sailors of the *Carl Vinson* strike group?

CHAPTER 40

"You wanted to see me, Admiral?" his COS asked as Admiral Robinson motioned him into the cabin. It'd been six hours since the shoot-down of Fighting Redcock 100. The appropriate messages had been sent. The wing commander back in NAS Lemoore—VFA-22's home base—had personally notified Commander McCabe's wife, as well as Lieutenant Bacon's fiancée.

Diplomatic protests were flying regarding the shoot-down, but the Islamic Republic was claiming, and it appeared the United States was buying, the story the aircraft had strayed into Iranian airspace and was inadvertently shot down.

Maybe U.S. policy makers had gotten themselves in a bind. This was too much like the shoot-down of the Syrian Foxbat, and America didn't want to be accused of playing by a different set of rules when it found itself on the other side of an aircraft shoot-down.

Perhaps the United States didn't want to tip its hand before the strike on the terrorist training camps. If it made a lot of noise about the Super Hornet shoot-down, perhaps the Iranians would be more alert and looking for the attacks on those camps. U.S. policy makers might make all manner of excuses, but this wasn't just a singular event—this was a long and sordid history of vacillation. Robinson determined it had gone far enough.

He hadn't fully worked out in his own mind precisely how he intended to carry out his plan, but he was determined to act. He needed to set the wheels in motion and start events moving in the direction he wanted them to go or it would be too late.

"Admiral?"

"COS," he began. George Sampson had been a loyal and trusted number two man for Robinson and lying to him pained him greatly. But it was a means to an end, he told himself. "I wanted to tell you where we stand regarding strikes on Iran. Please sit down."

Sampson sat and turned on his tablet.

"I've just gotten off the phone with the Fifth Fleet commander. This is all verbal now—we will see message tasking soon—but we must act quickly, so I want you to assemble the war council."

"Yes, Admiral."

"I've spoken with Admiral Flowers and we'll be getting orders soon to conduct strikes against the Islamic Republic. We didn't discuss details, since those communications will have to be carried over top secret channels, but suffice it to say these strikes will devastate Iran."

Sampson's fingers flew over the keys of his tablet.

"I got the distinct impression that these will be massive strikes using all our assets. I can't answer the 'when' part, we'll just have to wait and see. What I want to do now is get a jump-start on the planning and have our strike teams start detailed work on target folders."

"WILCO, Admiral, we can set that in motion. It will be good to get that tasking message with more specifics on our mission."

"We can't sit around waiting for that," Robinson replied. "I was here during Iraqi Freedom. We had a long buildup then, but even at that, we were getting target folders at the last minute. We never did get it exactly right. We won't have nearly that much time now. We need to start planning immediately."

"Yes, sir, I'll get right on it," Sampson replied.

Sampson was perplexed. He'd watched his boss do battle with the Fifth Fleet commander as Flowers had tried to make the strike group take a more aggressive stance in the Gulf, only to see Robinson shot down whenever he suggested using his strike group in a more conservative manner. Now his boss was leaning forward, ordering them to begin detailed planning for strikes in advance of any formal tasking from the chain of command.

"Good, COS. I need a bit of time alone now. Let me know when you can have everyone assembled."

"Yes, sir," he replied. Sampson was as loyal as the day was long, but the admiral's actions were giving him pause.

CHAPTER 41

"Ladies and gentlemen, the president," the national security adviser announced as he preceded Patrick Browne into the Cabinet Room. The president strode to his seat at the head of the table.

"All right, what do we have, Michael?" the president asked.

"Mr. President, this will be a presentation on Operation Resilient Response, our attack on nine terrorist training camps in the Islamic Republic of Iran. The DNI will provide background on what we've done to discover the smoking gun held by the Islamic Republic. Admiral Monroe will then go through the detailed operation plan for our attack on the camps."

"Let's just get on with it," the president responded wearily. The bombing of the InterContinental was the low point of his presidency. The Khobar Towers, the embassies in Kenya and Tanzania, none of those attacks on American interests abroad had been as devastating—and this had happened on *his* watch.

"Certainly, Mr. President. Mr. Hernandez will begin the briefing."

Peter Hernandez stood and began a detailed briefing on the activities that took place in the Iranian terrorist training camps. The president marveled at how the United States could gather such comprehensive knowledge of something that happened in a foreign country.

Hernandez put up slide after slide, speaking in a dull monotone. After he finished, he asked the president if he had any questions.

"No, Peter, good brief, thank you."

"Admiral Monroe," the national security adviser said.

"Good morning, Mr. President," the JCS Chairman began. Like Hernandez before him, Monroe put up slide after slide, describing how *Carl Vinson* Strike Group would attack the terrorist training camps. His briefing didn't hold the president's attention any more than Hernandez's.

"Do you have any questions about our plan, Mr. President?"

"No, Admiral, not at all. Outstanding brief. Thank you."

Other briefings followed. Finally, they were finished. There was silence. The president sat with his chin propped on his extended fingers.

"Mr. President?" Michael Curtis said as gently as possible.

"Yes, I know. You all are waiting for a decision."

"We are, Mr. President."

"Admiral Monroe, is this the plan General Lawrence favors?"

"Yes, sir," Monroe replied.

"Good, then I think that we should approve it, don't you?"

"Yes, sir, I do."

"Fine, thank you," the president said as he stood. The others rose, and then just stared as Patrick Browne strode out of the room. They had given their briefings. The president had listened, and he had approved their plan. It was over just like that. Quick. Antiseptic.

Several minutes later, the national security adviser followed the president into the Oval Office. Instinctively, Patrick Browne knew what Curtis was going to say, and he spoke first.

"Michael, I know you were looking for a little more dialogue in there, but there wasn't much else to say. You all had the plan pretty well laid out. Within the operational constraints we're working with, time this for the maximum impact on the evening network and cable news shows."

"Mr. President, thank you for endorsing this plan. I know this isn't something you relish doing. It is the right thing, though, and we can carry it out effectively—though with some risk—"

"There's always risk, Michael," the president snapped.

"There would be less if we rolled back the Iran's military capability first!" There, he'd said it. He had been brooding since the last time he met with the president on this issue. He had hoped—no, he had done more than that—he had planted just the right words with the chairman of the joint chiefs and others. He wanted to ensure that as questions were asked about striking just the terrorist training camps, the president would consider first striking Iranian military targets. That hadn't happened. This was his last chance.

"Sit down, Michael!"

Curtis sat in the chair in front of the president's desk.

"When we last discussed this issue, I told you I'd been well-served by your brilliance, and that now I needed your loyalty. That loyalty extends into the private as well as the public realm. You didn't second-guess me publicly, and I commend you for that. Now don't do it privately. I've made my decision. Now, I'm sure that you have more important things that you need to do rather than just sit here."

With that the president rose, giving Curtis the unmistakable signal he should leave. He couldn't remember ever being kicked out of the Oval Office.

* * *

Had they been on firmer ground, Minister Velayati and General Najafi would have been angry they were being summoned to President Habibi's office so frequently. But they weren't on firm ground. They didn't have full control of the forces of the Islamic Republic. They each had their own agenda, but they couldn't carry it out if their underlings kept letting things get out of hand.

The bombing of the InterContinental had been too much, too soon. Velayati had supported Jahani in his desire to unleash his operatives to strike at American interests in the Gulf, but he had gone too far. So many Americans were killed in such a spectacular fashion. World opinion had turned strongly against the Islamic Republic.

Velayati and Najafi now faced a fuming Habibi again.

"So, General, you say you don't understand yet why your I-Hawk battery shot down the American jet."

"I don't, Mr. President. I've ordered a full investigation and have summoned all those in charge of the missile batteries to Tehran to explain why this happened."

"You may not have had that intention, General, but the result is that the Americans have lost their plane and their pilots with it. We can forget any thought that they might stay their hand against us."

"They wouldn't stay their hand with or without this shoot-down, or for that matter, with or without the bombing at the InterContinental," Velayati began. "Surely you recall we sat in this very office not that many days ago and warned you the Americans were conducting this aggressive exercise dubbed 'Swift Sword' that directly threatened us."

"We've told the international press the American aircraft strayed over our territorial waters and was heading right for our territory. It's well known the

Americans operate their jets aggressively. It's not too much to believe they would violate our territory," Najafi added.

"It matters not what the international press thinks, General. We should care what the Americans think!" Habibi shouted.

"Mr. President," Velayati continued, "again, we don't know if the *Carl Vinson* will attack us. But if it attacks once, it will have to strike many, many times to really harm our Republic. Jahani has his men in place, and they're ready to strike when ordered to do so. One attack by an American plane or a missile and American citizens will start to die. The strikes by the United States will stop immediately after that."

"And if they don't? What if the Americans just attack again with more weapons?"

"Then my aircraft will destroy the American aircraft carrier."

The dialogue continued for a long time, with each man trying to convince President Habibi the mission could be accomplished. When they left his office, they weren't certain he believed they'd succeed. But there was no doubt in their minds they would.

CHAPTER 42

One of the things United States military does best is develop and update war plans. These are "on the shelf" plans with detailed directives for either quick strikes or sustained campaigns against various countries around the globe. The planning that goes into determining what targets to hit, with what types of weapons, and in what sequence, is a Byzantine science practiced by analysts and planners working in the bowels of the Pentagon on the Joint Staff, as well as at the headquarters of the Unified Commanders responsible for specific geographic regions of the world.

For a few select countries—rogue nations that threaten American interests most directly—the war plans on the shelf are detailed and have numerous iterations. Such was the case with Iran. The long-term threat to U.S. interests presented by the clerical regime necessitated the evolution of a series of war plans. These campaigns had numerous subsets that would destroy targets over various geographic areas. One subset of the overall Mountain Crucible campaign designed to bring the entire Islamic Republic to its knees was called Mountain Divide.

Mountain Divide didn't attack regime stability—it attacked only military targets. That name was circulating through his warfare commanders, as well as through a few key players on Robinson's staff. That's what the men around the table were about to discuss.

"Gentlemen," Admiral Robinson said as they took their seats, a group of laminated maps of Iran serving as a multi-layered, multi-colored tablecloth for the admiral's conference table.

His closest advisors, his own chief of staff, ops officer and intel officer were joined by CAG, *Carl Vinson's* skipper and the DESRON commander. Mountain Divide had to be so closely held these were the only people who needed to know about the operation at this juncture. As they got closer to execution, others would be "read in" to the plan.

"Admiral, over the past several hours we've taken a look at what you've given us and we have a few questions," Wizard Foster began. As CAG he was the strike commander, responsible for offensive strike warfare. He would have to take the detailed off-the-shelf contingency plan, add whatever additional, specific tasking the NCA—National Command Authority—the president and the secretary of defense, provided and vet these targets against the objectives the strike group had practiced against during Exercise Swift Sword. Time was the enemy. There was a great deal of planning that would have to be done in a short time.

"I'm sure you do, CAG. When we get this sort of short-fused tasking, especially when it's verbal, our planning process goes into overdrive. That's why I felt it was crucial to get this moving immediately—even in the absence of all the message traffic that will flow in time."

"We all appreciate that, Admiral," CAG continued. At his level he was far less concerned about the niceties of formal tasking from above—hell, it was too hard to get at those messages. They were all classified top secret and higher and never left the intelligence officer's tiny office in CVIC. Foster was under enormous pressure to get on with planning strikes that would get the mission done.

"Admiral, from the squadron's perspective, I can move our ships around to allow the shooters to be in their launch baskets when CAG wants them there," Jim Hughes said. "CAG, are you going to have every Tomahawk platform shoot during this operation?"

"I am," Foster replied. "These are going to be massive strikes. I'm gonna need every weapon I can use—and then some."

"You got it. I'll move them when you give me the word."

"Okay," the ops officer chimed in. "I think we shouldn't move anything yet until we complete our planning and until the execute order is issued. That way we won't tip our hand, and—"

"Well, hold on now," Robinson interrupted. "I don't think our leadership is going to wait long before they order us to strike. I don't think we'd be tipping our hand if we moved our ships to the right areas."

"Of course not, Admiral," Durham replied. "The commodore will move them as you indicated. He can start doing that immediately."

"Good. Rocky, what do your intel boys say about the overall threat and whether this plan is executable or not?"

"Admiral," Jacobson began. "There are elements of what we've been tasked to do that closely resemble portions of Exercise Swift Sword. From the standpoint of having current target folders, from the perspective of aircrews being familiar with their targets, and regarding Tomahawk missions already being planned, we're ahead of the power curve."

"We are, Admiral," Foster added. "With the exception of the terrorist training camps there are very few targets, no more than a handful, not fully planned out. The camps themselves should be easy to take out—they're all soft targets—and with the exception of the camps near Tehran, none of them present any particular ingress or egress challenges. I think we can have this mission planned out and ready to go in thirty-six hours."

The dialogue between and among the key players continued, with Robinson giving no specific direction or orders. He wanted this to be their plan, one they would execute without question or hesitation.

At a very basic level, Robinson hated deluding these men, his closest advisors and his senior warriors. But he'd reconciled his decision. If his nation refused to take appropriate action for the death of his men and women, then he would. The shoot-down of Nasty McCabe's aircraft was merely the last straw.

Robinson had thought through how he'd put his plan in motion. He would allow his staff to plan out a full Mountain Divide campaign. That plan would be kept secret from the entire chain of command. Just before the order came to take out the terrorist training camps, he would instigate a provocation by the Iranians—he thought an attack on one of his ships would be sufficient—so he would be authorized to retaliate against the base that the attacking unit came from.

No further planning would be needed, as he'd let the campaign flow. After these events were complete, they'd finally recognize his plotting, but that didn't matter to him. He was a man on a mission operating with no authority but his own. There was only one more person who he needed to bring on board. He called his front office to put through the call.

"Yes, Admiral," Becky Phillips replied to the buzz of the intercom.

"Oh, Flag Sec, wasn't trying to reach you, I was looking for the flag lieutenant or flag writer. I want to place a call to Fifth Fleet."

"They aren't here, Admiral. I'm the only one in the office. I'd be happy to place it for you."

"That will be fine, thank you," Robinson replied.

"I'll buzz you when I get their front office on the line, Admiral."

* * *

"Admiral, call on the STU-III, Admiral Robinson is on the line," his aide said as he walked into Admiral Flowers's office.

"All right, send it in," he replied. He was so accustomed to calling Robinson to chew him out for one thing or another that when his subordinate called him it was surprising.

* * *

Back on *Carl Vinson*, Becky Phillips was stuck. She usually didn't get involved in placing calls for her boss. She'd worked in the Pentagon and had watched executive assistants for flag officers stay on the line to take notes for their bosses. She didn't know whether the admiral expected her to do that or not, and she didn't have the flag lieutenant or flag writer around to query. She was too embarrassed to ask the admiral whether she should. She decided it was easier to beg forgiveness than to ask permission and decided to listen to the phone call between the two admirals just in case she was expected to capture the conversation.

"Good afternoon, Admiral Robinson," Flowers said.

"Good afternoon, Admiral. I wanted to update you on our preparations for striking the terrorist training camps in Iran."

Flowers recalled how he had chewed Robinson out during their last phone conversation, but Flowers needed Robinson on board for the strikes on the terrorist training camps. He decided to soften his approach.

"I appreciate you keeping me in the loop. We haven't gotten the execute order yet, but I sense it's helpful to have more time for your planning."

"It is," Robinson began. "The extra planning time we're getting is being put to good use by our strike teams."

"That's good," Flowers replied.

Robinson paused before continuing. He was about to utter the most important sentences of his almost three-decade career. He recalled his earlier conversations with Flowers, remembered how the admiral was interested in enhancing the Navy's prestige in the Gulf, and how Flowers wanted him to use his strike group more aggressively. He remembered how the admiral wanted to lean forward, but how he was being hamstrung by the CENTCOM commander. And most importantly, he knew what Admiral Flowers *really* wanted—to strike Iran and strike hard.

"Admiral, I roger everything you told me in our last conversation about hitting the terrorist training camps—and only those camps. That's precisely what my strike planners are working on right now."

"That's good." Flowers was pleased Robinson was carrying out his instructions and even acting cheerful about it.

"Thank you, Admiral. What we're also working on are a series of pre-planned responses. We're playing out all of the 'what-ifs' that might happen after we strike the terrorist training camps. We're coming up with plans to retaliate against their ships if they strike us, as well as strikes against their naval bases if more ships appear ready to sortie."

"Well, yes, it appears that would be prudent, wouldn't it?"

"Yes, sir, it is. But I think we need this to be more than reactionary, because if that's all we do, I'm worried that we couldn't respond quickly enough. Now, if we knew, or suspected, one of their ships was about to attack us, we could plan a counterstrike against that ship."

"Yes, I suppose you could, if you were clairvoyant," Flowers responded. Robinson thought that he detected his interest being piqued.

"Yes, sir. We'd find it only prudent to go after the bases these ships came from to ensure that another unit wasn't coming out to attack us."

"Yes, I suppose you would."

"But, Admiral, you know how well coordinated our strikes have to be. If we're in the midst of hitting the terrorist training camps, and then we have to hit an Iranian ship that attacks us, and then if we have to subsequently go after a naval base—and we'd have to take out the IADS protecting that base—then those attacks would be terribly uncoordinated."

"Nothing you say is incorrect. What is the punch-line, though?"

"Admiral, if we were to get such a provocation by an Iranian ship—one that necessitated this level of response—right before the attack on the terrorist training camps, we'd be better served by a coordinated attack on the camps, the Iranian Navy, their IADS and their entire network."

"Robinson, this sounds a lot like something we've been told we wouldn't do," Flowers replied.

"It does, Admiral, but of course, it would only be for self-defense if we were attacked."

"You wouldn't initiate this without authorization, would you?"

"Not without your authorization. I do think we ought to be prepared for such an eventuality, don't you?"

Flowers now understood where Robinson was going. It was the best of all worlds. He'd be prepared to strike the Islamic Republic with everything he had, and he only needed to respond to a provocation. Fifth Fleet would just be a bystander. There would be no personal risk to him. Robinson would be the lightning rod for this action.

"What do you want me to do then?" Flowers asked.

"Well, I think I'd just want your okay to respond to a provocation against the strike group. I'd handle the rest. The Iranians are becoming aggressive at sea. When I receive an execute order for this operation, I'll be watching the Iranian Navy carefully."

"All right, but you keep me informed, is that clear?"

"Perfectly clear," Robinson responded.

After the conversation between the two admirals ended, Becky Phillips held the phone receiver up to her ear for what seemed like an eternity. What had she just heard?

CHAPTER 43

Harry Flowers wasn't an overly cautious man, but Robinson's phone call gave him pause. Initially, he was interested only in covering himself and ensuring the plan concocted by Robinson didn't implicate him. Once he was convinced that was accomplished, he had time to reflect on the overall feasibility of the plan.

Robinson's plan was straightforward, and was, though he hated to admit it, brilliant in its conception and easy in its execution. What puzzled him was the why: why was Robinson now hell-bent on wreaking havoc on the Islamic Republic, when a short while ago he'd seemed intent on keeping his precious strike group out of any action?

"Admiral, you wanted to talk to me about these fitness reports?" Bolter Dennis asked as he absently walked in through the private passageway between their offices. *The chief of staff must have been raised by wolves,* Flowers thought. He chafed at his constant interruptions. But now he thought he might turn this into an opportunity.

"Chief of Staff, we can do that a little later. I just got off the phone with Admiral Robinson. It appears all of the plans to execute strikes against the terrorist training camps are coming together nicely."

"I think they are, Admiral."

"I must admit, though, Admiral Robinson did seem a bit distracted. I know he's upset about the loss of his people at the InterContinental. He has every right to be. But there seems to be something more, something deeper."

"Admiral, I'm sure you know he's especially affected by the loss of his Super Hornet."

"Yes, but the aircraft was where it wasn't supposed to be. Tragic as that incident was, you have to understand that in the wake of the Foxbat shoot-down, we don't have a leg to stand on if one of our aircraft gets shot at or shot down because it encroaches on someone else's territory."

Typical non-aviator response, Dennis thought. The normal hazards associated with naval aviation were exacerbated by the tough mission in the Gulf where the rules of engagement were especially strict. Non-aviators expected a single pilot or crew to make perfect decisions the first time, every time, to keep from shooting down planes they weren't supposed to as they avoided getting shot down themselves, all while hurtling along in a cramped cockpit going close to the speed of sound. He needed to tell Flowers the full story.

"Admiral," Dennis began, "The squadron CO, Nasty McCabe, had been the admiral's nugget WSO when he had his squadron command. They made a combat cruise to the Gulf during Iraqi Freedom. He had been McCabe's mentor for a long time. I think that might be affecting him, especially since, after this happened, the National Command Authorities didn't do a damn thing about it and basically told him that it was McCabe's fault. We all know that's a crock!" Dennis stopped suddenly, realizing he was all but attacking Flowers.

So that's it. Now he thought he understood what was driving Robinson.

"Thanks for enlightening me, COS. I agree with you. Admiral Robinson has every reason to be upset. I don't understand everything there is to know about this shoot-down, but you need to understand the decision not to retaliate against the Iranians for this single act was not mine to make."

Dennis hurriedly replied, "Yes, sir," as he turned to leave.

Robinson's thinking now was clear, and so was Flowers's next action. He wasn't sanguine Robinson could pull this operation off as he intended to—even with his tacit approval. There was one more person who had to be brought onboard.

* * *

"Tom, are you there?" Flowers asked.

"I'm listening, Admiral. Your yeoman said it was extremely urgent. How can I help you, sir?" Perry sounded a bit perplexed—and groggy—since it was 0430 in Washington.

"Now just listen, Tom. Here is what I want you to do, and here's what I want you to tell Mr. Curtis...."

CHAPTER 44

Becky Phillips looked out on the Arabian Gulf as she pounded away on the stair stepper on the Flag Bridge. She usually listened to music on her iPhone, or brought a book or magazine to read when she worked out, but today she just pumped away and stared—and thought.

The conversation she'd overheard had been too strange to make any sense of. She'd tried to busy herself with paperwork when the flag writer returned, but she'd found it impossible to concentrate. She had to escape to think and working out always cleared her brain.

Admiral Robinson had always been so conservative. Was he now talking about disobeying the orders of the president? Was he deceiving the Fifth Fleet commander, as well as the entire chain of command? She couldn't believe any of this, but she was worried enough that she was unwilling to write it off. She decided she needed to do something, and she thought she knew just what to do.

* * *

Seven thousand feet above *Carl Vinson*, Anne O'Connor was in the tanker track again, refueling Airwing Seventeen's strike aircraft as they practiced mirror-image strikes in the Central Gulf.

The Airwing had ratcheted up the level of flying dramatically, now generating over one hundred thirty sorties a day and practicing strikes against the terrorist training camps. CAG Foster wanted to give his strikers practice flying the kind of profiles they'd fly getting to their targets. They used most of the length and width of the Gulf to simulate the substantial distance overland to reach their targets in Iran.

That was one of the reasons that O'Connor was flying this much. If the jets were going to go on a long overland mission, they needed topping-off prior to crossing the coastline. CAG was determined the Airwing would train like it was going to fight, and he wanted his pilots to go through the drill of tanking prior to flying over Iran.

O'Connor was still down, as were all on *Carl Vinson*, about the attack on the InterContinental. But she was feeling it a bit more directly. She had been one of the first on the scene and had worked alongside Rick Holden as they pulled broken bodies out of the wreckage. She had heard the cries of the wounded, and she had held the hand of men and women who knew that they were going to die.

* * *

Becky Phillips knocked on the open door of the chief of staff's tiny office adjacent to the flag staff wardroom lounge. A far cry from the admiral's cabin, which Heater Robinson found almost embarrassingly big, Sampson's area could be charitably described as a cubbyhole: it was five feet wide by about seven feet long, crammed with a desk, his chair, and a small chair for a visitor. A desktop computer, laptop, and two phones took up the majority of the space on his desk. He was hunched over his laptop answering an e-mail when Phillips knocked.

"Got a minute, Chief of Staff?" she asked. Sampson discouraged drop-in visits by the majority of the CSG One staff, but he worked so closely with Phillips and with the admiral's aide, Mike Lumme, they had open access anytime.

"Yeah, Flag Sec, what's on your mind?"

"Sir, do you mind if I close the door?" she asked.

When Sampson didn't object, she shut the door.

"Chief of Staff, I don't know where to begin. I overheard something, and I need to tell someone."

Sampson listened impassively. Phillips was a surface warfare officer like he was, the one "union" in the Navy that considered themselves the most professional—not "flaky," like some Airedales.

"Sir, you know Admiral Robinson has told us verbally we're going to strike Iran as part of Operation Mountain Divide."

"Yes, I know that," he replied. "How much are you read into?"

"Not all the details, COS, just enough to do my job as Staff TAO. But I have the basics down: strikes against the Iranian military, especially their Navy and their IADS, followed by attacks on their terrorist training camps. Do I have that about right?"

"Yes, you do," he replied, now more than a little bit puzzled.

"Sir, I was in the admin office when Admiral Robinson called to have us place a call to Admiral Flowers. The aide or the writer usually handle those, but both were gone, so I placed the call. Then…well…I got a little confused as to whether I was supposed to be an EA and take notes on the call. So I decided it would be best to listen in and then recap the conversation for the admiral."

Sampson had a quizzical look, but nodded for her to continue.

"Well, COS, I listened, and Admiral Robinson and Admiral Flowers discussed the fact that only strikes against the terrorist training camps were authorized. But then Admiral Robinson said that he was planning to find a way to strike at more targets: naval facilities, IADS sites, those sorts of thing—"

"Wait a minute," Sampson interrupted. "Do you know what you're saying? First of all, only a few people are read into the entire operation and unfortunately you aren't one of them. But, yes, the strikes against Iran involve more than just hitting terrorist training camps. Doing just that would put our pilots in terrible jeopardy. Are you sure you didn't misinterpret what you heard?"

"No, sir, I don't think so. I recall Admiral Flowers saying the plan was just to hit the terrorist training camps, and then Admiral Robinson telling him that he was going to continue to plan to hit everything at once and even find a provocation to do that."

Phillips wasn't backing down. As much respect as Sampson had for her, he couldn't make himself believe she'd heard what she thought she had heard.

"Okay, look. Let's suppose—and I mean just suppose—for a minute you actually heard what you think you heard. Do you know what that would mean? Do you have any *idea* what that would mean to our Navy? To our *country*?"

"Yes, I think I do," she stammered. Phillips didn't often lose her cool, but she was losing it now. The chief of staff wasn't listening any longer, he was lecturing.

"I don't think you do. If you *really* believe you heard what you think you heard, you're talking about sedition, and you're talking about treason. Is there anything Admiral Robinson has done or said in the time you've known him to make you think he would do something like this?"

"No, sir, there isn't, but—"

"Of course there isn't *Lieutenant Commander Phillips*," he interrupted. "Look, I think I do a good job of sheltering those of you further down the chain of command, but you *might* have noticed that Admiral Robinson is under enormous pressure courtesy of his boss, Admiral Flowers. Now this is never to leave this room, but our admiral has taken major, major hits from the Fifth Fleet commander and he's never complained. Does that sound like the kind of relationship that would lead to two people *conspiring*?"

"Chief of Staff, I don't know what to say."

"Look," Sampson continued. "We're all under a lot of pressure. You were listening in on a conversation that was probably a continuation of several conversations you didn't hear. It's easy to get things out of context if you don't have the big picture. I can understand how you might have gotten confused about this."

"Yes, COS, I suppose I could have."

"It's nothing you need to feel badly about. It could happen to anyone. The point, though, is there can't be any loose talk or speculation on your part. Think how the admiral would feel if he thought that one of his closest advisors could possibly consider this."

"Yes, sir, I see," Phillips stammered, looking down at the carpet.

"Good, then we won't hear any more of this," Sampson said as he stood up. He reached over and opened the door, latching it back.

Sampson gave her a friendly wave as she departed, and then he sat back down to continue his work. The incident was now in his rearview mirror.

* * *

Just forty feet forward, Brian McDonald stood hunched over a large table in the center of CVIC. The bulkheads around him were covered with charts and other planning tools and the other members of his strike team were in CVIC with him.

McDonald was one of the most junior strike leads in the Airwing. There were about a half-dozen strike leads senior to him and under normal circumstances he'd have been used as a secondary strike lead. But so many Airwing pilots had been killed or wounded in the attack at the InterContinental, he'd moved up in seniority and was now leading the planning for a strike against the naval base at Bushehr.

While he was honored to be doing this, McDonald chafed over the amount of time he was spending planning and how little time he was flying. He had last been airborne three days ago and that only for a short 1 + 15 ASR hop. He could feel himself getting rusty. He thought how ironic it was; he'd seen Anne O'Connor in the dirty-shirts wardroom earlier in the day—she was going up for her second hop of the day, her fifth of the week. He reminded himself to give her a bad time about flying so much while he slaved away in CVIC.

* * *

Becky Phillips couldn't go work out again to clear her mind. That would seem too strange, so she decided to take a walk around *Carl Vinson*'s cavernous hangar bay instead. She dropped down the three decks from the O-3 level and began to walk, weaving her way carefully around the aircraft undergoing maintenance. The chief of staff had been no help. What could she do now?

Was he right and was she wrong? Phillips ducked under a Super Hornet that was undergoing an engine change. She'd heard what she had heard. Had the chief of staff really listened?

As Phillips walked past elevator four and looked out at the horizon at *Shiloh,* she thought back to her previous sea duty tour aboard the AEGIS cruiser USS *Chancellorsville.* Her CO, Captain Terry O'Donnell, had written a letter of recommendation when she'd applied for the Flag Secretary job on the CSG One staff. She wondered where he was now.

Back in her tiny stateroom, Phillips clicked on her laptop. Through a series of satellite data-links she was connected on the SIPRNet—the Secret Internet Protocol Router Network—and with literally hundreds of commands DOD-wide. She had one address she needed to find.

Phillips thought she remembered that O'Donnell was serving on the Joint Staff. A short time surfing the Joint Chiefs of Staff web page confirmed his billet—the J5 Strategic Plans and Policy Directorate, phone number, and e-mail address. Phillips began to put her concerns in an e-mail. She typed and then erased and then typed some more. Finally, she had something she thought made sense.

Hello Captain O'Donnell. This is Becky Phillips. It's been a while since we served in Chancellorsville together. I'm enjoying my job as Flag Secretary on CARGRU One staff, and I appreciate you helping me get it.

Captain, I have a bit of a dilemma here. I almost don't know how to begin. It all involves the terrorist attack on the InterContinental. I know we're going to strike Iran; I just don't know what the extent of these strikes will be.

I guess there's a limit to how specific I can get, but Captain, here's where I am really confused. Our admiral briefed our staff and our warfare commanders that we're going after a full range of targets in Iran. But some time later, I overheard the admiral talking with the Fifth Fleet Commander and alluding to the fact only strikes against the terrorist training camps were authorized, but that he was then going to cause some kind of provocation and use it as an excuse to attack other targets. I tried to tell my chief of staff about it, but he just blew me off. Can you tell me what the real story is?

If it's true that we're supposed to strike only the terrorist training camps, then something's really wrong out here. If we're supposed to hit all these other targets, then I've completely misunderstood what's going on, and I apologize for bothering you. I look forward to hearing back from you, sir.

Very respectfully, Becky.

P.S. Sir, please respond as soon as you can.

Satisfied with what she had composed, she took a deep breath and hit the Send button.

CHAPTER 45

The action onboard *Carl Vinson* was hectic. Wizard Foster stood next to the captain's chair on the bridge and waited for Craig Vandegrift to complete his conversation with his air boss.

"Sorry, CAG, air boss is working hard, and I don't want him to miss anything," the captain said.

"No worries. I reckon he could use some help. First time our sortie count's going to climb past one-forty this cruise. We doing okay?"

"Yeah, we can handle it. Kids on the flight deck are working awfully hard, though. You know, we can talk with the admiral again about this, but he was pretty adamant about getting ready for these strikes against Iran. I think he's gonna keep putting a ton of planes in the air every day so we're tuned up."

"I'm all for getting tuned up, but some of my pilots are getting burned out," Foster replied. "They're trying to make up for the pilots we lost by just working harder and flying more sorties. I know some of the squadrons are shading crew rest rules already—and that's just based on what some of the pilots admit. I keep seeing that thousand-yard stare when I walk through the ready rooms."

"I know what you're saying."

"I haven't been really worried until the last two days, Craig. I don't know how much longer we can keep up this pace."

* * *

The morning flag brief—and the subsequent warfare commanders' meeting—had finally ended. Both had been exceptionally long as the admiral had insisted on wringing out all of the details of the preparations for the strikes against Iran. Foster and Vandegrift stayed behind after the meeting to talk with Admiral Robinson.

"Okay fellas, what's on your minds?" Robinson asked. Both men could see the admiral was distracted, almost distant. Something had changed, but neither man could tell what it was.

"Admiral," Foster began. "We're watching the sortie count ramp-up. We think we may be pushing the outer limits of what we can sustain, and we think we may want to turn down the gain just a bit."

"You think that we're flying too much, CAG?" the admiral asked. It sounded more like an accusation than a question. "You think so, too?" he continued, looking at Vandegrift.

"I do, Admiral," Vandegrift replied. "People on the flight deck are getting a little ragged. I'm not sure how long we can sustain this before we have another accident."

Robinson paused for a long while before he spoke.

"Look, gents, the concerns you raise are legitimate. I know our people are getting tired. But it is only a matter of time—a very short time I think—before we get the order to strike Iran, and I've got to be sure we're absolutely ready. Everybody needs a final tune-up before the real thing. We may have to buy some element of risk."

"I know that, Admiral," Foster replied. "But with our losses at the InterContinental, I can barely make the flight schedule and that's with double and triple cycling a lot of folks."

"Same thing on the flight deck, Admiral. I'm seeing the same type of fatigue, maybe worse, that I saw when we lost Petty Officer Parker," Vandegrift added.

"All right, I get it. Look, we all flew during Iraqi Freedom. We all got tired. But we all made it. Now we need to be just as ready."

His officers knew that there was no use in arguing.

* * *

Anne O'Conner's jet was on short final approaching *Carl Vinson's* flight deck. The deck was stable, she was flying a good approach, and there were few calls from the LSO.

"Power."

"Right for lineup."

SLAM! The Super Hornet caught the three-wire. *Perfect,* O'Connor thought as the wire ran out and jerked her aircraft to a halt.

O'Connor was ready for the rack. The fatigue was beginning to show in the Stingers' ready room. Her hop had been a double-cycle armed surface recee hop—two-and-one-half hours. She'd launched just after 0900, and they were back on deck shortly before noon. A debrief in CVIC, finish the paperwork at maintenance control, some chow, a fast shower. She figured that she could be in the rack by 1330 and get a few hours of sleep before her late afternoon tanker hop. It would be similar routine that Chrissie Moore would go through after she landed.

O'Connor was worried about her roommate. She had looked more and more worn down over the past several days—even more so than most of the other Stingers' officers. She was living on little more than a few hours' sleep a night. Worse, she had drawn tanker duty today, and the replacement tanker went down on the cat. They decided to "yo-yo" Moore—refuel her, and send her up to tank again—while Stingers' maintenance control sorted out the aircraft situation.

O'Connor finished her paperwork in maintenance control. As she was about to leave, she asked the maintenance control chief if Moore had landed yet.

"No, ma'am," the chief replied. "Board says she's coming back with this recovery. She'll probably be last down."

"Rog, Chief, thanks," O'Connor replied.

It had been a while since O'Connor had had "tower flower" duty serving as the squadron pilot assigned to be in *Carl Vinson*'s tower to assist with any situation that came up with a squadron aircraft. Some sixth sense told her to head up the seven decks to the tower to see Moore land.

O'Connor arrived in the tower as the air boss was catching the last half-dozen aircraft in the recovery. Brian McDonald was up there already, taking his turn as tower flower for the Fighting Redcocks.

"Gear set three-six, Hornet," the air boss intoned, letting everyone in the tower know that an F/A-18C would be landing next, and repeating what the tower phone talker had heard from the phone talker in the arresting gear machinery room.

"Two-zero-five, Hornet ball, four-point-four."

"Roger, ball, Hornet, working twenty-seven knots," the LSO replied. His voice calls were being piped into the tower.

The next few aircraft all trapped successfully. As the maintenance control chief predicted, Moore was the last in the groove. She'd been flying for four-and-a-half hours. O'Connor knew she had to be exhausted.

"Four-zero-six, Rhino ball, five-point-eight."

"Roger, ball, Rhino, working twenty-seven knots," the LSO replied.

It wasn't the smoothest approach O'Connor or the others in the tower had ever seen. Moore was wobbly; she was overcorrecting as she came down the glide slope. Paddles was giving rapid instructions.

"Four-zero-six, you're lined up left."

Moore responded, but overcorrected.

"You're drifting right."

Just get it down on deck Chrissie. This doesn't have to be the greatest pass you've ever made. Just get the jet on the deck, O'Connor thought.

"Power!"

Moore responded to the power call, but not in the right way.

SLAM! Moore's aircraft hit the deck, but she bunted the nose forward as she dove for it. As the Super Hornet's nose pitched forward, the tail hook lifted away from the deck just enough to miss the arresting wires.

"Bolter, bolter!" the LSO shouted.

The Super Hornet skidded down the flight deck and lumbered back into the air.

In the tower, O'Connor shot McDonald a worried glance. The look he fired back wasn't encouraging. Even if Moore hadn't boltered, her pass had looked pretty awful.

As the tension mounted in the tower, Moore turned downwind for another try. Davison tried mightily to keep his voice calm. He reminded paddles to do the same.

"Okay 406, you just had a little hook skip there, bring it around and we'll trap you. The deck's all yours," Davison said.

Moore rolled final.

"Four-zero-six, Rhino ball, five-point-two."

"Roger, ball, Rhino, working twenty-eight knots," Paddles replied.

Moore was a solid, experienced, second-cruise pilot, but everyone understood the strain the increased flying tempo was causing throughout the Airwing. They knew how long Moore had been flying that day, as well as how shaky that last pass had been.

"Deck's steady, working twenty-eight knots," paddles continued. His voice was calm, almost a whisper. He wanted Moore to feel like he was in the cockpit with her. She drifted left in-close.

"Right for lineup," the LSO commanded, but Moore made too big a correction and was now right of course.

"Don't overcorrect; back to the left."

Moore was controlling the Super Hornet erratically; her scan was breaking down.

In the tower, O'Connor, McDonald, the air boss—as well as all the others—stood frozen in anticipation. It was a helpless feeling as they watched the Super Hornet gyrate down the glide slope.

"You're on glideslope," paddles said, although he knew he was stretching it. Moore was all over the sky.

"Don't settle."

Paddle's calls were coming more rapidly now as the Super Hornet passed inside a half mile. At 135 knots, Moore would be over the deck in less than twenty seconds.

"You're on glideslope."

"Little power…a little more power…you're settling."

Moore's reactions were sluggish. She was behind the aircraft. She was no longer flying the jet, it was flying her. The fingertip touch on the stick had degenerated to a hand wrapped tight around it. Her hand on the throttle had the same tight grip. Her eyes no longer danced, scanning her gauges and scanning the deck and the meatball.

"Power," paddles said, his voice raising several octaves.

The Super Hornet was settling, and Moore was much too slow with the power.

"POWER, POWER!" Paddles was now insistent, demanding.

"POWER, POWER, POWER!" the backup paddles shouted as the aircraft approached the ramp. In that instant both LSOs knew Moore had no chance of making a landing. They both did the only thing that they could.

"WAVE OFF, WAVE OFF, WAVE OFF!" the LSO yelled as he hit the switch turning on the flashing red lights surrounding the meatball.

It was too late. The aircraft was settling below the ramp. Even as Moore slammed the throttles to full power, she couldn't overcome the laws of physics. Her aircraft had settled too far below the glide path. No amount of power, and no movement of the controls, could keep the Super Hornet from striking the ramp.

Paddles saw it first and issued his next, fateful order.

"EJECT, EJECT!"

It all happened too fast for Moore. Only a handful of the five thousand men and women on *Carl Vinson* had ever seen a ramp strike, but they all knew, instinctively, what was about to happen. Everyone on the LSO platform dove into the net just below the platform. On the flight deck, people started running away from the ramp, trying to put as much distance between them and the aircraft about to impale itself on the ship.

SLAM! The Super Hornet hit the ramp with a sickening thud, breaking its back, and causing an instant fireball as the fuel tanks ruptured and the 5,000 pounds of jet fuel ignited. Pieces of aircraft shot a hundred feet in the air and aircraft parts hurtled down the deck like missiles.

O'Connor's eyes grew wide with horror as everyone in the tower instinctively ducked for cover, even though it was unlikely any of the flying debris would reach that high and forward—let alone penetrate primary's thick, shatterproof glass windows. Seconds after the initial impact, everyone in the tower peeked over the console to see, they hoped, a chute carrying Moore to safety. There was none.

O'Connor began to shake, almost uncontrollably. She turned and ran out of primary. McDonald stood stunned for a moment and then ran after her as she bolted down ladders and away from the scene.

CHAPTER 46

General Najafi walked up to one of the low concrete block buildings on the outskirts of what had once been an active base for the Army of the Islamic Republic. He had flown from Tehran to Qom via military transport and then had been driven the forty miles from Qom to this facility.

The base had once been a bustling training facility, but now it was officially closed—another victim of the desperate economic times facing his country. While it was no longer a training base, it was secretly used for another purpose.

He was met at the outer door by the facility's chief scientist, Doctor Bani Hashemi.

"Welcome, General," he began. "We're honored to have you visit us; I think you'll be pleased with what we have to show you."

"I'm sure I will be," Najafi replied.

"Here we have the receiving areas," Hashemi said as he shepherded the general through the building. "Here on the right is our calibration laboratory. Right this way is the main assembly area."

The reason for the general's visit had been unspecified—and short-fused—and Hashemi was doing his best to anticipate what he might want to see.

"Here we are," the chief scientist said as he ushered the general past a blast-proof door and into the main assembly area. It was half as big as a soccer field, well lit, with white-washed concrete floors. The general paused to take it all in as Hashemi continued to babble away.

"So, Dr. Hashemi, you've done well with this project. How soon will you be ready to put the weapon on one of our aircraft?"

The chief scientist was shocked by the question. They had been given a timeline and they were slightly ahead of schedule.

"General, as you see, our assembly is nearly complete. Working at this pace, we'll have it put together in a week-and-a-half to two weeks."

"At this pace?" Najafi asked.

"Yes, General. We aren't funded for even two shifts, let alone around the clock operations. We put in an efficient eight to ten-hour day," he continued. "Once we finish the assembly, we must complete the testing. There are fidelity checks to run, other more complicated tests—"

"How long will those tests take?" Najafi interrupted.

"It is almost impossible to say, General—"

Najafi interrupted again. "Dr. Hashemi, is this absolutely the best you can do?"

The chief scientist had dealt with the bureaucrats in the Ministry of Defense for years. He'd been assigned to this project two years ago and had dedicated almost every waking moment to ensuring its success. He had prevailed in spite of every obstacle. The drawings the North Koreans had given them had been flawed. They hadn't gotten all the material in time. Their technicians had too little training. Now he was close to completion. This was the Islamic Republic's first nuclear weapon. He wouldn't allow some military fool, even if he was the head of the armed forces, hurry his work.

"General, it is, and may I say, we are working extraordinarily hard just to make that schedule."

"That's good that you are working hard, Doctor," Najafi said sarcastically, "but I need you to work harder. I want this weapon ready to load on my transport plane in ninety-six hours."

There was a collective gasp in the room. Then a murmur. Then Hashemi spoke.

"General, that's impossible."

"Impossible?"

"Yes, General, quite impossible."

"Doctor Hashemi, who is your deputy?"

"My deputy, General?"

"Yes, your deputy, your second in command."

"I am," one of the white coats said as he stepped forward. "I am Dr. Mohammad Samimi; I am the chief scientist's principal assistant."

"Good," Najafi replied. "Good," he said again as he went over to shake the man's hand. He stepped back from the man and turned back toward the chief scientist.

"This is the best you can do, Doctor?" he asked.

"Absolutely, General," he replied firmly, giving Najafi a defiant stare.

Najafi said nothing as his right hand reached down and undid the clip holding down the flap of his service revolver holster. With a smooth motion he took the gun out of the holster, brought it up parallel to the floor, pointed it directly at the chief scientist, and fired.

The bullet hit Hashemi square on the forehead and the back of his head came off, sending bone, skin, and blood everywhere. Hashemi dropped like a rock, his lifeless eyes wide with shock.

"Doctor Samimi, you have ninety-six hours," Najafi said as he strode out of the room.

* * *

At the Iranian naval bases of Bushehr and Bandar Abbas, sailors strained to load stores and supplies and prepare their vessels to get underway. Though the Iranian navy had numerous ships and craft conducting naval exercises in the Gulf at least yearly, its ship's crews weren't accustomed to leaving port on short notice.

If the Americans attacked in retaliation for the bombing at the InterContinental, the Iranian military didn't want to have their ships in their ports to be sunk at their piers by American airplanes. That made sense to the senior Navy captains and commanders. What made less sense was the high-priority mission assigned to two ships' captains, Commander Mohammad Mohtaj on the Saam Class frigate *Sabalan*, putting out to sea from Bushehr and Commander Farhad Kani on another Saam Class frigate, *Alborz*, putting out from Bandar Abbas.

Mohtaj called his executive officer into his cabin.

"Abbas Sohrabi, you're my right-hand man. My orders are to not share this information with anyone, but as my second in command, I must tell you.

"Yes, sir," Sohrabi replied.

"While many of our Navy vessels are putting out to sea simply so they're not sitting ducks for an American attack, we—along with *Alborz*—are to find the American aircraft carrier *Carl Vinson*."

Sohrabi gasped. He was as brave as anyone, but this was tantamount to suicide—their frigate taking on an American carrier.

"I can see the concern in your eyes, but don't worry. Our orders are only to observe the American ship. Our leaders fear the Americans may order a preemptive attack. Our role, and that of *Alborz,* is to observe the actions of the carrier and listen to its transmissions. It's unlikely it will be able to hide the fact it's launching a huge number of aircraft to strike our country."

"But, Captain," Sohrabi replied, "we've learned that the Americans value their carriers above all else. Given the level of tension between our two countries, is it likely that they'll let us operate near them?"

"We're merely patrolling in international waters. We can come close to their ships with impunity. There's nothing that they can do."

"Yes, Captain, I understand," Sohrabi replied without enthusiasm.

* * *

Four hundred and fifty miles away from Bushehr, General Najafi was escorted into President Habibi's office.

"General," Habibi began, "I understand you've visited the site where the nuclear weapon is being built."

"I have, and I've told them I wanted the weapon completed in ninety-six hours. We'll be ready to deliver the bomb against the American aircraft carrier."

Habibi paused. The general was leaning forward—that he could abide—but he was now taking national policy into his own hands.

"When did you intend to deploy this weapon, General?"

"Why, immediately after it's completed, Mr. President. We'll eliminate the danger to our Islamic Republic in one blow."

Habibi had trouble believing what he was hearing. Najafi was getting way, way out in front.

"General, we're not sure if the Americans intend to attack us, and even if they do, we have ample ways to respond and we'd have world opinion on our side. Is this something you've carefully considered?"

Najafi was confused. He thought he had carte blanche to defend the Islamic Republic as he saw fit. Now Habibi was temporizing.

"Mr. President, my sole purpose in life is the defense of the Islamic Republic. We need to defang the Americans before they can attack us."

"General, it's *crucial* that you not move with undue haste. You told me the location of the facility where your weapon is being prepared. You're secure from attack by the Americans. They have far more inviting targets at our naval bases and our military airfields."

Najafi continued to listen.

"You've also told me how you'll have your ships shadow the *Carl Vinson*. You'll know if they intend to attack, and you can unleash your weapon then. If we attack preemptively with a nuclear weapon, we'll be the scourge of the international community. Wait for the Americans to move, and we'll see the world rally to our cause."

Najafi sat silently. He was beginning to see Habibi's point.

"Mr. President, your words carry wisdom," he said as he rose.

Habibi stood silently, wondering if he'd convinced the general.

* * *

A short distance away from where Habibi was using his powers of persuasion, Foreign Minister Velayati had no such concerns. He and Jahani were of like mind. He'd told Jahani to put his agents where they could have the greatest impact and do the most damage, and Jahani had instructed three men to deploy in New York City, in Washington, D.C., and in San Diego, California.

Each man was a trusted underling who Jahani felt would gladly give his life for the cause. Each had been provided a quantity of deadly VX nerve agent and directions on how to release it. Each was instructed to pick a crowded public place to release this gas. Once they had reported where this place was, they were each to take a small hotel room close to the location where their gas would ultimately be released and wait for Jahani to contact them on their disposable cell phones. They were to be ready day or night to carry out their tasks. Now all they had to do was wait.

CHAPTER 47

Captain Terry O'Donnell started at his computer monitor and read Becky Phillips's e-mail message for the third time. Could this really be happening on *Carl Vinson*? He hit "Print," and as soon as the single page appeared, he grabbed it and rushed out into the Pentagon corridor.

His boss, Air Force Colonel Dave Laird, was in a meeting. O'Donnell paced nervously outside his office. The wait gave him time to sort through his thoughts. What would he tell Laird? If Phillips's story was true, it was a matter of the utmost urgency. But what if it weren't true? What if she had somehow misunderstood the conversation between Robinson and Flowers? He wanted to do the right thing, but he didn't want to take the bullet for a mistake made seven thousand miles away.

The meeting broke up and O'Donnell walked into Laird's office.

"What is it, Captain? I didn't expect to see you up here today."

"I needed to see you right away. There may be a development aboard one of our aircraft carriers."

"A development aboard an aircraft carrier?" Laird asked a bit sarcastically. "You forget, we're the J-5 Directorate...we're not much into current operations. Why did this *development* hit your desk?"

"This is why," O'Donnell replied as he handed Laird the e-mail.

Laird read it quickly and then read it again slowly.

"Have you shown this to anyone else?" Laird asked.

"No, you're the first one. Do you know what she's talking about?"

"Only scuttlebutt. The guys in the Current Ops Directorate are dealing with this situation. I've heard—and it seems logical—we might strike Iran, but where and when is being run by the J-3 and CENTCOM."

"What should we do?" O'Donnell asked.

"This may be nothing, but we can't sit on it. We need to get this to the Current Ops Directorate right now. I know General Allen's executive assistant. I think his EA can get us on the calendar today."

This was happening too fast for O'Donnell. He could be minutes away from seeing the director of operations for the Joint Chiefs of Staff. *And some complain about bureaucratic inertia.*

"Don't you think we ought to talk about what we're gonna say?" O'Donnell asked. "We may want to run it through lower levels first—"

"We're the lower levels," Laird interrupted. "I don't know how you Navy guys work, but if we had two Air Force generals conspiring to attack somebody we didn't authorize them to attack, we'd sure as hell not stand on ceremony." Laird dialed the phone.

Fifteen minutes later, both men had passed through a maze of offices and were ushered into the office of Lieutenant General Robert Allen, director of operations for the Joint Staff. He was the primary link to the Unified Commanders worldwide. In time of crisis, he became the focal point for much of the nation's military efforts.

"Morning, fellas. My EA said you needed to see me right away."

"General," Laird began, "we wouldn't have bothered you unless we felt this was crucial, real-time information you needed to have."

"I'm sure you wouldn't have, Colonel. Well, let's have it."

Laird began to pour out his story—everything he and O'Donnell had discussed. Finally, he produced Phillips's e-mail.

Allen read it slowly, and then looked up at O'Donnell.

"You know this person, Captain?"

"Yes, sir, I do."

"Is she some kind of wild-eyed, impressionable flake?"

"No, sir, she's a solid officer. She served in my command. If she's gone outside the chain of command like this, I think there's a problem."

"You all stand by. We're going to see the chairman."

Within an hour they'd seen the chairman. Admiral Monroe had been incredulous. A short while ago he'd defended Robinson's shoot-down of the Iraqi Foxbat. Now this had happened. He decided that the best course was to have Allen call Robinson and get to the bottom of what was going on.

Back in his office, Allen had shooed Laird and O'Donnell away and told them to stand by. After getting Robinson's direct-dial number from one of his assistants, he left instructions not to be disturbed.

It was 1100 Washington time, 1800 in the Arabian Gulf. Heater Robinson was sitting at the head of the table in the Flag Mess beginning the evening meal. The Stu III rang three times at Robinson's desk before tripping over to his admin office. His flag writer answered the phone. After a polite skirmish with General Allen's secretary, she walked into the Flag Mess to get the admiral.

"Admiral," she began, "General Allen of the Joint Staff is on the phone for you."

"Bob Allen? We were at National War College together. What's he want? 'Scuse me," he said as he got up. "I'll take it in my cabin."

Robinson strode the few steps to his cabin. The operations director on the Joint Staff was calling him. Maybe the operation to strike Iran was a "go." He sat down and picked up the secure phone.

"Robinson?" Allen said.

"Good to hear from you, General. It's been a long time since the National War College."

"Admiral Robinson, I'm calling to ask you about your preparations the upcoming operation against Iran."

This wasn't a call to give him an execute order, Robinson thought. *What was the general driving at, and why call him directly?*

"Yes, General, we're working it every day. We're doing mirror-image strikes and preparing for an execute order. I thought you might be calling about that."

"No, that'll come in due course. What I'm calling about is any potential misunderstandings about what those strikes will entail. You've gotten the warning order, and you're clear these strikes will be against the terrorist training camps, and only against them, correct?"

So that was it, Robinson thought. His mind raced. How did Allen know this? Had Flowers ratted him out? He and Flowers were the only ones who had discussed this.

"Correct, General. Only against the terrorist training camps."

"There's a concern here that there might have been conversations suggesting hitting other targets. We want to ensure that isn't the case."

Now he knew someone had let Allen in on his conversation with Flowers. Flowers? No, he was implicated, it wasn't him. There must be a leak somewhere...somewhere internal. *Think, Mike, think.*

"General, you know that we go to great lengths with operational deception to keep the Iranians off balance. The last thing we want to do is telegraph our exact plans. We're all-but-certain they're monitoring our radio communications. My comms experts suggested I have a conversation with the Fifth Fleet commander talking about strikes that weren't going to happen. Admiral Flowers isn't an aviator, and I had to coach him through the dialogue—but we made it work. We're just trying to keep the Iranians confused about our real intentions."

Allen had listened intently. At first skeptical, he was brought around by Robinson's seemingly sound logic.

"I see, Admiral. If you'd let someone on the Joint Staff know you were doing this we could have turned off the alarm bells before they got too loud."

"That would have been a better idea; we'll do that next time. Do you have any insights into when we'll get an execute order?"

"Not yet. We'll let you know. You keep us informed, hear?"

"Good-bye, General."

Satisfied with Robinson's explanation, Allen hung up the phone. Still cha-grined he hadn't checked this out more thoroughly before raising it to Monroe's level, he called in Laird and O'Donnell and had a large piece of their butts.

Certain that he had derailed this crisis, Robinson rejoined his staff at the dinner table. Buoyed that he had extricated himself from this trap, he was in a chipper mood. But he was thinking; *Who had done this?*

"Welcome back, Admiral. Anything up, sir?" his COS asked.

"No, nothing important." Looking around the table and seeing the empty chair, he asked, "Where's Commander Phillips?"

"Oh, she excused herself right after you got up, admiral," his COS answered.

"I see," Robinson replied. "Ops O, pass that steak sauce," he continued, changing the conversation. *Was this just a coincidence?*

Forty feet away, Becky Phillips sat alone in the admin office. As soon as she'd arrived, she'd dismissed the flag writer. Then she furtively picked up the phone and listened to the entire conversation between the admiral and General Allen. Now she had no doubts.

CHAPTER 48

Becky Phillips sat alone in her stateroom shortly after reveille and read her e-mail. What stared back at her from her screen was so frustrating it was hard to believe.

> *Dear Becky. Thank you for your e-mail. I appreciate your contacting me with your concerns. I ran this up the chain right to the top. However, in the final analysis, we're convinced Admiral Robinson fully grasps JCS direction on this matter. He understands he is to attack the terrorist training camps and only those camps. Any conversations he may have had with Admiral Flowers were for operational deception purposes.*
>
> *Becky, please don't take this the wrong way, but perhaps you should take such matters up with Admiral Robinson himself before going outside the lifelines. That way, any confusion generated can be resolved at the source before it bubbles up and gets out of control.*

How could they be so naive? Phillips thought. *Operational deception* indeed! Robinson had deceived the Joint Staff lock, stock, and broomstick. Allen had bought Robinson's lies. She had heard the entire conversation and she knew the truth. She put on her uniform and headed to the admin office.

* * *

Admiral Robinson sat at his desk as Radioman First Class Mike Lopresti explained the procedures and answered the admiral's questions.

"To use this older phone I key on the lighted buttons, is that correct? When one of these lights up, it indicates there's a conversation on that line. I just need to press the button and pick up the handset. Neither caller will know that I'm on the line because my handset speaker has been disabled. Do I have this about right?"

"Precisely, Admiral," Lopresti replied. He had wondered why the admiral was having another phone system put in his cabin.

"Wish I could tell you precisely why we're doing this, but all I can tell you is we're trying to plug a security breach, and I need to get involved. Remember, you're not to discuss this with anyone."

Yes, sir, I understand," Lopresti replied.

"Very well, you're dismissed."

Robinson stared at the Plexiglas buttons Lopresti had numbered. One for the flag lieutenant's number, two for the flag writer's number, three for the flag secretary's number, four for the operations officer's number and so on down the line. He had his suspicions, and he would be watching line number three.

* * *

As flag secretary, Becky Phillips was the senior person in the admin office. When she wanted to, it was her prerogative to order the other people there to carry out duties in other parts of the ship.

This day she waited until evening chow on the mess decks when all of her yeoman would be gone. The flag lieutenant was working out. Only the flag writer remained. She asked her to give her some time alone, and the chief complied. It was almost 1700 aboard *Carl Vinson,* and 1000 in the Pentagon. She'd found his number, and dialed it. The phone rang only once.

"J-5 Directorate, Captain O'Donnell, speaking."

"Captain, this is Becky Phillips."

"Becky, I'm surprised to hear from you. This connection sounds really good. Did you get my e-mail?"

"Yes I did, Captain."

"Well, I hope it explained everything. I appreciate your trying to do a good professional job, but I think this might be a case where you may have misunderstood what was said."

"I didn't misunderstand anything."

"Becky, look, I probably shouldn't even be discussing this with you, but we have assurances there's nothing untoward happening here."

"Captain, I listened to the entire conversation between General Allen and Admiral Robinson. What Robinson told him was pure, unadulterated bull. It was a lie, and your general bought it. I know what's going on here. The strike group is planning major strikes against Iran's military infrastructure. I know because I have friends in the Airwing who are on strike teams. They're carrying around target folders and they're for much more than terrorist training camps."

"Becky, this process is very convoluted. Perhaps these people are part of the operational deception plan. Don't you see, you're challenging a strike group commander, a man who has given his life to the Navy. Why in God's name would he do something like this?"

"Why do you have to ask?" Becky shouted. This wasn't turning out the way she wanted it to. Captain O'Donnell was supposed to be on her side. Why did he doubt her?

"Becky, look, I'll take your story up the chain one more time. If we hadn't served together for as long as we did, I wouldn't do this. You understand that, don't you?"

"I understand, and I appreciate your running with this. I think we'd better hurry. I have a feeling that these strikes will be happening soon."

"We'll hurry it up at this end, Becky. You just be careful."

"Don't worry about me," she replied as she hung up the phone.

* * *

Across the passageway, less than fifty feet from where Phillips sat, Heater Robinson placed the phone back in its cradle. He hadn't missed a word.

* * *

On the flight deck, the first plane shot down the cat, with Brian McDonald in Fighting Redcock 104. It was the first of four night launches for practice strikes. Every pilot was flying every day and night—except for Anne O'Connor.

CHAPTER 49

Captain Terry O'Connell sat at his desk in his Pentagon office with his head buried in his hands. Two days ago life in the J-5 Directorate had been fairly routine. Now, after an exchange of e-mails with Becky Phillips, a lightning series of meetings with the most senior officers on the Joint Staff—including the chairman himself—and the phone call from Becky, he was adrift as to how to proceed.

It hadn't been this way during his command of an Aegis-class destroyer during Iraqi Freedom, when he had peppered Iraq with Tomahawk cruise missiles, or during his command of *Chancellorsville,* when he had been the air defense coordinator for the *Nimitz* strike group. During those tours he had made major decisions every day. He'd been responsible for the lives of his three-hundred-plus sailors.

He couldn't remember making a decision in the last eighteen months—his time on the Joint Staff. He had written countless position papers, floated up numerous ideas, "chopped" the point papers of others and had gone to hundreds of meetings where he did nothing more than listen. He was a staff officer who didn't make decisions.

But he had to make one now. He thought the issue was put to bed, but what Phillips had told him was alarming. He tried to convince himself that maybe she was overreacting—but he couldn't. He knew her too well and what she'd told him was too compelling.

He could go see Colonel Laird, and they could repeat the route up the chain of command again. But at any step along the way one officer in the chain could say enough—table the discussion and put it to bed—and he would be done. He felt that he had only one recourse.

The chairman's office was on the Pentagon's E-ring. It was far from O'Donnell's office, and he was winded when he arrived there. While the chairman's office was on the outboard side of the E-ring, his waiting room was across the corridor on the inboard side of the ring. O'Donnell stood in the corridor between them. Scylla and Charybdis.

He entered room 2E872 and walked up to the chairman's executive assistant. The man looked up, startled to see someone he hadn't expected just standing there.

"May I help you, Captain?" the EA asked. The Chairman of the Joint Chiefs of Staff had a small army of assistants who micro-managed his schedule down to the minute. Having anyone, even a three or four-star officer, drop in unexpectedly was anathema. Having a mere captain standing in front of the desk of the chairman's EA a bizarre occurrence.

"Captain O'Donnell of the J-5 Directorate. I was up here yesterday with General Allen. We had some unfinished business with the chairman, and I'd like a moment of his time if you can arrange it."

"Yes, Captain, I remember you, but I don't see you on the chairman's calendar today," the EA replied matter-of-factly.

"No, you don't. This is a follow-up, and I just need a minute with the chairman."

"Well, the chairman *is* very busy, *Captain.*"

"I wouldn't be here unless it was important. Please, just work me in. Anytime today would be great," O'Donnell said.

"Look, *Captain,*" the EA said. "I work my ass off to try to squeeze in three-stars who want to get in with the chairman a week from now—and he knows every one of them personally. What makes you think that I could work you in—even if I wanted to?"

"This is a matter of national security. I need you to work me in, and I need you to do it now."

"Captain!" the EA shouted. "Hell could freeze over before I tried to get you on the chairman's calendar, today, or any day."

"I'll wait until the chairman comes out if I have to."

"The hell you will!" the EA replied, standing for the first time, and now pointing his finger at O'Donnell.

"Watch me!" O'Donnell shouted.

"Beat it, Captain, before I call security!" the EA shouted back.

"Not gonna happen, man," O'Donnell said.

Suddenly, Admiral Monroe walked into the office.

"Gentlemen!" he said loudly. "Just what the hell is going on here?"

"Mr. Chairman, this captain is trying to force his way onto your calendar," the EA began. "I was just explaining that's quite impossible."

"Captain, I see from your badge that you work here on the Joint Staff. You must know we have procedures for requesting meetings."

"Yes, Mr. Chairman, I do—" O'Donnell began, but Monroe interrupted him.

"Wait a minute. Weren't you here yesterday with General Allen?"

"Yes, Admiral, I was."

"Yes, 'that matter.' We had closure on that, didn't we? We had a misunderstanding by one officer, and I think we cleared that up."

"It wasn't cleared up, Mr. Chairman. It's worse than we thought."

"Maybe you'd better come into my office, Captain." Turning to his EA, he said, "Carl, hold all my calls and then come in too."

Seated in a chair in the chairman's office, O'Donnell told the chairman of his latest conversation with Becky Phillips as the EA took notes. Finally, he finished. The chairman took a long, deep breath.

"This is worrying, Captain. It's most disturbing, because I just got an e-mail from Admiral Beard at COMNAVAIRFORCES. He's asking the CNO to move assets from AIRLANT to fill urgent requisitions for Airwing Seventeen. He says CAG is asking for a large number of weapons, far in excess of anything he needs to strike a few terrorist training camps. CAG is telling him he needs a ton of spares, too, and we see he's flying almost one hundred and fifty sorties a day. It doesn't look like he's ramping up just to hit some camps."

"That's because he's not, Mr. Chairman. I quizzed Lieutenant Commander Phillips when she called me. She knows what's going on aboard *Carl Vinson*. Sir, we can check out her story if we want to, but I know what she's telling me is true. I'd stake my career on it."

"If what you say is true, then there's a hell of a lot more at stake than your career."

With that, the chairman rose. "All right, Captain, thanks for coming forward. I may need you again soon, so please stay put in your office. Carl," he said, turning to his EA, "I need to see the national security adviser right now. No phone call—this has to be in person. Use whatever means you have to and make that happen."

"Will do," the EA replied as he turned and left.

O'Donnell tried not to smirk.

CHAPTER 50

Heater Robinson sat in his cabin and waited. He knew the staff's routine, and he'd planned accordingly. He'd told his chief of staff he was skipping dinner, something he occasionally did when red meat was offered in the Flag Mess.

Shortly after 1800, when most of his staff were seated for the meal, he walked up to the Flag Bridge. As he expected, it was deserted and dark. The sun had set forty-five minutes ago, and nightfall had already made the Gulf a dark shroud. He looked out on the smooth water. If he was going to cast the die, he would have to do it now.

* * *

Five decks below the Flag Bridge and far forward, Anne O'Connor sat in the dirty shirts wardroom finishing dinner. She sat with Mike Hart, Fred Barber, and Laura Meechan. They were all in a somber mood, still mourning Chrissie Moore's death. Though they all were down, O'Connor was feeling it most, having been so close to her roommate. In spite of the Stingers' intense flying, her skipper had elected to keep her grounded for one more day.

O'Connor wanted desperately to be back in the air, but she knew she wasn't one hundred percent yet. She would see the flight surgeon first thing in the morning and hopefully get her "up-chit." She finished eating a bit before her squadron-mates and got up to leave.

"Anne, hang in there with us, we'll be finished soon," Barber said. "We'll walk back to the ready room with ya."

"Thanks guys, but I gotta stop by my stateroom. I'll see you all back there in a bit. What time did the ops o say the AOM was?"

"All officers meeting is at 1900," Hart replied.

"I'll be there, thanks."

Rick Holden was finishing up his meal with a group of the HSM-73 bubbas and saw O'Connor leaving. As she moved toward the door, he got up and started to leave. As she reached the door at the after end of the wardroom, he held it open.

"I got it shipmate, good to see you."

"Oh, hi," O'Connor said absently. "Good to see you too, how've you been?" she continued as she walked aft and Holden followed.

"I've been okay. The question is; how've you been?"

"Been better, to tell you the truth."

They stopped in an alcove to let a few sailors pass by. Holden had an idea.

"You got five minutes you can spare?"

"I guess so," she replied.

"Great, let's follow these guys out onto the catwalk."

"Okay," she said as she followed along behind him.

Once outside the skin of the ship, they leaned on the catwalk rail and stared out at the sea. Finally, Holden spoke.

"Look, Anne, we hardly know each other, and if I'm being too forward just tell me to shut up and I'll bug out," he began.

"It's just that I think I understand how close you and Chrissie were. I know this is tearing you up inside. I've lost buddies in situations like this. I know Chrissie's death is probably the worst thing that's ever happened in your life—"

"It is," she replied, interrupting him. "I just have to deal with it."

"I know you do, and I don't rate telling you what you should or shouldn't do. I just wanted you to know that I'm in your corner and rooting for you, that's all."

Holden started to question himself. Was all of his babbling making any sense to her—or to him?

O'Connor knew he was right, and she knew she had to get on with it. But she also knew she couldn't keep this inside forever, she had to get it out. If not him, who?

"Rick, you don't know how much I appreciate what you're saying," she began. "Chrissie was more than a roommate; she was my soulmate. I shared everything with her. Maybe you understand in a general sense, but you couldn't have known how close we were. Our flight surgeon says I'm in denial. I just may be."

"He might be right. But we need you, Anne. Your squadron needs you back in the air. We *all* need you back. I want to help. For now, let' just get you back to your ready room."

* * *

On the Flag Bridge, Heater Robinson picked up the Bogen phone and hit 24, connecting him to Flag Admin. He knew who would answer.

"Flag Admin, Lieutenant Commander Phillips."

"Flag Sec, Admiral here. I'm up on the Flag Bridge trying to get some paperwork finished. Thought I'd look at the end-of-tour award for *Shiloh's* CO. Do you have it ready yet?"

Phillips had been word-smithing that award all afternoon. It had made it through the chief of staff and was finally ready for the admiral's signature. She wondered why he wanted it now—it was dark up there and all the admiral had was a small red reading light above his chair.

"It's ready, Admiral. I'm on the way up."

Two minutes later, Phillips was on the Flag Bridge. She looked toward the admiral's chair and saw the one white star on a blue background decorating it, but he wasn't there. No one was on the port side of the Flag Bridge. It was dark, with only the lights on the flight deck making a reflected glow.

She walked forward and looked across to the starboard side of the bridge. It was dark over there too, but she thought she saw something.

"Admiral?"

"Over here, Flag Sec," came the voice. She had just come from inside the ship, and she had no night adaptation.

She continued to the starboard side of the Flag Bridge and saw Robinson sitting in the chief of staff's chair.

"Hello, Admiral," she said.

The admiral sat in total darkness—a form more than a person.

"Hope I'm not taking you away from anything important."

"No, Admiral, you're not," she replied, handing him the package.

Robinson reached up and turned on the small red spotlight over the chair. The glow of the dim red bulb framed him in just a hint of light.

"Thanks for this," he said as he looked at the folder.

While Robinson studied the document, Phillips looked at the aerobic equipment clogging the entire starboard side of the Flag Bridge. How little time—but what big events—had passed since she came up here after hearing Robinson's conversation with Admiral Flowers.

"Well, this is a typically outstanding Phillips' product. You do terrific work, Becky, and you have a bright future in the Navy."

"Thank you, Admiral."

"There are some issues that we need to clear up, though," he said as he got out of his chair.

"Issues, Admiral?" she asked as she backed up a step.

"Yes, Becky, issues. It really goes to our staff being a team. You know, not taking our issues outside the lifelines of this ship."

"Admiral, I'm not sure what you mean," she replied, suddenly feeling her skin crawl.

"Well, I think you do. It goes to the issue of when friends on the same staff know things they should keep among their fellow friends. It goes to keeping absolutely everything to ourselves here on the staff."

She thought she finally knew what Robinson was talking about, while hoping against hope she wasn't correct.

"Admiral, I think I take great pains to keep everything we do here private. I'm not sure what you're referring to."

Robinson was under too much stress to be coy with Phillips any longer. Taking a step toward her, he laid his cards on the table.

"Commander, were you or were you not listening to my phone conversation with Admiral Flowers?" No longer the fatherly mentor, he was the accuser. "And didn't you subsequently call someone on the Joint Staff and relate your version of events to him?"

Phillips was trapped. She couldn't lie about it now. Robinson probably knew everything. How? Had he been listening to her conversation with Captain O'Donnell?

"Admiral, it's clear to me what you're doing. Don't you realize you have to stop? You can't take national policy into your own hands. I heard your conversation with Admiral Flowers by mistake—I really did. But once I knew, I couldn't *not* do anything. Please stop doing this. We can get everything back to normal and just do what we're supposed to do."

"Now, look, Becky," Robinson began, softening his tone. "I think you might have misunderstood what Admiral Flowers and I were discussing. We were just talking OPSEC. We thought that the Iranians might have been listening, and we wanted to throw them off." He moved even closer toward Phillips.

"Admiral, God, please, don't lie to me," Phillips said, backing away. "You just need to stop. You need to stop thinking about hitting these other targets and just hit the terrorist training camps. You haven't done anything wrong—yet."

Ah, the blissful ignorance of youth, Robinson thought. *What was she thinking?* If he admitted one scintilla of this, he would be off the ship within twenty-four hours—relieved in disgrace—but more importantly, no longer able to exact revenge on the Islamic Republic.

"Becky, you have to understand. This is all part of a much grander scheme that has support right up to the top of the chain of command. If you will just give me time and let events play out, you will see. It will become clear to you—"

Phillips couldn't stand being next to the man for a moment longer. "Admiral, we've talked enough; I'm leaving."

Robinson moved a step closer and grasped her arm, turning as he did to place himself between her and the passage back toward the port side of the Flag Bridge. As Becky tried to shake her arm free, he just squeezed it tighter.

"Admiral, you're hurting me. Please let go of my arm."

He just held her arm tightly and said, "Come on, Becky, think about what you're doing."

He was inches from her now. She could feel the heat of his breath. She shook her arm violently and momentarily broke free. She moved for the back of the Flag Bridge and for the freedom the door at the end of the passage would bring her. She took two steps, trying to work her way around the aerobic gear, but it impeded her progress.

Robinson had her left arm again. There was no time to think—only react.

"Becky, stop!" he shouted.

She wheeled, and with her free hand, struck him in the face with her right fist. She heard an audible *pop* and watched the admiral flinch as he released his grasp on her arm. She jumped up on the treadmill and tried to work her way toward the door—and freedom.

"Arrughh," came the cry from behind as Robinson lunged at her. His 240 pounds fell on top of her as he tried to tackle her to keep her from leaving. With a resounding crash, they both fell—half on the treadmill and half on the deck. Robinson lay still for a moment, and then pushed himself up and got ready to grab Phillips, but she didn't move.

Robinson stood there heaving, trying to catch his breath. Phillips still didn't move. He knelt down beside her and started to balance himself on one hand, but as his hand hit the ground, it was immediately covered by something wet and sticky.

Robinson turned her over and immediately recognized what the wet, sticky substance was. It was blood. Her face was covered with it, and even in the dim light of the bridge, he could see that her skull was cracked open. It had evidently hit the side of the treadmill.

Robinson panicked. What had he done? What would they think? Then, primal instincts took over. Someone knew Phillips was calling the Joint Staff. They would draw the only possible conclusion if she were discovered dead. Robinson looked up toward the door at the back of the Flag Bridge—the door that led to an outside platform.

His mind racing, adrenaline coursing through his body, he picked up the lifeless body of Becky Phillips and headed for the door. Holding her body on his hip, he opened first the joiner door, then the blast door, and got out onto the platform.

Robinson was working only on instincts. He stripped her uniform off and dropped her shirt and pants on the metal grating. Then, using all his strength, he picked her up and thrust her lifeless body over the guard rail and into the waters of the Arabian Gulf.

He grabbed her uniform and went back inside to clean up the blood on the deck. It was difficult to see, but he held his penlight flashlight between his teeth and worked mightily to get it all up. That mission complete, he returned to the platform and cast the uniform into the sea.

CHAPTER 51

They spoke in hushed tones, speculating in groups of two or three what the turn of events would bring. They knew Michael Curtis was with the president at that moment, and that he'd join them soon.

Among such high-powered people there were no real secrets. Each of them had well-developed networks of associates who kept them informed. The price of not having real-time information was just too high.

They knew that there was a crisis in the Arabian Gulf, and that it involved USS *Carl Vinson*—the same ship that was preparing to conduct strikes against terrorist training camps in Iran. They knew there'd been a number of emergency meetings within the Joint Staff, and that Admiral Monroe had briefed the national security adviser earlier that day.

Curtis entered, and everyone took their seats. He strode to the head of the table and tossed his briefing books down.

"All right," he growled. "We might as well get started. Bad news doesn't get any better with age. I had a meeting with Admiral Monroe early this morning," he continued, looking toward the JCS chairman, "and my immediate staff filled in some details throughout the day."

Although many of them thought they knew most of the story, they wanted to hear it straight from him.

"I've just spent almost an hour with the president, and he insists on immediate and decisive action. We're here to determine precisely how to do that. Admiral Monroe is closest to the issue. I'll let him bring all of you up to speed."

"Thank you, Mr. Curtis," Monroe said as he stood. He had no slides and no notes. "As you know, planning has been ongoing to attack nine terrorist training camps in Iran. It's come to our attention the strike group commander has, for reasons known only to him, decided to attack not only these terrorist training camps, but also a number of military targets in Iran."

There was a gasp by those in the room who didn't know even this much of the story.

"After consulting with the national security adviser, my recommendation is we immediately relieve Admiral Robinson of his duties. We need to have Admiral Harry Flowers, the Fifth Fleet commander, replace Robinson immediately," Monroe said.

"The president concurs with Admiral Monroe's recommendation," Curtis added. "We just need to get on with it."

Michael Curtis had reason to be agitated. He had pressed hard for robust strikes against Iran. Secretly, he had hoped Iran would do something provocative that would cause the United States to rain down attacks on the Islamic Republic. Now this renegade admiral, for reasons not clear to anyone, was threatening to do this on his own, and the president was ordering them to stop him. Any hopes that Curtis had of ratcheting up the crisis were dashed.

"Admiral, we need to continue planning for the strikes against the terrorist training camps, but we'll take no action until Admiral Robinson is off USS *Carl Vinson*. You need to have Admiral Flowers relieve him and take control of the strike group. The president wants to be notified when Admiral Flowers has taken charge."

"We'll make that happen, Mr. Curtis," Monroe replied. The JCS chairman could feel the chill. Curtis' tone and body language conveyed that the military—and specifically the Navy—had screwed this up.

Monroe was torn. He and Robinson were professional and personal friends, but now there seemed to be compelling evidence that Robinson was operating as a maverick. What Flowers had heard Robinson say was consistent with what had been reported from other sources. Monroe couldn't understand why Flowers hadn't relieved Robinson on the spot for even suggesting what he had, but that was water over the dam now. It was time to get on with it.

CHAPTER 52

In three cities in the United States, three men with the same mission were each doing the same thing. They were waiting for a call they were certain would come.

None of the three men knew each other. That was by design. Though there was little chance of any of them being caught, no link to any other was provided. Each was to be contacted individually by Jahani, directed to commence his mission, and not communicate with anyone until after his mission was complete.

In New York, Mejid Homani had picked the spot on the United Nations concourse where he'd release his nerve agent. He had spent the better part of the previous day observing the patterns of movement, evaluating his ability to hide the gas, and balancing that against having it released where it would kill the most people.

His choice of location complete, he holed up in a room in a nearby hotel. A small television sat on the bureau. Homani had the TV tuned to CNN, waiting and hoping to see news of a United States attack against the Islamic Republic. Could America have kept an attack secret? He doubted it, but wondered nonetheless.

* * *

In the nation's capital, Hala Karomi walked out of Union Station for what he thought would be the next to last time. When he returned, it would be to release his nerve agent and then immediately jump on the Metro and return to his hotel room. Jahani had instructed him to take a hotel room close to the station, but Karomi was put off by the high cost the upscale hotels near Union Station and concerned about the police presence in and around the station. He thought that by disappearing into the Metro he could shake any pursuers.

That was the one part of the mission that Karomi hated the most—staying in Washington after the attack he was about to unleash. He knew Americans treated their capital city with near reverence. He would never feel safe until he was on an airplane back to the Middle East. But he also knew Jahani wanted to control this operation from start to finish. Soon, he was back in his hotel room waiting while CNN droned on.

* * *

In San Diego, California, home to scores of ships of the U.S. Pacific Fleet, Achmed Boleshari stood on the ground floor of Horton Plaza, a shopping mall less than two miles from the U.S. Navy base. It was the perfect location. Crowds streamed by throughout the day and the traffic was heavy in the late afternoon. Above him, multiple levels of the shopping plaza stood exposed to any gas that would waft upward.

He wanted desperately to be somewhere else—to be at the nearby Navy base. There, the ships that threatened his nation stood idly at their piers—their crews not alerted, their billion-dollar ships inviting targets for the havoc that he knew he could wreak. But it was only a dream. Above all, Jahani taught obedience, and Boleshari put those thoughts out of his mind as he returned to his hotel room, just a block from where he would act. How long would he have to wait?

* * *

Hossein Jahani sat in his hidden location, a location known only to a handful of his underlings and to no one else—not to Foreign Minister Velayati, and certainly not to President Habibi. If the United States attacked the Islamic Republic, he would release these men on their mission. He wouldn't hesitate, and he certainly wouldn't ask permission of those politicians.

CHAPTER 53

"Admiral, we have the principals assembled in the War Room," George Sampson said as he cracked open the door to the admiral's cabin. It was 0900, and no one had seen Heater Robinson since Bill Durham had brought him the night orders at 1930 the night before.

The ops officer had mentioned that the admiral had looked shaken. Sampson had attributed it to stress. Shortly after that, the admiral had called the Staff TAO to tell him he was retiring for the evening and had locked his doors.

"On the way in, COS," he replied. Robinson *was* shaken. Rationalizing he was performing a higher duty by ratcheting up what were intended to be surgical strikes against terrorist training camps to a wholesale attack on another nation, that was one thing. Killing another person, let alone someone who had been one of his closest advisors, was something else again. He had taken twice the normal dose of sedatives he had browbeaten out of the flight surgeon and had finally gotten to sleep. He had only been awake for a half hour and was still groggy.

His warfare commanders were standing behind their chairs when the admiral entered the War Room. He sat down, and the others followed suit. CAG stood to begin the briefing.

"Admiral, this is an overview brief for the strikes against Iran. We're going to conduct a three-day rolling campaign against the main naval facilities, air defense units, major airfields and then the terrorist training camps. This briefing is classified Top Secret."

Robinson was silent, so Foster continued. "Our planning has mimicked the campaign plan for Operation Mountain Divide. In the absence of detailed instructions or an execute order, this is our best recommendation as to how to conduct these strikes. We made a few adjustments to the Mountain Divide campaign plan to take maximum advantage of our aircraft weapons systems and Tomahawk load-out."

Even in his state, Robinson could tell Foster was fishing, expressing his frustration that all of this was being done based on verbal guidance—in direct contravention to the way they'd trained. Robinson knew once he blessed this plan detailed discussions might tip their hand to others outside the staff. He had a plan for that, too.

"Right, CAG. We have no indication from Fifth Fleet when we might get that definitive guidance by message," he replied. "For now, I just have to take the word of the Fifth Fleet commander."

"Yes, sir. I'll present the overall plan and discuss the aircraft strike packages, as well as the details of the Tomahawks we intend to shoot. Then Commander Tallent and Lieutenant McDonald will brief the day-one strikes."

"Fine, CAG, just proceed," Robinson replied.

* * *

Sixty nautical miles east-south-east of *Carl Vinson*, Commander Farhad Kani stood on the bridge of *Alborz* and looked over the shoulder of his radar operator. The sailor did his best to relate the information that his captain wanted.

"Is that the *Sabalan* standing out of Bushehr?"

"Captain, according to the coordinates we've been given and the track that was predicted for her, that should be *Sabalan*."

"Captain Mohtaj told me that he'd make fifteen knots and proceed due west. Is that the speed you have him going?"

"Yes, Captain."

"Officer of the Deck, increase your speed to twenty-four knots, set a rendezvous course to intercept *Sabalan*." Turning to his executive officer he said, "Captain Mohtaj is the senior among us and I'll follow his directions. We'll join on him, and then we'll approach *Carl Vinson* from both the east and the west and observe her movements."

"Yes, Captain," his exec replied. "What if the American carrier wishes to silence us? We'll be no match for her attack planes."

"No, we won't, but we'll have done our duty. The admiral informs me that a terrible vengeance will be launched against the Americans."

His exec merely nodded as the captain turned to other matters.

* * *

Petty Officer Andrew Tyson looked at his radar display in *Carl Vinson*'s Combat Direction Center. What he saw was interesting enough to call over his supervisor, Chief House, to take a look.

"What do you have, Tyson?" the chief asked.

"Look at this. We usually have guys going about six, maybe eight, knots up and down the Iranian coast, usually dhows or small tankers. See this guy over here," he said, moving his cursor to rest on top of *Sabalan*. "He's making fifteen knots, heading due west. On this course, he'll pass within about ten miles of us."

"I see him," the chief replied.

"But down here," Tyson continued, putting his cursor on *Alborz*, "this guy is doing over twenty knots, making a beeline for our first guy."

"Okay," House replied. He was going off watch in fifteen minutes and didn't want to generate any additional excitement.

"Should I report this to the TAO, Chief?"

"Naw, not unless you have something more significant to tell him. Continue tracking and point them out to Chief Butterworth when he relieves me."

"All right," Tyson replied. He was troubled by the contacts, but the chief had the last word.

* * *

Just thirty feet from where Petty Officer Tyson held these two contacts, the strike briefs were finally nearing completion.

"Admiral, that about wraps it up," CAG said. "We'll take on board your comments and make the adjustments you indicated."

"Good," Robinson replied. "Now we need to deny the enemy any opportunity to learn the details of this plan."

"Commo?" he continued, looking at his staff communicator, Lieutenant Commander Susan Wright.

"Yes, sir," she replied.

"I think that it's time we executed emission control for radio transmissions. Can you make that happen?"

"WILCO, Admiral," she said as Robinson rose to leave.

The rest of his people let this order sink in. They were going to go into total radio silence in preparation for the strikes against Iran. This would keep them from giving away their position. Tactically, the move was sound. Robinson had another agenda none of them could suspect.

Robinson shuffled back into his cabin. He was gathering his thoughts when the door to his cabin opened and his flag writer entered.

"Sir, we've got things backing up in the office, waiting for Commander Phillips' chop," Chief Weaver said. "I was told she had an urgent mission at Fifth Fleet, but it's not like her to just leave without instructions for the rest of us to carry on while she is gone."

Robinson sensed danger. Did they know anything?

"Well, Chief, she probably didn't have time to tell you all because I told her to get her bags packed and get on the COD with about fifteen minutes' notice. We've got some awards snafus at Fifth Fleet and I've gotten tired of dealing with Admiral Flowers about things that are supposed to be handled three to four pay-grades below mine. She'll get it straightened out now that she's there."

"Do you know when she'll be back, Admiral?"

"She'll get back when she gets these damned awards straightened out, Chief!" Robinson snapped.

"Yes, sir," Weaver responded as she hustled out of Robinson's cabin.

Heather Robinson continued to think of how he would precipitate a full-blown attack on the Islamic Republic. He needed a provocation of some kind, something that would threaten *Carl Vinson* and the entire strike group. If he got that provocation, he could unleash his attacks. He had been watching his GCCS display and the appearance of two unknown surface contacts validated an idea that had been bubbling in his brain.

CHAPTER 54

The last twenty-four hours had been a blur for Harry Flowers. He had had been extraordinarily careful about what he had said. He had taken every precaution to distance himself from what Robinson was plotting. He would have plausible deniability. It was only a matter of time until events would play themselves out.

He had just finished berating his flag lieutenant for some protocol miscue when a yeoman burst into his office.

"Admiral," he began. "I have Lieutenant General Allen's office on the line."

"The Joint Staff?" Flowers asked, recognizing instantly who was calling. The yeoman responded it was the Joint Staff operations director.

"Yes…well…wait. Don't put him through yet. You can wait outside, I'll buzz you when I'm ready to take the call," he said.

Flowers felt his heart beat faster. Had someone found something out? Did they suspect he had something to do with what was being planned aboard *Carl Vinson*?

He sagged deep into his chair. What would he say? He needed time to think. Should he have the yeoman say he wasn't in his office? No, it was too late for that. After hesitating for as long as he dared, he buzzed the yeoman. Within seconds, General Allen was on the phone.

"Admiral Flowers, is that you?"

"Yes, General, it is. How are things in Washington?"

"Busy, Admiral, but they're about to become busier in your AOR."

Allen began to pour out everything they had learned about Robinson's actions, information they had gained from Phillips's e-mails, as well as the fallout from Flowers's secretive communications with Tom Perry. Flowers listened, exhaling only when Allen stopped. He had made no accusation against the Fifth Fleet Commander.

"General, that's an astounding story. I thought I knew Admiral Robinson a lot better than I evidently did."

The suspense was driving him mad, so he pressed. "General has...has...my performance been...been satisfactory?"

"Of course it has. That's the reason I'm calling and what I was getting to. The chairman, Admiral Monroe, has directed that you fly out to *Carl Vinson* and relieve Admiral Robinson on the spot."

Allen paused to let this sink in, but he didn't wait long enough to allow Flowers to respond.

"You are to take control of the strike group, cancel any strikes against the Iranian military infrastructure—*any* of it—and conduct attacks against the terrorist training camps."

Flowers was relieved—relieved beyond words—he hadn't been found out. But now he was going to *take over* the strike group?

"Admiral, did you hear me?"

"Yes, General. I'll do so immediately. Please convey to the chairman my thanks for this vote of confidence—"

Allen didn't need to hear any more of this gratuitous dribble. "Look, just get out there and report back when you've taken charge."

"Will there be any written follow-up guidance once I do this?"

"Flowers, dammit, just do it and do it fast, man!" Allen shouted as slammed the phone down.

Flowers buzzed his chief of staff.

As soon as Dennis walked in, Flowers said, "I think I need to pay Admiral Robinson a visit. Let's see if we can get me out there."

"Certainly, Admiral," Dennis replied. He was shocked. Flowers hated flying and didn't enjoy visiting any of his ships. "When would you like to plan to visit, Admiral?"

"Today, COS."

"Today, sir?" Dennis asked. A visit by a flag officer was a well-orchestrated event that involved detailed planning. A week was usually the minimum lead time needed—and that was pushing it.

"TODAY!" Flowers shouted. "Don't patronize me, chief of staff. Call the ship, tell them to send in one of their helos or that claptrap C-2, I don't give a damn which, and get me out there this afternoon, clear?"

"Yes, sir," Dennis replied as he rushed out of the executive spaces and headed for TFCC, grabbing the ops officer on the way.

"Get *Carl Vinson* on the command circuit right now," Dennis said to the watch officer as soon as he entered TFCC.

Dennis and Carl Mullen watched as the harried watch officer called *Carl Vinson* several times on the strike group command net. Thwarted in his attempts, he turned toward the chief of staff.

"COS, it's no use. It looks like *Carl Vinson Carl Vinson* may be in radio silence. We haven't heard any calls from them in the last four to five hours."

"Great, how do we get to them? We've got to get them to send an aircraft to pick up the admiral and take him out to the boat," Dennis said.

"Sir," one of the other watchstanders chimed in, "there's one COD at the Aviation Support Unit. Their flight plan says they're going to take a load of cargo out to *Carl Vinson* late this afternoon. Maybe we could tell them to hurry their preps and take the admiral out as soon as he wants to go."

"He wants to go now," Dennis replied. "Call the COD crew and tell them to get ready for VIP transport and tell them to hurry it up."

CHAPTER 55

The activity on the floor of the national military command center was intense. Generals and admirals moved about, issuing orders and looking at displays on various monitors. Brigadier General Roger Kissel commanded a small watch team that comprised the action arm of NMCC.

General Allen had become a permanent fixture in the command center. Kissel initially chafed at the constant presence of the Joint Staff operations director, who was directing virtually every effort. Then again, he thought, with as many times as the chairman and several other of the joint chiefs had been in the NMCC insisting on being updated on the situation in the Gulf, maybe it was better that Allen was the one who had to field their questions and fend off their attempts to micro-manage the situation.

It was relatively calm—no high-powered visitors for the moment—when the Army major manning one of the phones announced, "General, I have Admiral Flowers's office on the line."

Kissel moved toward the phone, but Allen quickly preempted him. "I'll take it, Major."

"Allen, here."

"General," Flowers began. "I wanted to update you on what I'm doing to carry out your orders to relieve Admiral Robinson. It seems that the strike group commander has put the carrier into total emission control. We haven't been able to raise them on any circuit."

Allen was stunned. He had given Flowers explicit orders to do something—something the National Security Council had directed. Was this admiral now telling him he hadn't begun to carry out these orders?

"Admiral Flowers, we spoke hours—*hours*—ago, did we not? I'm astonished you're calling me from your headquarters and not from *Carl Vinson*. I expected you to be on the ship. This is a national emergency, Admiral, a national emergency!"

"Yes, General," Flowers replied. "I'm flying out to *Carl Vinson* shortly. Since I wasn't able to contact *Carl Vinson*, they couldn't provide an aircraft. Unfortunately, both of our CH-53E helos are down for maintenance—"

"Admiral, I don't give a tinker's damn about your helos or your problems. Relieve Admiral Robinson. Do it right now! Don't give me a bunch of minutiae about how you're going to do it."

"Yes, General," Flowers replied. "I will be lifting off—"

"DAMMIT FLOWERS; just friggin' get there!" Allen shouted as he slammed down the phone.

Several large screen displays in the NMCC carried network and cable news stories about the crisis in the Gulf. The shoot-down of the Syrian Foxbat had been a footnote, the ongoing standoff with Iran a bothersome fact of life, the continuous over-flights of Syria a nuisance at best. But the explosion at the InterContinental had galvanized America. Citizens from every walk of life had demanded the perpetrators be found and justice done.

Elsewhere in the NMCC, on a monitor mimicking the display Allen and Kissel were watching, a Navy commander and an Air Force major watched the large screen. It showed the *Carl Vinson* Strike Group proceeding along a predictable northwest to southeast track. It also showed dozens of other tracks moving about the screen. Ominously, it showed two high-speed tracks converging on *Carl Vinson*. The commander picked up the phone connecting him with the general.

CHAPTER 56

Aboard *Carl Vinson*, in a cool, dimly lit corner of CDC, Petty Officer Tyson continued to track the two fast-moving contacts he'd picked up a little over an hour ago. He remembered his guidance from Chief House, and called Chief Butterworth over to his screen.

"Chief, I pointed these guys out to Chief House just before you relieved him, and he told me to continue to track them. I've been doing just that and nothing has changed. They continue to converge and will come together just fifteen miles southeast of us. We don't have any ESM on them," he said, referring to electronic surveillance measures. "Think that we need to let the TAO know, Chief?"

Butterworth looked over Tyson's shoulder and assessed the situation. He called another OS chief over to validate what he saw. After a few moments of conferring, they made their decision.

As soon as the TAO evaluated what his team was presenting him, he picked up the Bogen phone and called the captain.

* * *

At the Aviation Support Unit several miles away from Fifth Fleet Headquarters, Captain Dennis had just finished an angry confrontation with the COD pilots. Only by issuing them a direct order was he able to convince them to fly out to *Carl Vinson*. The unpleasant conversation still rang in his ears.

"Captain, we can't take off until we file a flight plan with the carrier, and we can't do that until we talk with them," the first pilot said.

"You can file in the air, dammit," Dennis responded.

"We can, Captain," countered the second pilot, "but we're not sure where *Carl Vinson* is, and we can't fake the hand-off from the Bahraini air controllers.

They always want to know exactly where we're going. You're an aviator sir; you know where we're coming from."

"You're damn right I'm an aviator, son, and the reason I've gotten where I have in my career is that I haven't offered some pussy excuse every time a mission I was assigned wasn't exactly to my liking. I'm going to make it easy for you. This is a direct order. You are to fly Admiral Flowers to *Carl Vinson* immediately. Is that clear enough for you?" he asked, finishing with a flourish.

"We'll do what you say, *sir*, but I'm doing this because you've made it a direct order—that's the only reason."

"That's all the reason you need," Dennis replied.

Now Dennis stood near the maintenance hangar waiting for Admiral Flowers to arrive as the COD sat on the field with both engines turning and the ramp down.

* * *

Aboard *Carl Vinson*, Craig Vandegrift sat in his bridge chair and listened as his TAO reported the approach of the two suspicious craft. The timing couldn't have been worse. He was pointing into the wind, about to launch a major package—eighteen aircraft—and then had to recover twenty-one others. The wind in the Gulf was almost dead calm, and he was making almost thirty-two knots to generate enough wind over the deck to safely launch and recover his bomb-laden aircraft.

"If I keep doing this, TAO, where will these guys be right after the launch?"

"They'll be about ten miles from us, Captain, maybe less."

"Okay, I've got it. I'll tell the handler to get those armed surface recce Hornets off the deck early. I'm turning them over to the commodore—he needs them now."

"Yes, sir," the TAO replied. He called the commodore and told him that the third aircraft coming off the cat would be an ASR Hornet up for his control.

* * *

A few frames forward of where the CDC team was keeping a wary eye on the worrisome contacts, the CSG One TAO received a call from *Carl Vinson*'s TAO. Concurrently, Vandegrift called the admiral to report the developing situation. Within moments, Robinson made his decision. The strike group was still in

EMCON—emission control—so the staff TAO had *Carl Vinson* contact the carrier's shotgun ship via flashing light.

"*Shiloh,* this is X-ray Bravo, over," the flashing light signal began.

"X-ray Bravo, this is *Shiloh,* roger, over," was the flashing light reply from the cruiser.

"*Shiloh,* do you hold the two fast-moving contacts coming up from the south-south-east?"

"Roger, hold them on the SPY," *Shiloh* replied, referring to the AN/SPY-1 radar system.

"*Shiloh,* X-ray Bravo, you're directed to keep those contacts away from *Carl Vinson.* Use whatever means necessary."

"This is *Shiloh,* roger, out."

* * *

Admiral Flowers listened with a pained expression as the COD crew chief delivered the standard safety brief, while his aide fumbled with the gear the admiral was bringing along. It included a large envelope containing a formal letter relieving Robinson.

Flowers sat in the front seat of the COD, but that meant looking backwards. Essentially the same airframe as the E-2D, the C-2A Greyhound was anything but a greyhound. It was slow, ponderous, and had the aerodynamics of a truck. The admiral tried to do what he could to get comfortable.

* * *

Aboard *Sabalan,* Mohammad Mohtaj had seen multiple aircraft heading to the northwest—they were aircraft moving toward the carrier's marshal stack—confirming in his mind the large contact in that direction was *Carl Vinson.* He signaled that fact to Farhad Kani on *Alborz.*

Together, they decided *Alborz* would go west of *Carl Vinson* and *Sabalan* would go east, each ship giving the American carrier a respectable five-mile standoff. From those vantage points they'd watch its every move. Both ships proceeded at flank speed.

* * *

The level of intensity aboard *Carl Vinson* was picking up. The launch was complete. Now the jets overhead were reaching critical fuel states and had to be recovered. The ship steamed into the wind when Petty Officer Tyson shouted, "Chief Butterworth!"

The chief appeared quickly and asked, "What ya got, son?"

"Chief, these guys I'm tracking have picked up speed."

"Tell the TAO now," he commanded.

* * *

Aboard *Shiloh,* Captain Jake Busch had both Iranian ships on his SPY radar. He saw that the ship to the west would come closest to the carrier. Convinced it was the most immediate threat, he proceeded in that direction. He was also working to get his Seahawk helo launched so he could visually ID the contact. At ten miles away in the Arabian Gulf haze, all he could tell was that it was a warship. That was enough to make him decide to close at full speed.

His orders were to keep these ships away from *Carl Vinson.* But what did that mean? He hoped his mere presence—he intended to place *Shiloh* between the ship to the west and the carrier—would suffice. But what if it didn't? What if the Iranian ship continued to close? These people had bombed a hotel and shot a Super Hornet out of the sky. *They were capable of anything.*

The rules of engagement were still murky. Shoulder the ship? Fire a shot across its bow? Busch had never spoken to the admiral directly about his intentions. He was basing his actions on the flashing light message. He ran through his options as *Shiloh* and *Alborz* converged at a combined speed of almost fifty knots.

* * *

Kani was the junior captain among the two Iranian ship commanders. He knew Mohtaj, many years his senior, was watching, and he was expected to close the carrier as he'd been ordered. Kani stood in the center of his bridge and gripped the gyrocompass. He gave the order.

"Helmsman, turn right forty degrees. Point your bow at the starboard bow of the aircraft carrier and keep it there."

* * *

Shiloh's bridge team saw the sharp maneuver. They were now less than four miles from the Iranian ship. The Iranian was making a beeline for the carrier. It defied belief. Jake Busch ordered flank speed as *Shiloh* took a course to place it between the Iranian warship and *Carl Vinson*.

* * *

Kani steeled himself for the confrontation. He knew he was now committed. This American cruiser was attempting to keep him from complying with his orders. He could not fail. He held his course.

* * *

Busch saw *Carl Vinson* was still recovering aircraft—aircraft that were low on gas. He knew Vandegrift had to hold the carrier on a steady heading that would put him dangerously close to *Alborz*. As he got closer to *Alborz*, Busch called the Iranian ship on bridge-to-bridge radio warning him off, but he received no reply.

When Busch saw the Iranian unmask his batteries, he made his move. He set *Shiloh* on a course to take the ship inside of *Alborz's* port bow, which would cause it to collide with *Alborz* if the Iranian didn't change course. Then he pointed his gun at Kani's ship and activated his fire control radar.

* * *

Kani heard the warning over bridge-to-bridge at the very moment he heard the alarmed voice of his combat information center officer. "Captain, the American ship has lit us up with his fire control radar."

Kani panicked. The American captain yelling at him, his ship on a collision course, and now a definite hostile act—locking him up with a fire control radar. He knew Mohtaj was watching. He made his decision in an instant. "Fire a warning shot ahead of the American's bow."

His men were keyed up. His gunner didn't pause to ask the captain how far in front of *Shiloh* he should shoot, or how many rounds he should fire. He pumped out three rounds in quick succession, two passing just ahead of *Shiloh*. The third, though, struck the cruiser's bow.

Jake Busch wasn't the type who needed to be told something twice before he got the message. He gave the order to his gunners.

Flames leapt out of the barrel of *Shiloh*'s five-inch, fifty-four caliber gun, as round after round found *Alborz* with deadly accuracy. The lightly-armored Iranian frigate was no match for this concentrated fire. Holes were ripped into the ship's superstructure. Fires broke out everywhere. *Shiloh* kept firing as *Alborz* slowly decelerated.

* * *

Aboard *Sabalan,* Captain Mohtaj watched in horror as his sister ship took a merciless pounding. He was eight miles from *Shiloh*, and did the only thing that he thought he could do: he pointed his ship directly at the American cruiser and told his gunners to prepare to fire. Win or lose, he'd not let the American cruiser pound one of his ships with impunity.

* * *

Aloft in his Super Hornet, Lieutenant Mike Doyle was watching the surface action. He broke radio silence and called the Zulu Module, talking directly with Commodore Hughes.

"Commodore, Fighting Redcock 105, I've got a bead on the Iranian ship moving toward *Shiloh*, request weapons release."

"Granted, 105."

Doyle screamed out of the sky and headed directly toward *Sabalan.* He put the frigate in his sights as he hit the pickle switch and pulled up. Four Mk 82 500-pound bombs rained down.

* * *

Captain Mohtaj never saw the Super Hornet screaming down at him. He was completely focused on *Shiloh*. His radio operator was already calling Bushehr, telling of the American attack on *Alborz*.

Mohtaj felt the explosion before he heard it. Every man on *Sabalan* was knocked off his feet. Ominously, the engines wound down, and *Sabalan* slowed precipitously, mortally wounded. Mohtaj knew immediately he'd lost his ship.

* * *

In TFCC on *Carl Vinson*, Heater Robinson stood behind his TAO and watched the surface action. *Shiloh* had handled one contact, and the commodore took out the other with a Super Hornet. It was crisp, almost antiseptic, as the Iranian ships were taken out of action.

For Robinson it was an ominous sign. Were the Iranians conducting a wholesale assault on his strike group? If so, it meant the entire Iranian fleet was sortieing from its ports. That would defeat his attack plan to catch all of those ships at their moorings. He decided Operation Mountain Divide couldn't wait.

* * *

The COD sat on the tarmac at Bahrain International Airport. Harry Flowers sat in the back of the rumbling aircraft, sweat pouring off him. His aide tried to explain that the pilots were trying to get clearance from the Bahraini air controllers who seemed to take great delight in delaying the launch of American military aircraft. There was nothing the pilots could do to speed the process along.

CHAPTER 57

"Captain, look at this?" Lieutenant Colonel Bill Mansalo said.

"I see it, but I don't believe it," Captain Mike Ruggles replied.

The two officers were monitoring their worldwide GCCS display on the floor of the NMCC. Their team had focused on the Northern Gulf and on the area immediately surrounding *Carl Vinson*. They had tracked the carrier south-south-east as two unknown surface contacts continued to close. They had watched with concern as the symbology for the two tracks had changed from "unknown" to "hostile."

Now one of the tracks had disappeared.

Mansalo saw it first and asked Ruggles to confirm his suspicions.

"Do tracks just drop out of the system like that?"

"Not likely. Let's see what corroborating evidence we can find," Ruggles replied. Moments later, they heard a loud voice.

"OPREP Three Pinnacle/Front Burner from USS *Shiloh*. *Shiloh* reports engaging an Iranian frigate threatening *Carl Vinson*. *Shiloh* also reports a *Carl Vinson* aircraft is attacking another Iranian frigate!"

What had precipitated the attacks? Watching the displays just prior to the contacts' disappearing as they converged on *Carl Vinson* fueled intense speculation—from preemptive attacks against the Iranian vessels by *Shiloh*, to a defensive response to an Iranian attack.

The last half-century had seen U.S. naval engagements covering a wide spectrum—from the Tonkin Gulf incident off Vietnam, to action against Libyan surface craft, to action against the Iranian Navy decades ago—where the first reports were often wrong. They hoped the follow-up OPREP messages would provide more accurate information.

Soon, the OPREP messages from *Shiloh* and *Carl Vinson* appeared. They painted a comprehensive picture of the way the strike group had defended itself from the attacks by the Iranian frigates. While no one knew why these Iranian ships had attacked, the consensus was the strike group had done the proper thing in defending itself.

While the voice reports and the more comprehensive message OPREPS had been a good start, they hadn't been enough. What they wanted to hear, but what was conspicuous by its absence, was a voice report by Admiral Robinson with a recap of what had gone on—a formal OPREP THREE PINNACLE FRONT BURNER from the admiral himself, providing his assessment of the situation. They knew Robinson had put the group in emission control to make it more difficult for the Iranians to locate his ships, but they needed him to communicate directly with them. He hadn't. Beyond that silence, the watch team noticed something else.

"Richards, what do you make of these ship posits?" Ruggles asked a member of his watch team, Lieutenant Commander Hank Richards.

"Let me put up some overlays, and I'll try to tell you," he replied. Richards was an expert in Tomahawk employment. He was searching for overlays depicting the geographic area where each of the Tomahawk ships would have to take position to launch its missiles. Richards manipulated the GCCS display for another minute.

"There they are, Captain," he replied as he drew wind through his teeth.

"Yeah, I see it; it's every one, isn't it?"

"Sure is. They've got every TLAM shooter positioned where they need to be to launch strikes against Iran."

"Are you sure it's not just a coincidence that they happen to be where they are?"

"No way, Captain, look at this," Richards replied as he moved his laser pointer around the screen. "These two guys down here are tucked in close to the Iranian land mass, someplace that they'd never be unless they were going to shoot Tomahawks at Iran."

"I see. Are they the only ones in odd positions?" Ruggles asked.

"No, Captain," Richards continued, "they all are, and he's got tremendous overkill with his Tomahawks."

"How so?" Ruggles asked.

"Sir, I've sat in on some of the targeting sessions for the strikes against the Iranian terrorist training camps. TACAIR is providing most of the firepower; we're only shooting twenty-six Tomahawks against the camps. He could get that from one ship. He's got every Tomahawk shooter—with a total of over three hundred twenty-five missiles—in position ready to fire against Iran."

"Maybe he just wants backups in case some missiles fail," Ruggles replied.

"That would be a stretch. What this really looks like is the force laydown for Mountain Divide."

"You're right. It's just like we've war-gamed it."

"We need to tell the boss," Richards said.

"I agree," Ruggles replied as he reached for the phone.

As the reports from these watchstanders worked its way up through the Joint Staff, it confirmed what those near the top of the chain knew already—Robinson was planning to attack the Islamic Republic with massive strikes. What made the situation more ominous was the fact the admiral had already placed his TLAM ships in position to fire their deadly missiles.

* * *

General Allen burst into the chairman's office with the latest news. "Admiral," Allen began, "it appears Admiral Robinson may be preparing to launch attacks against Iran sooner than we anticipated."

"It looks like he may," the chairman responded. As a naval officer and former strike group commander who had led a strike group in the Arabian Gulf years ago, Monroe knew what was about to happen.

"Any further action on my part right now, Mr. Chairman?" Allen asked.

"No, we've got it from here," Monroe replied.

As Allen departed the chairman's office, Monroe told his EA to get the national security advisor on the line. They knew what Robinson was planning. Now it appeared he had moved up his timeline. Monroe had Admiral Flowers in an aircraft headed out to *Carl Vinson*. But what would happen when Flowers got there? Would Robinson listen to Flowers or just ignore him? Would he even let him land? Monroe's EA let him know the national security adviser's office was waiting.

"Admiral?" Curtis began, "My secretary said it was urgent."

"It is, sir. The timetable for events in the Arabian Gulf has picked up. I believe we need an emergency meeting of the NSC immediately."

"Is this about the Iranian ships that just threatened *Carl Vinson*, the ones that got taken out?"

"That and more, Mr. Curtis. Please, we need to move on this one."

* * *

Within an hour, the principals were reconvened in the Cabinet Room, waiting for Curtis. They were getting weary of these meetings. There wasn't time to do all the things they had agreed upon—or, more accurately, that Curtis had directed them to do—before they were meeting again to take on new actions.

The principals rose as Curtis and Monroe entered.

"Thank you all for coming on such short notice," Curtis began. "I assure you the urgency of the situation made this a necessary meeting.

"Based on some good analysis by watchstanders in the NMCC, the evidence *Carl Vinson* is going to launch attacks against a range of targets in Iran is now overwhelming. What's more, the timetable for these attacks could be more imminent than we initially thought.

"Admiral Flowers is airborne en route to *Carl Vinson* to relieve Admiral Robinson. We hope this relief goes smoothly. However, if it doesn't, we need to hedge against that possibility and be ready to take other action. I've assembled all of you here to discuss options."

There was silence in the room. They weren't prepared for this meeting. Their staffs hadn't had time to craft the usual position papers. They were left to their own instincts and their own wits.

Curtis surveyed the sea of faces. No one made eye contact.

"Ideas?" Curtis asked, his voice betraying his annoyance.

"All right," the national security adviser said. "Maybe it was unfair of me to gather you all so soon. Shortly, we'll know if Admiral Flowers was successful in his mission. Admiral Monroe will keep us posted. Meanwhile, I want you to come up with contingency plans."

As they filed out, they heard Curtis shout after them, "Four hours. I want to reconvene in four hours to evaluate your options!"

CHAPTER 58

The C-2A lurched down runway 30 at Bahrain International Airport and lumbered into the air. A terrified Harry Flowers faced aft, sitting next to one of only two small windows in the cabin. The Bahraini air controllers had delayed them for over forty-five minutes and then had had them taxi the length of the twelve-thousand-foot taxiway to take off northwest on runway 30. His khakis were already soaked through, and they still had thirty to forty minutes in the air before they reached *Carl Vinson*.

Flowers hated to fly and had the disposition of a doomed man. Only by reminding himself he was about to command a carrier strike group—a position that had eluded him during his career—was he able to keep his spirits up.

Sitting in the Greyhound's cockpit, Lieutenant Frank Barrett and Lieutenant Steve Green discussed their options.

"I'm really pissed that we got browbeaten into doing this mission, Frank," Green, the junior pilot of the two, said.

"I am too, and I know it was my call as aircraft commander, but Captain Dennis gave us a direct order, and the admiral sure rubbed it in when he got to the plane. Let's just get him to the boat and get back to base. I'm filing a report with the skipper. This shit has got to stop."

"First we've got to find the boat," Green replied. "The chief of staff said he thought they'd be just south of Bushehr. We'll look there first. Why don't you pick up a heading of 050 magnetic?"

"WILCO, but we'll have to get right on top of them. This order by the chief of staff to turn our transponder off so our arrival is a surprise is total bullshit, but I don't give a damn anymore. I just want to get this over with."

"Me too, buddy, me too," Green said as the COD droned ahead.

* * *

Carl Vinson and *Shiloh* continued northwest toward the furthermost corner of the northern operating area, trying to put as much distance between themselves and the Iranian naval bases and airfields to buy as much reaction time as possible should the Iranians try a major attack. Both ships remained at General Quarters.

Heater Robinson kept the group in radio EMCON, the only exceptions being his direction to each of the group's TLAM shooters to remain in their launch baskets and await further orders, as well as the brief OPREP report of *Shiloh* disabling *Alborz* and of the Super Hornet sinking *Sabalan*. Once that was complete, he re-imposed radio silence and charged his staff to ensure there were no transmissions.

The tension aboard *Carl Vinson* and aboard *Shiloh* was palpable. Although they had "won" the engagement with the frigates, they weren't convinced they could so handily defeat multiple attacks by similar units. More ominously, there was concern these attacks had been mere probes—sacrificial attacks to test the group's defensive systems—precursors to massive coordinated Iranian attacks.

* * *

Admiral Flowers's aide crawled up into the cockpit of the COD. "The admiral wants to know when we're going to get to *Carl Vinson*."

"We've got to find the damn boat first," Green replied as the COD did a lazy circle in the central Gulf, scanning the horizon for a ship that wasn't there.

"Well, can't you call them?" the aide asked.

"We could," Barrett snarled, "if my fricking radio hadn't just gone sneakers up."

"Shit!" Green shouted, "What now? We wrote up that radio last flight, and the techs said they fixed it. It worked back on deck at Bahrain International."

"Yeah, we got the bargain fix," Barrett groused. "Let's just get to the boat, dump the admiral, and get this goat rope over with."

As the admiral's aide returned to the COD cabin to deliver the report to Admiral Flowers, Green turned to Barrett, "Okay, Frank, you're the aircraft commander, what next?"

"I was afraid of this," he replied. "These yokels gave us bum gouge about the carrier being here. I'm gonna take us northwest up to where *Carl Vinson* usually operates. We'll find her there."

* * *

Carl Vinson and *Shiloh* had been at General Quarters for several hours. In the Stingers' Ready Room, Anne O'Connor sat in her chair watching the pace of activity and thinking. Early that morning she'd gone running with Rick Holden, and he had followed up on his earlier advice. No advice she hadn't asked for, just wise counsel as they'd pounded out three miles on the steel deck. What he had told her had made sense, and he had listened too. She knew she needed to make a decision.

* * *

As the COD continued to fly northwest, the pilots had no knowledge of the recent surface action, but they felt vulnerable nonetheless. It was one thing to fly out to an aircraft carrier—even one that had been their home for months—without filing a flight plan. It was another to be searching for the ship. But the most unsatisfactory part of this mission was flying without their IFF—identification friend or foe—transponder on, the one sure way that they could identify themselves as a friendly aircraft. Now their radios were useless, compounding their challenge of even getting the admiral to the carrier.

Sure, a three-star admiral was aboard and his aviator chief of staff had ordered them to launch on this mission. He had told them this wasn't a routine visit and Admiral Flowers wouldn't be returning from *Carl Vinson*. Maybe some huge operation that required the presence of a three-star admiral was in the offing. That thought gave them some comfort as they pressed on at 9,000 feet and 240 knots.

* * *

Carl Vinson and *Shiloh* remained on alert, scanning the seas and skies around them. Visibility was less than five miles, and the anxiety level was high. Petty Officer Sandy Martinez, manning his scope in *Shiloh's* CDC, was the first to spot it.

"I've got an airborne contact bearing 130 for eighty-five miles. Course 325, speed two hundred forty knots, altitude nine thousand feet. No modes, no codes." The last part of the report told her superiors that they were interrogating the aircraft with IFF, but it wasn't responding.

"Roger," the watch supervisor replied.

The watch supervisor passed this information to the TAO who evaluated what he'd heard. When he finally made his report to the captain, the contact was at less than seventy miles away.

"What do you think, Alan?" *Shiloh's* commanding officer asked.

"We need to watch this one, Captain," Lieutenant Commander Alan Mellon replied. "It came from the vicinity of Bushehr. Slow speed tells me it probably isn't a high-performance fighter or attack plane, but they could be going this slowly deliberately to throw us off."

"I agree; break radio silence and contact the Flag TAO aboard *Carl Vinson*."

"WILCO," Mellon replied.

* * *

Aboard *Carl Vinson*, the Flag TAO called Admiral Robinson. An unknown aircraft inbound with "no squawk" was a serious concern. Robinson appeared in TFCC and watched the aircraft on both the ACDS and GCCS displays. As the contact closed to within fifty miles, he broke radio silence again and directed *Shiloh's* CO to issue level one warnings to the aircraft and directed *Carl Vinson's* CO to launch Alert 7 fighters.

* * *

Aboard *Shiloh*, the captain ordered his TAO to issue level one warnings. He did so, but there was no response and the plane kept coming.

* * *

The action on the flight deck was frenetic as *Carl Vinson* turned into the wind to launch the Alert 7 fighters. Lieutenant Rudy Garcia in Shrike 306 got his Super Hornet started first and followed the yellow shirt director to head to cat 3. A minute later, Lieutenant Pat Whaley in Shrike 302 started his aircraft and was ready to taxi to cat 4. The two Shrike pilots had been surprised by the call for the alert launch and were a bit behind. It had been five minutes since the alert was called away and they were worried about busting the seven-minute limit.

The flight deck yellow shirts usually moved aircraft with well-choreographed precision, but they were feeling the effects of the tremendous ramp-up in flight tempo over the last several days. They didn't cross-check as they usually did. The yellow shirts directing Whaley got him moving just a bit too fast and overshot the corner to bring him on to cat 4. The air boss caught it first and grabbed the 5MC.

"On the flight deck, yellow shirt directing Shrike 302, emergency stop. I say again, emergency stop!" the air boss shouted.

But it was too late. With a sickening crunch, the radome of Shrike 302 smashed into the right wing of Shrike 306 as it turned up on cat 3. The flight deck crew scrambled for cover as Whaley desperately slammed on the brakes. Pieces of aircraft flew everywhere as both Whaley and Garcia quickly shut down their aircraft. Mercifully, no one on the flight deck was seriously injured by the flying debris. Someone thought they saw smoke coming out of Shrike 306, and the crash cart crew sprayed a layer of foam to fight the nonexistent fire.

* * *

One deck below, *Carl Vinson*'s TAO and the Flag TAO watched the flight deck camera in horror. Beyond their concerns for the safety of those on deck, they realized that there would be a delay in launching interceptors. The unknown air contact was now at forty miles, headed directly for them.

* * *

Aboard *Shiloh* the tension was palpable. Level one warnings had not deterred the aircraft.

The TAO issued level two warnings: "Unidentified aircraft bearing 125 at thirty miles from my position and flying at nine thousand feet, on course 305, speed approximately two hundred fifty knots; you are approaching a United States Navy warship operating in international waters. Your identity is not known and your intentions are unclear. You are standing into danger and may be subject to United States defensive measures. Establish communications now or alter your course to remain clear of me. Alter course to 090 to remain clear!"

No response.

"Again," the captain said. He could feel his palms sweating.

"Unknown aircraft ... to remain clear!" the TAO shouted, repeating the warning.

Again there was no response.

* * *

Green and Barrett were still searching in vain.

"Frank, the haze is getting pretty bad up here; do you want to try to break out below, maybe the visibility will be a little bit better."

"Let's try it. What have we got to lose?"

"WILCO," Barrett said as he pushed the yoke forward.

* * *

Heater Robinson grabbed the UHF radio and called *Shiloh.*

"X-ray Whiskey, this is X-ray Bravo. Emergency on *Carl Vinson's* flight deck. Unable to launch DLIs. Unable to launch DLIs. We show the air contact still closing the force. Request intentions."

* * *

Aboard *Shiloh,* the captain was about to respond to the admiral, when the petty officer manning the scope made her call.

"Airborne contact at twenty-eight miles, two hundred seventy knots descending rapidly, passing through seven thousand feet. It looks like an attack profile sir!"

"Take it with birds!" the captain shouted.

His order was repeated back, and within seconds, two SM-2 ER—standard missiles extended range—leapt out of *Shiloh's* vertical launch magazine.

Almost thirty feet long, and weighing almost 3,000 pounds, the SM-2 ER is accurate out to over twenty-five nautical miles. The missiles proceeded with deadly precision toward the COD. At two-and-a-half times the speed of sound, they would be airborne less than a minute-and-a-half.

* * *

The AWACS airborne over Saudi Arabia had been tracking the COD from the time it departed Bahrain. Long accustomed to the transit of these aircraft between Bahrain International and aircraft carriers in the Gulf, the operators on board didn't focus intently on the aircraft. They thought its flight path was a bit circuitous and ascribed that to those Navy boys just not telling each other where they were.

They noticed the aircraft didn't seem to have an operating transponder, something they could easily write off to Navy pilots lack of pride in their gear and a baffling willingness to fly their aircraft in a degraded mode. They almost missed them, but finally picked up missiles streaking up from USS *Shiloh* and impacting the aircraft. After a moment of stunned silence, they began to communicate with higher echelons.

CHAPTER 59

"General, it's an OPREP Pinnacle/Front Burner voice report from *Carl Vinson*."

"What does it say?" General Allen asked the NMCC watchstander. He had watched the GCCS display and thought that he knew what the report would say.

"Sir, *Shiloh* reports shooting down an unknown aircraft with negative squawk that was closing *Carl Vinson* and descending on an attack profile."

"Shot down with *Shiloh* birds?"

"Yes, sir."

"Any visual ID?"

"No, General. An accident on *Carl Vinson*'s flight deck prevented them from launching any DLIs. *Shiloh* shot beyond visual range."

"I see," General Allen replied. "I'll call the chairman. Make sure this is passed to the White House Situation Room."

"Yes, General."

Allen had just departed the NMCC, leaving his deputy in charge, when another OPREP Pinnacle/Front Burner report arrived.

"Admiral," the watchstander said to Rear Admiral Walt Morrin, "OPREP just received from the AWACS over Saudi Arabia."

"Go ahead," Morrin responded.

"Sir, they report *Shiloh* just shot down the COD aircraft that was flying from Bahrain out to *Carl Vinson*."

"No, that can't be; the AWACS crew must be confused. *Shiloh* just shot down an Iranian military aircraft approaching from Bushehr."

"Admiral, the AWACS crew said they tracked this aircraft from the time it departed Bahrain International. They double-checked with Bahrain Approach, and they confirmed the COD took off at exactly the time the AWACS began tracking it. They said there's no doubt."

"SHIT," Morrin shouted. "Get General Allen back in here now!"

"Yes, sir."

"And have someone get back on the net and have *Carl Vinson* and *Shiloh* patched back in. We need to sort this out."

"Admiral," the shaken watchstander responded, "the strike group has gone back into radio silence."

"DAMMIT!" Morrin yelled as he rushed out of the room.

Within minutes, the Joint Staff was mobilized to try to de-conflict the two radically different stories about the aircraft shoot-down. Phone calls were made, tapes reviewed, and aircraft specifications double-checked. Within twenty minutes they'd made their assessment. It confirmed their worst fears.

General Allen sat in the chairman's office as Admiral Monroe called the national security adviser. He could see the chairman had trouble even expressing himself. Allen knew the NSC was about out of options. He felt more confident the plan they were going to propose, draconian as it was, would be accepted.

* * *

The principals took their seats in the Situation Room. The mood was beyond somber; it approached despair. Michael Curtis was in his seat, staring straight ahead as the others filed in.

"You àll know why you're here," he began. "I assume the word of the shoot-down of Admiral Flowers's aircraft has reached each of you. Admiral Monroe will briefly recap these events. Admiral."

"Thank you, Mr. Curtis," Monroe replied. One of his aides placed a map of the Arabian Gulf on an easel, and the admiral recapped the chain of events. Afterward, there were several obligatory questions, but there was no doubt as what had occurred. All eyes turned toward Curtis.

"When I sent you away to come up with a backup solution to removing Admiral Robinson from *Carl Vinson,* the worst scenario I envisioned was his refusing to yield to Admiral Flowers's authority. We...I...had no idea the strike group commander would shoot his plane out of the sky and kill seven innocent people. You're going to hear two options briefed this evening that will sound radical. I hope that you will agree with me the nature of this crisis demands we carefully consider both options. Admiral Monroe will begin, followed by Mr. Hernandez."

* * *

Monroe stood up once again as aides put up different charts on a set of easels. They showed a now-familiar chart of the Arabian Gulf, a picture of USS *Carl Vinson,* and a picture of a submarine. The admiral let his aides finish setting up and then had them leave the room before he spoke.

"Ladies and gentlemen," he began, "Admiral Robinson has *Carl Vinson* in position ready to conduct massive strikes against Iran. He could conduct these strikes at any moment, though we suspect he will most likely do so sometime in the next twenty-four to thirty-six hours. The key is to prevent him from doing that by disabling the aircraft carrier and negating its ability to conduct these strikes."

Monroe paused to look around the room. Every pair of eyes was on him.

"USS *Jefferson City,* one of our Los Angeles-class attack boats, is in the Southern Gulf. We propose to have her make best speed north and disable the carrier by shooting torpedoes into her screws. If the carrier can't make way through the water, it can't launch and recover aircraft. While not an ideal solution, given the urgency of the situation, it's our best option."

The admiral went on to explain some of the technical details of *Jefferson City*'s capabilities, the specifications of her torpedoes, and how the sub would conduct the attack. He then asked for questions.

"How can you be sure that the torpedo won't sink *Carl Vinson?*"

"These are highly accurate fish; we can place them precisely where we want them."

"Can the sub actually find the ship?"

"We'll give *Jefferson City* locating data on the carrier's position."

"After the screws are hit, how long will the carrier be disabled?"

"As drastic as this might sound, replacing the screws on an aircraft carrier— or any other ship for that matter—is relatively straightforward. It's much less complex than repairing hull damage from a torpedo."

"What about the strikes on the terrorist training camps?"

"Once Admiral Robinson is removed from *Carl Vinson,* we'll order his replacement to attack the terrorist training camps with Tomahawk cruise missiles."

The admiral continued to field questions until Curtis weighed in. "Before we get into too much more detail regarding Admiral Monroe's option, I want you to hear from Mr. Hernandez."

* * *

Peter Hernandez stood up. He had neither charts nor assistants. His body language conveyed the fact he didn't like doing what he was about to do. There was silence in the room.

"Ladies and gentlemen, the option I propose is quite simple compared to that offered by Admiral Monroe. We've had a CIA operative embarked in *Carl Vinson* since the beginning of her deployment. He's assigned there as a Navy SEAL and has been with the SEALs for several years. He recently completed a mission for us in another area, and our intent was to keep him on hold for a while, conducting his normal Navy duties until we needed him again."

Hernandez could tell by the look on their faces they had no idea where he was going with this proposal.

"My CIA Director's people are in contact with this man. We propose to communicate with him and have him disable Admiral Robinson—by whatever means necessary—to prevent him from conducting these attacks. We assess the ship's crew isn't behind Robinson, and it's likely he's duped them into believing a full-blown attack against Iran has been ordered by competent authority. We believe that once he's disabled, order can be restored."

The questions came hot and heavy.

"What if he refuses to do it?"

"This individual has put his life on the line for his country before. We have no doubt that he'll carry out his orders."

"Can one person accomplish this, no matter how capable he is?"

"He's is a uniquely qualified individual. He can do this mission."

"Who will be in command if Admiral Robinson is disabled?"

"Temporarily, his chief of staff, Captain George Sampson, will be in charge as the next senior man. However, the Navy is preparing to send another flag officer to take his place soon after that."

"Will this individual just incapacitate, or will he kill, Robinson?"

"His orders will be to disable him by whatever means necessary."

There were a few more questions for the director. Finally, there were no more, and Curtis stood up.

"Ladies and gentlemen," he began, "these are draconian proposals, but they are necessary because we must stop Admiral Robinson at all costs. I think the urgency of the situation demands we put both plans in motion right away. We can afford to have redundancy in this mission; we just can't afford to fail."

Chapter 60

The chief of naval operations, Admiral Jack O'Sullivan, convened an emergency meeting of his close advisors immediately after the NSC meeting. He had made his suggestion to the chairman of the Joint Chiefs of Staff not expecting it would be accepted. Now that this option had been endorsed by the NSC, it was up to him to make it happen.

Once they reconciled the fact that a U.S. Navy submarine was going to fire torpedoes at a multi-billion-dollar Navy aircraft carrier, there was nothing complex about making this happen. They decided the order should come from COMSUBFOR, with a concurrent message from the CNO.

* * *

Seven time zones away from the Pentagon, Commander Joe Willard stood in the control room of USS *Jefferson City*. Willard loved this boat, and loved what *Jefferson City* could do as a war machine. Armed with a mix of Mark 48 wire-guided torpedoes, as well as Tomahawk cruise missiles, and possessing sophisticated weapons control and sonar systems, *Jefferson City* was more than a match for anything in or on the oceans. She could stay submerged indefinitely and her two turbines could propel the boat at over thirty knots.

Willard was in his sixth straight day outside the Iranian port of Bandar Abbas, watching to see if any Iranian Kilo-class submarines got underway. It was a mission that prevented him from training to hone his crew's skill. Willard could feel the barnacles growing on their readiness. He was roused from his musing by his executive officer.

"Captain, SPECAT message has just come in. RM2 Campbell is standing by outside of your cabin."

"SPECAT message?"

"Yes, sir."

Willard hurried back to his cabin and grabbed the message from the radioman. He signed for it and dismissed Campbell.

He closed the door and opened up the message.

FLASH
FROM: COMSUBFOR
TO: USS JEFFERSON CITY
BT
TOP SECRET SPECAT PERSONAL FOR COMMANDING OFFICER FROM COMSUBFOR//Nooooo//
SUBJ/ (TS) JEFFERSON CITY MISSION//
1. (TS) COMMANDER, THIS IS NOT A DRILL. UPON RECEIPT YOU ARE TO PROCEED AT BEST SPEED TO THE NORTHERN ARABIAN GULF. UPON ARRIVAL YOU WILL LOCATE USS CARL VINSON. YOU WILL SET UP FOR A DELIBERATE ATTACK TO DISABLE THE CARRIER. YOU WILL DO SO BY FIRING TORPEDOES INTO THE CARRIER'S SCREWS. THE REASON FOR YOUR TASKING SHALL NOT BE DIVULGED TO ANYONE. THE STRIKE GROUP COMMANDER HAS ELECTED, FOR REASONS KNOWN ONLY TO HIM, TO ATTACK THE ISLAMIC REPUBLIC OF IRAN. YOU MUST DISABLE CARL VINSON BEFORE HE CONDUCTS THESE ATTACKS. BEST ESTIMATE OF THE TIME OF THESE ATTACKS IS 24 TO 36 HOURS FROM NOW. THE IMPORTANCE OF YOUR MISSION CANNOT BE OVERSTATED. THIS IS NOT A DRILL. DEUTERMANN SENDS.
DECL/X4//

Willard read the message three times, then grabbed a sheath of yellow legal paper and started to fashion a response. Twenty years of submarine service hadn't prepared him for this. He wrote and scratched and wrote and scratched. There was a knock on his door.

"Yes," he replied.

"Captain, Petty Officer Campbell. Sir, another SPECAT for you."

Thank God, Willard thought. Surely this was another message from SUB-FOR canceling the original message. He grabbed the message from Campbell, hastily signed for it, then closed and locked the door. He opened the message, his anticipated relief already welling up.

FLASH
FROM: CHIEF OF NAVAL OPERATIONS
TO: USS JEFFERSON CITY
BT
TOP SECRET SPECAT PERSONAL FOR COMMANDING OFFICER FROM
CHIEF OF NAVAL OPERATIONS//Nooooo//
SUBJ/ (TS) MISSION VALIDATION//
1. (TS) YOU HAVE JUST RECEIVED A SPECAT PERSONAL FROM COM-
SUBFOR. UNDOUBTEDLY, IT HAS GIVEN YOU PAUSE AND PERHAPS
MADE YOU WONDER IF THIS IS SOME CRUEL JOKE VESTED ON YOU
AND YOUR CREW. LET ME ASSURE YOU IT IS NOT. I HAVE SAT WITH
THE CHAIRMAN OF THE JOINT CHIEFS OF STAFF AND THE NATIONAL
SECURITY ADVISER AND GIVEN THEM MY ASSURANCE YOU ARE THE
RIGHT MAN FOR THIS EXTRAORDINARILY DIFFICULT ASSIGNMENT.
YOU AND YOUR CREW ARE ALL THAT STANDS BETWEEN EVENTS SO
CATACLYSMIC THEY DEFY EXPLANATION. ACKNOWLEDGE RECEIPT
OF THIS MESSAGE. GO FORWARD AND DO YOUR DUTY. REGARDS,
O'SULLIVAN.
DECL/X4//

As he did with the message from COMSUBFOR, Willard read this message over and over, and then scribbled on the yellow legal pad. He locked both messages his safe and emerged from his cabin. He handed his radioman the two pieces of yellow legal paper and then strode into the Control Room and looked directly at his officer of the deck.

"We've been ordered to break off this mission. Turn northwest, and when clear the shallows, make your speed twenty knots. Have the exec gather the department heads in the Wardroom."

* * *

The two men had never been in the CIA director's office. They knew if they were being called there it had to have something to do with their "friend." Their jobs as field agents would never result a meeting like this, at least without first briefing four levels of the bureaucracy first.

Like the chairman of the joint chiefs, Peter Hernandez had presented his recommendation under extreme time duress. He had offered it as an option, not thinking it would be given serious consideration. But it had been accepted. He needed to act quickly.

Hernandez had called the CIA Director and given him the order. Bradley Garner had been the director for three years, and thought he had seen and heard it all, but the call from the DNI had stunned him.

They stood as he entered the room.

"I know you're wondering why I called you in. It regards the other mission you two have been assigned. What I'm about to tell you must never be broached outside of these channels.

"You are to contact your friend aboard the *Carl Vinson*. He is to conduct a mission that is so crucial that we've spent the last four hours writing and rewriting explicit and detailed instructions. You are to e-mail this information to him, then destroy this paper, and then purge your e-mail files. Once your friend acknowledges receipt of this message, you are to contact me immediately."

He pushed a single piece of paper across his desk. They both read it. They waited for further explanation regarding what they were to do. There was none, and they didn't know how to ask for any.

"I can only guess what you are thinking," the DCI said. "These are astounding instructions, and I wish I could explain more to you, but I cannot. Transmit the message."

With that, he rose, and the two men departed.

* * *

Rick Holden returned to his stateroom tired but satisfied. The level of intensity onboard *Carl Vinson* had reached fever pitch, and he was happy to be part of something important. His training with HSM-73 had been intense, and they were more than ready for any CSAR mission.

He was also satisfied he had been getting through to Anne O'Connor. There was no good reason why he was caught up in this, he just had an intuitive sense he was doing the right thing. Getting her through the loss of her best friend and back flying was a huge challenge.

The confluence of these two "missions"—preparing to save his fellow warriors and returning O'Connor to her full professional duties—had another leavening effect on Holden. It helped him to push the agency even further into the background.

He sat at his desk and looked at his laptop. Just a few minutes for his daily e-mail check, and he'd hit the rack. He logged on and prepared to read the typical two lines. He read something else.

Holden, you've been assigned a mission that you must complete in the next 18 hours. These orders come directly from the National Security Council, and from the DCI, who has authorized us to transit this message to you—code word—"Houseboat."

The admiral commanding the strike group has disobeyed military orders and intends to conduct massive attacks on Iran. He has deceived his staff and duped them into believing he has orders from higher authority to conduct these attacks. Only attacks on the terrorist training camps were authorized and now these must be held in abeyance.

The NCA sent the Fifth Fleet Commander to relieve him in person, but Admiral Flowers' aircraft was shot out of the sky. The admiral concocted a story it was an Iranian aircraft bent on destroying the group. It was not. You are to consider the admiral unbalanced. Do not try to reason with him. Find him, disable him, and if necessary, kill him. Then explain the contents of this message to his second in command, Captain Sampson.

Code word "Houseboat" applies. Acknowledge receipt of this message only with "message received." Good luck, Holden.

He stood up, paced around his tiny stateroom, sat down, and read the message again. He had to get a grip long enough to respond to his handlers. Was he prepared to do this? Had he been living a normal existence too long?

CHAPTER 61

Bolter Dennis stood in TFCC at Fifth Fleet Headquarters and held the phone receiver a few inches from his ear, certain that he would still be able to hear the loud voice of the four-star general. This was the third call from General Lawrence in the last hour. While these calls were ostensibly to get more information about the COD shoot-down, as well as the overall situation with respect to the *Carl Vinson* Strike Group, the questions from the CENTCOM commander always seemed to turn into accusations. The fact that Dennis had browbeaten the pilots into launching on this mission made his guilt and grief for those lost even stronger.

"Dennis, are you there?" Lawrence asked.

It wasn't a shout; it was a normal voice.

"Yes, General, chief of staff here."

"Captain Dennis, we all mourn the loss of your commander and the other professionals in the C-2 that was shot down. There's information I need to share with you. Can you take this call in private?"

"Yes, sir. I'm in TFCC, but I can have this transferred to my office. If I may put you on hold for about two minutes, I'll sprint back there."

"Thank you, Captain. I'll wait," Lawrence replied.

Dennis was perplexed by the request and was astounded by the change in the general's tone. He hurried to his office.

"I'm at my desk now, General."

"Captain Dennis, what I am going to tell you is to go no further than you as acting commander. Is that understood?"

"Yes, General, of course."

"Good. The OPREP sent by *Carl Vinson* at the same time the COD was shot down indicated the aircraft was an Iranian fighter out of Bushehr threatening the strike group. That story made sense to us then. However, a short time later, a report from the AWACS working over Saudi Arabia indicated it had tracked the COD from the time it took off from Bahrain International until the time it was shot down twenty-five miles from *Carl Vinson*."

"The AWACS is sure of that?" Dennis asked.

"Absolutely positive. What's more, the preliminary analysis here and in Washington is that, given the systems onboard *Carl Vinson* and *Shiloh*, particularly Link 16 and the SPY radar, it's all but inconceivable this fact was not known on both of those ships."

"General, I'm not certain what you're suggesting."

"Captain, given the strange behavior Admiral Robinson has demonstrated thus far, and given the fact Admiral Flowers was flying out to relieve him of his duties, the possibility—and I would make it a significant possibility—exists Robinson intentionally had Flowers's aircraft shot down. We can't know that with certainty, and won't until we get someone aboard *Carl Vinson*, but for now we have to assume the worst and act accordingly."

"General, I roger everything you say. What actions would you like us to take here?"

"Nothing right now, Captain. But it's important you get your casualty control people moving to make the proper notifications to the families of the people we lost. I know Mrs. Flowers is still in Washington, D.C., and that the CNO has visited her. I'll leave it to you to take care of the rest of the people."

"We'll do that, General. Is there anything else?"

"Yes, there is. Due to the nature of these events, I need to be in theater, and I don't need to be in the middle of the Saudi desert. My people will give your folks details, but I'll be boarding an aircraft within the hour. Expect me at your headquarters in about eighteen hours."

CHAPTER 62

Aboard *Carl Vinson*, her crew braced for a full assault by the Islamic Republic. Rocky Jacobson and his people were peppered for information about what the Iranians would do next, but it was information they couldn't provide. Jacobson and his people lived in a world of capabilities—orders of battle, military strengths and weakness, what the enemy *could* do if he intended to. But they could not divine intentions.

Admiral Robinson was shaken by the fact that an Iranian aircraft had come within weapons release range of his flagship before it was shot down, and he was worried the Iranians might mount a full-scale attack on his strike group. He decided on his own what he would do. Normally, this was a decision he would make with his warfare commanders. Not now. He could no longer look these men in the eye. He sat at his desk and picked up the Bogen phone connecting him to his chief of staff.

"Chief of staff," Sampson responded.

"COS, this attack by the Iranian aircraft is worrisome, and Rocky and his boys can't tell us a damn thing about what to expect next. We need to accelerate our timeline for attacks against Iran before they lash out at us again."

"We can do that, Admiral, I think. I'll have to get with CAG and with our surface strike people. Bomb buildup is proceeding on schedule." Sampson knew making these attacks earlier than planned would be extraordinarily difficult. "Would you like me to gather the warfare commanders in your cabin?" he asked.

"No, I think this is something you all ought to be able to figure out without having another group-grope. Just get with CAG and decide how much earlier we can push H-hour and then get back to me."

"Yes, Admiral," he replied as he wheeled out of his office and headed across the passageway to talk with CAG. Sampson knew this wasn't going to work, and he dreaded having to hear CAG vent when presented with yet another demand.

* * *

Anne O'Connor would be on the flight schedule tomorrow. She'd decided her period of mourning for Chrissie Moore was over. She'd loved Moore like a sister, but she needed to get back in the cockpit. It wasn't just her love of flying; she needed to hold up her end of the log. Her fellow pilots were carrying the load for their shipmates lost at the InterContinental, and now they were carrying it for Moore. They couldn't carry it indefinitely for her as well.

As O'Connor headed for her destination, she reflected on the fact she hadn't made this decision on her own. She didn't know if she could have done so—at least she didn't think that she could have made it this soon. Rick Holden had been the one person who had helped her work through this tragedy. He'd been through this before and he'd helped her. Not only had he enabled her to make this decision with confidence, but this assurance had also spilled over during her interview with the Airwing flight surgeon, with her XO, and finally with her skipper. They all agreed O'Connor should be back in the cockpit.

Now she was looking for Holden. She needed to share the good news and thank him. She remembered from the day's Air Plan that HSM-73 had several CSAR training events. Holden would certainly be involved, and she headed down to the Battlecats' Ready Room to look for him and tell him that she was flying again.

O'Connor walked aft down the starboard passageway and arrived at the back door of the HSM-73 Ready Room. The briefing for the CSAR event was over. Holden was out the back door and headed aft toward the Battlecat paraloft to draw his gear. He breezed by O'Connor without looking up, missing her completely.

"Rick," she called out.

"Anne, I sure didn't expect to see you here. Miss the turn for the Stingers' Ready Room?" he joked. O'Connor's ready room was next door to HSM-73's. Occasionally a yeoman delivering a flight schedule, or others not fully aware of their surroundings, would venture into the wrong one—but never a pilot.

"No, I really wanted to see you and speak with you for a minute."

"Anne, we just briefed for this mission, and I'm gonna be late if I don't hustle up to the flight deck. I'll talk with you later, okay?"

It wasn't really a request, it was a statement. Holden walked away from her and toward the paraloft. Was he that busy?

"Rick?" she said as she ran the few steps to catch up with him outside the door to the paraloft.

"Anne, not now!" he hissed and disappeared inside the door.

O'Connor's instincts were on overdrive. This wasn't someone who was just busy. There was something else on his mind, and she wanted to know what it was. She wheeled to go back to her ready room, determined she would find out.

CHAPTER 63

Patrick Browne was in a foul mood as he sat in the Oval Office waiting for his meeting with the national security adviser. The crisis in the Arabian Gulf was spinning out of control. Michael Curtis had asked for a private session and had asked for a full hour.

"Come in, Michael," the president said wearily.

Curtis powered up his tablet and held it on his lap. "Mr. President, a great deal has happened in the last forty-eight hours with this crisis in the Gulf. I know you've been kept up to speed, but I'd like to recap recent events and then brief you on the recommendations we evolved in our NSC meeting."

After almost a half-hour of constant talking, with very few interruptions, Curtis concluded, "These are our two plans, Mr. President. I've put both of them in motion concurrently."

"These plans are moving forward now?"

"Yes, Mr. President, but we won't fully execute them without your final approval."

"Are you certain that these are the only solutions to this crisis?"

"Yes, Mr. President, and having these solutions available was a very near thing. We were lucky *Jefferson City* was in the Gulf, and we were lucky this CIA agent was onboard *Carl Vinson*."

"Yes, that sounds fortunate," the president began. "I shudder at the thought of one of our subs attacking our aircraft carrier, but I think I see this is a way to stop any aircraft strikes. And I see Admiral Robinson must be stopped, but I cannot—I will not—condone murder. My God, Michael, we have *laws* about assassinating other heads of state. To condone murdering one of our own flag officers, no, I won't have it."

Curtis had anticipated this reaction.

"Mr. President, the orders to this agent were to disable the admiral if at all possible. He will do that and then report the details of the situation to the strike group chief of staff. Once Captain Sampson takes control the chairman has another Navy admiral ready to take over."

"All right, I see your point. But make sure this agent understands his mission explicitly."

"Yes, Mr. President. Sir, there is one other matter. In the event Admiral Robinson isn't stopped in time, we might want to consider informing the Islamic Republic of what might happen so they don't think this attack is being ordered at the highest levels of our government."

"Is this your recommendation?"

"No, it isn't, Mr. President. It would be a good hedge, but it's impractical."

"Then let's not do that."

* * *

Less than two miles from where the president and the national security adviser were discussing these matters, a nervous Hala Karomi made his fourth trip to Union Station. He'd already made his decision as to where to place his agent and now it was time to wait. Still, he couldn't sit in his hotel room, so he returned to see where he would carry out his work.

He watched the hundreds of commuters stream by and tried to imagine what would happen to them as soon as he released his nerve agent. He felt neither compassion nor hatred, just indifference.

CHAPTER 64

Aboard USS *Jefferson City*, Joe Willard sat in his stateroom, trying to decide how to tell his crew about this mission. The SPECAT messages had been explicit, but he knew the level of detail his people needed to know far better than anyone else. The chairman and the CNO could be excused for not knowing what he had to tell his men—they weren't submariners. But COMSUBFOR should know better. Then again, it had been many years since Admiral Deutermann had commanded his own boat.

Willard left his cabin and walked the few steps into the control room. He asked his quartermaster to lay out chart 62032, which depicted the entire Arabian Gulf. He looked at the position of their boat, now thirty-five miles west of Bandar Abbas. He let his eyes wander up the chart toward the extreme northern Arabian Gulf where *Carl Vinson* was operating. What he saw was not what he wanted to see—vast stretches of clear, deep ocean depths. Instead he saw shallow water and a sea full of obstructions—seamounts, wrecks, and oil platforms—massive rigs that were sturdy enough to break his boat. Maneuvering in these waters at high speed was going to be a challenge.

His exec broke him out of his musing. "Captain, I have the department heads assembled."

"Good. Lead on, XO," he replied as they headed for the wardroom.

* * *

Just over three hundred miles north, Rick Holden sat in his tiny stateroom and opened his e-mail, hoping to find a message from his "friends." To his chagrin, there wasn't one.

He had e-mailed his handlers twice. The first time he expressed his aston-ishment at his tasking, asked for more details, and was told to complete his mission as ordered. The second time he was more specific, asking questions about follow-on actions. Their failure to respond disturbed him. They owed him more than this—at least an explanation at some level of detail.

He didn't appreciate the fact his handlers had told him not to get "hung up" on the semantics of whether he was going to kill—or just disable—Admiral Robinson. Semantics? How could they be so cavalier about what happened to another human being—even one *suspected* of doing what Robinson was being accused of doing?

CHAPTER 65

"Welcome, General," President Habibi said as the secretary ushered the general into his office. He knew this would be a difficult meeting.

It almost surprised him that General Najafi had waited this long for an audience and didn't blame the general for pressing him. Ultimately, it was Najafi who was charged with the defense of the Islamic Republic. It was his job as president to rein in the general when necessary.

"Mr. President," Najafi began, "the Americans are becoming more aggressive, and I fear that they may attack soon."

"What makes you so certain of this?"

"The American bandits have sunk one of our ships and crippled another. Our ships weren't threatening the Americans. They'll make up some sort of cover story about us shooting first, but I assure you we did not. We've reviewed the tapes of the radio transmissions from both *Sabalan* and *Alborz*. The Americans attacked without provocation."

"I understand that, General. How many sailors did we lose?"

"We're not certain yet. *Alborz* was shot up badly but is still seaworthy under her own power, while *Sabalan* was sunk. *Alborz* is looking for survivors from *Sabalan*. Commander Kani tells us that they've lost many men from *Alborz* and that it is too early to tell how many have been lost from *Sabalan*."

"What did the Americans do after the engagement?"

"Nothing, Mr. President. They just withdrew from the area and kept launching airplanes. They did nothing to help search for survivors."

"Nothing?"

"No, Mr. President, nothing. Once the American carrier was well clear of the area we sent our Orion aircraft to drop life rafts and medical supplies. We've also gotten another ship underway from Bushehr to assist *Alborz*."

"This was a tragedy to be sure, General," Habibi replied. "The Americans are telling the international media we attacked their carrier. I wonder what credibility they have now that they've proven so trigger happy that they've shot down one of their own aircraft."

"This is troubling, Mr. President. The Americans are portraying this shoot-down of their C-2 transport as a mistake, and it surely was, but we think they shot down this plane because they thought it was one of ours. They're afraid we'll see they're about to launch strikes against us. That's why we must act now."

"General, I have no doubt you've looked at this carefully, and I understand the Americans harbor ill will toward us. But isn't it possible the Americans are just trying to protect their carrier? Do you really think an attack against us is imminent?"

"I do, Mr. President."

"I tend to agree with you, General, more than I did just a day ago. But still, we cannot attack the American carrier without their first striking our homeland."

"Mr. President!" Najafi shouted. "You must reconsider—" But Habibi wouldn't let him finish.

"General, you told me earlier your weapon was 'almost' ready. Is it fully prepared yet?"

"No, Mr. President, but I'm confident it will be—and soon—perhaps today and certainly by tomorrow."

"Fine, then finish assembling the weapon and load it on your aircraft. Tell your crew to be ready on short notice to do what we've discussed, but don't do this preemptively."

"Mr. President—"

Habibi raised his hand and cut him off. "Our diplomats are attempting to shape world opinion in our favor. The American attack on *Sabalan* and *Alborz* is tilting the scales our way. But drop a nuclear weapon on their carrier, and we'll not only incur the wrath of the world for starting a full-scale war, but we'll be censured for letting the nuclear genie out of the bottle. I will use this weapon if we're attacked—but it will only be used to stay the hand of the Americans."

"As you wish," Najafi replied.

As Najafi departed, it occurred to Habibi that if only they had a diplomatic opening to the United States, they might be able to defuse this crisis. That was in the hands of the foreign minister. At this point in these escalating hostilities,

Minister Velayati should be talking with the American secretary of state and eventually, as president of the Islamic Republic, he should be talking with the American president.

Habibi brought himself back to reality. There was no channel between him and the American president because Velayati had done nothing to open up a rapprochement with the United States. Hostage to the ayatollahs, Velayati had used all manner of excuses to spurn feelers from the Americans.

It was one thing to be ideologically pure and not associate with the United States. It was another to not have the means to defuse a crisis like this. Habibi knew what Velayati was doing. He and this madman Jahani were no doubt plotting further terrorist attacks against America. Habibi knew they'd already taken this too far, but he was at a loss as to how to stop them. He had to regain control, and he eventually had to find a way to speak with the American president.

Chapter 66

"Admiral, we're ready," Mike Lumme said as he opened the door to the admiral's cabin.

"Okay, Mike, let's go," the admiral replied as he rose and headed for his place at the end of the War Room table.

After they all sat down, he looked at the sea of faces and could see the strain of the last few days was taking its toll on them. It still grieved him he had to delude them.

"Ladies and gentleman, I've just spoken with Admiral Flowers and he has received the execute order for Operation Mountain Divide. The attacks are on. Fifth Fleet will give us a no-earlier-than and no-later-than time for these strikes. I expect the no-earlier-than time to happen soon, so we should prepare to execute these strikes within the next six to twelve hours at the outside. We need to assess our ability to do that."

"Admiral, we've completed our practice strikes and the Airwing is ready to conduct these attacks," Foster began.

"Good, CAG," Robinson responded. "Captain?"

"Admiral, we have most of the ordnance built up and staged. I still have some in the magazines, but once I load most of what I have on the flight deck, I can bring that up. We can support the launch plan for a good two to two-and-a-half days of sustained operations."

"Good," Robinson replied. "Will you have enough sea room?"

"Yes, sir. Wind has been out of the northwest, and I've got just enough room."

"Got it. Jim?"

"Admiral, our shooters are in their launch baskets," Commodore Hughes replied. "They're ready to go."

"Good." "Ops O?"

"Admiral, our overall assessment is we're ready. It's almost disconcerting Iran isn't at a higher state of readiness and anticipating these strikes. But we're ready to go."

"Okay, Ops, thanks. George, you're the cleanup hitter."

"Admiral, I agree with Ops O," Sampson replied. "The strike group is ready. Our folks are mighty tired, so I think that the sooner we get this going the better off we'll be."

"I agree with you," Robinson replied. "All right, let's get to work."

* * *

Sampson walked back to his office thinking he would just return to his usual mound of paperwork. He found CAG, the commodore, and Craig Vandegrift waiting for him.

"What's up?" Sampson asked.

"COS, we've been good soldiers about all of this and have gone along with the admiral's plans to prep for this attack," Foster began. "But you have got to talk with him. We can't attack without a hard-copy execute order. You know that. If this is that sensitive that CENTCOM or Fifth Fleet can't transmit it to us via the normal channels—even back channel means—then, hell, get your flag sec on an aircraft and have her bring it out. She's been in there for two days, hasn't she?"

Sampson knew the idea of Becky Phillips bringing the execute order out was a good one. He was still puzzled about the admiral sending her to Fifth Fleet Headquarters on a special mission. He had looked for an opportunity to ask the admiral about it, but Robinson had been so non-communicative he decided not to ask.

"Look fellas," Sampson began, "we can't get wrapped around the axle about the niceties of what the textbooks say about how the JOPES system works," he continued, referring to the Joint Planning and Execution System. "If the admiral says he's talked with the Fifth Fleet commander about this, that's good enough."

"We hear you, COS." Hughes replied. "We just want to be sure we get it right."

"I know, fellas, and I appreciate your cautions. Let's just press ahead."

Satisfied they had raised the issue to the proper level, the three men left to complete their work.

* * *

A hundred frames forward, Anne O'Connor stood outside the door of Rick Holden's stateroom. There was no way to sugarcoat it; he had blown her off in the passageway outside their ready rooms. Was this the same man who had patiently guided her back to flight status?

If he hadn't done so much for her, his actions would be easier to understand. She figured maybe he'd just had a bad moment. She checked with Jake Roach and found out that Holden wouldn't be going on his CSAR training mission for another several hours. She figured he'd be back in his stateroom. Maybe he'd want to talk with her now.

O'Connor knocked.

"Who is it?"

"Rick, its Anne. I just wanted to talk for a minute."

There was a long delay, and then he opened his door a crack—but only a crack.

"Hi Anne. Look, I really can't talk now. I've got something I've got to do. You understand, don't you?"

O'Connor looked at Holden, and could see that he looked stressed and even drained. This wasn't the confident—even cocky—SEAL she knew.

"Sure, okay, I understand. I may come back later, all right?"

"Later would be good, thanks," he said as he shut the door.

CHAPTER 67

What had attracted Patrick Browne to politics was power—the power to make decisions, the power to control events, the power to do great things. This was the reward that made all the campaigning, all the fund-raisers, and all the compromises worthwhile.

The president felt none of that power now. He felt like a hostage to his national security apparatus. He felt they were being overtaken by events and were powerless to be masters of their own destiny.

Michael Curtis was shocked by the short-notice summons to the Oval Office—the president usually didn't work this way. Inside the Oval, he was surprised to see the president already talking with Secretary of State Philip Quinn.

"Hello, Mr. President. Mr. Secretary," Curtis said. *What did the president want? Why was the secretary of state here?*

"Michael," Quinn said as he nodded. The secretary looked so self-assured Curtis began to worry that he and the president had already evolved a decision that might muck up his own plans.

"Michael, please sit down," the president began. "I asked Secretary Quinn to come over and brief me on our diplomatic options vis-à-vis the Islamic Republic. I wanted to know what we could possibly do to make some sort of rapprochement with President Habibi."

So that was it. At the eleventh hour, the fuzzy-headed diplomats at Foggy Bottom thought they had a better idea about how to defuse a crisis the rest of them couldn't. Dammit, he didn't like getting blindsided like this.

"Options, Mr. President?" Curtis asked. "I thought we'd addressed that in our previous meeting. If we tip our hand to the Islamic Republic, we could put our military forces in jeopardy. No, sir, I stand by my previous recommendation.

Job one for us is to stop Admiral Robinson from launching these attacks. Next, after we reassert control of the strike group, we need to follow through with our original plan to strike the terrorist training camps. Iran can't be allowed to think terrorism can stand without consequences. Beyond that, I think Secretary Quinn is right to seek a long-term dialogue with the Islamic Republic."

"Michael, I agree with you up to a point," the president began, "and you should know Secretary Quinn didn't initiate this meeting, I did. I know how strongly you feel about the prospects for more normalized relations with the Islamic Republic, but my concern is more immediate. Whatever we do to Iran must have a purpose, and I must be able to communicate with President Habibi and try to end this crisis."

"Yes, Mr. President, your point is well-taken."

"Michael," Quinn added, "as you know, our ability to communicate with Iran is limited. When we've wanted to talk with them we've used the good offices of other embassies, but that's not an effective way to communicate."

"I understand, Mr. Secretary,"

"Then you also understand." Quinn continued, "President Habibi is a voice of moderation in Iran. He may be approachable, and he may want to open up a dialogue with the president. I'm sure you know how his foreign minister, Velayati, and the head of his armed forces, General Najafi, operate almost autonomously. But Habibi was elected with a huge popular mandate, and we think if the president communicates with him and gives him all the facts, he might be able to force a more moderate approach by these people. We just need to communicate."

Curtis was no neophyte. He knew this was what the president wanted. He'd stand aside and let Quinn work this issue.

"Mr. Secretary, I agree opening up this path is important—once we follow through with our plans to retaliate for these terrorist attacks. At some point, yes, the president will have to enable President Habibi to back down from his country's aggression against us."

"Good, Michael, I'm glad you agree," the president said. "Now, please tell us about the progress we're making in stopping Admiral Robinson before he carries out these strikes."

"Certainly, Mr. President," Curtis replied as he recapped USS *Jefferson City* progress, as well as Rick Holden's.

Chapter 68

After briefing his department heads, Joe Willard laid out their current track—one that would take *Jefferson City* north to find *Carl Vinson*. After turning over their overwatch of the Bandar Abbas port to USS *Preble* and her two MANTAS USVs, *Jeff City* left its gate-guard position and had gone south to remain clear of Qeshm Island. Clearing that, they took up a west-south-westerly course remaining just north of the Salah Oil Field.

Turning more westerly now, Willard maneuvered south of the Western Traffic Separation Scheme, slipping through the deep water south of the Greater and Lesser Tunbs and north of Abu Musa Island. He maintained five knots as he crept between Forur and Bani Forur Islands. West of these islands, the water depth became a more comfortable eighty-five meters, and he increased speed to fifteen knots. He maneuvered in a northwesterly direction in order to use Kish Island as a navigation landmark.

Willard again met with his exec, operations, and weapons officers, this time to review their options. "Captain," his exec began, "I know our goal is to temporarily cripple *Carl Vinson* so she can't launch airplanes but not permanently damage her."

"Right," Willard responded. "What do you see as the most effective way to accomplish that?"

"Captain, as you know, the Mark 48 is a capable torpedo," his weapons officer began. "We recommend a close-in shot, aiming right for her screws. That will definitely stop her or at least slow her down—"

"What about permanent damage? Screws are difficult to repair," the captain interrupted.

"Screws are pretty major, Captain, but they're replaceable in a dry dock and it's the kind of job that could be done in a week or so. Under the circumstances, it's the best option."

"Can we get in close enough to take that shot?"

"It'll be a gamble. It all depends on whether we're spotted."

"I've got to think their defenses will be good. You all know what a carrier strike group brings to the table."

"We know that, Captain," his ops officer replied. "Biggest thing we're depending on is them knowing Iran's three Kilo-class submarines are in-port Bandar Abbas. If they know that, they shouldn't suspect an attack. If a Kilo does get underway, then that changes things, and they'll be alert and searching for a sub."

"Fine. We can refine our tactics as we go north. Let's hope those Kilos don't make a move."

CHAPTER 69

Rick Holden had spent a long time in his stateroom reconciling his mission. Reluctant as he was to admit it at first, he now recognized Admiral Robinson had to be stopped.

How to do it was the conundrum he faced. He was glad they had seemingly acceded to his suggestion regarding disabling—rather than killing—the admiral. The next great unknown was whether the admiral was acting alone, or whether he had co-opted his entire staff.

Holden only had snippets of information—scuttlebutt—passing through the ship's junior officer circuit. There was word that the admiral was taking medication for stress, that he had lost a pilot who he had mentored, and that he'd been sequestered in his stateroom for days. These and other hints led him to suspect Robinson was acting alone.

He didn't know how to begin his mission. He didn't even know much about the area where the admiral worked—the Blue Tile Area. He needed to learn more, so he left his stateroom and went aft for some initial scouting.

* * *

As much as Anne O'Connor had confidence in her ability as a naval aviator to "compartmentalize" things and not bring personal problems into the cockpit, her concern about Rick Holden was too big an issue for her to leave unresolved and then go flying. She returned to stateroom 03-45-4-L. She knocked but got no answer. Another knock and the same silence. She thought she'd timed it better. Holden wasn't flying; she'd checked the Battlecats flight schedule. Flight ops were going on, so he couldn't be jogging on the flight deck. Maybe he was working out in *Carl Vinson*'s gym. Even he couldn't do that forever.

She tried the doorknob. It turned and she opened the door. The room was empty.

O'Connor shut the door and flicked on the light. Holden had the room to himself for about ten days while his roommate was in Kuwait for an exercise. It made the room less cramped and made it easier for her to decide to wait for him there. She knew it would look odd if someone else came along, but she needed to talk with him right away.

O'Connor paced for a few minutes, but she finally sat down at his tiny desk which held his laptop computer. She stared at the screen-saver with the Navy SEAL logo. As she turned to examine her surroundings, she bumped the desk and the slight movement disabled the screen-saver. What she saw on the screen was his e-mail account with a string of e-mails in his inbox, as well as an e-mail opened up off to the side.

She was sensitive to invading his privacy, but maybe what was upsetting him had come by e-mail. Her curiosity overcame her, and she started to read the open e-mail. She thought she'd give it a quick scan—maybe it was that dreaded "Dear John" letter from a girlfriend, or a message from a family member describing an illness—anything that would help explain his recent actions. She read the short message.

> We are sensitive to your concerns as to whether you should kill the admiral outright, or whether it is possible to just disable him. We have run this up through the highest levels. You may disable him, but you must not fail in your mission. He must be stopped. This must be accomplished within the next 24 hours. Acknowledge receipt of this message. YFATA.

What had she just read? This had to be some kind of SEAL thing—some cryptic exercise or something else she didn't understand.

She had to find out more. She looked at the return address on the e-mail she had just read: walkerk@corg.com. She scanned the list of e-mails he had saved in his queue, looking for ones with the same address. She found one from the day before and opened it.

> We have received your reply. This is not a mistake. You are to carry out your mission. There is no other alternative. YFATA.

YFATA? A name? An organization? Someone—or some entity, or some country—was telling him to do this. Her heart was pounding. She closed that e-mail and looked at the list of incoming e-mails for another one with the same return address. There was one right above, and she saw it was only about six hours older than the one she had just read.

> *It's time for you perform a mission for us. You must neutralize Admiral Robinson. We cannot give you any more information at this time. You must move now, before he attacks the Islamic Republic. YFATA.*

Not let the admiral attack Iran? Was Holden an agent for a foreign government? Impossible? She needed to see his responses to these e-mails. She closed the e-mail she was reading and opened the Sent e-mail queue. She looked at the door. What would she say if he walked in now? She looked at the Sent e-mail screen, but there were no e-mails. He probably deleted those e-mails once he sent them.

* * *

Rick Holden walked across the athwartships passageway outside of Strike Ops and Plans—which marked the forward boundary of the Blue Tile Area—as casually as he could. *Remember where doors are,* he told himself, *remember where the admiral's cabin is and where the closest ladders are. Notice which doors have regular locks and which ones have cipher locks.*

He didn't have unlimited time. The timeline YFATA—"your friends at the agency"—had given him was short. He'd return in the middle of the night for a final check. He still wasn't sure exactly how he would take down the admiral, but first he had to get the basic lay of the land. He had put on a regular khaki uniform, figuring he would better blend in with the CSG One staff.

He turned right at the end of the athwartships passageway and entered the Blue Tile area. The door to the Flag Mess was on his right. He knew he couldn't just stop, but he decided if he gave way to everyone else who came through the passageway it would slow down his movement and let him absorb as much as possible. Doing this at night would be easier, but if red lighting was used here at night, he'd be able to see very little. Going through here later with a flashlight was a non-starter—that would surely attract the kind of attention he didn't want.

Two officers were coming the other way, and he ducked into the small alcove outside the Flag Mess and let them pass. He nodded as they blew by him. He could see the flag admin office up ahead on his left as he made a mental map of everything he saw.

Twenty feet up ahead, a crowd of officers emerged from the War Room—a meeting had evidently just broken up. Holden stopped in his tracks as the passageway momentarily went into gridlock. He happened to stop right in front of the admiral's cabin.

He saw the master-at-arms assigned to stand in the tiny alcove outside the admiral's door.

"May I help you, sir?" the man said.

"Just passing through, mister, thanks," Holden replied. The crowd outside the War Room was breaking up, and people were starting to move again.

"Sir, this passageway is for Flag Staff only. Do you have business here?"

He didn't need this kind of challenge—not now.

"Right, just moving out, Sailor."

Maybe it was his tone that made this sailor—a second-class petty officer who normally wouldn't challenge a lieutenant—take offense.

"Who do you have business with, *sir*?" the MAA asked.

"I don't have business here, Sailor, just passing through."

"Sir, I'll have to *respectfully* request that you turn around and go the other way. This passageway is only for the admiral's *immediate* staff."

Holden glared at the man.

"*Sir?*" the MAA said, his tone and body language conveying that he didn't intend to back down.

"Sure, Sailor, no problem," Holden replied.

A full look at the Blue Tile passageway would have to wait.

* * *

Anne O'Connor had tried several options, but couldn't find a way to retrieve any of Holden's sent e-mails. She was nervous; he was sure to return any minute. She couldn't have a normal conversation with him now. She quickly reread the three e-mails she'd seen and then returned his laptop to its original configuration. She stood up and put the chair back where she remembered it had been. She opened the door. The passageway was deserted. She pulled the door closed and hurried away.

CHAPTER 70

Michael Curtis sat at his desk and fumed. So much had happened in such a short time that he was having difficulty just keeping track of things, let alone controlling them. All he was doing was lurching from event to event. That fact alone made him angry. He'd decided to use his most-trusted assistant as a sounding board and was relieved when he knocked.

"Come in," Curtis said.

"I came right over. Your secretary said it was urgent," Perry began.

"Not urgent from an action standpoint, Tom, but there are issues we need to sort out—issues that can't wait."

"It's been an eventful few days, sir," Perry replied.

"Tom, what do you hear from your contacts at State? Secretary Quinn is on a mission to establish a link between the president and President Habibi. Is that moving forward, and are we going to get some last minute peace offering that will cause us to stop our strikes against the terrorist training camps?"

"No, sir. Reestablishing a dialogue with Iran hasn't been as easy as Secretary Quinn first assumed. I think they'll eventually get there but it will take a while."

"I see; so nothing in the offing right now on that score?"

"No, nothing soon at all."

"The other thing on my mind is how this whole process of stopping Admiral Robinson is going. We bought into two concurrent plans, hell I *sold* the president on those plans. But now that we've let the Pentagon run with their plan, and the DNI run with his, it's like getting blood out of a stone to get them to keep us informed. Do I have to convene multiple meetings a day just to find out what's going on?"

"No, sir, you shouldn't have to do that."

"When does the Pentagon think their sub will get to *Carl Vinson*?"

"*Jefferson City* is making steady progress on her journey north. She should be there in about twelve to fifteen hours. I'm certain *Jeff City* understands the urgency of the situation. I know the skipper, Joe Willard. He was two years behind me at the Academy. He has his orders; he'll carry them out as swiftly as he can."

"Okay, fine. I just wish we'd get more frequent updates from the Pentagon. How about this agent Peter Hernandez thinks can stop the admiral? What's the latest on him?"

"My source at CIA tells me that at first the guy on *Carl Vinson* didn't believe they were assigning him this mission. He finally acknowledged he has to stop the admiral, but we have no way of knowing what progress he's making. The agency just told him to get it done."

"Not a lot to go on, is it?"

"No, sir, it isn't."

"So when it comes right down to it, we have no idea which one of these actions will happen first—if either one of them happens at all. Damn, Tom, this is a hell of a mess."

"It is, sir."

"I need to have Admiral Monroe and Mr. Hernandez talk to me. Things are moving too fast to have me getting information third or fourth hand."

"We'll make that happen, sir," Perry said as he left the room.

Chapter 71

Anne O'Connor didn't remember how far or how long she'd walked after leaving Rick Holden's stateroom. She remembered walking all the way forward and down a deck to the fo'c'sle, and then going down to the hangar bay, and finally coming back to her stateroom and throwing herself on her bed. The pressure of all the flying, Moore's death, and now the one person she thought she could talk to might be an...an... *assassin.* It was almost too much to bear.

She didn't know how long she'd slept, but her head felt a bit clearer. Holden had always changed the subject on the few occasions when she'd asked about his past. He'd never been clear about how he'd been commissioned, or how he had come to be assigned as OIC of the SEAL platoon. He was older too, over thirty at least, while other SEALs who had his type of job were just a few years out of college.

She knew she couldn't deal with this by herself; she needed to talk with someone else, someone with more experience and perspective. She knew Brian McDonald would listen and she knew where to find him.

She walked aft from her stateroom down the starboard side passageway. She reached CVIC and paused outside of the intel complex. She tried to be unobtrusive and busied herself reading the bits of information displayed on the intel bulletin board. She was counting on McDonald showing up soon.

She spotted him coming around the corner. He was in the lead with about six other pilots and WSOs.

"Hi, Brian, you got a minute?" she asked as casually as possible.

"Oh, hi, Anne," he replied as they both moved to let the other aircrew continue into CVIC.

"Brian, I have a problem, and I need to speak with you."

He could see that she was worried. Her face was flushed, her eyes looked red, and she seemed stressed.

"Anne, I want to talk with you too, but I'm just heading into CVIC to give the strike brief for our attack on Bushehr. CAG moved these briefs up so that everyone will have more time at their unit briefs. I've got to give this brief, and I've got to give it right now."

"Sure, Brian," she replied. "I'll catch you after the brief, okay?"

"That would be great. I really do want to speak with you."

With that, he turned and walked into CVIC.

* * *

In his stateroom, Rick Holden brought up his e-mail account. It bothered him that the mission was still a go. He paused, feeling something was odd about his room. Something was different. Was it a scent? Had he encountered it before?

He couldn't tell. He decided to erase the messages from his friends and then left his stateroom. He would try the Blue Tile Area again in a little while—perhaps hit it from the other end away from the sentry.

CHAPTER 72

Jefferson City continued to work her way north. Joe Willard had briefed his crew on their mission and its importance, and despite any misgivings anyone might have, his crew had risen to the task.

Eventually, the boat reached a predetermined point where he felt he needed to take another visual fix.

"Up periscope," he commanded.

Willard was on the handles of number one scope as soon as it rose to the level of his shoulders. Slowly, he moved in a circle.

"There it is. Mark Shah Allum Shoal Light, bearing 082," he said.

"Shah Allum Shoal Light, bearing 082," the OOD replied.

"Range, approximately eight to ten miles."

"Aye, Captain."

"Down periscope."

"Fathometer?"

"Sixty meters, Captain."

"Make your heading 330 degrees true," he said. He would head slightly more to the north-north-west in order to avoid the large collection of oil wells approximately fifty miles north of the tip of Qatar.

Willard had been back in his cabin for about fifteen minutes when there was a knock at the door.

"Enter," he said.

"Hello, Captain," his chief of the boat, Sonarman Senior Chief Nikola, said.

"Hello COB, what's on your mind?" The chief of the boat, or COB, was the senior enlisted man on a U.S. submarine and was the one man the captain depended upon to have the true pulse of the boat—to know what the crew was thinking and what they were worried about.

"Captain, I've been talking to the men. Ever since your announcement, they've been seeking me out in droves."

"I imagine that they have been, COB. This is an extraordinarily important mission. I hope they appreciate the fact I gave it to them straight."

"They do, Captain. But, sir, the long and short of it is that the men want you to warn *Carl Vinson* before we fire any torpedoes at them."

Willard just stared at the COB, not believing what he was hearing.

CHAPTER 73

Anne O'Connor looked at her watch. It was finally lunch time. She needed to eat, and she needed to get out of her stateroom. Normally a place of refuge from the hectic pace on an aircraft carrier, her stateroom was evoking too many memories of Chrissie Moore. Her ready room and the camaraderie of her fellow officers was a better place, but for now she just wanted some time to herself. She headed to Wardroom One.

She pushed her tray through the serving line, grabbed a burger, and found one of the small tables at the after end of the wardroom. She looked forward to just a few minutes of alone time. She was two bites into her burger when she sensed a figure and then heard a familiar voice.

"Mind if I join you?"

"Uh, hi Rick," she replied. "Sure."

Her mind was racing. Did he know that she'd been reading his e-mails? Had he come to see if she would admit she'd been in his stateroom?

"Good burgers?" Holden asked as he sat down.

"For you SEALs I'm sure this is haute cuisine. This has to be better than the food you have out in the field, isn't it?"

"That's an understatement. Those box lunches we get on our CSAR training missions leave a lot to be desired."

"I bet. Do you have a training mission today?"

"No, not today. I have some other stuff I have to take care of."

"Oh, what's that?"

"Just some things. I've been wrestling with a lot of stuff."

"There's a lot going on out here, Rick."

"Yeah, there is," he replied. "It's just there are major things happening that none of us have visibility into down here at our level."

"That's the truth, isn't it?"

"Yep. We're all brought up believing our senior leaders are doing what's right for the Navy and for the nation. I don't know; sometimes that may be too much of a leap of faith."

"You're probably right," she replied. "I think at least out here at the strike group level we're pretty focused on just doing our job."

"Do you think the right thing is to lay waste to Iran's entire military infrastructure? That's going to put a lot of pilots at risk and it won't be something we can take back once we start it."

"I think it may but that's our mission. That's what has been handed down from higher authority."

"I know. But I wonder if we ever stop to ask if the people at the top—at the very top—are doing the right thing. There are situations where those people have to be stopped."

O'Connor realized Holden was really reaching. Maybe he was being forced to do this and now he was having second thoughts. She was now certain that he intended to do something to Admiral Robinson.

"There are all sorts of issues out there. I really have trouble dealing with some of this big picture, political stuff," she replied.

"Well, the politics of the situation is probably driving all of us to do the things we do."

There was a long, pregnant pause as they both munched away. O'Connor now thought she knew what Holden was going to do, and she was sure she needed to do something about it.

"Rick, it was good seeing you, but I'm flying in a little while, so I'd better get down to my ready room. I'll see you around, okay?"

"Sure, Anne, sure," he replied. "Fly 'em safe."

"You bet," she said as she got up.

O'Connor walked out of Wardroom One in a daze. She'd learned a lot from this chance encounter, and there was only one place that she could go with this information. She didn't have much time to do it.

CHAPTER 74

The neon sign outside his window flashed every second and sent a surreal glow into his hotel room. Mejid Homani lay on his bed with his remote in his right hand, idly clicking through the channels but always returning to CNN. He slid his left hand to his side feeling for his iPhone. It was still there. It was still silent.

Homani was only twenty-three, but he had been a soldier for Jahani for almost seven years. Homani had trained diligently and had proven himself against men a decade older.

But that's all it had been for all of those years—training. He'd done the same repetitive things month-after-month, year-after-year, always being promised he would be given a mission "someday." Now, "someday" had come, and he'd been selected, he was sure, for his devotion and his willingness to die for his cause. He'd followed his instructions to the letter. Now he just had to wait.

Homani returned to CNN, and was about to continue scanning the channels, when he saw a map of the Arabian Gulf appear behind a reporter:

And in the Arabian Gulf, the simmering crisis between the United States and the Islamic Republic of Iran continues and threatens to intensify. Yesterday, two Iranian frigates attempted to attack the carrier USS Carl Vinson in the northern Gulf. The Navy cruiser USS Shiloh, shown here, severely damaged one frigate while attack planes from Carl Vinson sank the other. There were no U.S. casualties.

Later that same day, USS Shiloh shot down an Iranian aircraft closing the strike group in a threatening manner. The aircraft did not respond to warnings Shiloh's warnings, was in an attack profile, and was coming within weapons release range. Iranian officials deny one of their aircraft was approaching the strike group.

Meanwhile, at the United Nations, the Iranian UN ambassador decried the attack on the Iranian frigates, saying that they were operating in international waters, and calling the Americans 'pirates and bandits' for attacking these ships.

He called for a United Nations resolution condemning the United States for these barbaric acts.

Pentagon officials declined to comment on the action in the Gulf, indicating only the matter was under investigation. These officials would not speculate regarding possible American attacks on Iran in the wake of the bombing of the Muscat InterContinental Hotel and the shoot-down of the Navy Super Hornet aircraft off the coast of Iran.

Meanwhile, at the U.S. Capitol....

Homani hit the mute button. He didn't want to hear any more. The American pigs were sinking Iranian ships and killing Iranian sailors. They were shooting down his homeland's airplanes whether his government wanted to admit it or not. But he was not yet unleashed. He fingered his iPhone once again, as if he were trying to coax it into going off. How long would he have to wait?

He didn't know how long he'd been asleep. It was dark. The neon light outside of his hotel room, dim in the daylight, was now a bright pulsating strobe that flooded his room in waves. He shot out of bed. Had he missed a call from Jahani? His iPhone was on. No message.

Homani couldn't stay in the tiny hotel room any longer. He needed to do something. What were they waiting for? He checked on his agent. It was safely under the hotel bed, hidden in a box labeled Jewelry Samples. He hurried out of the room and locked the door behind him.

Homani walked the three blocks to the United Nations Plaza. It was 2100, and the plaza was virtually deserted. He walked up to the glass doors leading to the concourse and put his nose against the glass. He could see where he would place the agent. It was ideal. He had studied the traffic patterns and understood what the effect of the gas would be on those busy workers and visitors who would be the victims of his attack. He couldn't have planned it any better.

CHAPTER 75

Anne O'Connor needed time to think, so although it went against all her professional instincts, she decided she needed to come off the flight schedule. She had to get to the bottom of what Holden was doing and she couldn't do it in the air.

She also needed help. If Brian McDonald was unavailable—for good reason—then she would tell her squadron skipper and then depend on his good judgment to help her stop Rick Holden.

The ready room wasn't packed, just the usual assemblage of pilots getting ready to go fly.

"Hey, Anne," the duty officer, said. "Brief goes down in fifteen minutes. Good to have you back flying."

"Yeah, thanks," she replied without enthusiasm.

O'Connor continued forward, scanning the front row of ready room seats.

She didn't see a head rising over the top of her skipper's chair. As she reached the front of the ready room, a voice piped up, "Hello O'Connor; welcome back."

It was her XO, Bingo Reynolds. He was slouched in his chair reading the day's messages on his tablet.

"Thanks, XO. Good to be back," she began. "Sir, is the skipper around?"

"No, he's still flying. Something I can help you with?"

She wanted to talk with her skipper. He was easy to talk to, and she needed to have this be easy. The XO—well, he was just the XO—and he didn't seem to have her best interests at heart. But this couldn't wait.

"Actually, XO, there is." She looked around. There were about a dozen other officers in the ready room. She knew that because she was standing in front of the ready room talking with the exec, almost everyone was listening to her conversation. "XO, this is a delicate matter," she continued in a whisper. "Could we discuss this in private?"

As difficult to get along with as Reynolds was, he recognized this was something he needed to accommodate. He rose. "We can do that. Let's talk out in the passageway."

She followed him out the front door of the ready room. They passed Stingers' Maintenance Control. It wasn't the place to try to talk.

"Looks a little jammed here, O'Connor. Let's go down to my stateroom."

She followed him aft for a few dozen frames. At his stateroom, Reynolds pushed the door open, letting O'Connor enter first. He flicked on the neon overhead light and shut the door behind him. He motioned for her to sit in his desk chair as he sat on the edge of his pull-out bed.

"Okay, O'Connor, what's on your mind?"

"XO, I don't really know where to begin. For right now, I think I need to come off today's flight schedule."

Reynolds knew how much O'Connor loved to fly, so he understood that something was seriously wrong.

"We can make that happen. Is there something else you want to share?"

She was never comfortable with the exec, but she decided she couldn't wait for the skipper; she had to tell the XO.

"XO, I think that I've walked into something I'm having trouble dealing with. It's complicated, but I think we have a big problem."

"Problem? What kind of problem?"

"XO, this may take a while," she replied.

As Reynolds listened with rapt attention, she poured out the details of the e-mails she had read in Holden's stateroom, and then she related the lunch conversation she'd just had with him. She reinforced all this by telling the XO it was Holden who'd helped her through her crisis after Chrissie Moore's death as a way of assuring him she knew Holden well enough to know something had changed, and that she was certain he was going to do what the e-mails told him to do.

"O'Connor," he said once she was finished, "I don't know where to begin. This is the most troubling story I've ever heard. But first things first, we do need to get you off the flight schedule. Walters has been whining that he isn't getting his fair share of flight time. I'll have the ops o stick him into your slot. Then we'll dig into this other matter."

Chapter 76

Michael Curtis didn't remember how many times he'd been in the Oval Office during the years he'd worked as the president's national security adviser. In all of those previous times he never could remember feeling he'd been summoned.

Curtis breezed by the president's secretary as he entered the Oval. His aides had related the president's exact words: "I think you better come over here right now."

The president had his back to the door. His desk was clear. Curtis had seen him do this before—whenever the president faced a serious crisis, he cleared his calendar and tidied his desk.

"You wanted to see me, Mr. President?"

"Yes, Michael. I don't feel like I'm getting brought up to speed on events in the Gulf fast enough. I know that we often joke about CNN being ahead of our intelligence people in reporting world events, but in this case, I think it might be true."

Curtis couldn't get the Pentagon or the agency to keep him updated frequently enough. Yet the president came to him, and him alone, to vent his frustrations regarding *his* not being kept up to speed.

"Mr. President, events are moving rapidly. Admiral Monroe is executing his plan to send the submarine to stop *Carl Vinson*, and the DNI has had the CIA Director give his agent instructions to stop Admiral Robinson."

"Yes, I understand all that. But with all the communications networks we have, you'd think we could do better than being in the dark about what's happening and when it's happening."

"You would think we would, Mr. President." "I've taken every measure I can to get updates from Admiral Monroe and Mr. Hernandez, but I get all manner of reasons why they can't keep us informed."

Curtis's didn't want to look or act like he was putting his colleagues on report with the president, but he was under too much pressure as it was to take the heat for two senior national security officials who ought to know better than to keep him in the dark.

"I know it's frustrating, Michael, but there are larger issues to deal with than just what the Pentagon and the agency are working on."

"I know that, sir."

"I'm not certain you do fully. I'd discussed with you all the idea of letting the president of the Islamic Republic know what was happening with the *Carl Vinson* Strike Group. You convinced me then not to."

"Yes, sir, and I think that was sound advice at the time."

"But now? Is it still sound advice?"

"Mr. President, I—"

"No, Michael," the president interrupted, "it's absolutely terrible advice.

"Michael, I never pretended to be a grand strategist, or to be especially knowledgeable about military matters. That's why I brought professionals like you to work here. But there are some basic things I think you all are missing."

Curtis wanted to respond, but he held his tongue.

"I know this terrorist attack on our people was a dreadful, barbaric act. And I know the subsequent shoot-down of our aircraft was a hostile act, as was the fact that those Iranian ships attacked *Carl Vinson*. I understand all that."

"Yes, Mr. President."

"But you are seeing right now how much trouble we have just getting subordinates to merely inform us of their actions.

"So here we have Iran, which as near as I can figure doesn't have one power center, it must have several. Yet we assume their president has full control of his military, his police, his foreign policy apparatus, everything. Do you really believe he does?"

"He may not, Mr. President."

"Exactly. I'm not convinced President Habibi condoned any of these actions against us. But we have a mad admiral who may rain destruction down on military bases and airfields and God knows what else, and you all *insist* I not contact Habibi and warn him that there's a part of our arsenal we may not have full control of!"

The national security adviser saw where the president was coming from. For Curtis, this was the toughest professional conundrum he'd ever faced. His loyalty to his president was absolute. Curtis believed fervently the Islamic Republic posed a compelling long-term danger to the United States. And if...and only if...they failed to stop Admiral Robinson, and he delivered the attacks they now knew he was planning, Iran's ability to threaten the United States would be dismantled for a least a decade—perhaps more. Importantly, the United States could then be absolved of any responsibility—they could blame it all on a renegade military officer. It was the opportunity of a lifetime.

But if the president made overtures to President Habibi, the Islamic Republic might have a better chance of blunting the American attacks, and more importantly, of dispersing their naval and air forces. Robinson likely would attack with full force over a short time period. If the initial flurry of attacks hit empty naval facilities and deserted air bases, it was doubtful he would have enough weapons to conduct an ongoing campaign to attack these dispersed units. Moreover, by that time, one plan to stop the admiral would surely have been successful.

"Mr. President, you have a valid point. We need to establish a way for you to contact President Habibi. I know Secretary Quinn has been working on upgrading our diplomatic networks to reach out to the Islamic Republic. I recommend we get this line established right away."

"Good, then we're agreed, Michael. Shall I call the secretary?"

"No sir, I'll be talking to him soon on another matter. I'll ensure he gets on this right away."

"Thank you, Michael."

Curtis would speak with Secretary Quinn—in due course.

CHAPTER 77

Wizard Foster was trying to make sense of the strange story Bingo Reynolds and Anne O'Connor had just told him. He was sure the others—Deputy CAG, O'Connor's CO, and the ship's XO—were as well.

"You've told us an amazing and shocking story, Lieutenant," CAG began, "Thank you for coming forward. Would you mind giving us a few moments? I'd appreciate it if you'd stand by in your ready room."

"Yes, sir, CAG."

No sooner had O'Connor left the room than Foster asked, "Impressions?"

"It's the same story she told me earlier. I think she really believes Holden is out to assassinate the admiral," Reynolds replied.

"I think we need to get to the bottom of these e-mails," *Carl Vinson*'s XO added. "We need to see exactly what they say."

"Good idea, XO," CAG replied. "Can you find a window to do that when Holden isn't in his stateroom?"

"Should be soon, CAG, I was scanning the Air Plan. HSM-73 is flying several practice CSAR missions, and Holden will likely be in the air for one of those. I'll check for sure and then look at his e-mails right away."

"Good, XO," Foster replied as Carl Vinson's XO left his cabin.

"Skipper?" CAG asked, looking at the Stingers' CO.

"CAG, Lieutenant O'Connor is one of my best nugget pilots. She may be my high-time pilot this month—"

"So she's flying a lot?" CAG interrupted.

"Really banging out the hops. I took her off the flight schedule after Lieutenant Moore's death. She got cleared by medical and was ready to fly again...at least until she talked with the XO just now."

"Lots of pressure doing that much flying, especially here in the Gulf. How close was she to Moore? Wasn't she her roommate?"

"She was. I'd say they were really close, wouldn't you, XO?"

"They were, and she took Moore's death hard. She was in the tower when Moore hit the ramp."

"I didn't know that," CAG replied. "How has she been dealing with being one of our few women aviators, Skipper?"

"I think she's been doing, okay, CAG. O'Connor is a little unique. She's the only woman in the squadron who isn't either married or attached to a significant other. The other women don't seem as hell-bent to excel every minute."

"CAG," Reynolds added, "the scuttlebutt is that she's been seeing Holden, but that's just talk among the JOs."

"Is there talk there's some sort of romantic involvement?"

"Yeah, you know, the usual stuff."

"I see," CAG replied.

CAG's deputy, Stretch Purcell, had listened impassively to the entire conversation. The dialogue about a possible romantic link struck a responsive chord.

"CAG," Purcell began, "I was getting a burger in Wardroom One a little while ago, and I saw O'Connor and Holden having lunch together in an out-of-the-way corner. Why would she have been having lunch with the guy in a quiet corner if she thought he was an assassin?"

"I don't know, Deputy, I'm getting a little confused myself."

They continued to "what if" the situation for some time. *Carl Vinson's* XO stepped back in. He started talking immediately. "As soon as I left here, I confirmed Holden was flying with HSM-73. I went down to his stateroom. His laptop was open and on, just like O'Connor had told us. I went to his e-mail account and found about two dozen incoming e-mails sitting in his queue. I scanned every one of them. There wasn't one that was even vaguely like the ones O'Connor described. There wasn't one telling him to *do* anything."

"Are you sure, XO?"

"CAG, I'm sure. Look, I'm not a computer genius, but I gave it a good look. I opened all his files. It didn't take long, because he doesn't have much on his machine. There's nothing in there that could lead anyone to believe that Holden is involved in anything untoward."

"Nothing?" CAG asked.

"Nothing. I suppose we could turn this over to our legal department, formally charge him with a crime, confiscate his laptop, and have some IT experts go through it. But I think I may have some insight on where O'Connor is coming from."

"I see, go ahead."

"CAG, there were three e-mails in there from someone named 'Laura.' They're not mushy, but it sounds like there is a serious relationship. She's evidently a semi-steady girlfriend."

"Did they look like they've been on his machine for a while?"

"They do. The most recent one is from two days ago and the others are a little older."

Deputy CAG chimed in. "So, XO, are you thinking maybe O'Connor read those e-mails?"

"I don't want to jump to conclusions, Deputy," the XO said, "but that's my general train of thought. Skipper and XO here tell us she's kind of 'seeing' Holden. She goes down to his stateroom, and she reads these e-mails from some other woman. I guess I could understand she'd be a little peeved. Maybe it's a stretch, but I could see where she'd be pissed enough to try to get him in some kind of trouble. Making up a story that he's trying to take out Admiral Robinson might seem like a big leap, but who knows. I'll defer to her skipper and XO. If they say she's been under a lot of stress, maybe she stopped thinking and snapped."

"I had a girlfriend once who would rat me out to God if she thought I ever looked at anyone else," Reynolds said.

"Whoa, we're really taking a leap here," CAG replied. "I'm not sure we want to cashier O'Connor quite yet."

"I'm not saying we should, CAG," O'Connor's skipper chimed in, "but she's our officer, and now I'm concerned about her. I think, at a minimum, we should have her evaluated. I think our CAG flight surgeon and the senior medical officer need to give her a thorough psychological evaluation. I don't want her tripping over the edge."

"I'll leave that to your good judgment," CAG responded. "Now, what do you all think we should do regarding Holden? If these accusations are true, we obviously need to do something. Do we think that there's any chance they're true?"

His deputy spoke first. "CAG, based on what we know right now, there doesn't appear to be a shred of evidence against him. The only 'evidence'

O'Connor related just doesn't exist, and now we have reason to believe she just might have reason to manufacture these charges—"

"I don't think we ought to hang that on O'Connor yet," Reynolds interrupted. As much of a hard-nose as the Stingers' XO was, when it came to accusing one of their JOs, he drew the line.

"All right, XO, we're not *accusing* her of anything. We're trying to decide if there is enough to go on to accuse Holden of anything—at least accuse him formally—and where she's coming from plays into that."

"I think that we'd be on shaky legal ground doing anything to Holden based on the info we have thus far," *Carl Vinson*'s XO added.

"Okay, okay!" CAG shouted. "We're getting a little far afield here. Here's what we're going to do. Skipper, XO, I want you to get O'Connor checked out. Big XO, Deputy, I want you to work with whatever investigators we have onboard and see if we can at least keep track of what Holden's doing until we get a handle on this. I need to take everything we know to the chief of staff. Let's get this resolved soon. We have a fight about to start and we all need to stay focused."

* * *

Anne O'Connor's CO and XO found her in the Stingers' Ready Room. Her eyes grew wide as her skipper began to tell her what they were going to do.

CHAPTER 78

Joe Willard sat with his COB for over an hour listening to his concerns. They discussed the mission over and over again, trying to come up with options that were less draconian than what he was about to do. There was no easy answer.

The captain reflected that when COB had first broached the subject of warning *Carl Vinson,* he had been taken aback. He had—for a moment—been bitterly disappointed that his crew wasn't a hundred percent behind the mission he had laid out to them. Upon reflection, he began to recognize that these men were right to have doubts about an order to torpedo a U.S. Navy aircraft carrier.

"Captain," the COB said, "I think the men would be satisfied if you went back up the chain of command and at least asked the question again to see if warning *Carl Vinson* was an option."

"COB, I can ask the question. But I've got two messages here—from COM-SUBFOR and from CNO—that tell me I must attack *Carl Vinson.* They don't authorize me to warn the carrier."

"But they don't tell us we can't do that," the COB replied. "That's all the men are looking for, just that you've asked the question again."

Willard was silent for a moment, and then the COB continued.

"Sir, this crew would follow you anywhere. I think all they need to know is that you asked higher authority for clarification. Captain, you and I both know what we're going to be told when we ask the question—they're going to tell us to complete our mission and tell us explicitly not to warn the carrier. We know that, but they don't, sir."

"You really believe the crew thinks we would ever be authorized to warn the carrier?"

"Captain, most of the men came into the Navy when the Cold War was just a memory. They don't know anything about the clandestine ops we used to be involved in. They think we can make combat a casualty-free video game. We just need to keep faith with them, that's all."

"All right, COB, let me think about this for a minute, will you?"

"Sure, Captain. I'll be standing by when you need me."

Willard knew he needed to complete his mission, but he also needed to keep faith with his men. He reflected for a long time, and then he pulled out his yellow legal pad and began to write.

* * *

Willard stood in *Jefferson City*'s Control Room and continued to monitor his boat's progress north. He'd never felt the weight of command more than he did at this moment.

As the periscope reached the full up position, Willard rested on its outstretched handles. He saw nothing but the one light he hoped to see.

"Navigator."

"Yes, Captain."

"Ra's Tanura Racon, bearing 012, mark."

"Ra's Tanura Racon, bearing 012. Estimated distance?"

"Distance three, no, four miles."

"Yes, Captain."

"Fathometer?"

"Fifty-two meters."

"Down scope."

"Make your course 316, speed ten knots."

"Make my course 316, speed ten knots, aye," his officer of the deck responded.

Willard left the Control Room and walked the few feet to his cabin. When he arrived, RM2 Campbell was waiting for him.

"I have the message ready, Captain."

"Good, let me see it."

He sat down and laid the message on his desk.

FLASH
FM USS JEFFERSON CITY
TO COMSUBFOR

BT
TOP SECRET SPECAT PERSONAL FOR COMSUBPAC FROM WILLARD//
Nooooo//
MSGID/GENADMIN/JEFFERSON CITY/
SUBJ/ (TS) JEFFERSON CITY MISSION//
RMKS/1. (TS) ADMIRAL DEUTERMANN: JEFFERSON CITY HAS BEEN
PROCEEDING NORTH AS ORDERED IN ORDER TO INTERCEPT AND
ATTACK CARL VINSON.
2. (TS) THERE IS CONSIDERABLE CONCERN ON THE PART OF MY
CREW REGARDING TORPEDOING A U.S. NAVY SHIP. A POSSIBLE AL-
TERNATIVE WOULD BE TO FIRST WARN CARL VINSON PRIOR TO
FIRING TORPEDOES AT HER. THIS WOULD ENABLE HER CREW TO
VOLUNTARILY ELECT TO CEASE THIS MISSION, BUT FAILING THAT,
WOULD ENSURE THEY ARE PREPARED TO TAKE PROPER DAMAGE
CONTROL MEASURES TO KEEP FROM LOSING THEIR SHIP. DUE TO
THE EXTRAORDINARY NATURE OF THIS MISSION, I RESPECTFULLY
REQUEST YOU CONSIDER AUTHORIZING US TO MAKE THIS WARN-
ING TO CARL VINSON.
3. (U) VERY RESPECTFULLY, JOE WILLARD.//
DECL/X4//

He read the message carefully, and then said, "Send it."

Willard waited at communication depth for COMSUBFOR to send his answer. Less than twenty minutes later, it came.

FLASH
FM COMSUBFOR
TO USS JEFFERSON CITY
BT
TOP SECRET SPECAT PERSONAL FOR COMMANDING OFFICER FROM
COMSUBFOR//Nooooo//
MSGID/GENADMIN/JEFFERSON CITY/
SUBJ/ (TS) JEFFERSON CITY MISSION//
1. RMKS (TS) CARRY OUT YOUR MISSION AS ORDERED.
2. (U) REGARDS, DEUTERMANN.
DECL/X4//

CHAPTER 79

"Hello, sir," his weapons petty officer said as Rick Holden found Petty Officer First Class Ed Vickers in Hangar Bay One.

"Hello, Vickers. How's business?"

"Booming, sir, booming," Vickers said, smiling.

Edward Vickers had been a SEAL for sixteen years. He had seen action in Iraq and Afghanistan. He'd been in enough scuffles on liberty, however, he was never going to be selected for chief petty officer. He was just serving out his last four years before he could retire. Although he thought the request was a bit strange, he figured he could bend the rules a bit when it came to issuing weapons to his fellow SEAL team members—especially his officer-in-charge.

Hell, Vickers thought, these ship drones could set all the damn rules that they wanted to, but he and his fellow SEALs were probably going to be on the ground in the fight soon if there was a CSAR mission. They needed to be ready to shoot straight on the first mission—there was no batting practice or warm-up game. If he had to bend the idiotic rules the ship had about issue control, so be it. He wasn't a glorified equipment manager.

"That's good. I hope we're not making your job any harder than it has to be."

"Not at all, L.T.," he replied, using the common abbreviation for lieutenant. "Any intel on when the strikes are gonna happen?"

"No, nothing exact, but I'd be surprised if it was any later than tomorrow or the next day at the very latest. All the signs are there."

"We'll be ready for CSAR sir—or for anything else."

"I know we will, Vickers. Now I need to be ready to do my part. Not gonna be much of an example if the lieutenant can't shoot straight."

"That's for sure, sir. What's your pleasure today?"

"I think I'll work with the nine millimeter and a forty-five caliber. Better give me enough ammo to get warmed up. That way, once I start using them, I don't have to come looking for you again."

"That's not a problem; I'm here whenever you need me."

Holden put both weapons and the ammo in his aviator's helmet bag the HSM-73 bubbas had given him and started aft.

"See you, Vickers."

"See ya, L.T. And remember, if there's gonna be any action, don't forget who your best killer is."

"I won't, Vickers."

Passing through *Carl Vinson*'s hangar bay, Holden thought about how he could complete his mission to stop Admiral Robinson.

He needed to be alone so he could think. He worked his way past a Hawkeye parked in Hangar Bay Two and started up the port side ladder. As he closed the hatch behind him he had the feeling someone was following him. He looked around, but didn't see anyone.

Holden slipped into his stateroom with his weapons and ran through his options. He could just shoot the Admiral outright and be done with it. He would be taken into custody, but then he would tell his story to the chief of staff—the next senior man—have him to check the veracity of his story with the agency and then wait for justice to lurch ahead. The planned strikes would be called off and the nation would be saved a bloody conflict with an enraged Islamic Republic.

But that wasn't what he wanted to do. That was why he'd lobbied his handlers to let him disable Admiral Robinson instead of killing him.

His thoughts flashed back to the hangar bay; had someone been following him? Who, someone on the admiral's staff? If he was being followed, he couldn't stay in his stateroom any longer. It would be too easy to trap him here. He had to move.

Holden put the nine millimeter inside the front of his waistband, while he put the forty-five between his waistband and the small of his back. The camouflage uniform was sufficiently baggy it hid both weapons. He then distributed the extra ammo in the pockets of his jacket. He was ready. He just needed one more thing.

He dropped back down to the hangar bay. As he moved, he looked around furtively, looking for anyone who might be following him. He went forward and found Vickers again.

"Hi, sir, come back for another weapon?"

"Nope, just want to get a walkie-talkie. We're gonna need to do some coordination with the ship."

"No problem, sir. I have one right here, all charged up."

"Thanks, I won't lose it."

"No problem, L.T. If you do, it'll come out of your pay, not mine," Vickers replied with a Cheshire Cat grin.

Holden gave him a wave and looked for somewhere to complete his planning. He had to assume they might be on to him. The walkie-talkie would let him eavesdrop on the actions the ship might be taking to find him. More importantly, he knew that the master-at-arms force used these to alert each other of the admiral's movements so they could make sure the route he picked to travel was clear.

He walked aft through Hangar Bay Two. As he did, he continued to look over his shoulder. *Damn,* he thought, *there is someone watching me. I just know there is.*

CHAPTER 80

Achmed Boleshari sat bolt upright in his bed in his tiny hotel room just two blocks away from Horton Plaza. The "Special Report" on CNN had just appeared with a lead-in featuring a picture of both the American and Iranian flags. He flicked the volume up and listened:

> *Iranian Foreign Minister Ali Akbar Velayati again condemned the United States for its attacks on two Iranian frigates in the Arabian Gulf. Velayati denounced "America's Rambo actions in attacking these ships in international waters, as well as America's total disregard for customary international law by not picking up survivors of Sabalan." Minister Velayati went on to note, "a total of one hundred thirty-four sailors died in this action, many of whom would have not perished had the U.S. Navy ships attempted to provide any assistance."*
>
> *At the United Nations, the Iranian ambassador renewed his call for a resolution condemning the United States for these attacks. Further, he petitioned the United Nations Secretary General to demand monetary compensation of six hundred and seventy million dollars—five million dollars for each victim—for the families of those lost. He indicated unless or until this compensation was paid "the Islamic Republic will wage a worldwide fatwa against the United States."*
>
> *At the Pentagon, U.S. military officials insisted the attacks on the Iranian frigates were strictly in self-defense. One high-ranking official, speaking on condition of anonymity, noted he could not think of a plausible scenario that wouldn't result in retaliation by the United States for the attack on the Muscat InterContinental Hotel.*
>
> *In the United States House of Representatives, Congressman Parker Jay of California called for "immediate attacks on the Islamic Republic of Iran," citing "over three decades of extreme hostility toward the United States, as well as a pervasive pattern of supporting terrorism." In a remarkable bipartisan response,*

over two hundred and thirty-seven Republicans and one hundred and fifty-four Democrats representatives joined Parker in this resolution.

The talking head continued, and Boleshari could feel himself becoming more and more enraged. One hundred and thirty-four of his brothers slaughtered. He knew he could kill twice that number of American sailors if he was unleashed on the American Navy base just a ten-minute taxi ride from his hotel. He certainly had enough nerve agent to attack a ship and then also conduct the planned attack in Horton Plaza.

What would they do? Condemn him? He thought not. No, he would forever be a hero of the Islamic Republic—revered for his determination and his bravery in taking the fight to the United States in a way that retaliated most directly for the heinous attack on *Sabalan* and *Alborz*. He closed his eyes and envisioned these American sailors dying as they tried to find their way off their ship—trapped in a steel casket.

He knew he could get on the base. Their security, such that it was, was a sieve. Taxi drivers, pizza delivery men, contractors selling everything from soap to bombs, Federal Express, United Parcel Service, the list went on and on. Boleshari felt himself getting more and more worked up.

He flicked off the television, knowing whatever he missed on CNN would be played again and again, and packed his knapsack. Pausing only a moment to pray, he dashed out of his room and down the two flights of steps and came out on Market Street on the fringes of San Diego's Gaslamp District. He hailed the first taxi he saw.

"Where to, buddy?" the driver asked.

"San Diego Naval Station."

CHAPTER 81

Anne O'Connor sat alone in Exam Room Two in Carl Vinson's sick bay and stewed.

The interview with the ship's Senior Medical Officer came first. She asked him several times why she was being examined, but the SMO was evasive, saying only, "your chain of command was concerned about you." She kept her responses professional but curt. Finally, after a thorough examination, she asked if he'd found anything wrong. He said he hadn't.

Then Lieutenant Commander Cummings had grilled her. "So Lieutenant, you were saying you don't know why you're here."

"No, I really don't; maybe you could enlighten me."

"Well, it seems that your chain of command is worried about you, Lieutenant O'Connor, or may I call you Anne?"

"You can call me anything that you want, Doc. Why is my chain of command 'worried' about me?"

"It seems they note, first of all, you've been under stress—"

"All of us have, Doc. If you think I'm the only one stressed, you must not get out much."

"Well, yes, I know that many people, especially you pilots, are under a lot of stress. Of course, not everyone has witnessed their roommate and best friend die in a fiery crash right before their eyes."

"No they haven't, but you know what? I was checked out by your buddies right after that crash and given an up-chit."

"But recently, you asked to be pulled off the flight schedule. Could it have been because you had second thoughts about getting back into the cockpit?"

"No, Doc, it couldn't have been for that reason, but it *could* be because we have an assassin loose on the ship getting ready to take out Admiral Robinson!"

"Oh, that story," he replied.

"What do you mean, 'oh that story'?"

"I mean this idea Lieutenant Holden is an assassin is a fantasy."

"A fantasy? Try this, Doc. Why don't you go to his stateroom and read his e-mails—the ones telling him to kill Admiral Robinson."

"We have read his e-mails."

"And?"

"And, *Anne,* there are no e-mails saying anything incriminating—none. The XO himself checked."

"What do you mean? I saw them."

"They aren't there now—if they ever were."

"If they ever were? I'm tired of this bullshit, Doc, I'm outta here!"

"You will stay right here, *Lieutenant.* That's an order!"

She wasn't prepared for that. She seethed.

"What we *did* find were e-mails from someone named Laura. Does that ring a bell?"

"Laura? No. What's that supposed to mean?"

"Well, Anne, it seems Laura may be Lieutenant Holden's steady girlfriend. There were some things in her e-mails that might upset someone else who was *seeing* him."

"Seeing him? You think I'm *seeing* Holden?"

"It's nothing to be ashamed of. You are both young, independent people. There's no crime in seeing someone. It's only a problem if you let relationships get in the way of your judgment," he said soothingly.

"There is no f-ing relationship, Doc. What planet are you on?"

"All right; you say you didn't read any of this woman's e-mails, and you're not trying to retaliate against Holden out of jealousy. Good. Now convince me there's evidence enough to believe your story."

"There *were* e-mails there. Why else would I tell my exec?"

"Well, that's the part we're having a little trouble with. DCAG says he saw you having lunch with Holden after you were in his stateroom, but before you went down to your ready room."

"Okay, Doc, look; I don't have control of who goes where or who does what on this boat. I was sitting there and Holden just showed up. I thought it would look suspicious if I told him he couldn't join me."

The interview went on for another hour, Cummings always seeming to agree with her, seeming to be on her side.

Finally, he said, "Well, Lieutenant O'Connor, that about wraps it up—unless there's anything else you want to share with me."

"Holden is an assassin and you guys need to stop him. Now let me out of here and let's get on with it."

"Oh, I don't think you'll be going just yet. The CAG flight surgeon needs to see you—and I need to file my report."

"Your report? What's your *report* going to say?"

"I'm afraid that's privileged information," he said as he left.

She was left alone in the exam room for another ten minutes. Finally, Commander Alex Fitzgerald entered.

"Hello, Anne," he said.

"Hello, Doc," she replied. "Am I close to getting out of here?"

"We've conferred, and I'm about to release you. I'm going to ask you if you'd sit on the bench for a few days—no flying. Just to make it official, I need to give you a grounding chit."

"Fine," she replied.

"Anne, this means no flying, but it also means you need to return down here in two to three days for a reexamination. We want you to be back in the air, but I must tell you that Doctor Cummings's report is…well…troubling. I'm giving you the benefit of the doubt and giving you a few days to work things out."

She'd known Fitzgerald for over a year and liked him. But he was telling her she wasn't right mentally. That worm Cummings had worked his psycho-babble on the CAG flight surgeon.

These men not only didn't believe anything that she said, they were now treating her as if she needed to be "handled." Years of being a team player had socialized her to believe in the system. Now the system was cashiering her. She decided to take matters into her own hands.

"Okay, Doc. I get it. I agree with you. I just need a few more days to get over things. I'll come back in a couple of days."

"Good, I think that will be best for all concerned."

But as she hurried out of sick bay and bounded up the four ladders to the O-3 level, she was already planning her mission and how to enlist the help of one other person.

CHAPTER 82

George Sampson was becoming accustomed to people closing his door after entering his tiny office. Now it was CAG.

"George, there's something we need to talk about. One of our JOs just told me the wildest tale I've ever heard." He went on to report O'Connor's accusation, as well as his assessment she'd made the whole thing up.

"Damn, Wizard, that's quite a tale. You don't think that O'Connor is going to do something crazy, do you?"

"No, I don't. After meeting with the other docs, she had a good session with my flight surgeon."

"Good. But getting back to what she alleges, am I right in understanding no evidence supports her allegations?"

"None. As a precaution, I talked with the skipper and we're having his master-at-arms people watch Holden on the one-in-a-thousand chance there's something to what O'Connor is saying. But believe me, there's nothing there."

"But what if she's right? What if Holden really is after the admiral?"

"COS—"

"Even if it is a 'one-in-a-thousand' chance," he interrupted, "we have an obligation to protect the admiral."

The COS was a pretty good guy, CAG told himself, but he was a typical Blackshoe, overreacting to any stimulus.

"I said Craig has his guys watching Holden. If he is some kind of agent, we'll see what he's up to—"

Sampson interrupted him again. "But you may not be able to stop him in time. My responsibility is to the admiral. Look, we'll do it discreetly, but I'm going to have the staff protect the admiral."

"All right, George, you do what you need to do."

"Are you certain there's no way that we can lock up Holden—at least until we check things out?"

"We can do anything that we want to. But without any evidence, I think watching him will be a good compromise."

"All right, Wizard, but you and Craig better watch him closely."

* * *

Forty frames aft, Anne O'Connor sat in the Stingers' Ready Room watching the strike brief on SITE TV—the ship's internal video network. She hadn't spoken to any of her squadron-mates since returning from sick bay—she was too embarrassed. She knew it was common knowledge she was marched down to medical by her skipper and exec. How could she face her fellow pilots?

She was watching Brian McDonald. She knew he would have time to talk with her now. There was time built in between the overall strike brief, which he had just delivered to all ready rooms via SITE TV, and the element briefs for each squadron. She arrived outside of CVIC confident he would be out soon. In a few minutes, he appeared.

"Brian, I've got to speak with you. This is a matter of life or death."

"Anne, what do you mean?"

"Brian, please listen to me. We need to talk and talk now."

He could see the look of desperation on her face and the sound of panic in her voice. "Fine, fine. Look, let's go to your stateroom, okay?"

McDonald followed her down the starboard side passageway.

In her stateroom, he tried to be patient. "I can tell you're upset. What's the problem?"

"Brian, I'm going to give you the short version. Rick Holden is an assassin. My best guess is he's an Iranian agent. He is going to kill Admiral Robinson. We have to stop him."

McDonald couldn't find the words to respond.

"I know what you're thinking, but here's where I'm coming from...." With that, she related the entire story of what she knew and how she came to know it, sparing nothing.

"Anne, I don't know what to say. This is serious. We have to get the ship to do something to stop him. They need to arrest him."

"Brian, have you heard anything I've said? I've tried to go there, but I got shot down. They're not going to do a thing."

"Anne, you're talking about taking the law into your own hands. What are you going to do when you confront him? Do you think he's going to just stop? I...I don't know what you want me to do."

"You can help me stop him!"

"Anne...the strike...I mean; I launch in just a few hours. You know what this strike means to our overall campaign...."

"Brian, I hate to get you involved, but you're the only one I can trust. I almost wound up in a straightjacket when I tried this on my chain of command. If you won't help me, I'm going to go after him alone."

"I can't let you do that."

"Then help me, please."

"I've got to tell DCAG so he can drop me off the schedule. You know this is going to raise a ton of questions. I'll cover as best I can, but what we're doing may come out."

"And if we don't stop Holden, our admiral may be dead."

"I know. Look, just let me get out of this as gracefully as I can. Once I do, we can come up with a plan to stop him. Anne, are you—"

She cut him off as gently as she could. "Brian, I am absolutely certain. I read the e-mails. You've got to believe me."

"I do, I really do."

* * *

George Sampson found Admiral Robinson in TFCC and asked him if he and CAG could have a private moment with him. The admiral was reluctant to leave TFCC, but finally followed them into his cabin.

"Okay, COS, what's so damned important that it can't wait?"

Sampson poured out the entire story and watched the admiral's eyes grow wide with disbelief.

CHAPTER 83

Joe Willard was now spending virtually every minute in *Jefferson City*'s control room as he continued to work his way north. He was in the most dangerous waters of the Gulf. Double and triple-checking his navigation, he picked his way through the shallows west of Farsi Island.

He put his best conning officer on watch as they moved through the Lawhah Oil Field and remained at a heightened state of alert as they entered the Fereydun Oil Field which contained even more oil wells.

Willard had ordered the boat to slow to eight knots—a safer speed for picking his way through the maze of oil platforms. This was also a better speed to give his sonar gang a chance to hear *Carl Vinson*'s screws. *Jefferson City*'s sonarmen were trained to pick out the unique sound of a 100,000-ton aircraft carrier pushed through the water by four powerful screws.

"Officer of the deck, sonar. I have screw noises, bearing 335."

"Roger, Sonar," the OOD replied. The OOD consulted his chart. Bearing 335 pointed toward the massive offshore Sirus Oil Terminal where supertankers took on oil and began their journey to destinations in Europe, Asia, and North America. Willard didn't want to overreact—it might be the carrier—or it might be one of those supertankers.

"Sonar, give me a course recommendation," Willard ordered.

"Aye, aye, Captain," the petty officer manning the sonar stack replied. *Jefferson City* was heading on a course that didn't optimize the ability of her towed hydrophone array to hear contacts ahead of the boat. They needed to pick a course to unmask the towed array and allow it to have a clear listening path to the contact.

Willard consulted with his ops officer, Lieutenant Commander Walt Capen.

"Walt, what's your assessment?"

"I looked at sonar display; it could be the carrier. Once sonar gives us a new course to steer, we'll be able to resolve any ambiguity."

"I agree. Do you concur that we need to go to battle stations?"

"I do, Captain."

"Good. Pass the word. No announcements. Quiet ship."

"Aye, aye, Captain," Capen replied.

"Officer of the deck, sonar. Sonar recommends coming to course 070 to clear the towed array and give us a clear bearing angle."

"Officer of the Deck, aye," he replied as he moved to the chart table. Huddled with the captain, they decided 070 would be a safe course.

"Make it so," Willard said.

Jefferson City came around slowly, gliding through the water at eight knots. The boat had been settled on her new course for about ten minutes when the call came from sonar.

"Officer of the deck, sonar. Sir, this definitely sounds like an aircraft carrier."

"What's your range estimate?" Willard asked, suddenly appearing in the tight confines of the stacks.

"Captain, the max range we could hear a carrier in these waters is about eighteen thousand to twenty thousand yards, and that's if she's making twenty knots or so. Based on how faint this signal is, I'd estimate it's at about fifteen thousand yards right now."

"Roger, fifteen thousand yards. Continue to refine the bearing.

"Aye, Captain, contact now bears 328 degrees."

In their attempts to unmask the towed array and resolve the contact, Willard was moving the sub away from *Carl Vinson* on a tangent. He'd continue this dance for a short time longer to refine the tactical picture.

"Captain, screw noise is getting fainter; it sounds like the carrier is moving away from us."

"Roger, bearing now?"

"Bearing 325 degrees, Captain. Noise is getting fainter."

Willard needed to make decision: Close the contact rapidly, or continue to maneuver carefully and set up for a time when he was certain that the carrier would run south again. He knew the prevailing wind was typically from the northwest, and he guessed *Carl Vinson* was probably launching and recovering aircraft at this moment.

"Officer of the Deck, come left, steer course 325. Make your depth sixty feet. Prepare to raise the scope."

That order electrified the control room. At fifteen thousand yards and opening, they were too far for a torpedo shot, so his crew knew the captain wanted to ensure that this contact was the carrier before making an attack.

Jefferson City turned to her ordered course and came to periscope depth. Once the boat was stabilized, the captain gave the order.

The number one periscope came up rapidly, and the captain was already on it as it locked into place. He scanned the horizon in all directions. Satisfied there were no contacts close by, and no threats to his boat, he looked in the direction that sonar had reported the noise—325 degrees.

The visibility in the Gulf was as poor as ever. He strained his eyes, trying to make out the carrier. He thought he might have a contact, but he couldn't be sure.

"Officer of the deck, have a look."

The OOD stepped up to the periscope and looked. Nothing. He stepped back. Then he stepped forward again. Still nothing...no...wait.

"Officer of the deck, sonar, sounds are getting fainter, sir, I'm starting to lose contact."

"Officer of the deck, aye," the OOD responded. "Captain, there might be something out there, but I can't be sure. Look out here at 330."

* * *

Thousands of feet above where Willard was stepping up to his scope again, Lieutenant Tiny Baker and Lieutenant Dave Wallstadt piloted their Super Hornets back toward *Carl Vinson*. They'd been part of a simulated strike mission against the Iranian naval base at Bandar Abbas.

"Tiny, Dave!" Wallstadt shouted over their squadron common frequency.

"Go, Dave."

"Tiny, it's the damnedest thing, but I think I just saw a sub periscope down there."

"Where?"

"Just passed below us."

"Another look?"

"Roger, we'd better."

Baker, flying lead, broke left, and Wallstadt followed on his wing. They reversed the course they'd been flying to return to the carrier.

Both pilots scanned the water three thousand feet below them. Nothing. Then Baker saw it.

"Dave, you're right. Down there. One o'clock low. It looks like a periscope feather," Baker said, using the term for the small wake of white water a periscope makes. "Let's drop down to angels one to have a closer look."

Both pilots chopped their power and put their aircraft into a gradual descent as they began a shallow turn to arc around the periscope at 1,000 feet. They began to circle around it.

"Dave, you got any doubts?"

"None, Tiny. That's the real deal."

"I got it. I'm calling strike and reporting it."

"Roger, let's head back now. My fuel's getting near red line."

With that, they headed back toward *Carl Vinson.*

"Strike, Fighting Redcock 104."

"Go ahead, 104."

"Strike, we've just passed over a periscope. We're on *Carl Vinson's* 150 for eight point two miles. Returning to ship."

"Fighting Redcock 104, confirm a periscope."

"Affirmative, Strike. It's a periscope. We're certain."

"Roger, 104."

* * *

Aboard *Jefferson City,* neither Willard nor his officer of the deck could make out anything definite on the horizon. They were so intent on looking down the bearing line they didn't notice the aircraft overhead.

"Down scope. Make your depth one hundred seventy feet. Increase speed to twenty knots."

Jefferson City would put more noise in the water at this speed. But Willard had made his decision. He was going after his target.

* * *

In *Carl Vinson's* CDC, OS1 Sanders turned to his chief.

"I just got a report from one of the aircraft returning to the ship. He says he saw a periscope."

"Yeah, and I'm captain of this ship," Chief Brewer replied, his voice dripping with sarcasm. How many times before had these flyboys sent them a bogus report?

"Chief, he said both he and his wingman saw it, and they flew back over it a second time to be sure."

"Where is it?"

"About eight miles away, Chief."

"All right, tell the TAO, but don't get all excited. We're gonna find out there's nothing there."

CHAPTER 84

Carl Vinson's TAO, Lieutenant Andy Bogle, made Petty Officer Sanders repeat his story twice. After what the man said sank in, Bogle began to issue orders in rapid-fire fashion.

"Fred, call Flag TAO. Tell 'em the whole story—slowly—make sure that they get it."

"WILCO."

"Art, walk over to the SCC Module and tell them exactly what happened. I'm gonna call 'em over the battle group command net, but I want them to hear it from you first."

"Got it, sir."

"Chief Walton."

"Yes, sir."

"That's got to be an Iranian Kilo out there. Go down to CVIC and see if they can get the latest imagery on Bandar Abbas. We've got to know what information they have on all the Kilos."

"WILCO, Lieutenant."

Bogle picked up the red phone—the battle group command circuit that connected him to all the battle group's warfare commanders.

"X-ray Bravo, this is USS *Carl Vinson.* Aircraft from *Carl Vinson* have sighted a submarine periscope bearing 150, distance eight miles from the ship. Break. X-ray Zulu, acknowledge."

Bogle had used the most abbreviated shorthand, ensuring that the strike group commander—X-ray Bravo—knew what was going on, and that the officer who needed to take action—X-ray Zulu, Commodore Hughes—heard the report and needed to report back.

"This is X-ray Zulu. Roger out."

Seconds later, Bogle's phone rang. It was the captain. After a brief exchange, he hung up.

"GENERAL QUARTERS, GENERAL QUARTERS, all hands man your battle stations. Go up and forward on the starboard side, down and aft on the port side. Expedite setting Zebra. Repeat, expedite setting Zebra. Hostile submarine in the area!"

As Bogle had anticipated, Commodore Hughes was soon standing next to him.

"TAO, I need aircraft at the datum."

"I've already alerted CAG. First guy off the deck for you will be one of the HSM-73 helos. We need to run downwind for a while so we have plenty of sea room for the next launch."

"Okay, I need to brief the admiral."

As Hughes entered TFCC, Robinson turned toward him. "Submarine?"

"Yes sir. I need to get aircraft over datum immediately and check this out. In the meantime, I heard we intend to turn downwind as soon as we catch these last few aircraft. I'd like to request that we don't do that. I want to put as much distance between us and the sub as I can."

"Commodore, look at the GCCS display. The ship is going to run out of sea room in just a few miles. There's nowhere to go up here."

"Yes, sir, I know, but—"

"Look, Jim, just debrief those pilots when they land and get the rest of their story. Then get as many helos as you can over the datum. I need to get some sea room to get ready to launch my strikes."

Hughes could understand the admiral's skepticism. False sub sightings were an unfortunate fact of life in naval operations. Add the fact the Iranians had used their Kilos in their naval exercises, and it was understandable people could "see" a submarine that wasn't there.

"We'll find it and pin it down."

"I'm counting on you, Commodore."

After Hughes left, the chief of staff spoke to the admiral.

"Admiral, would you please consider moving from TFCC? We think that if this assassin is going to move against you, it's going to be here. We can protect you far better if we keep moving."

"I've got confidence you all can 'protect' me right here—that is, if I need 'protecting'—and I'm not certain I do. We're about to unleash the strikes that our president has directed us to conduct. My place is right here."

Sampson hoped the admiral knew what he was doing.

CHAPTER 85

As Operation Mountain Divide moved forward, the admiral asked his battle watch captain for a recap.

"Admiral, one of HSM-73's helos is heading to the datum under X-ray Zulu's control. We've got another MH-60R getting ready to launch, and *Shiloh's* bird is heading that way also. That should give the commodore enough assets to see if this is really a sub or not."

"Okay, got it. How's the timeline for our strikes?"

"H-hour is two hours and twenty-five minutes from now. We'll turn back into the wind and set up to launch well before that."

"How about our TLAM shooters?"

"All units are in their launch baskets. They'll execute on command at H-hour."

"Fine, any loose ends?"

"Nothing major, Admiral. Ship's TAO tells us that they're doing a little reshuffle on the flight deck. Seems the strike leader for the first attack on Bushehr, Lieutenant McDonald, dropped out of the flight at the last minute. CAG has put the alternate strike leader in charge of the mission. No real impact on the strike."

"We need to know what's going on at the sub datum."

"Got it, Admiral."

Robinson continued to monitor the action and was surprised when the chief of staff and the captain suddenly appeared in TFCC. Having the captain leave the bridge at such a critical juncture was highly unusual and the admiral's antennae went up.

Sampson began, "Captain and I wondered if we could drag you out of TFCC for a moment. There's something urgent we need to tell you."

"Do we have to do this now, COS? We're just getting spooled up for the strikes."

"It can't wait, Admiral," Vandegrift interjected. The admiral's antennae went up even higher as he walked with them toward his cabin.

"All right, what is it you need to tell me?" he asked.

"Admiral, it's about this alleged assassin," Vandegrift began.

"Not that again? Captain, I've just been through this with the chief of staff and CAG. What's this, the tag team approach?"

"No, sir, it's not. We've just come up with some new information. As you know, we'd all but discounted this story by Lieutenant O'Connor—she just has too many reasons to be confused, or worse, have an ax to grind—"

"Fine, I know all that," he interrupted.

"Yes, Admiral, but just as a precaution, we've been following Lieutenant Holden to try to determine if he's doing anything suspicious. We haven't put a close tail on him—didn't want to alert him to our efforts—but we've maintained a sense of where he's been and what he's done."

"So far you haven't told me anything that makes it worth me leaving TFCC when we're about to conduct the biggest military operation this country has conducted in over a decade."

"Yes, sir," the captain responded. "Admiral, we know Holden was in the SEALs' work area on the hangar bay. We talked to the petty officer who handles their weapons, and he told us Holden drew two weapons earlier today, a nine millimeter and a 45-caliber. He said he was going to practice firing them to get ready for his CSAR mission."

"So far I don't see anything all that alarming."

"Admiral, we don't let folks just shoot weapons any time they want to," Vandegrift continued. "We schedule FAM fires for our folks who use weapons—the MAAs, the SEALs and others—several times a week. There hasn't been a FAM fire time scheduled since Holden drew these weapons. The rules are clear: you draw your weapon right before a FAM fire, use it, and then return it right away. When you go on a mission you do the same thing. You don't just check out two weapons and keep them indefinitely."

"Has anyone asked Holden what he thinks he's doing?" Robinson asked. "These SEALs are kind of independent operators anyway."

"No, we didn't want to alert him," the captain replied. "The other disturbing thing, Admiral, is he checked out an awful lot of ammo—several boxes—and he checked out a walkie-talkie."

"That much ammo? Why would he want a walkie-talkie?"

"We're not certain. But it stands to reason he might be interested in knowing your exact movements. Admiral, we've got to at least complicate his efforts to reach you."

"All right, but we're going to have to keep me in constant contact with TFCC. We must stay on our timeline to launch strikes. And if we are this sure Holden is an assassin, Captain, don't you want your men to pick him up?"

"I do, Admiral. I talked it over with my JAG and with my master-at-arms. I think I can find a reasonable pretense to bring him in—just the fact that he's violated ship's policy on weapons should be enough to at least bring him down to the master-at-arms office for questioning. But while we do that, we have to keep you moving."

"All right. You two have made your point. I'll agree to move, but you have to come up with a way to keep me in contact with TFCC."

"We can use the walkie-talkies on a discreet channel. Unless Holden keeps changing freqs, he'll never land on yours. We won't do or say anything that reveals your location. All we'll do is provide a constant flow keeping you informed of the strike preparations."

"Let's do it that way then," Robinson replied. "COS, I want you here in TFCC. Captain, I know you need to be on the bridge. I'll travel with the flag lieutenant, the master chief, and one other person who can handle a weapon. Who do you recommend, COS?"

"Admiral, air ops is pretty good with weapons; I think he shot pistol at the Academy."

"Then grab him—one guy with a gun should be enough—and get him down to the armory ASAP so the captain can have his people issue him a weapon. I also want ops o with me while I'm on the move. I think the five of us can keep a low enough profile."

"Yes, sir, we'll make that happen," the chief of staff responded.

* * *

Four decks below, Rick Holden had planned his mission as best he could. He knew he could use his walkie-talkie to keep up to speed on the admiral's location and movements. He also knew that if he stayed on the fringes of the Blue Tile Area he'd be able to close in on him.

Holden hadn't worked this out precisely—there were just too many possibilities—but his initial thought was if he could catch the admiral in transit to or from the Flag Bridge, or catch him alone in his cabin, he'd have a good chance of disabling him.

Once he subdued him it got a bit murkier. He didn't want to kill the man. His hope was that once he subdued him he could tell him that the chain of command had found him out. After he'd done that, the admiral might just admit what he was doing. Keeping him from launching the strikes was the key.

This business with the submarine contact was puzzling. Was it actually a contact or just a false alarm? With the ship at General Quarters, his movements would be somewhat restricted—more hatches to open and close—but that wouldn't be a major factor. What he needed to focus on was stopping the admiral from launching strikes. He left the safety of the corner of the hangar bay and looked for a ladder to climb.

* * *

On the O-3 level, Anne O'Connor and Brian McDonald knew they needed to find Holden and find him fast. On a ship as large as an aircraft carrier, this effort initially seemed all but impossible. But as it sunk in that their mission was to keep Holden from attacking the admiral, they began to realize if they simply kept themselves close to the admiral they'd have a good chance of protecting him. But they had to be careful not to let Robinson or anyone on his staff know what they were doing.

The sub alert baffled O'Connor. It seemed inconceivable that an Iranian Kilo could have slipped out of Bandar Abbas undetected. The United States just had too many assets looking for these subs. She knew many of her fellow aviators were airborne looking for that Kilo.

"Anne, are we agreed on our plan?" McDonald asked.

"I think so. We'll cycle through the Blue Tile Area every fifteen minutes or so, close to each other, but not together. Between the two of us, if Holden is there, we'll see him."

"Do you still want to make first contact?"

"I do. I think it would be a lot more natural if I went up to him and started talking. Once I get him engaged, you can close in and help me stop him," O'Connor replied.

"We haven't really decided how we're going to do that."

"I think we might be a lot closer than we think. The thing he thinks he has going for him is surprise. If he's confronted, and if we tell him we're on to him, he might just give it up right there."

"I suppose that's what we've got to count on, but if it starts to turn into a fight, we—you—need to back away before things start to get out of control," McDonald replied.

"I'll watch out for myself."

"Okay, ready to move?"

"Yeah, let's go," O'Connor replied as they headed aft.

Chapter 86

Jahani was receiving calls from Velayati several times a day as the crisis continued to unfold. There could be no doubt now the Americans were preparing for an imminent attack. He wanted to ensure his men were ready to carry out their mission immediately after the pigs struck so that there would be no doubt in the Americans' minds they were paying for striking the Islamic Republic.

He was so sure they would have to act soon—perhaps within a few hours—he wanted to be certain they were ready. He decided to send them a short communication. He entered the first number.

* * *

It was not yet dawn. Hala Karomi was sitting on the Metro a few minutes out of Union Station when his iPhone went off. Karomi scrolled through the text message once, then twice:

> HALA, YOU ARE TO BE READY TO CARRY OUT YOUR MISSION IN THE NEXT FEW HOURS. WE WILL STRIKE HARD. READY YOUR AGENT AND BE PREPARED TO SET IT OFF.

Karomi looked at the message with relief and satisfaction; relief he wasn't ordered to carry out his attack now—this foolish riding back and forth on the Metro had put him in the worst possible position to do that—and satisfaction he was actually going to conduct his attack. As the train arrived at Union Station, he got off quickly to return to his hotel.

* * *

In New York and in San Diego, Mejid Homani and Achmed Boleshari received identical messages and felt a thrill similar to Karomi's.

Chapter 87

Carl Vinson had been at General Quarters since the sub sighting, and the ship was locked down with very little movement about her decks. Passageways and ladders that were typically full of people coming and going were now virtually deserted as all of the carrier's officers, chiefs, and sailors were at their battle stations.

Dressed in his desert camouflage uniform, Rick Holden stood out on the hangar bay, but he counted on the fact the crew was accustomed to SEALs being just about anywhere. He knew once he began his assent to the ship's upper decks, dogged-down hatches or groups of sailors in damage control parties would impede his progress. Therefore, he looked for a way to get to the Blue Tile Area as quickly possible. He walked aft until he spotted the Captain's Ladder. Reserved for the captain and the flag staff, he knew it would be unused during GQ. He could make his way up that ladder and get to where he thought he'd find the admiral.

* * *

On the O-3 level, Brian McDonald and Anne O'Connor were starting to exhaust ways to patrol the Blue Tile Area without looking suspicious themselves. They were in their flight suits, and both had gone to their paralofts to grab their helmet bags, survival vests and other gear so they could look like they were on the way to their ready rooms.

They were in the passageway at the far aft end of the Blue Tile Area. It led outboard to the Captain's Ladder going up to the flight deck. They had a clear view of the starboard side fore-and-aft passageway, as well as of the door to the Captain's Ladder.

"Anne, I think this MAA is getting awfully suspicious of our movements. We'd better go around to the port side for a while."

"I agree," she replied. "Maybe we don't need to cycle back and forth so often. We can split up, and one of us can watch each end of the passageway. There's no way he could get by us then."

McDonald reflected that this might put O'Connor in jeopardy if she ended up having to confront Holden alone. "No, I think that we should stick together for now."

* * *

Holden un-dogged the hatch, and began to work his way up the three ladders. He put his hand on the weapon in his belt—it was there. He reached behind his back and felt for the other one. It was there as well.

O'Connor and McDonald were ready to cycle back to the other side of the Blue Tile Area when the door leading to the Captain's Ladder opened. O'Connor was closest to it, while McDonald was on the other side of a half-bulkhead further inboard. Suddenly, Holden emerged.

"Anne!" he shouted. "What are you doing here?"

"Oh, just going down to my ready room," she lied. "I thought you'd be in the HSM-73 Ready Room getting ready for a CSAR event."

"I'm heading that way now. I just had to check with my guys down on the hangar bay."

Holden didn't like lying to O'Connor, that's why he'd fended her off when she'd tried to see him. He'd let his guard down when he'd sat with her over lunch, but the encounter with the MAA earlier had shaken his confidence and he was relieved to see a friendly face.

"Want to walk there together?" O'Connor asked.

She knew McDonald was on the other side of the bulkhead. She didn't think Holden saw him yet. They hadn't really thought this through beyond catching up with Holden. They just hoped he would stop doing what he was going to do.

"No, I don't want to hold you up. I may go up toward CVIC for a minute and then head on back," he said.

O'Connor knew if he headed forward he would be that much closer to the admiral. Putting her hand on his arm, she tried to delay him.

"Gee, Rick, I thought you could give me a minute or two. Can't you just walk me back to my ready room and talk for a minute? Honestly, it will just be a minute." She kept her hand on his arm.

"Look, Anne, I'd like to talk, but I have something important to do, and I need to do it alone." He gently pushed her hand away.

"Rick, I just need a minute."

"Sorry."

O'Connor wasn't getting anywhere with this tactic. Holden was almost at the bulkhead and would see McDonald. She swallowed hard and said, "I know what's up, Rick."

That stopped him.

She stepped toward him. "I know sometimes people may ask you to do something, and I know it may not always be something you want to do. I want you to know that if you don't want to do it, you don't have to."

Holden's mind was racing. What did she mean? Could she know anything about his mission?

"Anne, I'm not sure what you mean. Do you think I have some sort of an agenda?" he asked.

"Rick, I just think…well…people sometimes get put into positions they don't want to get put into and they make poor decisions. But until you do something wrong there's no harm done."

"I'm not exactly sure what you're talking about."

"There's nothing you've done that can't be undone. You can turn back now. Just don't do this."

How could she know? He was close to O'Connor now, as she had put her body between him and the hatch leading to where McDonald was lying in wait. O'Connor's sweating made her scent stronger. That scent. Holden had smelled that before. In his stateroom!

He grabbed her arm.

"Do what, Anne?"

"Rick, just don't do anything. You need to think it through before you act." She twisted her arm, but he didn't relax his grip.

"What do you think I'm going to do?"

"Ouch, Rick, you're hurting me. Stop!"

Suddenly, McDonald rushed out from behind the bulkhead.

"Let her go!" he commanded.

"You too?" Holden said, stepping back from O'Connor.

"It's over," McDonald said.

"I don't think so. You're meddling in something too big for you to even know about. Back away!" Holden shouted as he moved toward the hatch that led to the War Room.

McDonald put his body in front of him. "I said you're not going anywhere."

"Watch me!" Holden shouted as he pushed past McDonald and made for the opening. McDonald threw himself in Holden's way. Holden grabbed him and that was all it took. Both men were on each other. At first, McDonald held his own, but Holden started landing more and more blows, trying to beat McDonald into submission.

McDonald found the wall behind him with his foot and used it to launch himself at Holden, slamming his body against him and pinning him to the bulkhead. He heard the *crack* as Holden's head hit the steel.

Momentarily dazed as McDonald leaned his weight on him, Holden slumped, causing McDonald to loosen his hold. That was all Holden needed. He spun around and pinned McDonald against the bulkhead and began hammering him with his fists.

"You couldn't leave it alone, could you?" Holden gasped.

O'Connor hadn't been able to do much as two men went toe-to-toe, but now she leaped on Holden's back, locking her left arm around his neck while slamming his head with her right fist.

Having her on his back shocked Holden, but his adrenaline was so high that as McDonald slumped down against the bulkhead, he wheeled and flung O'Connor against the opposite bulkhead. As he did, the pistol in the small of his back fell out and clattered to the deck.

The combination of a few moments of relief from Holden's blows, and seeing him fling O'Connor off of him like a rag doll, fired McDonald with new energy as he came at Holden. They continued to pound each other.

O'Connor broke out of her daze and tried to grab the gun. Holden saw what she was doing and lunged at her, but McDonald grabbed Holden's leg, keeping him from reaching her.

O'Connor finally was able to grab the gun.

"Run, Anne, run!" McDonald shouted, and O'Connor scrambled away, heading back down the Captain's Ladder.

Holden slammed McDonald repeatedly against the bulkhead, trying to subdue him so he could catch O'Connor.

McDonald knew he couldn't fight back much longer and finally wrapped his left arm around Holden's neck and held on.

Holden ripped McDonald's arm away and threw him on the ground. Then he landed on him with both knees.

Snap.

McDonald suddenly went cold as Holden's knees snapped his arm right above the elbow.

Holden collapsed on the deck, panting.

Holden needed to ensure that McDonald was no longer a threat. He looked around for a place to hide him. He spotted the Captain's galley a few feet away. Rarely used when the ship was underway, the galley and the entire in-port cabin area were sure to be deserted during GQ.

Holden opened the door and dragged McDonald into the galley. He let him go, and he slumped on the deck. Ripping through the shelves in the galley pantry, Holden found a roll of duct tape and began to bind McDonald.

"Rick, look, it's not too late to stop. You can't do what you plan to do to Admiral Robinson. Don't you see, its murder, pure and simple? The officers around the admiral will shoot you if you try to get close to him, and the Navy will execute you if you succeed."

"How did you know I was going to do this?" Holden asked as he continued to wrap the duct tape around McDonald's feet. "Did Anne read my e-mails?"

"Yes, she did, but it's not her fault. She never intended to, but once she read them, what did you expect her to do?"

"Listen, I'm not necessarily trying to kill Robinson," Holden replied, "but I will if I have to. These strikes against Iranian bases you all have been practicing—they're illegal."

McDonald grimaced in pain as Holden moved his arms and bound them with duct tape.

"The only strikes authorized are the strikes against the terrorist training camps. The admiral is intent on starting his own war, and he's lied to everyone on the staff and to everyone on the ship."

"I don't believe you. Why do you want to assassinate him?"

"Come on Brian, think! How hard would it be to get a 'foreign agent' into a Navy uniform? And don't you think it's a little strange no one has seen an execute order for these strikes—it's all verbal between Admiral Flowers and Admiral Robinson? Do you think there's any other reason for the admiral to

put the entire strike group into radio silence for this long? Add it up. One man
has five thousand of you duped."

"Rick, no, you—" but McDonald was cut off as Holden wrapped the duct
tape around his mouth.

That complete, Holden dragged McDonald into the far reaches of the Cap-
tain's galley, laying him out in the most out-of-the-way corner he could find.
McDonald struggled against the duct tape, if for no other reason than to show
Holden his spirit hadn't been completely broken.

Holden turned off the galley lights and closed the door behind him. Then
he stood in the narrow passageway inside the captain's in-port cabin collecting
his thoughts. Where had O'Connor run away to? Should he go after her, or go
after the admiral?

CHAPTER 88

Jefferson City had lost contact with *Carl Vinson* as soon as Willard turned his boat's bow toward it and increased speed to twenty knots. His exec, weapons officer, and navigator now huddled over the chart table trying to come up with their best estimate of where the carrier might be. But every instinct told Willard he was closing the carrier.

* * *

Several miles south, Lieutenant Commander Bob Labuda, the pilot of Battlecat 705, was the scene of action commander at the datum that the two Hornets had reported. His Seahawk was armed with a full sonobuoy load and had arrived at the datum first. The helo's pilots were determined to locate the sub before it attacked their carrier.

Soon, another MH-60R from *Carl Vinson* arrived. The three helos continued working the contact area. They had seeded the area with an array of passive sonobuoys and were now using their dipping sonars to listen for the submarine.

* * *

Unbeknownst to the helos working the datum, *Jefferson City* had cleared the datum—by miles. Willard had no knowledge he was being hunted.

His exec came up from the chart table and stood at the captain's side. "Captain, by our calculations we've been closing the carrier for some time. We estimate we're now less than ten thousand yards away."

"Good estimate?" Willard asked.

"Really solid, Captain. We could even be a little closer. We all agree that we should take a look."

"Let's keep driving for a bit longer. I only want to have to take one look."

* * *

High above, Labuda continued to direct the actions of the helos at the datum. They had been joined by another helo, this one from one of their Arleigh Burke destroyers. The buoy field, however, remained completely cold and the dipping sonars were not finding a thing in passive mode.

* * *

"Officer of the deck, make your speed five knots, make your depth sixty feet."

The OOD repeated the order back and then gave his orders to the diving officer and the helmsman. *Jefferson City* slowed and began her gradual assent. Finally, she was at depth and on speed.

"Up scope."

The captain popped the handles of the periscope and spun 360 degrees. Finally, he looked in a northerly direction.

"There it is; it's the carrier! Bearing 342...range...eight thousand yards and opening. OOD, have a look!"

The captain moved away, and the OOD stepped up to the eyepiece. He nodded to the captain.

"Down scope," Willard ordered. "Make your depth one hundred feet, increase speed to fifteen knots."

* * *

"Ninety-nine, Saberhawk 48. Radar sinker, repeat, radar sinker. Bearing 350, range sixty-five hundred yards from my posit! Vectoring to the datum," the pilot shouted.

The news electrified the crews of each of the four helos working the contact area. If Saberhawk had actually seen a periscope, then the Kilo submarine was only a few miles from *Carl Vinson*. Labuda knew that he needed to get to the sub fast.

"Saberhawk, Battlecat 705, roger. When you get to datum, I want you to put in a four-buoy field and then put in the rest of your DIFAR buoys on a line just north of that. Then I want you to clear the datum and move to the east. You're carrying two torps, right?"

"Affirmative on the torps; we'll call as soon as we're clear."

"Battlecat 701, stand by to dip as soon as we get a buoy hot," Labuda ordered.

"WILCO."

"Okay folks, we're not gonna lose this guy," Labuda said.

The aircraft went through their procedures, spitting a new round of sonobuoys, knowing now that they had a fresh datum they would have a much higher probability of localizing and attacking the Kilo submarine that was after their carrier.

* * *

"Suggestions?" Willard looked toward his OOD and to the other officers standing in the Control Room.

"Captain, I recommend we continue on this course for six to eight more minutes. At that point we'll be set up for a close-in shot on her screws. Take one quick look when we get there, and we'll have a perfect firing solution," his OOD responded.

"I agree," his exec said. "We've got it set up just right, Captain. Thus far, I think they're unaware we're here."

* * *

"Battlecat 705, this is Saberhawk 48, hot contact, I say again, hot contact on DIFAR 13 and DIFAR 28. I say again, HOT CONTACT!"

Chapter 89

Anne O'Connor didn't know how long she'd been sitting in the Joint Air Operations Center. She'd retreated there after the fight. Holden's gun was beside her. It was dark inside the JAOC save for the glow of a few computer screens.

What had Holden done to McDonald? Had he killed him? She couldn't live with the thought. She wanted to go back up to the O-3 level and see what had become of him, but she couldn't do it, not yet.

Thoughts of McDonald and of how much he had done for her came rushing back. From his first intervention at the Naval Academy; to his continuing encouragement throughout her career as a midshipman, as a flight student, and as a naval aviator; to his agreeing to help her stop Holden; she thought back to how much she'd depended on him. Now she'd let him down and had caused him to be beaten to a pulp—or worse.

Those thoughts filled her with sudden resolve. Summoning up all the courage she could muster, she cracked open the JAOC door and listened. She had to stop Holden herself.

* * *

Admiral Robinson stalked out of TFCC again and entered his cabin, followed by CAG, the CO and XO of the Stingers, and his own chief of staff. He waited until the door closed, then exploded.

"Chief of Staff, what is so damned important you all have to drag me out of TFCC again!"

"Admiral, we've come up with more information that bears directly on Lieutenant Holden. While we doubted Lieutenant O'Connor from the beginning, we don't believe she doubted herself, because she's missing."

"You don't think Holden killed her, do you?"

"No, sir. We think she might have gone after Holden herself."

"That changes things, Chief of Staff," the admiral replied, He turned, left them behind, and headed back into TFCC.

* * *

O'Connor figured that the admiral was probably in TFCC, especially since the ship was at GQ. The MAA stood outside the door to the admiral's cabin. He wouldn't be in a position to stop Holden if he tried to get to the admiral while he was in TFCC. All Holden had to do was get into the War Room, and once he was in there, he had a clear path to TFCC.

How could she stop him? She figured if she confronted Holden when he came up to the Blue Tile Area, it might take him some time to get his bearings, come up with a plan, and then go after the admiral. She counted on that time to allow her to catch up with him and stop him.

Or was he coming after her? She had his gun. Was it the only one he had? If it was, he could do nothing to the admiral until he got it back. Would he be looking for her? She decided she couldn't count on his not having another gun and just wait for him to look for her. She had to go after him before he got to Admiral Robinson.

It occurred to her to check the gun she'd picked up. She hadn't fired a weapon since plebe year at the Naval Academy, but she felt confident she could handle it. She checked the clip. There was ammo enough for what she needed to do.

But could she actually do it? Could she shoot another human being—even one with such evil intentions—in cold blood? She didn't know what she would do. She hoped her instincts would take over. With that, she crept out of the JAOC.

CHAPTER 90

Mejid Homani could almost walk from his hotel room to the United Nations in his sleep. It was a half hour before dawn when the message to be ready appeared on his iPhone. He decided to go to the United Nations and wait for the final notification. He rolled out of bed and went to the closet. He unzipped the backpack. His agent was secure.

First light was just breaking as Homani walked along on the nearly deserted streets, the only signs of life an occasional jogger or the ubiquitous garbage trucks. He walked quickly, not just because he was focused on his mission, but because he feared the New York streets. He was happy his mission would soon be over, and that he'd be able to return to the Islamic Republic.

Homani had never been to the United Nations this early and was surprised to find the building was not yet open. Resolved to be as close as he could be, he walked across the street and entered a small coffee shop, selecting a spot where he could watch the concourse doors. He wanted to be one of the first to enter.

* * *

In Washington, Hala Karomi didn't have the same leisurely time that Homani had in New York. Near panic when his iPhone went off, he fidgeted nervously as the Metro approached Union Station. Why had he gotten into this idiotic habit of riding the train? Sure, it calmed his nerves, but now he was separated from his agent, and Jahani might instruct him to carry out his attacks at any time. This stupid diversion might cause him to fail to carry out his mission.

Karomi bolted off the train as soon as it entered Union Station. He crossed the overpass and headed down the stairs to wait for the train that would take him the three stops back to his hotel. He would then have to rush up to his room, grab his agent, get back on the Metro, and return to the spot he had selected to release his agent. Karomi prayed fervently that he'd make it back to Union Station in time.

* * *

In San Diego, Achmed Boleshari was awakened from a deep sleep as his iPhone went off. It was only three-thirty in the morning, and he knew there would be no shoppers in Horton Plaza at this early hour.

He hoped Jahani understood the time difference between San Diego and Iran. If Jahani gave his next order in just an hour, Boleshari would be releasing his agent in a deserted plaza. Surely he didn't intend this. Jahani had emphasized how critical timing was to every operation and how important it was to carry out his instructions to the letter. Now those two considerations collided.

Boleshari was questioning his own courage and that thought pained him. He had reconciled what he intended to do, and had wanted to deploy his agent on a U.S. Navy ship at the San Diego Naval Station. He had thought it through during the taxi ride to the station's gate. But when he'd gotten to the gate, he'd been surprised. Instead of the lone sentry who usually manned the gate, a full security force: armed sentries, military working dogs, and Marines in full battle dress had confronted him. A sign announced the base was in "THREATCON ALPHA."

Boleshari had instructed the taxi driver to make a U-turn and drop him on Harbor Drive. After over an hour of agonizing, he walked north along Harbor Drive, back toward his hotel.

Now he cursed that decision. If he'd been bolder, he would be in position hiding somewhere on that sprawling base and would deploy his agent on one of the American ships. Now that wouldn't happen. Instead, he might be ordered to deploy his agent in an empty or nearly empty shopping mall. He was becoming increasingly frustrated as he trudged along the dark downtown streets. The only other humans there were the street people who slept in the doorways of the stores along Market Street and the area near Horton Plaza.

CHAPTER 91

"Admiral, we're ready to move."

"All right," Robinson replied. His staff could tell he still didn't like the fact he had to abandon TFCC.

"Chief of Staff, I want to know absolutely everything that happens. Work with the captain and CAG to try to move the strikes earlier."

"Will do, Admiral," Sampson replied.

"I want to know about this damned submarine, too. I see a lot of excitement, but all anybody has is passive contact. Has anyone debriefed those Hornet pilots who said they saw a periscope?"

"Yes sir," Bill Durham replied. "Intel officer says they were debriefed down in CVIC. Rocky says they're sure of what they saw."

"Has Rocky got any imagery of the base at Bandar Abbas to confirm that there's a Kilo missing?"

"Not yet, he's hoping to get something soon."

"Yeah, and I'm hoping to find a Mercedes in my driveway when I get back home."

"Yes, Admiral. The Master-at-Arms will precede us when we head up to the Flag Bridge. He has a side arm, and air ops has one too."

"I've got your walkie-talkie to keep us in contact with TFCC, Admiral," Mike Lumme said.

"All right, make sure you do."

* * *

Less than twenty feet away, Rick Holden moved furtively through the O-3 level port-side passageway. Normally a busy thoroughfare, it was deserted now that GQ was set.

328

Holden thought about using the back entrance to TFCC. Was it locked from the inside? He was fairly certain the admiral was in TFCC. But if he weren't, he would tip his hand.

He rejected that idea. He might confront and surprise the admiral, or he might just run into a group of his staff and then be stuck in TFCC vainly trying to explain what he was doing there. He decided he would continue forward, cross over via the athwartships passageway, and then approach the Blue Tile Area from the other direction.

Holden stole across the passageway. One person walking through could foil his plan. What would he say if he was asked what he was doing there? He couldn't begin to think of a believable story.

* * *

Durham opened the door and signaled the MAA to start moving aft. He followed, letting Lumme go behind him, followed by the admiral. Air ops brought up the rear.

CHAPTER 92

The words "hot contact" electrified every crew member in the four helos at datum, as well as everyone in the Sea Combat Commander Module. Their strike group had bloodied—and had been bloodied by—Iran. Well over a hundred Iranian sailors had met their deaths in these waters less than twenty-four hours ago in the duel between *Shiloh* and the two Iranian frigates. Jim Hughes believed this Kilo submarine intended to send *Carl Vinson* to the bottom of the ocean. The new datum was seven thousand yards astern of the carrier.

The four helos were flying close enough together for each to see all the others. Although Labuda had directed altitude separation between each aircraft, every pilot had to take on the additional responsibility of not colliding with one of his playmates.

Labuda had flown over—"on-topped"—DIFAR 28, one of the hot buoys, and made that the anchor of his tactical picture. From his perch at five hundred feet, he directed the actions of the other aircraft.

"Battlecat 701, take angels one, mark on top DIFAR 28 and then lay a barrier north of it, three-thousand-yard spacing."

"701, WILCO."

"Saberhawk, keep to the east while 701 spits his buoys. I want you ready with your torps once we localize this guy."

"48, WILCO."

Labuda continued to issue instructions.

"Battlecat 701, as soon as we get clearance from X-ray Zulu we'll bring you in to dip. When you do, I want you to dip right on the contact."

"WILCO" the pilot replied. Thus far, Labuda was conducting passive tracking of the sub, trying not to alert the Kilo to the fact that there were aircraft prosecuting it. Once the sub's location was fairly well refined, Labuda would ask the commodore for authorization to use active, pinging, DICASS sonobuoys, as well as the active mode of the helos' dipping sonar. Once the active sensors were deployed, he knew the Kilo would become evasive.

As Battlecat 701 spit out more passive sonobuoys, the other aircraft at datum continued to try to zero in on the Kilo's location and Labuda passed this information back to the Zulu module. They were coming closer to gaining an attack solution on the submarine.

* * *

Joe Willard continued to press toward *Carl Vinson*. At fifteen knots, his passive sensors had to contend with so much own-boat's noise they didn't pick up the sounds of the passive sonobuoys hitting the water.

Jefferson City was ready. Willard had trained these men, and he knew that once they got him in position to fire his torpedoes, they would find their mark in the carrier's huge screws.

* * *

"X-ray Zulu, Battlecat 705, we're only holding intermittent contact on our passive buoys. But it looks like the Kilo is continuing to close the carrier. We need to go active."

Jim Hughes took the radio himself. The Kilo was just fifty-five hundred yards behind the carrier now; there was no advantage in trying to remain passive. They had to go active and localize and attack him now.

"Battlecat 705, you're cleared to go active."

"This is 705, Roger. Request authorization to drop torpedoes when we have him localized."

Permission to conduct a torpedo attack was normally issued only after a contact had been localized with active buoys and sonars. The problem was moving too fast for that. Hughes needed to get this sub before it got the carrier.

"Battlecat 705, you have torpedo release!" Hughes shouted.

* * *

Once they heard the torpedo release call, the crew of Battlecat 701 didn't wait for further instructions from Battlecat 705. They knew Saberhawk was the only helo at datum with torpedoes and they knew it was their job to localize the sub with their dipping sonar. They descended rapidly from five hundred feet and arrived in a hover at sixty feet right on the best datum that they had.

* * *

Willard considered his options.

"Navigator, what's your estimated distance to the carrier?"

"Unless she's picked up speed, inside of six thousand yards, maybe less than five thousand."

"Weps, how do you feel about a torp shot from here?"

"Would like to get a little closer, but we can take it from here."

"We'll hit the screws?"

"Yes, Captain. I think that—"

"CAPTAIN, SONAR, I HAVE ACTIVE SONAR CLOSE ABOARD. SOUNDS LIKE A DIPPER!" the sonar operator shouted.

Now there was no doubt. Willard knew that helos were there, and worse, had them located. There was no time to discuss options or weigh alternatives. They had two choices: run or shoot.

* * *

It took several *pings* before the sensor operator in the back of Battlecat 701 had solid contact on the submarine.

"Pilot, Senso, I've got him! Bearing 035, twelve hundred yards, down doppler!"

"705, Battlecat 701, solid contact on my ball. Bearing 035, twelve hundred yards from my posit, down doppler."

Labuda assessed the tactical situation. The contact Battlecat 701 had was close, close enough to convince him they had the sub nailed. Down doppler meant that the sub was moving away from where the helo was dipping—toward the carrier. Before long, the helo would lose contact as the sub slipped out of range of its dipping sonar. Labuda made his decision. He keyed the mike.

* * *

Aboard *Carl Vinson*, Jim Hughes knew that in addition to the aircraft prosecuting the datum, the carrier had one other weapon to escape from the submarine—speed. He didn't need to consult with the admiral's staff to give the aircraft prosecuting the datum permission to use both active sensors and torpedoes; that was his job. However, he did need to motivate them to use that speed. He picked up the Bogen phone and called TFCC.

"Flag TAO."

"This is the commodore; I need to speak with the admiral."

Clack, clack, clack. The first aircraft shot down the catapult.

"Sir, he's not here," the TAO replied.

"Well, where is he?"

"He's on the move. Chief of staff is here. Do you want to speak with him?"

"Absolutely!"

The harried TAO handed the Bogen phone to Sampson.

"COS here."

"George, this damned sub is just five or six thousand yards astern. Aircraft are pounding him with active sonar and active buoys and are trying to get a torpedo shot off, but he may shoot soon. We've got to get the ship moving to the north as fast as we can."

"Commodore, admiral's not here now and he left explicit instructions to hold this course and speed. We're launching our strikers, and if we speed up, we'll run out of sea room before we get them all launched."

"If we don't outrun the sub, the aircraft we're launching may not have a carrier to come home to!" Hughes shouted.

"I know that. You've got four aircraft at datum pounding the hell out of him. I can't move the ship any faster, not unless I talk with the admiral."

"Well talk with him, dammit!" the commodore yelled.

"All right, Jim, all right! I'll call you back."

Clack, clack, clack. The second aircraft roared down the cat.

Hughes slammed the Bogen phone down. He was powerless to do anything at his end. It was all up to the aircraft at datum.

"Get the admiral on the walkie-talkie," Sampson said to the staff TAO, "and hurry up."

* * *

"Saberhawk 48, Battlecat 701 has solid contact, set up for torp drops," Labuda commanded.

The pilots of Battlecat 701 and Saberhawk 48 both clicked their radio transmitters twice, indicating they heard the order.

* * *

Willard balanced his two options and found one wanting. He made his decision. "Slow to five knots."

He wasn't going to run. He was going to shoot.

"Sonar, get me a solid bearing on the carrier. We'll shoot on that bearing."

"Roger, Skipper."

"OOD, I want two straight runners. Fire down the bearing line. Carrier is going to be moving away from us, so I don't want any delay."

"Yes, Captain."

They stood transfixed, waiting for *Jefferson City*'s speed to bleed off. Twelve knots, ten knots...the pinging of the dipping sonar and the active sonobuoys echoed in their ears. Eight knots...seven. The torpedo room reported the number one and number three tubes had been flooded.

"Captain, sonar has good contact on the carrier. Bearing 025."

"OOD, fire down the bearing line!" Willard shouted.

First torpedo, *whoosh.* The boat shuddered. Then another, as it shuddered again. The water slugs ejected the two huge Mk 48 torpedoes from their tubes. *Jefferson City*'s crew held on as the fish swam away.

"Officer of the Deck, let's get out of here," the captain said. "Turn, speed up, and go deep."

"Helmsman, come right to course 060. Increase speed to twenty-five knots. Make your depth one hundred fifty feet," the OOD commanded.

* * *

"TORPEDOES IN THE WATER, TORPEDOES IN THE WATER!" Flying at five hundred feet above the water, and dropping sonobuoys ahead of the contact, the crew of Battlecat 705 saw the torpedoes first.

Battlecat 701 had solid active contact on the sub, and Labuda had already ordered Saberhawk 48 to close the datum. Lieutenant Pete Howe and Lieutenant Frank Meyers bore down on the contact, ready to drop their Mk 46 torpedoes

"Drop 48, drop!" Labuda shouted, reinforcing the instructions he'd already given them.

"Fifteen seconds to fly-to-point," Meyers shouted. Howe continued to bear down, following the number one needle on his compass, while Meyers held his finger over the torpedo release button.

"Torpedo away," Meyers said as Howe wrapped the Seahawk into a hard right turn and began to time the first fish. They would drop a second torp as soon as the first had run out for the appropriate number of minutes.

CHAPTER 93

The dark blue curtain hanging at the end of the Blue Tile Area gave Rick Holden perfect cover to observe what was going on. He could see up and down the fore-and-aft passageway. He saw the MAA standing in front of the door to the admiral's cabin. There had been no movement for a while. He knew strike aircraft were being launched, and he didn't have much time. The sound of the catapult shuttle was incessant, with aircraft being launched a minute apart.

He'd decided if he circled around on the port side again he could approach the Blue Tile Area from the other direction and then bolt into the War Room before the MAA saw him. He'd learned the combination to the War Room door cipher lock listening to staff members tell others who were new to the staff how to get in. Once in, he'd have a clear path to the admiral.

Holden was about to begin circling around when the he saw the MAA heading aft away from him. Soon, other figures emerged—the admiral, the aide, and others. The group headed aft, and he saw them take a left turn and head outboard toward the Captain's Ladder. As soon as the last person in the group turned the corner, he set out after them.

* * *

Anne O'Connor had reached the top of the Captain's Ladder and turned the handle of the door leading to the passageway she'd been in a short time earlier. She looked left and right. No one was in sight. She walked a few steps that way, into the passageway outside of the captain's galley. No McDonald. She was elated. If Brian McDonald wasn't lying dead or wounded in this passageway, she hoped it meant he'd escaped from Holden. She felt relief beyond words.

But where had Holden gone? She wasn't sure, but she thought he might be moving toward TFCC. As she looked forward, she saw a group of people emerging from the War Room with the MAA leading the way. What should she do? She didn't want them to see her stalking around the Blue Tile Area with a weapon.

She took a left and hid behind the dark blue curtain marking the aft limit of the Blue Tile Area. She peeked through the narrow crack between the curtain and the bulkhead.

She recognized Admiral Robinson. She pressed herself against the bulkhead. If they continued straight ahead beyond the curtain, they'd be on top of her. She prayed they'd turn left and miss her.

She heard the footsteps continue to come nearer. *Please, oh please, let them turn left.*

She sensed the entourage turning left, probably going to the Flag Bridge. She peered through the crack between the curtain and the bulkhead to try to identify the people following the admiral. As her eyes left the last man behind the admiral, she let them drift back up the passageway. She saw another figure. It was Holden. He'd found the admiral and was sneaking up behind him.

She flattened herself against the bulkhead. She had only one recourse; she had to follow Holden. If the admiral wound up on the Flag Bridge and Holden caught up with him, he'd be a sitting duck. She was now sure he had a weapon; otherwise, he wouldn't be following the admiral.

She waited until she no longer heard his footsteps and then peered around the curtain. He was gone. Now it was up to her stop him before he shot the admiral. There was no more stalking and no more finesse. It had to be a headlong rush to stop him.

She gripped the weapon as she swung out from behind the curtain. No Holden. She wound her way around the passageway, past the Captain's Galley, and finally up to the Captain's Ladder. She headed up the ladder and then hesitated before she opened the door to the O-4 level. She cracked the door open and peered out. No Holden.

She started up the next ladder. When she reached the top, she cracked open the door the same way she had opened the previous one. She saw no sign of life as she stepped out onto the O-5 level passageway.

Had she missed them? Why was she so sure that they were headed for the Flag Bridge? Maybe they were just outdistancing her. She picked up her pace.

She turned the corner on the O-5 level and moved up the next ladder. Halfway up, she looked up and saw feet on the exposed ladder above her and saw the hint of a desert uniform stuffed into tan desert boots. It had to be Holden. He was almost on the O-7 level, just one away from the Flag Bridge.

Still holding her weapon with two hands, she turned and covered the few steps to the next ladder. When she was three steps up the ladder, she brought her gun up and pointed it at Holden.

As she got to the middle of the ladder, Holden heard her and turned around. His eyes met hers, uncomprehending. His weapon was still tucked in his belt. There was no way he could draw it in time to shoot her before she shot him. He bolted and headed up the last ladder toward O-8 level.

O'Connor chased him. He was out of her sight in seconds. She bounded up the ladder and got ready to turn the corner—

WHAM. The sound was deafening as a shot rang out in the narrow passageway. She heard a shout, then a loud clattering as Holden tumbled down the ladder toward her.

Momentarily panicked, she ran down ladder after ladder and back toward the O-3 level. She was relieved—the admiral's men had stopped Holden—but her relief was short-lived as she heard the 1MC blare, "Torpedo in the water, I say again, torpedo in the water astern, ship is maneuvering, stand by for heavy rolls!"

CHAPTER 94

Joe Willard stood in the control room with a stopwatch, listening to his two Mk 48 torpedoes run out, estimating the time of impact. Willard knew he couldn't stay around for follow-on shots—at least not until he shook his pursuers.

He was maneuvering away from the datum. Speed and depth were his allies now. The pinging by the helo sonar was getting less intense; they may have escaped the net—

"CAPTAIN, TORPEDO IN THE WATER!" the sonar watch shouted. The call was the most dreaded a submariner could hear. Now they were no longer the hunters—they were the hunted—and the aircraft above them had every intention of sending their boat to the bottom.

"Activate countermeasures!" he shouted.

"Launch the Mk 2 torpedo decoy," the OOD ordered.

"Flank speed! Make your depth one hundred forty feet."

The water depth in this portion of the Arabian Gulf was only one hundred sixty feet. The captain was coming perilously close to bottoming the boat. And, at flank speed, it only took a momentary sticking of the diving planes to drive the boat into the mud—a watery grave they'd never escape.

The crew knew what the captain was trying to do. He was trying to lure the torpedo to the bottom. If the torpedo homed in on them it might not be able to pull out of its dive and might head straight into the bottom. *Jefferson City* pushed her speed above thirty knots and dove.

* * *

The stern lookout watched in horror as the two Mk 48 torpedoes, one leading the other by about a thousand yards, bore down on the ship. *Carl Vinson* was

339

turning rapidly but was not gaining much speed, the skidding turn bleeding off much of the energy gained by the increase in torque of her screws. The aft lookout talked rapidly.

"First one is at five o'clock, less than one thousand yards."

On the bridge, the bos'n mate took the reports

"First torp now moving through six o'clock," the lookout continued. "Think it's gonna pass just astern, not by much though."

"Second one is at six o'clock. This is gonna be really close!"

"First torp missed. It missed. It's outbound!"

A five-second pause.

"Second torp is close aboard starboard side. Six o'clock, six o'clock. It's gonna hit!"

* * *

Four miles away from *Carl Vinson*, *Jefferson City* had a torpedo on her tail as the OOD punched out countermeasures. The MH-60R helo had dropped a second torp two minutes after the first, and the sub's sonarmen heard the distinctive sound of a second set of screws.

WHAM! The first Mk 46 torpedo struck *Jefferson City* in the after part of her sail. The shock wave knocked most of the sub's crewmen off their feet, and the boat suddenly went dark. Gear went flying and alarms went off.

"Damage estimates!" the captain shouted.

Reports started to stream in. The initial reports were encouraging. The boat still had propulsion, there was only relatively minor flooding, and most systems seemed to still be functioning. The captain leveled the boat at one hundred twenty-five feet and continued ahead at thirty knots.

"TORPEDO IN THE WATER! TORPEDO IN THE WATER!"

"Activate countermeasures!" the OOD commanded.

"Sir, countermeasures are completely expended."

* * *

"It's headed right for us!" the after lookout shouted as the torpedo continued to bear down on *Carl Vinson*. "It's inside of five hundred yards. It's gonna hit!"

The captain grabbed the 1MC mike from the bos'n mate.

"Torpedo inbound. Torpedo inbound. All hands brace for shock!"

KABOOM! The huge Mk 48 torpedo hit *Carl Vinson*'s number one screw. Sailors were knocked off their feet, gear shattered, and lights blinked off and then on again.

* * *

"Hard right rudder," the OOD shouted as he tried one last tactic, putting a knuckle of bubbles created by the boat's churning screw into the water to try to lure the second torpedo away from the sub.

Jefferson City continued to turn as the torpedo homed in on the boat.

WHAM! The second torpedo struck, but this time the jolt was much more severe, knocking most men down. Willard heard water rushing into his boat. They'd been hit hard. He had only one choice to save his boat.

EMERGENCY BLOW!

Slowly, *Jefferson City* rose, her role as a hunter finished, her crew desperately hoping their boat could get to the surface of before coming apart and sending them to a watery grave.

* * *

Aloft, the ASW aircraft knew they'd scored a hit when they heard the underwater explosions. They didn't know how well they'd done until they heard the transmission from Battlecat 705.

"Ninety-nine, Battlecat 705, sub is breaking the surface. I say again, sub is breaking the surface!"

The airmen watched as *Jefferson City* appeared. There was silence on the net until Labuda shouted, "It's not a Kilo. It's not a Kilo! It's a U.S. Los Angeles Class boat!"

CHAPTER 95

Anne O'Connor had reached the O-5 level when she felt the jolt of the torpedo. The ship shuddered.

"Torpedo hit aft! Torpedo hit aft!" the 1MC blared.

She continued to scamper down the ladder, not certain if Holden was dead or just wounded. Was he following her? Were they following her? If they saw her with a weapon, would they think she was an assassin working with him? She didn't have time to wonder; she just needed to get away, and she continued down the ladder.

* * *

In the Captain's galley, Brian McDonald was still bound with duct tape. He had passed out, but the torpedo explosion and the 1MC announcements roused him, and he managed to pull himself up and stand against the counter in the Captain's galley.

He was confident Holden was no longer nearby. Now his thoughts turned to getting out of this space. He struggled against the duct tape, but he was bound so tightly he had trouble moving at all.

He looked at the door. The push-in lock held it shut. Straining, he retrieved a fork from the counter and picked at the lock. Finally, he got the button to pop out. He slapped at the door handle with the back of his hand, trying to get it to turn. It wouldn't budge. There was nothing that he could do to turn the handle. Out of frustration, he slammed his left shoulder against the door The metal door resonated with a heavy clang.

This might be his chance. The door made a loud enough sound when he hit it that it might attract someone's attention. He continued to bang against the door, biting back the mounting pain.

* * *

Anne O'Connor made it down to the O-3 level unsure of what to do next. She didn't hear Holden or any of the admiral's men following her, but she wanted to be sure. She stopped on the O-3 level, confident she would see who was coming through the door on the O-4 level in enough time to slip away before they saw her.

She'd been waiting at the bottom of the ladder for just a few moments, confident no one was coming down after her, when she heard a clanging. She listened carefully. It was a dull noise of something against metal. It had a rhythm to it. A clang, a few seconds wait, another clang, the same number of seconds, and a clang again. She moved closer to the Captain's Cabin. The noise got louder. Was it coming from inside?

She looked back at the Captain's Ladder. No one was there. She decided to crack open the door to the Captain's Cabin. The noise got louder. What was it? She opened the door wide and now heard the noise clearly. It sounded like it was coming from the captain's galley. She called out.

"Who's there?"

The pounding increased in magnitude and the noises came much closer together. Was there someone who'd responded to her voice?

She moved to open the door to the galley. She heard scuffling inside. She swung the door open.

"Brian!" she heard herself cry out.

Near tears, she undid the duct tape.

"Brian, I thought...thought he had killed you!"

"Anne, I thought you were in trouble. Did he come after you?"

Their joy in finding each other alive and relatively intact overwhelmed both of them for a moment before McDonald continued talking.

"Holden told me an incredible story as he was tying me up."

"I'm not sure I'd believe anything he said," she replied.

"I wouldn't either, not earlier. I told him why we were after him. He looked shocked when I accused him of doing something wrong. He told me the strikes against the Iranian military bases are illegal. He said the only strikes authorized are those against the terrorist training camps. He told me the higher echelons in the Pentagon think Admiral Robinson wants to start his own war for some unknown reason. He said they don't know why he wants to do this, but he told me that he'd been ordered to stop him."

"And you believed all this?"

"At first, no, but then I started to think. Why would he lie to me? I was going to be tied up and helpless. But I'll tell you; these strikes have come together in a strange way. There's been no execute order. It's all being done on the fly based on phone calls between Admiral Robinson and Admiral Flowers. His story is starting to make sense to me."

"Look, Holden was after the admiral. I was after Holden and was about to catch him, but the admiral's men shot him. I don't know if he's dead or alive. I just got out of there as fast as I could."

"But what about the admiral? What about the strikes?"

She knew McDonald had been through a harrowing ordeal, and she didn't want to rub in just how wrong he was. Holden was an assassin—that was all there was to it.

"Okay, Brian, look. Let's take it a step at a time. Before I heard you, I was heading to the SCC Module to see what's going on with this Kilo that nailed us with the torpedo. Come over to the Module with me; then we can figure out what to do next."

* * *

High above *Carl Vinson*, three-quarters of the strike aircraft were overhead the ship and already refueling from their mission tankers. The leads were talking with Strike, trying to decide whether to push with the aircraft they had in the air, or wait for *Carl Vinson* to pick up speed and launch her remaining aircraft. Miles away from *Carl Vinson*, each Tomahawk shooter began the countdown for their deadly missiles.

CHAPTER 96

Twenty miles west of Bushehr naval base, the Iranian Orion flew its daily maritime patrol. Purchased from the United States during the shah's regime and maintained for decades with parts obtained on the black market, the P-3 was the eyes and ears of the Islamic Republic over the Gulf. U.S. forces had become so accustomed to the daily MARPAT missions that they paid little attention to them.

Khalil Sadr had been a plane commander for only a few months. He was elated to be in command of the huge four-engine plane, but he felt incredibly vulnerable as he flew above the Gulf.

The Islamic Republic and the United States were at war. There was no formal declaration, but to Sadr that meant nothing. Word of the sinking of one of their frigates and the disabling of the other by U.S. Navy ships had spread like wildfire. Now, the U.S Navy carrier was preparing for massive strikes against the Islamic Republic. Sadr's mission was to fly a profile that looked exactly like a typical MARPAT mission and alert his headquarters if the carrier launched strikes.

Sadr was no fool. He was well aware the Americans knew about these MARPAT flights. He was certain that if the Americans wanted to shoot him down they could do so, either with a missile from one of their AEGIS ships, or with one of the fighters from *Carl Vinson.* Sadr thought about ways he could flee before he was targeted and shot down.

He'd been airborne for about a half hour when he noticed them. They had been gathering continuously and now there were almost thirty that he could pick out—aircraft that were holding slightly east of the American carrier. There could be no other reason for it—they were preparing a massive strike. Sadr keyed his mike and made his report.

* * *

President Habibi listened impassively as his chief of staff reported the news. This was what Habibi had feared more than anything else—a massive air attack by American carrier jets.

Habibi railed against his own indecisiveness. He had told them he wanted to have a way to communicate with the American president. They had dragged their feet and offered all manner of excuses. Now he could wait no longer.

* * *

Foreign Minister Ali Akbar Velayati smiled as he put the receiver back in its cradle. He knew his country was about to suffer devastating attacks, but he was confident about its ability to absorb the blows. After all, Saddam had absorbed strikes by the United States for over a decade, and each time he'd come back stronger.

What the attacks would do was give him license to carry out the final step of his plan. Oh, he would step away from it and deny responsibility, saying it was that madman Jahani run amok, but it would achieve his goal—make the United States leave the Arabian Gulf for good. He picked up the phone to call Jahani.

* * *

General Najafi had had time to reflect on what he was about to do. It had been well over a half-century since the United States had let the nuclear genie out of the bottle. The so-called Cold War between the American and Soviet empires had been about keeping that genie quiet. Now, he was going to be the one to unleash it.

The general reconciled what he was about to do with the urgent need to defend his country. How could anyone fault him for using whatever means he had to make these aggressors back off? Najafi phoned the base. The officer picked the phone up on the first ring. He assured the general the plane would launch immediately.

CHAPTER 97

Commodore Hughes and his team were still getting over the shock of the call by Bob Labuda that the submarine that they had attacked was a U.S. Los Angeles Class boat when Anne O'Connor and Brian McDonald staggered into the SCC Module. The pair listened for a few moments before they were noticed.

O'Connor was still cradling her weapon and McDonald was beaten bloody. The commodore gaped at the pair. O'Connor finally spoke.

"Did I hear you correctly, sir? Did you say one of our boats fired on us?"

"Yes, USS *Jefferson City*," Hughes replied. "Her skipper is Joe Willard. I know him. We just sent one of our helos to pick him up and bring him here so we can get to the bottom of why he fired at us."

"Perhaps he mistook us for an Iranian ship," O'Connor offered.

"Perhaps. It's the best I can figure. Otherwise, it's the biggest screw-up in U.S. naval history. We'll know for sure when he arrives."

O'Connor started to put a number of disparate pieces together. They'd been attacked by a U.S. submarine—and by a sub skipper whom the commodore personally vouched for—but attacked in such a way as to only cripple *Carl Vinson*, not sink her. McDonald had been convinced by the story Holden had told him, a story she'd rejected out of hand—then.

"Commodore, I need to talk to that sub skipper now."

"He'll be here in ten minutes or so. We'll get him down here for a debrief, and we can all begin to try to piece this together."

"I need to talk with him right now. There may not be time to wait while we bring him back here. I'll explain it all in a minute."

Hughes had worked closely with her over the past year. He trusted her instincts, but she'd better be right.

"All right, let me talk to Battlecat first," he said.

347

"Battlecat 705, this is X-ray Zulu, over."

"X-ray Zulu, Battlecat 705, roger, over."

"Battlecat, I need you to put on the sub's captain on the net."

"Seven-zero-five, roger."

Within moments, Willard was on the line.

"Joe, this is Jim Hughes. We're vectoring *Shiloh* to assist you. She should be there soon. Are any of your men hurt?"

Willard was surprised to hear the voice of someone he knew. "No sir, they're all basically okay. I saw *Shiloh* on the horizon when they lifted me off the boat. She should be there soon."

"All right, Joe. Look, you'll be onboard in a few minutes and you can tell me more then, but I've got one of our pilots here who wants to speak with you. I'm putting Lieutenant O'Connor on."

"Skipper, can you hear me?" O'Connor said after the commodore handed her the headset.

"Yes, I can."

"Sir, I know there's a lot to sort out, but I need to know why you were attacking *Carl Vinson*."

Willard was concerned about what he should or shouldn't say over the radio, even on a secure net.

"Lieutenant, I think maybe I'd better wait until I can see all of you and Commodore Hughes face to face. Then I can—"

"Skipper, we can't wait for that. We're forming up strikes to devastate Iran. We have only minutes to stop the person who's orchestrating them—if you confirm what I think you're going to confirm."

"The strikes are going now?"

"Yes, our strike aircraft are overhead getting ready to push."

Willard lost any reluctance to talk. "Lieutenant, I don't know where you fit into the overall scheme of things, but I'm just going to lay it out for you and trust that you'll pass it along to the right people."

"Fair enough, sir."

"I received tasking from COMSUBFOR ordering me to attack *Carl Vinson*. The orders were to disable the ship, not sink it, that's why I shot at the screws. The message said the strike group commander had decided to attack Iran, and I needed to disable the carrier before that happened. I got another message from the chief of naval operations himself confirming my mission...."

O'Connor continued to listen.

"Even with these two messages in hand, I still sent a message back to COMSUB-FOR and asked for confirmation. I was told to complete my mission as ordered. I still find it unbelievable that a flag officer would do something crazy like this."

"We'll ensure you get a full brief when you get onboard, Skipper," she replied. She ripped the headset off her head. That was all the confirmation she needed. Admiral Robinson *was* conducting unauthorized strikes against Iran. Holden had been on a righteous mission all along.

Now she knew there was only one thing to do.

"Come on, Brian," she said, pulling McDonald toward the door.

"O'Connor, what did you find out from Commander Willard?" the commodore asked.

"No time, Commodore," she replied. "The skipper will be aboard in a little bit and tell you the whole story—"

"But, wait!" Hughes shouted as they departed.

O'Connor steered McDonald as they moved aft in the passageway. They exited the Blue Tile Area and went by the same blue curtain she had hidden behind earlier. "Brian, you were right about Holden. That conversation with the sub skipper confirmed everything he told you."

"We've got to stop the admiral."

"You can barely move. I've got to stop him."

* * *

The MAA worked his way down the ladder to the O-7 level, his weapon ready, prepared to put rounds into the supine figure. When he was a few feet away, he said, "Freeze."

No answer. He moved a step closer. Still no movement.

"Get up."

No sign of life. He approached the body and pushed it with his foot.

"Ooohhhh."

The MAA jumped back a few feet. He signaled the air ops officer at the top of the ladder to come down toward him as he called the admiral's aide on the walkie-talkie.

"I'm over Holden now, sir. He's alive, but barely moving. I think it's safe to move out."

"Roger."

The MAA and the air ops officer bent over Holden. He had taken a slug in the shoulder and was barely conscious.

"Admiral, Holden isn't a threat anymore," the air ops officer said. "The MAA will tie him up and stay with him. I think we can move out."

"Let's go," the admiral replied. "Ops O, where are we with TFCC?"

"COS says that the strike aircraft are overhead tanking, and getting ready to push for their missions. Captain and CAG were trying to decide whether to launch the remaining strikers—there are about seven or eight more to go—or send these guys ahead."

"That's my decision, not theirs. We need to get down to TFCC," the admiral replied. Turning to his aide, he said, "Lead on, Mike."

Lumme led the admiral and ops officer off the Flag Bridge. They walked down the first ladder and saw the MAA tying up Holden. Air ops fell in with them, and the four men headed down the ladders.

CHAPTER 98

National intelligence systems pick up an incredible amount of data every day—vastly more than the intelligence agencies can possibly process, let alone turn into any useful information. During a major crisis the efforts of analysts are shifted to allow them to focus on specific, critical information. Such was the case with the Gulf today. The action in the Gulf was so frenetic it outpaced the ability of the National Military Command Center and the White House Situation Room to keep track of events, let alone analyze and interpret them.

No one fully understood what was going on in the Gulf until the OPREP THREE PINNACLE messages began to arrive at the NMCC from both *Carl Vinson* and *Jefferson City*, indicating both units were under attack. A few watch-standers in the NMCC knew *Jefferson City* was on a highly classified mission.

It was clear—but it wasn't clear. *Carl Vinson* had been hit by *Jefferson City*. *Jefferson City* had been hit by torpedoes dropped by helos under control of *Carl Vinson*. A large gaggle of aircraft was forming up near *Carl Vinson*, apparently headed for Iran. And to make matters worse, there was no report from the CIA agent aboard *Carl Vinson* as to what was happening with regard to his efforts to stop Admiral Robinson.

Admiral Monroe was a fixture in the NMCC. He was one of the few who were read into *Jefferson City*'s mission, and he was able to steer watchstanders trying to evaluate the information that they did have without speculating on what they didn't know.

* * *

At the National Counterterrorism Center, Peter Hernandez pressed the control officers at CIA to try to find out what Rick Holden was doing. Hernandez was enough of a bureaucrat to know there was no point in standing in front of the president and admitting he didn't really know what was going on.

* * *

There was no one at the White House of sufficient rank or stature for President Browne to vent to except Michael Curtis.

"Michael, every time I walk down to the Situation Room I come away more confused about this operation. What else have you heard since our briefing an hour-and-a-half ago?"

"Nothing, Mr. President." "I've pressed the chairman for more information, and he tells me that reports are still coming in regarding action between *Carl Vinson* and *Jefferson City*."

"Is Secretary Quinn making any progress getting a communication network set up with President Habibi?"

"He's working on it, Mr. President," he lied. Curtis had reached a low-level functionary and had made this request. The man probably would take days just writing his memo to send up the chain. By then it would be too late.

"Well tell him to get it done, dammit! Get it done now!"

"I'll see to it, Mr. President."

* * *

One hundred and twenty miles as the crow flies from the waters of the Gulf, an aircraft was launching.

"Four thousand feet remaining...three thousand feet...you need to rotate now, Mohammad—"

"Airspeed isn't high enough yet, Fahim—"

"Less than two thousand feet now, you must rotate; rotate now!"

"No, we'll stall—"

"ROTATE, ROTATE, or we'll run off the runway!"

His hands frozen on the yoke, Mohammad Sallihab pulled back gently and lifted the C-130 off the deck at Shiraz Airport. The weapon was primitive and was enormously heavy. His calculations told him he should make it. It wasn't supposed to be this close, but there had been absolutely no wind and that had complicated things.

Sallihab climbed slowly and began a turn to join the airway. He would climb to the correct altitude and go at the right speed as he headed his aircraft toward Kuwait, knowing he and his crew would never reach there.

Chapter 99

In the skies above Carl Vinson, the thirsty aircraft sucked gas from the refueling tankers. The Airwing had scrambled to put enough tanker aircraft aloft to give the strike aircraft full bags of fuel so they could fly deep into Iran and deliver their weapons.

DCAG was the senior aviator in the air and was on the radio with *Carl Vinson's* CO, dealing with the issue of whether to wait to launch the remaining strike aircraft before pushing toward Iran. There was a limit to how long they could wait—and they were reaching that limit.

Once DCAG and the captain had made their decision, the captain passed it to TFCC to get Admiral Robinson's concurrence. They reached the chief of staff, who gave them a "wait out."

In the absence of guidance from the admiral or his staff, Craig Vandegrift decided to launch a total of six more strike aircraft and send them aloft to join DCAG's group.

* * *

Battlecat 705 touched down on spot 4 on *Carl Vinson's* flight deck, and a crewman assisted Joe Willard in getting out of the helo. He was whisked down to the SCC Module.

"Joe, I wasn't privy to your side of the call with Lieutenant O'Connor," Jim Hughes began. "I expect you told her just what in the hell you are doing shooting at *Carl Vinson*."

Willard was a little off balance already, and the commodore's comments only made him more so. He had laid everything out for the lieutenant; hadn't she told the commodore anything? Or maybe she had.

"Commodore, as I told the lieutenant, I received a message from my boss at SUBFOR, and another from the CNO himself, directing me to fire a torpedo at *Carl Vinson* and disable her. The message from SUBFOR told me the admiral on board the carrier was going to conduct an unauthorized attack against Iran and this was the only way to stop it from happening. I questioned that order by sending a message back to COMSUBFOR, but I was told I was to carry out my orders to the letter."

"What did you do after they confirmed your mission?"

"I worked my way north through the Gulf to get in position to attack the carrier. I don't know what damage, if any, I've done to *Carl Vinson*, but I can tell you that my boat is in bad shape. The first torp hit my sail. The next one hit my hull, and I had to surface or risk losing the boat. I need rescue and assistance parties to help me save it."

"*Shiloh* should be there soon," the commodore replied. *Could Willard's tale be true?*

"Commodore, you said my torpedo hit *Carl Vinson*?"

"Yeah, got us in the number one screw. Now tell me more about this...this... accusation in the message you received from COMSUBFOR alleging that the admiral was going to conduct unauthorized strikes."

"As I told the lieutenant, the message from COMSUBFOR was clear. It said, 'the strike group commander had elected, for reasons known only to him, to attack the Islamic Republic of Iran.' I know what the message said. I must have read it a dozen times."

"I'm sure you did. But did you know that our orders were to conduct those very attacks that SUBFOR told you weren't authorized?"

"No, I didn't. There must be some incredible mix-up somewhere that dwarfs any other kind of military snafu I've ever heard about."

"Commodore," his chief staff officer chimed in, "the orders for us to do these strikes have all been verbal. No naval message has come down from the chain of command—"

Now it was Willard's turn to interrupt. "You're conducting these strikes on verbal orders?"

"They're verbal orders that the admiral received directly from the Fifth Fleet commander."

"Commodore, even so, this casts doubt on the entire mission," his CSO continued. "Don't you see? If we're going on *verbal* orders to attack, and the skipper here has *a naval message* telling him that this isn't what's supposed to be happening, then something is wrong. We need to ask the chain of command what they really want us to do."

"We're in radio silence for a reason. We have to disguise our position and our intentions from the enemy."

"I think we might be disguising more than that, sir," Willard said. "Can't we break radio silence long enough just to check with Fifth Fleet as your CSO suggests?"

"I'll talk with the chief of staff. The admiral is on the Flag Bridge now. Yes, I think we can make a case for contacting Fifth Fleet."

"I just hope that we do whatever we're going to do soon," the CSO said. "And we need to find out what was wrong with O'Connor and that other pilot she was in here with," he continued.

CHAPTER 100

He dared not use his name. "My friend, as I speak, the American jets are preparing to drop their deadly bombs on our homes. Our brave seamen have died dueling with them, and we shot down one of their fighter jets before it crossed our coast. Their AEGIS cruiser shot down another aircraft that they only could have thought was ours," barked Ali Akbar Velayati. He didn't intend to give Jahani a tutorial. He hadn't planned on saying more than a few sentences, but he was enraged over the recent chain of events.

"Yes, Mr. Minister."

"They do all of this and their government doesn't even attempt to contact ours. Do you know why they treat us with such disdain?"

"I do not, Mr. Minister."

"They do this because we don't threaten them. We experimented with ballistic missiles that could reach the United States but they never lived up to their promise. The Americans laughed at us—our country wasn't advanced enough to have such missiles. We cannot hurt them, so they continue to act with impunity. You understand, don't you?"

"Yes, Mr. Minister."

"The time has come. You are to instruct our men in the United States to release their agents. We will take this fight to the enemy. As bombs are raining down on our country, Americans will be dying in the streets."

"It will be done."

"I know it will. But they all must release their agents at precisely the same time."

"They will."

"Good. It is now 1030 Greenwich Mean Time. They are to carry out their attacks at precisely 1145 GMT. Can you ensure that?"

"Yes, Mr. Minister. We're ready to carry out your orders."

"Excellent," he replied.

"Is there anything else, Mr. Minister?"

"Yes, my friend, Allahu Akbar," he said, using the familiar term for "Allah is greater."

Jahani put the phone down and pulled out a sheet of paper. He scratched until he had the words he wanted—

THE AMERICAN PIGS ARE ATTACKING OUR ISLAMIC REPUBLIC. YOU ARE TO CARRY OUT YOUR ATTACKS. YOU ARE TO RELEASE YOUR AGENTS AT PRECISELY 1145 GREENWICH MEAN TIME. NOT BEFORE. NOT AFTER. THE SUCCESS OF OUR NATION'S DEFENSE DEPENDS ON YOU. ALLAHU AKBAR.

—and entered the first number.

* * *

In New York, Mejid Homani left the coffee shop and crossed the street as the sun rose over the East River. He would try the doors to the United Nations. Maybe they would be open.

* * *

Hala Karomi received the message just as he was boarding the Metro to head back to Union Station, his agent tucked firmly under his arm. He was relieved. He would arrive in time.

* * *

Achmed Boleshari read the message and calculated what this time translated to in San Diego. It would barely be dawn. Horton Plaza would be nearly deserted. What was Jahani thinking? He couldn't believe this was what he wanted him to do.

CHAPTER 101

Anne O'Connor and Brian McDonald leaned against the steel bulkhead debating what to do next.

"Once I get the drop on the admiral," O'Connor began, "I can tell the senior officers on the staff what's going on and we can end this."

"But what if they're in on it too? What if they're part of the plot?"

"That's too big a stretch to think a whole group of people could have decided to do this. You know guys like CAG. There's no way."

"We thought we knew the admiral too, and he's gone off the deep end. If he could, then so could everyone else," McDonald replied.

"I doubt it. The messages Holden got, and what *Jeff City*'s CO told me, make it sound like the admiral was working alone."

"Where do you think he is now?"

"I gotta think he's still on the Flag Bridge. That's where he was headed when I saw Holden following him. Then I heard shots and saw Holden fall down the ladder. They're probably waiting to see if the coast is clear. Wait, there's one thing I have to check," O'Connor answered.

O'Connor took a few steps forward and peered down the passageway toward the admiral's cabin.

"What were you doing?" McDonald asked when she returned.

"I needed to see if the MAA was there. He wasn't, so I figure the admiral is still on the Flag Bridge. If we wait here, he'll have to pass by us to get back to TFCC. He's bound to go back there soon."

"So what's your plan? You—"

She raised her hand to silence him. She'd heard voices close by. They both pressed themselves against the bulkhead.

The voices got closer, and now they could pick out words.

"Keep moving, flag lieutenant, I don't want to get to TFCC after all the strikes are finished."

"Yes, sir."

The voices were closer and were moving toward the fore and aft passageway where they hid. In a few feet, the group would have to turn. If they turned right, they would stay in the Blue Tile passageway and head for TFCC. If they turned left, they'd be on top of them.

The voices grew louder.

"Ops, as soon as we get to TFCC, find out the status of the strikers. I want to know where they are and when they plan to push."

"Yes, sir."

"And I want to know where the TLAM shooters are on their countdown."

"Got it, Admiral."

The voices were almost on top of them. O'Connor held her breath.

"I don't know why the hell we went up to the Flag Bridge anyway. Chief of staff convinced me against my best instincts—"

The voices were right there. They dared not breathe or move.

"Admiral, we'll be in TFCC in just a moment," his ops officer said. The voices were growing softer. They were moving away.

The footsteps and the voices grew fainter still as the four men moved away down the passageway. O'Connor hazarded a peek from behind the curtain. They were almost to the War Room.

There was no waiting now. O'Connor started to move forward.

McDonald grabbed her arm with his good one. He mouthed the words "Be careful," then he released his grip. O'Connor wrapped both hands tightly around her weapon and moved.

CHAPTER 102

Mohammad Sallihab had followed the airway for over one hundred miles. He knew he would have to leave the airway, descend rapidly, and then find *Carl Vinson* in the perpetual haze hanging over the Gulf. Then he would have to penetrate the carrier's defenses and crash his aircraft on its flight deck, exploding his weapon.

He didn't fear dying, nor did his copilot. For them, martyrdom was the highest calling. It had taken many days of intense instruction to teach them how to fly the C-130 transport, at least enough to get it off the deck and to its destination. The Americans would be powerless to stop them.

* * *

Miles from where Sallihab's aircraft was about to cross the coastline, Jake Busch stalked back and forth in *Shiloh's* Combat Direction Center. *Shiloh* had been at General Quarters for longer than Busch could remember ever being at GQ. *Shiloh's* SPY radar scanned the crowded skies around *Carl Vinson*. They were shotgun for the carrier and needed to be prepared to deal with any hostile aircraft attempting to reach *Carl Vinson*. Busch turned toward his TAO.

"I'm going up to the bridge to oversee this rescue and assistance effort. If you get anything hot down here, let me know ASAP."

"Yes, sir," his TAO replied.

Petty Officer Alex Davillo sat at his console and did his best to sort out the airborne traffic. In addition to the over thirty aircraft milling around getting ready to push off on their strike mission, there was the traffic on nearby commercial airways. *Shiloh* had the airways depicted on her large-screen displays, and Davillo and his fellow OSs were confident they could sort friend from foe out of the maze of aircraft.

* * *

Sallihab was over the water now. His copilot held the nautical chart in his lap while he held the aerial chart in his right hand and continuously cross-checked the two. Their superiors had marked the spot on the nautical chart where the carrier was supposed to be. He kept up a running dialogue with Sallihab, telling him where he was and where he thought the carrier was located.

For his part, Sallihab concentrated on keeping his aircraft on the airway and traveling at the prescribed speed.

His copilot lifted his eyes from his charts and looked at Sallihab.

"We're at the closest point of approach to where the carrier is supposed to be. Here's the spot where you must turn," Fahim said.

"Turn to what course?" Sallihab asked.

"Turn to course 205."

"Course 205. I'm starting my descent," Sallihab replied. "I'm leaving ten thousand feet. I'll level out at one thousand feet."

"Yes, Mohammad."

With that, Sallihab pushed the yoke forward and turned sharply.

* * *

Aboard *Shiloh,* Davillo stared at his radar scope and eased forward to the edge of his chair. He blinked. Then he changed scales on his radar. Then he changed back to the original scale. It was still there.

"Chief."

"What is it, Davillo?"

"Chief, I've got this airborne contact at 035. He was on the airway, but he dropped off. He's headed right at us and descending rapidly. I'd better tell the TAO."

"Do it!" the chief shouted. It took him only seconds to make the same analysis that Davillo had. The aircraft that had been innocently plodding along the commercial airway was now making a beeline for *Shiloh* and *Carl Vinson.*

"Mr. Long!"

The TAO, Lieutenant Bob Long, walked up behind him. "What is it, Davillo?"

"Right here, sir," he said as he held his cursor over the spot. "Chief confirms it. This contact is headed straight for us at two hundred thirty-five knots."

"Did he come off the airway?"

"Yes, sir, he did."

"Is he squawking emergency?"

"No, sir, he's not squawking anything."

Long pressed the bitch box toggle that connected him to the bridge. "Captain, TAO, we need you in CDC!"

* * *

They were descending through eight thousand feet when Shalliab shouted, "There, Fahim!"

"Where?"

"There, there, at one o'clock low. There must be thirty of them. All over the sky!"

"Yes, I see them, Fahim replied.

Sallihab praised Allah and praised the intelligence men who had plotted the likely position of *Carl Vinson*. If those aircraft were all milling around, the carrier must be close by. While the Gulf haze often limited visibility near the deck to a half-dozen miles, above the haze Sallihab could see to the horizon. The aircraft circling high above *Carl Vinson* were difficult to miss.

"I'm turning ten degrees to head directly toward them. Now that we know where the carrier is, we must get under the clouds before those aircraft see us."

* * *

Jake Busch was standing next to his TAO within thirty seconds.

"What do you have?"

"This contact, Captain. No squawk. Coming right at the carrier—"

"Give him level two warnings. Don't waste your time with level one."

"Captain?"

"DO IT!" Busch shouted.

"Unidentified aircraft bearing 035, six thousand feet, on course 205, two hundred thirty-five knots, you are approaching a United States Navy warship operating in international waters. Your identity is not known and your intentions are unclear. You are standing into danger and may be subject to United States defensive measures. Request you establish communications now or alter your course immediately to remain clear of me."

No answer.

"Again."

"Unidentified aircraft...." The TAO repeated the instructions verbatim.

Still no answer.

"Take him with birds!" Busch shouted.

"Captain, we need to ask X-ray Bravo!"

"No we don't, dammit, DO IT NOW!" Busch had almost waited too long the day before when the other Iranian aircraft had approached them. That one hadn't made the devious move this one had in trying to look like a commercial airliner. Within seconds they felt first one jolt, and then another, as the deadly SM-3 missiles leapt from the vertical launch magazine.

$$* * *$$

Sallihab held the yoke forward with all his might as the C-130 shuddered violently, protesting the rapid descent. He looked at his attitude gyro, trying to keep his wings level and keep the aircraft in balanced flight....

CHAPTER 103

Anne O'Connor started down the passageway, gun in her hands. Ahead, the ops officer and air ops officer entered the War Room. The admiral's aide and the admiral were still a few steps behind.

She closed to within ten feet of the admiral and held her weapon at arm's length. She knew she couldn't miss from this distance.

She had a clear shot at the back of his head. All she had to do was take the shot, the admiral would be dead, and this ordeal would be over. Her finger slowly started to put pressure on the trigger....

She couldn't do it, not in the back of the head. She shouted, "Admiral!"

Robinson turned. He froze, his eyes wide with disbelief.

Mike Lumme had turned when the admiral had. As he did, he inadvertently let go of the handle to the War Room door and it slammed shut. Lumme moved, putting himself between Robinson and O'Connor.

"Lieutenant, don't do this," he said. "I don't know what you're doing, but you have to stop." He was slowly moving closer as he spoke.

"That's far enough. Stop right there!" O'Connor shouted, bringing her gun up just a little higher.

"Look, Lieutenant, you don't want to shoot anyone."

She took a step back to buy time, but Lumme moved closer.

"Stop, stop right there!" she shouted.

"You're not going to do this," Lumme said as he stepped toward O'Connor.

Suddenly, from behind O'Connor, there were heavy footsteps. McDonald had been watching and had crept up the passageway unnoticed by the other three. Cradling his broken arm, he brushed by O'Connor and crashed into Lumme, knocking him to the deck. As they hit the deck, he rolled on top of Lumme and began to pummel him with his good arm.

When McDonald brushed by O'Connor, he knocked the gun out of her hand. It slid along the deck toward where he and Lumme fought.

Robinson used the momentary chaos to try to escape. He was at the War Room door and only feet from safety. He grabbed the handle and turned it. It wouldn't open. He tried to think of the combination to the cipher lock.

Lumme saw the gun on the deck and started to belly-crawl toward it, but McDonald grabbed his leg and held on.

Robinson finally remembered the combination and was about to punch it in when he was knocked off his feet. O'Connor had hurdled the two struggling men and had thrown herself headlong into the admiral. The two came crashing down on the deck.

The adrenaline rushing through her body let her get the upper hand. She used the advantage to lay into him, delivering blow after blow.

While O'Connor struggled with the admiral, Lumme continued inching toward the gun as McDonald hung on to his leg, fighting him for every inch that he crawled.

Suddenly the door to the War Room opened, and the chief of staff and the air ops officer looked out on the commotion. The air ops officer drew his own gun and shouted, "STOP IT, STOP IT RIGHT THERE. EVERYONE FREEZE!"

"Admiral, are you all right?" the chief of staff said as he rushed to help the admiral to his feet.

The air ops officer saw the gun on the deck, and said to Lumme, "Flag Lieutenant, pick up that gun."

"Yes, sir," Lumme replied as he pulled free of McDonald.

"Admiral, did they try to shoot you?" the chief of staff asked.

"She did," he said, pointing at O'Connor. "How many damn assassins are there on this ship, Lieutenant, besides you, and Holden and him?" he asked, looking at McDonald.

The air ops officer kept his weapon trained on O'Connor and McDonald as O'Connor slowly got to her feet. McDonald struggled to get up, his arm now hanging grotesquely at his side.

The chief of staff took charge. "Flag Lieutenant, help the admiral and get into TFCC so he can monitor the strikes. Then call the ship's Master-at-Arms office and get several MAAs up here."

"Yes, sir," he replied.

"You two are under arrest," the chief of staff continued. "You are traitors, both of you, and you'll pay for your crimes—"

"NO WE'RE NOT!" O'Connor shouted.

McDonald forced himself up.

"McDonald, is that you? You were supposed to be leading one of these strikes, what the hell are you doing with this...this...woman stalking me?" Robinson asked.

Before McDonald could answer, they heard noise coming toward them from the back end of the Blue Tile Area. The commotion of the fighting had gotten the attention of the people in the SCC Module. The commodore and Joe Willard appeared.

"Commodore," the chief of staff said, "these two assassins tried to kill the admiral. They almost succeeded. We shot one of their co-conspirators up on the O-7 level just a few minutes ago."

"I have something to tell you and you'd better listen," Hughes began.

"This is Joe Willard, George, skipper of *Jefferson City*. He's told me why he was ordered to shoot at this ship—and shoot to wound us— not to sink us. I'll let him explain."

Ordered? Sampson asked.

"Chief of Staff. I've received messages from both COMSUBFOR and CNO telling me to disable *Carl Vinson* before the carrier launched strikes against Iran. I was told the admiral had taken matters into his own hands and was directing completely unauthorized strikes. As I told the commodore, I questioned those orders, but was told by Admiral Deutermann I was to proceed with my mission."

"George, don't you see what's happening?" the commodore asked.

"I *see* this is very strange," the chief of staff replied. "We're authorized to conduct strikes. We have orders directly from Fifth Fleet."

By now, McDonald had recovered enough to speak. "Sir, the Airwing has been planning these strikes based on verbal authority only. All of our doctrine, all of our training, tells us these kind of strikes are never tasked verbally. There is just too much that can go wrong. We must have hard-copy naval messages."

"I'm the one who read Holden's e-mails," O'Connor added. "He had the same kind of instructions the skipper of the sub had."

"It's all bullshit!" Robinson shouted. "Lock them all up!"

"Admiral, how do you expect to prove all these people are wrong and that you're right?" the commodore asked.

"I DON'T HAVE TO PROVE A GODDAMNED THING!" Robinson shouted. "Chief of Staff, are you going to order them locked up or do I have to do it myself?"

Sampson stood frozen in disbelief.

"Wait," McDonald said, "there's one way to find out what's true."

"What's that?" the chief of staff asked.

"We've been in radio silence for an extended time. There's no reason to be there anymore We won't give our position away any more than it's known already. Break radio silence, Chief of Staff. Call Fifth Fleet. They know what has or hasn't been authorized."

Sampson thought for a moment and then looked at the commodore for validation.

"Do it, George," Hughes said.

"No, Chief of Staff, you're not authorized to break radio silence, you are not authorized!" Robinson shouted.

"Admiral...I—"

"Do it, George, do it!" Hughes urged. "Do it, or I will!"

Sampson stood frozen, unable to go against the admiral's orders. Hughes pushed by him and headed into the War Room.

Bill Durham was directing the group in TFCC as the strikers moved toward the coast of Iran. The aircraft striking Bandar Abbas had pushed first due to the long distance involved in getting to the southern part of Iran. CAG was in TFCC with him, giving directions to the other strike aircraft. They were startled when Hughes burst in.

"Commodore, great job nailing the sub. What's up now?" Durham asked.

"We've got a crisis, Bill. We need to call Fifth Fleet about these strikes."

"Commodore, we're in radio silence. We can't break that now, not without the admiral's permission."

"We have to and we will!" he shouted. "Either you do it in here, or I'll do it from my module. It's these strikes and what we're supposed to hit. At this point this has all been based on verbal orders—conversations between the admiral and Admiral Flowers. Now there's doubt about what was actually ordered. We need to get to the bottom of—"

"But Commodore, the admiral—" Durham interrupted.

"You do it, or I'll do it!" Hughes shouted, interrupting Durham again. Durham finally decided he needed to make the call from TFCC. He picked up the Battle Group Command Net.

"Alpha, Alpha, this is X-ray Bravo."

"X-ray Bravo, this is Alpha Alpha," the startled Fifth Fleet watchstander replied. *Carl Vinson* had been off the net for a while, and they were surprised that they were initiating a communication.

"This is CSG One Ops Officer, Captain Durham. I need to talk with your ops officer, Captain Mullen, ASAP."

"Yes, sir, stand by," he replied.

The wait was only minutes. "Captain Mullen here."

"Carl, this is Bill Durham. We have multiple crises working here, and I don't have a lot of time to explain. I need clarification, and I need it now. Tell me about these strikes against Iran we're launching. There's a ton of confusion. What's authorized, and why didn't we get a hard copy of these orders? All this was supposedly worked out between Admiral Robinson and Admiral Flowers, but now there are unanswered questions. These strikes are on their way now; what's going on?"

Members of the military have a sixth sense for snafus, and Mullen's was tingling.

"Bill, we have a crisis here as well, and it all involves *Carl Vinson*. Admiral Flowers is dead. Your guys shot down his COD! You're supposed to be doing strikes against the terrorist training camps, that's all. We have the execute order here, but you all are in radio silence and we can't get it to you. Those are the only strikes authorized, nothing else. What are you all doing out there?"

Durham's spine went cold. Only the strikes against the terrorist training camps were authorized?

"Carl, I—"

"Bill, General Lawrence is on his way to our HQ to take over. He arrives in a few hours. Admiral Flowers was flying out to *Carl Vinson* to relieve your boss because there was proof that he was a renegade doing completely unauthorized things. You've got to be the one to stop it. Don't let those strikes keep going."

Durham couldn't believe what he was hearing. Could the admiral have been lying to all of them this entire time?

"Carl, I'll do everything I can to call them off. I'll leave CAG on the line with you; I've got to do something right now."

"All right, just stop those strikes."

"I will," Durham replied. Then, as an afterthought, he said, "I know we've been in radio silence, but we've been waiting for you to send info back with our flag sec, Lieutenant Commander Phillips."

"Phillips? Your flag sec? She isn't here."

"Sure she is. She went in on the COD three days ago."

"Bill, she's not here, never has been. I'd know about those things. Why did you think she was here?"

"Carl, the admiral—" But he caught himself. What else was the admiral hiding from them? He turned to Hughes. "Let's go, Commodore," he said, and the two of them left TFCC.

Durham and the commodore appeared again in the Blue Tile passageway as the chief of staff and the air ops officer continued to hold their weapons on O'Connor and McDonald. Admiral Robinson stood there too, telling the air ops officer what to do with the two "prisoners." He wasn't making a lot of sense to anyone and the entire scene had a surrealistic feeling about it.

"What did they say, Bill?" the chief of staff asked.

The ops officer didn't answer immediately, so Sampson turned toward him. Durham was white.

"Bill?"

"We shot down Admiral Flowers's plane and killed everyone on board."

"We what?"

"Remember that contact *Shiloh* shot down yesterday? The one that wouldn't respond to warnings? That was the COD. Admiral Flowers was on it."

"My God!"

"And another surprise, COS. Becky Phillips isn't at Fifth Fleet Headquarters. She never was, according to them."

"But admiral," George Sampson began, "you told us ..."

It came together for Sampson in a flash. Phillips had come to him, making wild accusations against the admiral. And it was the admiral who had told him about her being at Fifth Fleet on a "special mission." And now the Fifth Fleet ops officer had told Durham the verbal orders that Admiral Robinson had supposedly gotten from the Fifth Fleet commander hadn't happened—and couldn't have happened because Admiral Flowers was dead when Robinson was ostensibly talking with him.

"Admiral, these are pretty serious charges. Sir, tell me that none of it is true." Sampson asked

"Don't you all see?" Robinson began. "Iran is the real enemy. They've murdered our shipmates—on the ground and in the air. They must be destroyed. We hold the hammer. If we don't act now, our country will never have the will again. How many more people will have to die at the hands of terrorists? Our leaders didn't have the guts to move forward, so I moved forward without them. Each of you would have done the same thing in my position.

"Work with me on this," the admiral continued. "There shouldn't be any reason to turn back now. These people have our long-term destruction uppermost in their minds. We have to hit them first. I've tried to do it alone—that was a mistake—now I need you to join with me."

No one said anything for a tiny eternity.

"Air Ops," Sampson ordered "take the admiral into custody. Put him in his cabin under guard."

CHAPTER 104

"Get me the national security advisor!" Admiral Monroe said to the watch officer. The man dialed the number and handed the phone to the admiral. After a quick skirmish with the watchstander at the White House Situation Room, he was on the line with Michael Curtis.

"Yes, Admiral, what is it?"

"Mr. Curtis," he began, "I just got off the line with the acting commander at Fifth Fleet Headquarters. They finally received a communication from CSG One aboard *Carl Vinson*."

"You mean the carrier is finally out of radio silence?" Curtis asked.

"Yes, sir, and Captain Dennis had a great deal to report. I'll head to the Situation Room and brief you more fully there, but for now, here is what we know. Admiral Robinson has been taken into custody—"

"He has?" Curtis exclaimed.

"Yes, sir, but a lot has happened in the interim. USS *Jefferson City* attacked *Carl Vinson* and put one torpedo in her screw, but did only minor damage—the carrier is essentially operating as before. *Carl Vinson*, in turn, put two torpedoes into *Jefferson City* and almost sank her. She was forced to the surface but is still intact."

"Was anyone killed?"

"No, sir, not there. Onboard *Carl Vinson*, the Navy SEAL who was sent to take out Admiral Robinson was shot by Robinson's staff before he could complete his mission, but two other officers, for reasons we can't yet figure out, attacked the admiral and stopped him. Between what these officers told him, and what the CO of the submarine reported, the chief of staff and the commodore decided to break radio silence and call Fifth Fleet.

"They were told the strikes that Admiral Robinson claimed had been authorized by Admiral Flowers were not authorized at all. It was only then that the staff on *Carl Vinson* found out they'd shot down the COD carrying Admiral Flowers."

"Go on."

"There's been other action, sir. In addition to the running gun battle *Shiloh* has had with the Iranian frigates, she also shot down an Iranian aircraft making an attack on *Carl Vinson*. We're not certain what one plane—and one traveling at a relatively slow speed—was hoping to accomplish, but one theory is that it was a suicide aircraft. If the Iranians were resorting to that, it might have been the last card they had to play. They may not have anything else to throw at us."

"Admiral Robinson is in custody and the CSG One staff is talking to Fifth Fleet, and Iran is no longer threatening the strike group. Is everything settled then, with the strikes and everything? Are we sure that they aren't going to strike anything until they are authorized to do so?" the national security adviser asked.

"No, sir, that part isn't completely settled yet. The strike group will tell the Tomahawk shooters to hold fire. But the aircraft have all pushed off toward their targets. *Carl Vinson* is attempting to call them all back."

"Attempting to call them back?"

"They're trying, sir, via every means available. But these strikes were timed to happen simultaneously to ensure military surprise. The strikers that had the furthest to go—the ones that were assigned to attack Bandar Abbas—pushed first. They're the ones they may have trouble getting to hold off. I'm trying to get more information to clear this up."

"You damn well better," Curtis snapped. "I'm not going to go to the president with some half-cocked story."

"You won't have to do that, sir; I'll see to it personally."

"You need to, and you need to do it right now."

"Yes, sir." He needed to get on the net directly to the strike group and to whoever was in charge at the moment.

In the Situation Room, Michael Curtis announced, "I'll be with the president," and headed upstairs.

CHAPTER 105

Admiral Robinson sat on his sofa with his arms folded. One MAA sat at the other end of the sofa, while two other MAAs stood by the door to the War Room and the door to the Flag Mess. The admiral didn't speak to them, and they were ordered not to initiate conversation.

Just twenty feet away, George Sampson used his watchstanders to do the multitude of things they needed to do almost instantaneously. Sampson did so with considerable angst, trying to put out of his mind the role he may have played in Becky Phillips's disappearance. She had confided in him and had tried to get him to help her get to the bottom of her suspicions, but he had treated her like some rattled schoolgirl. And what had happened to her? Given the other things the admiral had done, Sampson feared the worst.

"John," he said to the Flag TAO, "you and your team contact each of our five TLAM shooters. Tell them to cancel their missions and power down their missiles. Talk to each CO individually. Get positive affirmation that they understand, got it?"

"Yes, sir."

"Good. That's the long pole in the tent. Aircraft we can call back. Tomahawks we can't."

"Paul," he said to Lieutenant Paul Barton, who was manning the air display console, "I want you to get me the Hawkeye crew. Tell them to call me on the J-1 circuit. I'm going to use them to reach the strikers and have 'em call back each strike group individually."

"Will do, sir," Barton replied.

"John, I want reports from *Shiloh* right away with a reconstruction of the track of the aircraft they shot down. I want to know where it came from and exactly why they felt threatened."

"WILCO, COS."

"CAG," he said, turning to Foster, "work with Craig to find a way to get this many aircraft back aboard safely. Tell him what's happened here, and tell him he can start moving southeast again—I know he doesn't want to get trapped in the shallow water up here."

"I'll work with him on that, COS."

"Chief of Staff, I've got the Hawkeye crew on the J-1 circuit," Barton said.

Sampson picked up the handset. "This is Captain Sampson, chief of staff for CSG One. Who's on this net?"

"Captain, Commander McCarthy, Sun King CO here. I've got primary air control. What is it, sir?"

"This is directive K.T. so I'm going to say it slowly. The strikes that just pushed are being recalled. I say again, the strikes are being recalled. You are to contact each of the strike leads ASAP and direct them to return to *Carl Vinson*, is that clear?"

Sampson knew the CO of the E-2D squadron well, and they recognized each other's voices.

"I got it, Chief of Staff."

"Get back to me as soon as you get confirmation you've turned them all around."

"Will do, sir."

Satisfied he dealt with the crucial operational issues, Sampson turned to other matters. "Mike," he said to the flag lieutenant, "what have we done with Lieutenant O'Connor and Lieutenant McDonald?"

"Sir, Lieutenant McDonald's arm is in really bad shape. They've got him down in medical right now, and the surgeon is working on him. Lieutenant O'Connor was a little shaken up, but she's basically okay. She's in flag admin now, telling her story to our legal folks."

"What about Lieutenant Holden?"

"I know he was alive when we went by him. The MAA was guarding him. I'll have to check on that."

"All right, we can find out more about that later. We shot the guy, and now it turns out that he's a hero for trying to do his duty."

Sampson picked up the Bogen phone and hit 28, which connected him instantly to the captain on the bridge.

"Captain," Vandegrift said.

"Craig, COS here. We're recalling the strikes and CAG is going to talk to you in just a minute to try to figure out how to recover all the strikers. But for now, we're not threatened anymore, so I think it's okay to stand the ship down from GQ."

"Will do, COS."

"Craig, would you do something for me?"

"Sure."

"There's a Lieutenant Holden one of your MAAs is guarding up on the O-7 level. He's been shot, but he's one of the good guys. Can you get someone there to get him medical help ASAP?"

"Can do, COS."

"Thanks, I'll get back to you."

"Chief of Staff, I have the E-2D mission commander on the J-l," Barton said.

"Great, give me the handset."

"COS, K.T. here."

"Go ahead, K.T. Have we got all the strikers turned around yet?"

"No, sir, not yet. There's a problem. I'm contacting our guys on our fleet air defense net, but they don't believe me. They think it's either some sort of Iranian ruse, or I'm confused and don't know what I'm talking about. The best I've been able to do is to get some guys to hold at their present position. If I don't convince them, they're gonna push."

"You've got to convince them!"

"I'm trying, but we're losing time, and that's not the worst news."

"Not the worst news? What is?"

"I've called the strike group heading toward Bandar Abbas a half-dozen times. They don't respond. They may be too low and too far away already. We may not be able to contact them at all!"

"Dammit, K.T., we need to be able to reach them!"

"DCAG's not too far from the southern strike group. I'll talk to him and see if he can reach them. In the meantime, we need to come up with a way to convince the strikers they're supposed to turn back."

"I'm going to give you a 'wait out' for a minute, K.T., until we sort things out down here. In the meantime, keep trying to convince your boys to turn around."

"WILCO, sir."

Sampson looked around TFCC. "All right," he began, "Our Hawkeye skipper is telling me not all the strikers want to turn back. They think this latest order is an Iranian ruse. Worse, he says the Bandar Abbas strikers group isn't responding to his calls. He mentioned DCAG trying to reach them. Jesus Christ, CAG, what does it take?"

"Chief of staff, here's what I propose. I'll raise DCAG. He's in a Super Hornet and he can try to catch the southern strike group. While he's en route, he can tell everyone else they should be turning back. Hearing it from him in the air, and on a covered net, will help."

"Will help?" Sampson asked.

"Right, Chief of Staff, but you need to put this out to everyone, and put it out on Guard. The guys in the air will understand if it comes at them that way."

"Okay, I'll do that," he replied.

Sampson huddled with his ops officer and air ops officer. Within a few minutes, they settled on what they were going to say.

First, Sampson picked up the J-l net.

"Sun King 600, X-ray Bravo."

"Go ahead, sir."

"K.T., here's the plan. CAG is going out to DCAG to get him to tell everyone to call off the strikes, catch up with the southern strike group, and tell them to return also. I want you to go out on the net one more time and tell them to return to *Carl Vinson*."

"WILCO, sir."

Sampson instructed his watch team to bring up a radio on Guard. What he said would be heard by every aircraft airborne, as well as by everyone with a UHF radio. He keyed the mike.

"All airborne units, all airborne units, this is X-ray Bravo on Guard. All units have been contacted by the Hawkeye, this message confirms that order. Do not, repeat, do not conduct any attacks against Iran. All strike aircraft must return to *Carl Vinson* immediately. No attacks are authorized. Return to home plate."

Sampson un-keyed the mike for a moment, and then he continued.

"All strike leaders report to the Hawkeye you've received this instruction. Gentlemen, it is crucial that we call back all your strikes."

Satisfied he had done everything that he possibly could; Sampson picked up the J-1 net.

"K.T., chief of staff here."

"Yes, sir?"

"I want to know immediately when all of the strikers have checked in with you and are returning."

"WILCO, sir. CAG has put out his radio message, too, and I think the combination of his call and your transmission on Guard will do the trick. He's speeding south now trying to catch up with the Bandar Abbas strike group."

"We'd better pray he makes it."

CHAPTER 106

The driver braked the staff car to an abrupt halt outside the military headquarters where General Najafi was conducting an inspection, and his passenger got out. After a brief conversation with the general's aide, the colonel approached him.

"General, communications headquarters has an urgent message for you."

"Yes, what is it?" Najafi asked.

"We've intercepted transmissions from the American aircraft carrier. They didn't try to be covert, but transmitted this on their Guard frequency—"

"The American carrier transmitted on Guard?" Najafi interrupted.

"Yes, sir, that's highly unusual as you know. But the nature of the transmission was even more alarming. General, the American carrier said strikes had been launched against our Republic and now those strikes were to be called back."

That the Americans were striking the Islamic Republic was not that astounding. That they were calling back their strikes was. He didn't know precisely what to make of it, but knew he would soon be called to the presidential Palace.

* * *

Foreign Minister Velayati was at his desk in the Foreign Ministry when he received the news. What could this mean? He also recognized that soon President Habibi would summon him. He didn't want to give him that satisfaction. Velayati called for his staff car.

For Velayati, the situation was suddenly extremely complex. A short time ago, the Americans were attacking, and he had directed Jahani to unleash his agents in the United States. Now the attacks were being called off. What was he to do? Should he call Jahani now, or wait until Habibi ordered him to do so? He decided he would force his hand.

***

President Habibi was pacing as the two men entered. They had arrived in his outer office almost simultaneously and were quickly ushered in. Habibi had received word of the extraordinary transmission from *Carl Vinson* earlier and had been trying to make sense of it. Habibi got down to business immediately.

"General, the American carrier now is recalling all of its aircraft. What do you make of this?"

"Mr. President, the carrier has been vigorous in defending itself. They had their bandit cruiser attack our ships. Our Orion aircraft reports they attacked a submarine that they thought was ours, but which turned out to be their own. They shot down our plane carrying the nuclear weapon. We expected them to lash out against us with their aircraft, and we were fully ready to defend our Republic to the last man—"

"Oh, I'm certain that you were, General," Habibi interrupted.

"Yes, we were, Mr. President. This could, of course, be an American ruse to throw off our defenders."

"General, I want to make this clear. I want you to take no provocative action. You are to do nothing to make the Americans believe we have hostile intentions. Is that clear?"

"Yes, Mr. President. It will be done as you direct it."

Habibi turned to Velayati. "Mr. Foreign Minister, I look at this as the beginning of an American effort to defuse this situation. I assume you have already canceled these attacks against American cities."

"I have not, Mr. President."

"You what?"

"I haven't canceled them, but will do so if those are your wishes."

"Yes, those are my wishes! Could there be any doubt? Are you deliberately dragging your feet?"

Velayati knew this was all a charade. He was dragging his feet, and knew Habibi knew he was.

"Mr. President, I will call off these men if you order it, but it is a decision of enormous consequences. Would it not be better if the Americans felt the full force of our wrath on their home soil? We have more than enough justification. Just ask the families of the sailors whose bodies lie entombed in our ship at the bottom of the Gulf."

Habibi was beyond rage Velayati would challenge him. He pushed the intercom button.

"Send them in," he ordered.

His secretary told the men to go in. The door opened and Colonel Mohammed Navez, assistant chief of the Tehran police force, entered with four of his men.

"Colonel Navez, you are to perform the mission we discussed early this morning. You are to escort Minister Velayati to his office. There he will contact an individual and direct him to call off his agents in the United States. After he does this, you will 'assist' him in establishing the communications path directly with the United States that I instructed him to establish some days ago."

"Yes, Mr. President."

"You are to stay with him as he establishes communications with the U.S. Department of State. He will inform them of our peaceful intentions. Then he will connect with the office of the American president, President Browne, and state my wishes to speak with him. If Minister Velayati fails to do any of these things, you are to place him under arrest. Do you understand these instructions completely?"

"Completely, Mr. President."

Velayati was furious and off-balance. Furious because of what was happening, and off-balance because of the carefully scripted dialogue between Habibi and the police colonel.

* * *

Six-hundred-and-fifty miles from Tehran, Lieutenant Commander Bill Weaver led his eight-plane strike group of on a course of 130 degrees, roughly paralleling the coast of Iran. They had just refueled south of *Carl Vinson* and were on the deck at two hundred feet above the surface of the Gulf. Weaver's strike group was the first to push and would be the first to hit the naval facility at Bandar Abbas.

There was an urgency to their mission, for once the Iranian vessels sortied from their port, they'd be extremely difficult to find and kill. Catch them at their piers and they'd be easy targets.

Weaver turned his strike group east as they passed Qeshm Island, which pointed like a dagger directly at the southern tip of the port of Bandar Abbas.

Once they reached the eastern end of the island, they would turn due north and run straight in at the port.

* * *

Back in Tehran, Velayati suffered the indignity of being escorted into his own Foreign Ministry. He couldn't hide his rage at Habibi and rambled to the police officers escorting him. After fuming for some time, he called Jahani.

"Yes, Mr. Foreign Minister."

"I have a simple message for you. President Habibi has ordered you to tell your agents in the United States to stop—to call off their attacks. They are not to release their agents. Is that clear?"

"Perfectly clear, Mr. Foreign Minister. But, you see, this may be quite impossible. These men have already been given the go-ahead."

Velayati looked up at the police officers surrounding him, eyeing the one officer who was discreetly listening on one of the other telephones in his office.

"It is not impossible." he raged at Jahani. "The hour we have designated for them to conduct their attacks is still twenty minutes away. You alerted them by phone to conduct these attacks; use the same method to tell them to stop. This is an order, Jahani, you will obey it!"

Jahani thought Velayati was losing both his control and his nerve—he had never used his name over a phone line like this before.

"As you wish, Mr. Minister. I will do as you say. These men have put themselves at great personal risk, but they will follow their orders."

"See that they do!" Velayati shouted as he slammed the phone down, more for effect than for any other reason. He wanted to ensure those standing over him would report back to Habibi he had done his bidding.

Jahani placed the phone back in its cradle. He wouldn't let his anger get the best of him as it had gotten the best of Velayati. He would make the calls. There would be other opportunities.

* * *

Weaver turned his strike group due north and pointed it straight at Bandar Abbas. The port facility was easy to pick out. It had a large, concentric breakwater, submarine and other piers in the wide outer harbor, and yet more piers in the restricted inner harbor.

The submarines would be the primary targets. Weaver and his wingman would attack first, followed by a section of Super Hornets that would re-attack. The other aircraft would fan out across the harbor and strike as many ships as possible. Working with data that was less than six hours old, they were confident they knew precisely where every vessel in the harbor was located.

Weaver felt especially good about leading the first attack against Iranian soil. Nasty McCabe had been his mentor, and Andy Bacon had been a good friend. He wanted to be the first to deliver cold steel against the Iranians who had murdered his shipmates. Four miles from the breakwater, without signal, each jet flipped its Master Arm Switch to Arm.

CHAPTER 107

Jahani sat alone in his tiny room. His head ached and his stomach churned after his conversation with Velayati. The man had no spine. They were so close to taking the fight to the infidels. He again considered ignoring Velayati's instructions, but rejected the idea. The foreign minister could make his life difficult. The funds he needed to support his camps were run through Velayati's Foreign Ministry. No, he reminded himself, there was a long-term war to be won; he would concede this skirmish. He scribbled out a message on a piece of paper:

YOUR MISSION HAS BEEN CANCELED. YOU ARE NOT TO RELEASE YOUR AGENTS. RETURN TO YOUR HOTEL ROOMS AND AWAIT FURTHER INSTRUCTIONS.

He sent the identical message to each of their iPhones.

* * *

Half a world away, three men watched the clock and prayed for the success of their mission. They didn't pray for their own safety—just that they might be successful and that they would somehow kill as many Americans as possible.

In New York, Mejid Homani sat on a bench in an out-of-the-way area of the large concourse on the ground floor of the United Nations. It was still early, and there weren't a huge number of people here, but there were enough—enough to die such that the infidels would recognize that the Islamic Republic could hit them where they lived.

He was surprised when his iPhone alerted him again. As discreetly as he could, he pulled it off his belt and looked at the message. He scrolled through the words, and then scrolled through them again. No, this could not be. Was this some American trick?

What if he just ignored the message? That was it! He could say later that he never received the message. He closed his eyes and prayed.

He opened his eyes. He couldn't do it. He got up, and, with his agent securely under his arm, he hurried out of the United Nations. He crossed the street and walked north on First Avenue. He couldn't go back to his hotel, not yet. He walked north, his head spinning.

* * *

Achmed Boleshari received the message in the coffee shop across the street from Horton Plaza. Like Homani, he was surprised at the message. What was going on? Did they know what they were doing? They issue an order and then change it an hour later?

He was disappointed the attack was being called off, but he was relieved in a way. The appointed hour to release his agent was in ten minutes, but Horton Plaza was still virtually deserted. If they were changing their minds like this, perhaps they would tell him to attack later when the plaza was full. Buoyed by this positive turn of events, Boleshari discreetly put the iPhone back in his pocket and signaled the waitress to bring him another cup of coffee.

* * *

In Washington, Hala Karomi got ready to get off the Metro, sweat pouring off his face. The next stop was his. It was going to be a close call whether he got to Union Station at the appointed time.

As he expected, the train was now jammed with commuters who jostled and bumped against one another. When the train lurched into the station, a dozen people stood between him and the door, and most didn't appear to be getting off at this stop. He squirmed out of his seat and started to make his way to the door even before the train stopped, now frantic to get off the train.

Pushing and shoving, he squeezed his body between the unyielding commuters. In desperation, he clutched his agent and wedged between the passengers and out of the door seconds before it closed. As he ran for the steps up to the street level and into Union Station, he looked up at the clock overhead. Only ten minutes before the appointed hour.

* * *

On the floor of the crowded train, a fallen iPhone went off. In the din of the now rapidly moving Metro, no one heard it, just as they hadn't heard it hit the floor after it was stripped off Karomi's belt as he pushed his way off the train.

Karomi stood outside Union Station for just a moment, composing himself. He wanted to appear calm as he approached the station and blend in with the other commuters.

Finally settled and with several minutes to spare, he walked to the news store in the center of the station and moved to the far corner of the small shop. He placed his backpack down on the floor and knelt next to it. No one was watching him. He broke the vial and pushed the backpack under a rack featuring sweatshirts with various logos of the Capitol region. He stood up and calmly walked away.

His training had told him the gas wouldn't release instantaneously, and he had time to exit the station without running. He forced himself to walk slowly. As he walked down the steps to the Metro, Karomi began taking deep breaths. When he reached into his pocket get his fare card for the train, he noticed his iPhone wasn't on his belt. Frantically he checked his pockets, and then realized it made no difference. He had delivered his agent. His masters would be proud.

CHAPTER 108

They were accustomed to being summoned to the president's headquarters. They'd been here so many times in the past several days they knew the surroundings as well as they did their own offices. But this time they hadn't been summoned. They had insisted on meeting with President Habibi and had bullied their way past his secretaries and other aides until they were ushered into his office. The president of the Islamic Republic clearly was not ready for this encounter and it showed. So much the better, General Najafi and Foreign Minister Velayati thought.

The general spoke first. "Mr. President, we must prepare to take further action. The Americans continue to confound us with their perfidy. They attacked our ships without cause and they shot down our plane, although the attack on our plane I can understand, since it was sent out to attack their precious carrier."

"What's your point, General?"

"I'm certain that by now you must have heard of the attack on our naval base at Bandar Abbas."

"I've been briefed on the attack, General. I'm told that our men acquitted themselves well in their efforts to defend the port."

"They did, Mr. President, and many died in that effort. But the point is that this attack came a half hour *after* there were radio instructions to the American aircraft to cease these attacks. We can deduce now these instructions represented an elaborate ruse to try to make our defenders let down their guard."

"I don't know why you're telling me this, General."

"The Americans are resorting to tactics which are repulsive to civilized nations. What they did was tantamount to walking up with a white flag and then shooting. Their actions cannot go unanswered, not while our nation still has the strength to fight at all."

"What do you propose?"

"The brave men who flew our C-130 cargo plane aren't the only martyrs we have. We have many more. They're prepared to launch soon to take the attack to the carrier once again, and this time they'll ride our jet airplanes not the lumbering cargo plane."

"You are talking about launching strikes against the American carrier?"

"Yes, I am. Until we disable the carrier, the Americans can continue to launch strikes against us!" he shouted.

"Sit down, General. If I hear another outburst you'll leave, and by the time you return to your barracks, you'll have no soldiers to lead."

"Minister Velayati?" Habibi said, now challenging the foreign minister to say something.

Velayati was unfazed by the dressing-down the general had just received.

"I've done as you've ordered. I've had the operatives in the United States contacted and directed to abandon their plans. I didn't agree with this, Mr. President, but obeyed your orders. Now, looking at what the Americans have done, I regret that decision."

"You regret it? Do you think the Americans have done everything to us they can do?"

"No, I don't, but—" He was interrupted in mid-sentence by one of the president's aides, who rushed in breathlessly.

"Turn on CNN," the man said. "Turn it on right now."

The man kept walking as he talked and moved to the large TV in Habibi's office. Soon the television was on and the picture was of a reporter in front of a large building. The caption read, *"Mindy Cole, Washington, D.C."* Her voice sounded hard as she gave her report:

Here at Union Station, the situation is chaotic. Early this morning, at the height of the morning commute, persons unknown released what appears to be a significant amount of a nerve agent inside Union Station. Emergency officials on the scene refuse to speculate on how many people may have been killed or injured, but the D.C. coroner is on scene. Many of those being removed from the station who are still alive appear to be very sick.

This attack comes only a short time after a reported attack by U.S. warplanes on the Iranian naval facility at Bandar Abbas. U.S. officials are refusing to say whether the Iranian regime is suspected of orchestrating this attack, but they would not discount this possibility.

District Police Chief Elmer Johnson has been on the scene and has requested the
assistance of the FBI in determining who perpetrated this crime. We are going
to follow the directions of the police and move further away from Union Station.
This is Mindy Cole, reporting live near Union Station in Washington, District of
Columbia.

Habibi turned to Velayati and hissed, "So you called off the attacks, Mr. Minister, did you?"

"I assure you I did. I gave explicit instructions these attacks be called off—"

The president cut him off. "Your underlings must not think much of the need to obey your commands. That's not what's important now. We have done this in their capital. Do you know how they'll respond?" Habibi's question was rhetorical.

"We will be prepared for anything, Mr. President," Najafi said.

"I'm sure you think you will, General. Only the foreign minister will do absolutely everything in his power to ensure you don't have to. Mr. Minister, have you obtained that direct link yet between me and the American president?"

"It is almost complete, Mr. President."

"Good. Until it is, you will remain at my headquarters and direct the efforts to finish it. Once that line is established, you let me know."

Velayati was beyond words. First he had been humiliated by being escorted to his Foreign Ministry. Now the president was making him a virtual prisoner in his offices until he completed this menial task.

"You are dismissed, General. See to your duties, Mr. Foreign Minister," Habibi said as he stalked out of the room.

CHAPTER 109

The emergency crews outside Union Station were aggressive in cordoning off the area around the station so ambulances and other official vehicles could pull up. However, they were having trouble keeping the hordes of media away. Every major national news network, as well as many local reporters, descended on the station. Reporters were pulled off every other story in the city and rushed to Union Station.

* * *

President Browne and his national security adviser sat in the Oval Office transfixed by the TV. The cameras moved periodically from the talking head to scenes of stretchers being carried out of the station. Many of the victims on the stretchers had blankets pulled over their heads—a grim reminder the death toll would be high.

The president and Michael Curtis continued to watch CNN as they waited for the secretary of defense, the secretary of state, and the chairman of the joint chiefs of staff to converge on the Oval Office. Curtis waited as long as he thought he dared before speaking.

"Mr. President, this certainly is an unbelievable tragedy. I'm afraid the number of casualties will be substantial."

"Yes, I know" the president replied.

"This attack has the Islamic Republic's fingerprints all over it."

"I know it appears that way, Michael, but we need to get to the bottom of it before making that determination."

"It could be weeks, maybe months, maybe years, before we catch the perpetrators. We can't wait, Mr. President!"

Patrick Browne simply didn't want to have this discussion with his national security adviser at that moment. "All right, Michael, you've made your point, thanks."

That hit Curtis exactly the wrong way, and he lashed back.

"Mr. President, may I remind you what has happened recently. *Iran* has reinitiated training at terrorist training camps. *Iran* viciously attacked the InterContinental Hotel and killed more of our men and women than had been killed in any previous terrorist attack on Americans except 911 and the bombing of the Marine barracks in Beirut, Lebanon in 1983. *Iran* attacked USS *Carl Vinson* with two of her ships. *Iran* shot down our aircraft when it was flying in international waters. *Iran* sent an aircraft to attack *Carl Vinson....*"

The president stopped looking at the television screen long enough to look at Curtis. Browne had never seen the national security adviser so animated. He was about to speak, but Curtis continued his harangue.

"And what have *we* done in response? Nothing. No, Mr. President, we've done *less* than nothing. We sent an American submarine to attack a U.S. Navy aircraft carrier. Not only that, but we unleashed an assassin to kill a Navy admiral who *might* have been getting ready to attack the same Islamic Republic that perpetrated these crimes. We've taken *extraordinary* pains to turn the other cheek, and every time we've done that, we've been slapped again and attacked again!"

The national security adviser continued his diatribe.

"Don't you see; we could have predicted this gas attack by the Iranians? They hit us, and we don't respond!"

"Michael, I'm only going to say this once, so I want you to listen," the president began. "I've followed your advice. I'm not saying you gave me bad advice, but I *am* saying I've never followed my instincts in an effort to get some sort of consensus among all of you."

"Mr. President, we all work for consensus," Curtis replied.

"But I've worked for it more than anyone. I have to do what I think is right. Ultimately, I'm responsible for the course this country takes."

"Of course you are, Mr. President."

"That's why I need to act. When the others get here, take them down to the Situation Room. Get updates on the tragedy at Union Station. I'm going to have a press conference, and I'll need details. I'll discuss this tragedy, and I'll discuss other matters."

"Other matters, Mr. President?"

"Yes, Michael, other matters. Now go; go meet the others."

CHAPTER 110

Hasan Ibrahim Habibi sat in his office alone. The phone on his desk was still silent. His aide had told him the president of the United States would be calling. Foreign Minister Velayati and General Najafi had been ushered from the presidential headquarters.

He would no longer listen to them. He was the elected president of the Islamic Republic. The only way he wouldn't have power would be if he abdicated it. Habibi was going to do what he thought was best for the country he loved.

He had brought in his communications chief, and the man had established a line that could connect him with anyone in the world. True, it wasn't a secure net, but there wasn't much that needed to be hidden—that could be hidden—anymore. It was too late for that.

* * *

President Browne had instructed the White House Communications Office to establish a phone line that could reach the Islamic Republic. The president asked for time to collect his thoughts before making the call. He refused to have an aide place the call, insisting he do it himself.

He picked up the phone and dialed the number for President Habibi. The phone rang twice, and then Habibi picked it up.

"President Habibi, speaking."

"Mr. President, this is Patrick Browne."

"Good day, Mr. President. There is much we should talk about."

"Indeed there is," Browne continued. "I think that this is a terrible state our nations find themselves in, isn't it?"

"It is, indeed. First, I must say I am very sorry for the deaths of your citizens in your capital city. I assure you the attack was not authorized by my government. It was done by a man acting on his own volition, and for this we are extremely sorry."

"I believe that is as you say it is, Mr. President. But I must ask you this. Was the attack on the InterContinental Hotel done by your nation?"

"I cannot deny that terrorists trained in my country probably perpetrated this horrible crime. We haven't controlled this scourge the way we should. It is my government's strong desire to pay reparations to the families of those who were lost at the InterContinental, as well as to the families of those people tragically killed in the attack at Union Station."

"That is very gracious of you. Our aircraft that attacked your naval base at Bandar Abbas were not authorized to do so. They were launched by a rogue admiral. He has been arrested and is no longer in a position to attack your nation. We express the deepest regret for the people you lost, as well as the damage done to your facility and to the ships there."

"This admiral you speak of, President Browne, why would he do such things without authorization?"

"We don't fully know that yet, but we're trying to get to the bottom of it. Sometimes men snap. In this case, it appears this admiral did. We did everything in our power to stop this man before he launched any strikes against you."

"I see, Mr. President."

"May I make a suggestion, President Habibi?"

"Yes, by all means."

"I suggest we have our forces disengage as quickly as possible. I will order *Carl Vinson* to exit Gulf and pass through the Strait of Hormuz as a signal to the world we mean the Islamic Republic no harm. We both have fences to mend. I think the sooner we do it, the better."

"I agree, Mr. President. I've let my country down by allowing others to make decisions for the Islamic Republic that are my responsibility and mine alone. That will no longer happen, not as long as I am in office."

"I, too, have been captive to my advisors. Often their advice is so earnest it is easy to go along with. Now I know that my instincts are often better than the advice I receive."

Epilogue

Patrick Browne sat at his desk in the wake of his phone call with President Habibi. He felt relieved beyond words the crisis in the Arabian Gulf had been defused and, most importantly, the killing had been stopped.

The president called his secretary into the room and dictated a brief agenda. First there would be the phone calls to the members of his national security team. Next would be the phone calls to several heads of state. After that, he would meet with his press secretary and prepare for his press conference.

* * *

Seven thousand miles away, in the presidential headquarters, President Habibi was already taking action. Iranian military forces were stood down and the terrorist training camps were shut down.

There was one action Habibi decided he needed to do in person. Within an hour of his conversation with Patrick Browne, he had Foreign Minister Velayati brought to his office. When Velayati arrived, there was already an assemblage of persons in the president's office, including the senior judge of the Iranian High Court.

Using legal language provided by the judge, Habibi cashiered Velayati for his complicity in terrorist operations, as well as his failure to derail these operations once they were ordered to be stopped. Velayati was given an opportunity to tell him about the whereabouts of Jahani, but he refused.

Velayati's failure to help Habibi ferret out Jahani prevented him from moving the Islamic Republic completely away from supporting terrorism. Although Habibi could see the camps were closed down, the fluid nature of the terrorist threat allowed Jahani to keep his network alive and moving from place to place—to be, in the end, an even more elusive target.

* * *

Michael Curtis was shocked by the president's phone call to President Habibi. A matter of such importance should have been discussed with him first—the president should have at least afforded him that courtesy. Patrick Browne told him a stated goal of his administration was now to mend fences with the Islamic Republic. The national security adviser received this message silently. He still believed that Iran still posed a deadly threat to the United States and its interests.

* * *

Secretary of Defense Bryce Jacobs called in the chairman of the Joint Chiefs of Staff and reviewed with him what they had been instructed to do. The military crisis in the Arabian Gulf had to be defused and Admiral Robinson had to be dealt with.

The first task was not easy. Blood had been spilled, people had died, bombs had been dropped, and military hardware had been destroyed. Disengaging two military machines that were at each other's throats took deft handling. Dealing with a volatile Central Command commander, who was now on station in Bahrain at Fifth Fleet Headquarters, made their job that much harder.

But this challenge paled by comparison with the really tough issue—how to deal with the strike group commander. Admiral Robinson had been relieved of his duties and was under house arrest aboard his own flagship. It didn't take long for the Naval Criminal Investigative Service to pin Becky Phillips' death on Robinson. If there were any silver lining—albeit a small one—in Phillips' dying at his hands, it was the fact that the headline-grabbing murder trial, and Robinson going to the military's Leavenworth prison for life, allowed the Navy to obscure the fact that one man almost started a conflict that could have threatened to engulf an entire region of the globe in a senseless war.

* * *

Far away from the weighty political and military matters being decided in the nation's capital, three young warriors began to deal with the aftermath of the crisis.

Anne O'Connor recovered from her injuries and was back in the cockpit flying within a week. Her love of flying was rekindled and would sustain her throughout her career. She even began to start to think seriously about applying for the U. S. Naval Test Pilot School.

Brian McDonald's injuries were more serious; his badly broken arm took him out of the cockpit and left him flying a desk, possibly for several months. His dedication and his heroism made those on *Carl Vinson* loath to lose him, and they were able to have him transferred from the Fighting Redcocks to Wizard Foster's personal staff.

Rick Holden was flown to Germany to recover from his gunshot wound. The medical evacuation to Germany got him off *Carl Vinson* and was the first step in having him go underground again. He had performed heroically, and once again, the powers that be decided he was too valuable an asset to cast off.

In spite of the order for the military pullback, and the damage done to various military units during the crisis, one constant stood out: USS *Carl Vinson* remained on station in the Mideast.

AFTERWORD

For Duty and Honor is a story woven around the awesome power of a U.S. Navy carrier strike group. For those unfamiliar with the operations of forward-deployed fleet units, the portrayal of the virtually autonomous power of a carrier strike group commander may appear to be a bit of a stretch. It's not.

The U.S. Navy is long accustomed to vesting paramount authority in the commanding officer of a Navy combatant ship. In a carrier strike group this happens on a far larger scale. The Navy and the nation entrust the lives of 8,000 people, national treasure in the tens of billions of dollars, as well as devastating firepower, in the hands of one carefully selected individual—the carrier strike group commander. No one person in any military organization in any nation personally controls so much destructive power.

Having worked directly for six strike group commanders over the course of almost seven years and through three deployments—including two deployments to the Arabian Gulf—I would be the first to admit that the scenario presented in this story is not one I lose sleep over. I never felt any of my bosses—all of whom were superb leaders—would ever be driven to the point Admiral Robinson of this story was.

But add the right mix of political circumstances, an unhelpful blending of military crises, a tense intersection of personalities, and a breakdown of checks and balances, and the scenario painted here could become all too real. Put another way, the question arises. Do we as a Navy and a nation try to produce an Admiral Robinson in this story? No. Could we collectively fail to pay attention, and push a military professional over the edge and create *Heart of Darkness* on an aircraft carrier? We might.

The overwhelming majority of military officers—especially senior military officers—focus exclusively on their duties and try not to be drawn into the

397

political arena. However, this is a situation that isn't always in their hands. They can be drawn into political and military intrigues not of their making. When this happens, they are typically treading on unfamiliar turf with less than fully developed instincts as to how to extricate themselves.

Like most stories, this one has a beginning, a middle, and an end. It has good characters and evil characters. Most are well defined. But what about Admiral Robinson? What about Michael Curtis? Who bears the burden of the events put in motion in this story? As in many things in life, the person out in front—the person taking or personally directing the action—is the most exposed. In this case, Admiral Robinson was cashiered while Michael Curtis continued serving as national security adviser.

And ships like USS *Carl Vinson* are on the line—every day.

Captain George Galdorisi
Coronado, California
July 2018

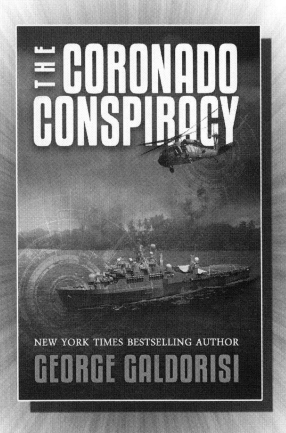

IT HAD ALL GONE TO HELL SO QUICKLY...

KEVIN MILLER

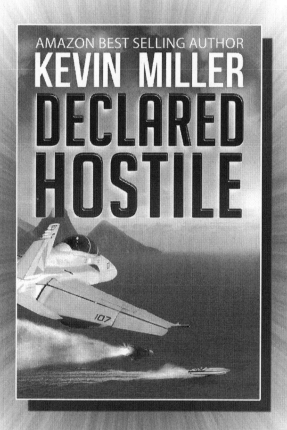

When does a covert mission become
an undeclared war?

www.braveshipbooks.com

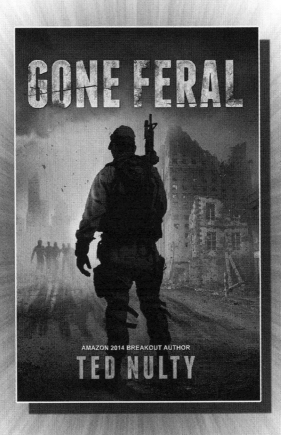

**THE THOUSAND YEAR REICH MAY BE
ONLY BEGINNING...**

ALLAN LEVERONE

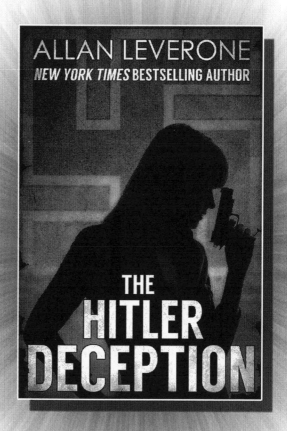

A Tracie Tanner Thriller

www.braveshipbooks.com

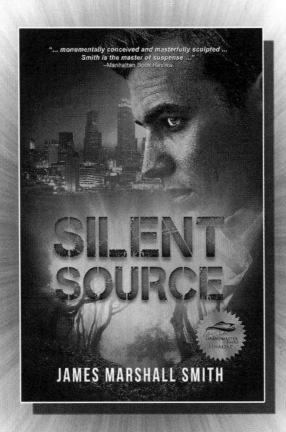

53953046R00250

Made in the USA
Columbia, SC
23 March 2019